Book
Title
Pop That Part 3

Author

Jamel Johnson

Jamelbronxny@gmail.com

<u>Chapter 1</u>

Vera walked back and forth in her bedroom. Three years she been drug free. For the first time in three years, today she woke up with that evil monkey on her back called, "Get High." She had done everything she could think of to get her mind off of wanting to get high. But nothing was working. Wanting to get high wouldn't leave her mind. She knew getting high again would be letting down her daughter Trina, and her grandson Quinn. Most importantly she would be letting down Solo her son in law. He went beyond the call of love for Trina and helped his mother in law get off of drugs. Did she went to disappoint them, no.

Looking at her watch Vera had thirty minutes before Trina would be at her house. Trina was picking her up so they could go out for their mother and daughter day. Biting on her bottom lip Vera began thinking to herself, "I can do this, no one will know. I can go cop some crack, get high, and be back here before Trina get here. I just have to move fast". Grabbing her car keys Vera ran out her house.

*****

Getting out her car Trina noticed her mother car wasn't parked in the driveway of the house. Using her own set of keys to her mother house. Trina let herself into her mother house. It didn't take her long enough to notice her mother wasn't home. Pulling out her cell phone Trina dialed her mother cell phone. Hearing a phone ranging in the kitchen. Trina saw that her mother had left her cell phone on the kitchen table. Hanging up Trina called Solo.

"Hey baby girl" Solo said answering his phone.

"Solo I'm at my mother house and she's not here. Have you seen her?"

"No baby girl. Why don't you call her cell phone?"

"I did and she left it in the house, and her car is gone too."

"Well Trina, your mother knew you were going to her house to pick her up. So I'm sure she didn't go to far."

"Solo If she didn't go far, she wouldn't have took her car. I have a whole mother and daughter day planned for us. We gonna be late for our body massage appointment!"

"Baby girl you getting worked up for nothing. I'm sure she'll be walking in her house any minute."

"She better! Because If we miss our appointment, I'm gonna kill her and you gonna need to bail me out of jail."

Solo bust out laughing. "Baby girl you know your man got you. If worst comes to worst, I always got the money for your bail. Listen I have to take care of some team business, so I got to go. Love you baby girl."

"Love you too" Trina said hanging up the phone.

Getting off the phone with Trina. Solo went to the back private room in the re-up apartment and closed the door. Booting up the computer he jumped on the internet. Putting in his code he looked up Vera gold chain he gave Vera two years ago. The same tracking device he had placed in all the chains of his team members. Pulling up Vera tracker map history. Solo looked at the computer screen confused. Seeing the address where Vera was at that very moment had Solo mind running a mile a minute.

"What the fuck is she doing over there" Solo said out loud turning off the computer.

Thinking to his self, Solo couldn't come up with a good reason to why Vera would be in Courtlandt Projects. Two thoughts ran threw his mind. "Courtlandt projects is where Mike drug spot is. Either Mike has my mother in law or she's back to using drugs." One or the other he needed to find out. Pulling out his car keys Solo left his re-up apartment to find out what was going on.

*****

Although Vera had been off of drugs for the past three years. She had been on drugs for over fifteen years before she finally got clean. She knew all the spots that carried good crack. Street hustlers had good stuff, but not better stuff then hustlers that sold crack out of projects. Solo ran the crack spots in Soundview projects. So she couldn't go there. Webster projects were shut down and about to be back up and running soon, with Solo team running those projects as well. The next closes projects that came to her mind was Courtlandt projects. She hated to cop drugs in Courtlandt projects. The dealers had more game with them then a toy store. If they gave you real drugs, because sometimes they stuff you. But If they did give you real drugs, before you left the building, they would stick you up and take it back along with any money you had on you. Yet having a evil monkey on her back. This would be a chance she was willing to take. She just hoped she could cop and get out the building with her drugs. Taking off her jewelry she put it in her purse. Pulling ten dollars out her purse, she got out her car.

Walking in the building the smell of piss smacked her dead in the face. Walking inside the staircase it was dark. The smell of piss seem to get even stronger. So strong it began to burn her eyes.

"Just two floors up, then I can get out of this staircase, go to the apartment, get my shit and I'll take the elevator back down" Vera said to herself.

Hearing someone walking up the stairs behind her. Vera began going up the stairs two steps at a time. The footsteps behind her seem to sound faster and closer. It was as If the person was running to catch up to her. Becoming scared before she could turn around, she felt someone grab her from behind. Placing their hand over her mouth. They pressed their penis against her back side, as they began dragging her back down the flight of stairs backwards. Kicking like a wild cat Vera tried her best to break free from the person tight grip. Seeing a man walking down the stairs towards her with a knife in his hand. Vera eyes grew large. Vera bit down hard, her teeth tore through the person hand that was holding her from behind. She felt warm blood fill into her mouth.

"Fucking bitch" the boy yelled out in pain letting Vera go.

Turning around Vera received a hard fist to her face. The in pack filled both of her eyes with tears as she fell backwards onto the stairs. The man coming down the stairs put the knife to Vera neck.

"Please don't do this! Please let me go!"

"Shut up bitch before I kill your stupid ass" the boy said pressing the knife harder into Vera neck.

Recovering from the bite to his hand the boy covered her mouth once again and got on top of her on the stairs. Pulling up her dress he pried her legs apart and ripped her panties in half. Vera could feel the boy penis poking at her pussy. Thinking fast Vera began moving her hips side to side making it even harder for the guy on top of her to get inside of her.

"Hurry up and fuck this bitch so I can get my turn nigga" the man said still holding the knife to Vera neck.

"I'm trying but she won't stop moving." Letting go of Vera mouth the boy punched Vera in her forehead. "Bitch stop fucking moving!"

Hearing someone coming up the stairs. The boy on top of Vera turned around, but not fast enough. Swinging the butt of his gun at the boy head Solo knocked him out cold. Falling on top of Vera, she pushed him off of her. The boy with the knife to Vera neck stood up in shock.

"Drop it and get the fuck out of here before I let one off in your ass" Solo yelled pointing his gun at the young boy. Dropping the knife the boy ran up the stairs at top speed.

A fresh pear of tears rushed out of Vera eyes seeing Solo. Standing up Vera wrapped her arms around Solo. Holding Vera in his arms Solo could feel Vera shaking in his arms.

"You a'ight?"

"Yeah" Vera answered as she sobbed into Solo chest. Pushing Vera back Solo looked at her.

"What the hell are you doing here Vera?"

"I…. I was…. Ummm…."

"Don't tell me you are back getting high again!"

"No! I was …." Vera put her head down in shame. "I was going to cop, but those two boys came out of no where and tried to rape me. But trust me Solo I won't try to cop drugs again. This was a sign from God. I'm still clean of drugs. Please don't tell Trina about this Solo."

"You want me to lie to my wife?"

"Please Solo" Vera asked with a heavy pleading heart into Solo eyes.

"Fine, I'll keep this situation between us. But I swear to god If I find out that your back on drugs. I'm done with you Vera and so is Trina. Now let's get out of here. You got a lot of explaining to do to Trina about where you been and what happen to your face. As for me I have to go back to work."

*****

Waking up to a pleasant aroma . Jay walked into his kitchen to find Erykah cooking breakfast.

"About time you got up Jay. Have a seat so I can feed my husband." Sitting down at the table Jay had the Gibbs million dollar smile on his face.

"So this is what it's like to be married, waking up to breakfast every morning."

"Jay, you make me happy. It's only right that I keep you happy in every way."

Placing Jay plate of food in front of him. Erykah sat down across from Jay with her plate. For the past two weeks Jay had been wanting to ask Erykah about something that had him puzzled. Feeling like this was the best time he cleared his throat.

"Erykah, me and you have been married for over two months now. I know we both jumped into getting married fast…."

"Jay don't tell me your having second thoughts about us being married now?"

"No, that's not what I'm trying to get at Erykah. I'm happy with the choice I made to marry you."

"That's good to know Jay because I feel the same way. But If that's not it, than what are you trying to get at then?"

"Well I'm a little confused about something you told me Erykah when we first met. Erykah, me and you are the same age, right?"

"Right."

"Erykah what you told me, and your age don't add up." Erykah looked at Jay with a confused look on her face.

"Jay are you trying to say I lied to you about something?"

"Erykah, I would hate to call my wife a liar. I'm just hoping that you could make some sense to me of what you told me."

"Okay Jay I'm all ears. What do you want me to clear up for you?"

"Well, me and you are both 24 years old. Please explain to me how you been a license therapist for fifteen years, and had your license to practice law for five years?"

Erykah bust out laughing. For a minute Erykah thought Jay had found out her secret.

"What's so funny?"

"Jay every time someone question me on my college degrees I laugh. Well for one Jay before you think it, let me tell you. My degrees are real, their not fake. I was sent to boarding school when I was two years old. Long story short I finished my schooling when I was eight years old. I got my associate degree in psychology when I was nine years old. After that I became bored and started studying criminal justice. The college wouldn't let me take my bar exam until I hit eighteen years old."

"Erykah so your telling me I married a genius?"

"I wouldn't say I'm a genius Jay. There's really nothing but schooling when your in a boarding school. With no friends and no family…."

"Were you adopted by your boarding school?"

"No, I was just left there to be raised. My mother had me when she was very young. After my grandmother dropped off the face of the earth. My grandfather put me in a boarding school and never looked back. Although my grandmother dropped off the face of the earth to the family. She kept in contact with me and came to visit me every two weeks while I was in the boarding school. My grandmother made me aware of who my mother is, but she never told me who my father is. Although I seen pictures of my mother. Me and her never spoke on it when I first met her when I got older."

While Erykah washed the dishes Jay began to get dressed in their bedroom. Hearing the doorbell Erykah dried her hands. Seeing that it was Rome, Erykah open the door.

"Hey Rome, come in, Jay is upstairs getting dressed." Walking in the living room Rome took a seat on the couch. "So Rome where are you and Jay off to today?"

"We going over to the hospital to pick up my mother. Then the whole team is going over to our drug spot to have a meeting."

"A meeting about what Rome?"

"Listen Erykah I'm not going to talk to you about my team dealings and business. I respect you as Jay wife and...."

"Rome please don't tell me you are still mad at me, for being your baby mother lawyer in your son custody case."

"Erykah it's not that, I'm over that. I just don't speak about my team business with people that are not down with my team."

"Rome, me being married to Jay doesn't that make me a part of your family?"

"Erykah being apart of my family and being apart of my team are to different things. Jay made you a part of my family. But the whole team has to agree to make you a part of, the team. With that said don't take me not wanting to talk to you about the team business personally."

Walking into the living room and seeing the look on Erykah and Rome face. Jay could tell there was some type of tension between them.

"Is everything okay?"

"Yeah, you ready to hit the road" Rome asked walking towards the front door.

"Me and you need to talk when you come back home" Erykah said walking to their bedroom.

Not liking the sound of that Jay followed behind her. Reaching the bedroom Erykah slammed the bedroom door in Jay face and locked it.

"Erykah!"

"I said, will talk when you come back home!"

Not wanting to push the issue Jay followed Rome out the house. No sooner then Jay got in Rome car, Rome pulled off. Looking over at Rome, jay noticed Rome was making it his business not to look over at him.

Rome do you plan on filling me in, or your just gonna keep acting like I'm not sitting in your car?"

"Fill you in about what?"

"Rome clearly you and Erykah seem to be having a problem. I hope you're not still hung up on her being Nicole lawyer that day."

"Jay I'm over that."

"If that's the case what's your problem with her?"

"Like I told her in the house. I don't have a problem with her. I told her; the team is going to have a meeting after we leave the hospital. She asked me, a meeting about what? I told her; I don't talk team business with outsiders."

"Rome, I can't say anything on that, because you're in the right about that."

"Jay, I don't have a problem with your wife. You my cousin and I have nothing but respect for Erykah. So let's drop it, a'ight?"

"Rome before I drop it. I want to talk to you about putting Erykah down with the team. What do you think about that?"

"I think that's something you should bring up in the meeting today. I can't make that choice, you can't make that choice, only uncle Solo can make that choice."

"I know that Rome, but I wanted to run it by you first. Hoping that you would back me when I bring it up to uncle Solo at the meeting today."

"Jay like I said, bring it up at the meeting later."

Chapter 2

Two months before Khia left New York. She sold her house that was on Anton block, and brought Erykah old house when Erykah moved in with Jay. Now that she was back in New York. She was glad she made that move to buy a new house. Khia had paid the movers to move all of her things into her house, and she told them how and where to place her things in her new house. Back in New York Khia unlocking the door to her new house. Walking in Tonya, Nicole, China, Trini, Cam, and Mellow, followed Khia into the house.

After Khia showed all six of them the five bedroom house. Tonya took a seat in the living room by herself. With a lot on her mind she needed some time to think to herself. During the plane ride from L.A to New York. Tonya noticed Khia seem to be acting a little bit funny towards her. Although Tonya hadn't been in Khia life as a mother for 21 years. Tonya knew that wasn't why Khia was acting funny towards her. For sure Tonya knew Khia was feeling some type of way because she was back and taking the spot of being the queen of the Sams drug operation from her. There wasn't a doubt in Tonya mind that she loved Khia. Yet at the same time Tonya had plans and would be damn If she let Khia mess up her plans. Three plans were running threw Tonya head. Getting her family back together, bring down the Gibbs drug operation, and making the Sams drug operation shine better then ever. Thinking harder to herself. Tonya needed a spot to set the Sams drug operation up at. Closing her eyes, Tonya open them quick. She knew the perfect place to set shop up at. Standing up Tonya called out to Trini, Tymel, Cam, and Mellow. Once all four of them was standing before her in the living room. Tonya told them, "to get in the car so they could set up their drug spot."

*****

Dropping Trini, Cam, Tymel, and Mellow off. Tonya headed to New Jersey to see Gail. Getting what she needed from Gail. Gail told Tonya, "a meeting would need to be set up for her to officially take the spot of running the Sams drug operation from Jo-Jo." Agreeing Tonya told

Gail, "to set it up, and let her know the date and time and she would be at the meeting." Giving Gail a hug and a kiss. Tonya got in her car and drove off.

Walking through the door Tonya through two duffle bags on the floor. Tymel take those two bags to the back office and get to bagging up. Pulling out her car keys Tonya through them at Cam.

"Go to my car and get the other four duffle bags and join Tymel in the back office." With out a word Cam went out to Tonya's car.

"You" Tonya said pointing to Mellow. "Get your ass out of here and tell every fiend you see in the streets. That were open for business and we got that Sky-High."

"Sky-High" Mellow repeated. "Tonya is that the name were gonna call our crack bags?"

"Yup! And Sky-High is the name our crew will be going by."

"Say no more Boss lady" Mellow said walking out the door.

Seeing how good the boys cleaned up their new drug spot. Finally only with Trini, Tonya smiled at him. Grabbing Tonya hand they both looked around as the memories came flooding threw their minds. The memory of their last time they were in this spot, was over 21 years ago. Tonya was surprised that Trini still had his keys to get into Joe store. She was even more surprised that the store hadn't been rented out.

"Well boys it looks like my plans are coming together slowly. The girls are at the house making phone calls to make our drug family bigger and stronger. As for you four I believe you four can hold things down here at the store. As for me I'm gonna head out. I have to go meet up with two old friends of mine."

"I take it these two friends of yours are part of setting your plans into motion fully" Trini asked.

"Indeed, why else would I go looking for people I use to know?"

"Tonya I would be glad when you tell me of these plans you have in that pretty little head of yours. You know how I hate not knowing what's going on Tonya."

"I know that Trini and in time you will know everything. Just bear with me sweetheart and we will be running the whole Bronx." Giving Trini a kiss Tonya left the store.

*****

Pulling up to a house that Tonya hadn't seen in years. Tonya parked her car and turn it off.

"Who the hell lives in this run down house" Tameka asked sitting in the passenger seat of Tonya car.

"A very good friend of mine Tameka, just like you are a friend of mine. So just hang tight and I'll be right back."

Getting out the car Tonya walked over to the house. Knocking on the old wooding door Tonya stood back.

"Girl who in the hell are you here to see" the man yelled opening the door.

"Hey Goody, long time no see."

Stepping a few feet back Goody eyes grew wide as he looked at Tonya. "Tonya" Goody whispered in shock.

"The one and the only" Tonya said with a smile.

"Girl did the devil let you come up from hell to come play with the living? I thought you was dead? Girl get over here and come in" Goody said hugging Tonya.

Walking in Goody house Tonya took a seat on the couch across from Goody in his living room.

"So do tell Tonya where you been hiding out at for over twenty something years."

"I been in L.A laying low until it was safe for me to come back to the Bronx. I'm sure you heard Carlos put a hit out on me some years ago."

"I did Tonya, that's why I thought you were dead."

"Well as you know Carlos was murdered so my life is no longer in danger."

"Tonya, I did business with Carlos for years with you bring me my drugs. I think it's safe for me to say. I know you very well. Carlos maybe dead but I'm more then sure Tonya. That your back in the Bronx to start some shit."

Tonya laughed at Goody comment. "You know me so well Goody. And yes, I'm back in the Bronx to start some shit. With your help hopefully Goody."

Goody looked at Tonya long and hard and began stretching at his chin. "Before I agree or disagree. Tell me what your trying to get into Tonya?"

"Well I'm back and will be running the Sams drug operation. I'm also in the Bronx to take Gibbs drug operation."

"Tonya I'm not gonna lie to you. I been wanting to get at the Gibbs team since Joe murdered all four of my boys. Me, Red, Moe, CK, and Shine, all grew up together. Joe murdered all four of them in my face. Not only that…." Goody stopped in mid-sentence when he saw his son walk into the living room.

"Dad who is this" Levi asked looking at Tonya.

"Levi this is an old friend of mine. Tonya was the wife of my old connect. She's back in town to take over where he left off at. She wants to take on the Gibbs drug operation."

"I'm in" Levi said sitting down.

"Not so fast Levi."

"What you mean not so fast Dad! Did you tell this woman how Supreme murdered my brother Tom?"

"No he didn't tell me about that Levi. Why don't you."

"Tonya I'm 31 years old and Supreme murdered my brother Tom Jones when I was eight years old. He shot my brother twice in his face, when my brother tried to stop him from pistol whipping another guy. Supreme got charged for beating up the guy but that case he somehow beat. When it came to my brother's murder, he never got charged for it. My brother had two close friends named Miguel and Ralph. They sent me to send a message to the Gibbs team. Me being so young at the time. They wild out on me and murdered Miguel and Ralph. Point blank miss lady If you're getting at the Gibbs drug team, I want in."

"Well that leaves you Goody. Are you in or out" Tonya said batting her eyes lashes at him.

Four eyes were on him as Goody began thinking to his self. Two eyes from Tonya, and the other two eyes from his son Levi.

"Tonya, I hope like hell you have done your homework on the Gibbs."

"I have Goody."

"Oh you have, so you know that damn family name rang bells throughout the Bronx when it comes to the drug game?"

"Yeah, I do know that, just like the Sams name use to rang bells threw out the Bronx years ago. And with your help Goody we can make the Sams name rang bells once again in the Bronx."

Goody took a deep breath then let it out slowly. "Fine, I'm in."

"Good because the Sams drug operation is having a meeting. Here's the address, date, and time" Tonya said passing Goody a piece of paper as she stood up to leave.

Chapter 3

"So Bev how does it feel to finally be released from the hospital today?"

"Solo, me being in the hospital for over two months. I'm more than ready to go" Beverly said. Looking around the hospital room. Beverly made sure she hadn't forgot to pack any of her things. While looking around the room Beverly noticed Supreme was being to quite. In no way was it like him to be so quite. Solo took notice that Supreme was being to quite also.

"You a'ight big Bro?"

"I'm good Solo. I'm just waiting for Bev to get her hospital release papers so me and her can go home.

"Home" Beverly repeated. "Supreme, Solo is having a team meeting at Soundview projects today. So we have to head over there first for the meeting. Then me and you can go home."

"Bev, I said, me and you are going home. If Solo want to have a meeting that's his right. But me and you are going home."

Beverly and Solo looked at one another, then looked back at Supreme. "You sure you all right big Bro?"

"Solo, I told you I'm fine. Me and Bev are done and were going home."

"Done with what Supreme?"

"Yeah, done with what" Beverly questioned as well.

"Done with the drug game! Me and you are done with the drug game Beverly. Rome is out too."

"Supreme what's wrong with you?"

"Word big Bro, you talking real crazy right now" Solo added in. "Big Bro getting money in the drug game is what we do."

"No! Wrong! That's what you do Solo! Me, my wife, and my son are out the drug game as of today."

Walking over to Supreme, Solo looked his older brother in the face. "Listen big Bro I don't want to argue with you or fight with you. You, maybe older than me Supreme, but I run our family drug operation, not you. You don't make the choice to tell me who's in and who's out the team. If you want out, fine, but Beverly and Rome can make their own choice."

Stepping closer to Solo, Supreme jaw muscles got tight. "Solo your right you run the family drug operation, but I run my family. Beverly is my wife and Rome is my son. If I say their out, than that's what it is."

Seeing that tension was growing thick between Supreme and Solo. Beverly got up and got between them. "Supreme, me and Solo understand that you are feeling some type of way because I was shot three times. And it was scary because you almost lost me. Listen, let's just all go to the meeting."

"Beverly you seem to be hard of hearing! This is not for a fucking debate. I'm out, you're out, and so is Rome."

"I'm not out of shit Supreme!"

Beyond pissed off that Beverly was going against him. Supreme snatched Beverly up by her arm, grabbed her bag off the hospital bed, and began dragging Beverly towards the door.

"Get off me" Beverly yelled trying her best to break away from Supreme grip.

Grabbing Supreme by his arm Solo stopped him from walking out the hospital room. "Get off her like that!"

Dropping the bag Supreme let Beverly arm go. Turning around Supreme stood face to face with Solo. "What fucking part of my family don't you understand?" With force Supreme mushed Solo in his face sending him halfway across the room. "Mind your fucking business!"

Recovering quick Solo rushed Supreme grabbed him by his shirt and slammed him against the wall. "Don't let your feelings get you fucked up in this room Supreme."

Grabbing Solo by his neck they saw a nurse and two security guards walking into the hospital room.

"Is there a problem in here" the nurse asked.

Letting one another go Supreme walked out the room and out the hospital. Not answering the nurse, Beverly signed her hospital release papers. Solo grabbed her bag and they both walked out the hospital without saying a word to one another.

Walking in the hospital parking lot. Beverly and Solo didn't see Supreme car anywhere, but they did see Rome and Jay pulling up in the parking lot. Getting in the car Solo beeped his car horn, waived his hand out the car window and pulled off. Beeping his car horn Rome followed Solo car to Soundview projects.

*****

In Soundview projects in their private re-up apartment. In the living room sat the whole team except Supreme. Not speaking Solo looked at each one of his team members. Beverly, Trina, Tone, Pit, Davon, Lloyd, Jo-Jo, Rome, Sierra, Corey, and Jay. As the whole team spoke to each other Solo sat quite. Multiple things were going through Solo mind. The most important thing that was on his mind, was the disagreement he had with Supreme. Supreme may have told him he was out the drug game. But no way in the hell was Solo going to allow him to leave the drug game. Solo would also be damn If he was going to let Rome or Beverly leave the team either.

"Okay, okay, let's get this team meeting started" Solo said standing up. Seeing that everyone in the living room was quiet and he had their full attention, Solo began speaking. "As everyone in this room know things with this team have been put on hold for the past two months. Why? Because our new queen of the Gibbs drug operation was in the hospital, from taking three bullets. Bev it's good to see you back up and running." Beverly gave Solo a wink and a smile. "With that said it's time we get things back on track. As promise Soundview projects now belong to Beverly. Thinking bigger were opening a drug spot in Webster projects. We will be setting up shop in our private apartment in Webster projects today. As of today this team will be split into two groups. Half of you will work under Beverly. The other half will be working under me at Webster projects. Bev who do you want to work under you?"

Beverly stood up and looked around the living room. "I want Rome, Sierra, Corey, Trina, and Jay. Solo you can take Tone, Pit, Davon, Lloyd, and Jo-Jo."

After Beverly split the team in half Solo stayed quite for a few seconds. "You foul Bev."

"Why you say that Solo?"

"Because you not slick Bev. You took members that are blood related to you, or married into the family, and left me with all friends of the family."

"She damn sure did Solo" Pit said.

"You get a position and already you being foul" Tone said.

Walking over to Tone, Beverly stood between his legs as he sat on the couch. "Me being foul towards the team, never that Tone. The reason why I split the team the way I did. Is because

I always think ahead. Yeah, I gave Solo all those that are friends of the family. I also gave him the muscles of our team to help him run and start up a new spot."

The more Solo listened to Beverly explain her reason for splitting the team the way she did. The more Solo realized it was a good idea how Beverly split the team. Looking at Beverly for sure Solo knew giving Beverly the queen of the Gibbs drug operation was a good idea. Taking a seat Beverly looked over at Solo.

"Listen people although it may have seemed like Beverly was being foul. Clearly she couldn't have split the team any better."

*****

On her fifth glass of wine. Erykah tried her best to forget about the conversation that she had with Rome earlier. Yet each glass she finished the more she thought about their conversation. Slamming the empty glass down on the table. Erykah poured herself another glass of wine. Slamming the bottle of wine on the table. Erykah looked at her glass for a few seconds. Standing up she almost fell back down in her chair but caught herself.

"Bullshit! You claim you don't have a problem with me. Bullshit! I know damn well you don't like me because I was Nicole lawyer against you in that custody case. I mean like damn! Get over it! I may have been her lawyer, but you won the custody case and kept your son. You don't want to get over it, fine! When Jay get home, I'm gonna tell him I don't want Rome in our house anymore until he can get over it. Yup, that's what I'm gonna tell Jay when…." Hearing someone knocking on the house door stopped Erykah from talking to herself in mid-sentence.

Without asking who was on the other side of the door. Erykah open the door. Seeing who it was Erykah eyes almost popped out of her head. Just as fast as she swung the door open, she tried to swing the door back closed just as fast. Stopping the door from closing in his face, he stuck his foot in the door and pushed it wide open. Being drunk the door knocked Erykah off balance and she fell into the wall. Stepping inside the house he closed the door behind him. Standing back up straight Erykah jumped in his face.

"I don't know how you found where I live, but you need to leave Henry."

"I'll leave when I damn well get ready to leave. And not a minute sooner!"

"Henry you need to just move on with your life. Me and you are over, I'm married now."

"I know all of that! So stop throwing that shit up in my face."

"If you know that then why are you here?"

"Because…."

"Because what!"

"Because I know your secret, or did you forget that? Not only do I know your secret. I been investigating your new boy toy Jay. And guess what I found out! Your little secret effects Jay. How do you think Jay would feel If he found out you are related to the Sams family?"

"I should have never told you any of my family business."

"Well you did Erykah! And If you want to keep your secret from Jay. You need to start lining my pockets with some of your boy toy money."

"What?"

"You heard me you foul bitch! You think you just gonna up and leave me for this new nigga and I'm just gonna lay down and deal with it? I don't think so! Your new man is paid and you gonna help me get paid too. So every Friday around this same time. You will be seeing me at your doorstep with head high with my hand out."

Hearing Henry say he going to blackmail her. Erykah wanted to spit in his face. Thinking twice Erykah decided against it and snatched up her purse. Pulling out five hundred dollars Erykah gave the money to Henry."

"This is a nice amount" Henry said putting the money in his pocket. Opening the door Henry turned around and looked at Erykah. "Make sure you have a thousand dollars for me every Friday."

Walking out the door Henry had a big smile on his face. Slamming the door closed Erykah wanted to scream. Walking back in the kitchen she picked up the bottle of wine and took it to the head. Emptying the bottle she slammed the bottle down on the table and picked up the glass and took that to the head as well.

Going in the cabinet Erykah reached for another bottle of wine. Before she could grab it, she heard her cell phone beeping, letting her know someone had just sent her a text message. Picking up her cell phone she read the text message: *"Be at your old house this Friday around 5 p.m."* The text message was from her grandmother Tonya. "This can't be good" Erykah said out load shaking her head.

*****

"Before I end this team meeting. Is there anything anyone want to say" Solo asked.

"I have something that I want to say" Jay said standing up.

"The floor is yours Jay" Solo said taking a seat.

"Well as everyone in this room know, I'm married now. With that being said I want Erykah to be a part of the team."

"Are you telling me that she's a part of the team or asking me can she be a part of the team Jay" Solo asked.

"I'm asking you Uncle Solo can Erykah be a part of the team?"

"No."

"What do you mean no, why not Uncle Solo?"

"Because I said so. Plus Erykah has nothing to bring to the team that we don't already have."

"She has a lot to bring to the team."

"Such as what Jay?"

"Well for one she's a lawyer."

"So are you Jay, and so is your grandmother. What the hell do we need three lawyers for?"

"You're not being fair Unc. Every man in this room that has a wife. Their wife is down with the team. Why?"

"Jay, I don't want to argue with you or go back and forth with you. As of right now Erykah is not getting down with the team."

"If my father Gutta was alive we wouldn't be having this conversation. You seem to forget the team was once my father's team."

Not liking Jay tone Solo stood up and walked over to Jay. "Your father is more alive than you know. And for the record yes Gutta use to run the team. But keep in mind my father Joe is who started the team, not your father. When my father was alive, I called the shots. When Gutta was alive I called the shots. Now that I have the team, I'm the only one that call the shots. If you have a problem with the way I run the team. Maybe you shouldn't be a part of the team any more Jay."

Beyond pissed off Jay snatched his coat off the chair and walked out the apartment. Turning around Solo stood face to face with the rest of his team members. "Tone, Pit, Davon, Lloyd, Jo-Jo. I want the five of you to go to Webster projects and start setting up shop. Here's the keys to our private re-up apartment in those projects. Pit, you are in charge of holding down that spot when I'm not around" Solo said throwing the keys to Pit. "This meeting is over" Solo said walking towards the back private room of the apartment.

<u>Chapter 4</u>

Beverly and Trina sat in the living room and watched everyone leave the re-up apartment after the meeting.

"Beverly, me and you need to talk."

"Trina don't tell me you are mad that Solo what me to be the queen of the Gibbs drug operation and not you when you are his wife."

"Beverly don't be stupid. Me and you are cousins. That position belong to you without a doubt. Plus I know damn well you wouldn't cross the line with my man. I trust both of you."

"Okay that's good to know. But what do you want to talk to me about Trina?"

Getting closer to Beverly ear Trina began whispering. I'm four months pregnant."

"Oh my god that's good!"

"Be quite Bev, Solo don't know, and I don't plan on telling him."

Beverly looked at Trina confused. "Why not Trina?"

"Because I'm getting an abortion. I told you Beverly after I had Quinn. One kid is good enough for me and I don't want anymore."

"If Solo find out that you killed his baby. He's gonna kill you Trina."

"He's not gonna kill shit because he's not gonna find out."

"Why couldn't you just go do it, why tell me Trina?"

"Because we family, why not?"

"Trina, you know how close I am to Solo. I don't like hiding secrets or lying to Solo."

"I know, that's why I'm not telling you what abortion clinic I'm going to. Just in case you can't hold your tongue."

"Trina, I don't need to know what clinic you're going to. Solo has eyes everywhere. It won't take him long to find out. Trina, I think you should have the baby. That's why I'm gonna tell Solo. Because I know once he know he will put a stop to it."

As Beverly stood up so did Trina. Pushing Beverly back down on the couch Trina ran out the apartment.

"You can run all you want but he'll find you" Beverly yelled laughing at the same time.

Getting up off the couch Beverly joined Solo in the back private room. Seeing Solo on his computer she walked up behind his chair.

"I thought everyone left. Why are you still here Bev" Solo asked without turning around.

"Well for one I thought I now run Soundview drug spot. Seeing how this is the Soundview drug spot and you no longer run it. The question is why are you still here Solo?"

"You right Bev, my bad. I'll be out your way in a minute."

Looking at the computer screen. Beverly noticed that Solo was on the internet checking on some of the team members chain trackers. For the past few years. Solo had a tracking device placed in the cross of every chain that each of his members were around their necks. The only ones that knew about the trackers were Supreme and Beverly. Taking a closer look at the computer screen. Beverly noticed Solo only had Supreme and Jay tracker maps up on the screen.

"You want to talk about it Solo?"

"There's nothing really to talk about Bev. I'm sure you will talk some sense into Supreme when you go home tonight. Right now his tracker map says he's at his strip club, Love it or hate it. Jay tracker map says he's on his way to the strip club. No doubt in my mind Jay is going over there to talk to Supreme about me. I'm sure Supreme will check Jay before he get to out of pocket."

"Solo, I agree with everything you just said. But I wasn't talking about none of that. I'm talking about that comment you made to Jay."

"What comment Bev?"

"You told him; your father is more alive than you know. Now I know Gutta is dead for a fact. So what did you mean by that comment?"

Turning around to face Beverly he had the million dollar Gibbs smile on his face.

"See that's why I made you the queen of the Gibbs drug operation because you don't miss a thing Bev."

"Solo not when I'm focus and believe me, I'm focus. So do explain that comment you made to Jay to me."

"Bev who is Rome's father?"

"Supreme, my husband, your brother."

"Bev I'm talking about who is his real father?"

"You, which only me and you know that. But what does that have to do with what you said to Jay?"

"Bev who is Jay's father?"

"Gutta."

"Wrong, I'm Jay's real father."

Beverly grabbed her mouth in shock. "How is that" Beverly whispered even though they were both alone in the apartment.

Solo smiled at Beverly again. "The same way I sexed you at that graduation party. I sexed Monique that same night."

"You are such a damn hoe Solo."

"Bev those are strong words coming from a person that fucked me and my brother in the same night."

Although Solo had a point Beverly still gave him the evil eye. Taking a seat Beverly looked at Solo.

"Solo, I was in the hospital for two months. I had a lot of time to think to myself. I died, and even though the doctors were able to bring me back. I really don't want to leave this earth without telling my son Rome who his real father is."

"What are you saying Bev?"

"I'm saying that we should tell Rome you are his real father. And now I also think you should tell Jay you are his real father too."

"Bev you should have let me do that years ago. Now it's been 24 years. Do you have any idea what type of problem it will cause now telling the truth? Hell I think Supreme would kill me and you. Not to mention how Trina would take the news. My marriage, your marriage, may both be over. On top of that Supreme may never speak to both of us ever again."

Taking a deep breath Beverly knew what Solo had just said was true. "Fine, we held these secrets all these years. We mind as well keep it this way Solo. But speaking of children you might want to check Trina tracker map."

Cutting his eye over at Beverly. Solo pulled up Trina tracker map. "What the hell is she doing at Plan Parent Hood Clinic" Solo said out loud. Looking at the computer screen Solo mind went into overdrive. "That's not where her doctor work. Beverly why is she at this clinic?" Beverly began looking around the room like she didn't hear Solo question. "I know damn well you heard me Bev!" Beverly continued to act like she didn't hear Solo speaking to her. "The only reason why people go to Plan Parent Hood. Is to get birth control pills, which she have them already. The other reason is to have an abortion. Abortion" Solo yelled jumping up from the computer. "Oh hell no" Solo yelled running out the apartment.

*****

Walking in Plan Parent Hood Clinic. Solo looked around the waiting room. Finally spotting Trina, he saw her sitting in the corner reading a XXL magazine. Walking up to Trina, Solo slapped the magazine out her hand. Looking up at Solo fair ran across Trina face. With the waiting room full to the max all eyes were on them. "What are you waiting for in this clinic?" Trina lips began moving but no words were coming out. "I can't hear you. Speak up!"

"Solo how did you find me?"

Her question seem to bounce off of Solo head. In no way was he going to answer that question. Nor was he in the mood to answer any questions."

"You in here trying to kill my baby."

"Solo listen…."

"Trina the only person that need to listen right now is you. You having an abortion is not gonna happen. If you do it, you can be sure you will meet that baby on the other side the same day. I love you; you love me, we are married. We have a four year old son together that we both love. We have more than enough money to take care of another child. If you feel you need help. I'm here to help, plus we can hire a nanny." Trina looked at Solo with tears in her eyes.

"The choice is yours baby girl. I'll be waiting in the car with my gun. Come out this clinic without my seed inside of you and I'm gonna leave you dead in the parking lot."

Walking out the clinic Solo left Trina sitting in the same seat he found her in. Trina wiped the tears from her eyes. Looking around the waiting room all eyes were still on her. A dark skin female stood up and walked over to Trina. By the look of the female. Her stomach look like she was way past the point of an abortion. Yet there she was, waiting to get an abortion just like the other girls in the room.

"Girl is you stupid or what" the dark skin female asked looked at Trina. Not waiting for a response the dark skin female continued to speak. "Girl do you have any idea how many bitches in here would wish the man that knocked them up. Would come up in here right now and say to them what your man just said to you. And here you are still sitting your stupid ass in that seat."

"I'm so fucking selfish" Trina said shaking her head. Standing up Trina walked out the clinic.

Stepping into the parking lot Trina got in the car with Solo. Looking over at Solo, Trina saw his gun on his lap. Leaning over Trina kissed Solo on his lips. Grabbing Trina by the back of her head gently Solo passionately kissed her back. Letting Trina go Solo looked at her.

"Trina, I swear to god if you ever pull another stunt like this. I'm gonna put a bullet in your ass."

"Solo I'm getting my tubes tied after I have this one."

Taking Trina hand Solo placed it on his penis. "Baby girl your man got the mandi go. Your birth control can't stop my soldiers. Hear me when I tell you my soldiers will untie your tubes too." Snatching her hand away from his penis. Trina couldn't help but to laugh.

*****

Up in Love it or Hate it. Walking through the strip club. Jay couldn't help but watch as some of the strippers made it clap for those dollars. Beating on the mic, DJ L-Boogie got everyone attention in the club.

"Party people we have a good treat for you. Coming to the stage. Unique! And Brown Sugar!"

Running onto the stage Brown Sugar and Unique came out wearing nothing but their birthday suits. Stepping in front of the stage Jay watched them work the poles and clap their ass. Two minute into their show Jay almost forgot what he was in the strip club for. Shaking his head from side to side. Jay walked away from the stage and headed straight to the club back office.

Knocking on the office door Jay heard Supreme tell him, to come in. Opening the door, Jay stepped inside and closed the door behind him.

"Unc, you got a minute to talk?"

Supreme pointed at the chair in front of his desk. Taking a seat Jay looked at Supreme and almost didn't know what to say. At times talking to Supreme was like talking to Solo. When he talked to Solo it was like talking to Supreme.

"I'm sure you didn't come here to just look at me. So spit it out, what's on your mind Jay?"

"Unc, I'm having a problem with Uncle Solo."

"Join the club" Supreme mumbled to his self. "What type of problem Jay?"

"I asked Uncle Solo can we put Erykah down with the team and he said, no. Which I don't understand why not? Every other man on the team wife is down with the team. Unc I need you to talk to Uncle Solo for me."

Sitting up in his chair Supreme looked at Jay for a few seconds before he spoke. "Jay no, I will not speak to Solo about Erykah. Nor do I think Erykah should be put down on the team."

"I knew it was a bad idea coming here to talk to you. Your just like Uncle Solo" Jay yelled standing up.

"Jay you maybe blood but I hope you didn't think I would go against my brother words. Not only do I agree with my brother I know how he think. I'm more than sure he told you, Erykah has nothing to bring to the team right now. It's not personal Jay. So don't try to take it like it's personal because it's not. There are three wives down with the team. Beverly, Trina, and Sierra. Beverly and Trina put in work when they wasn't asked to years ago. For that good deed that they did. They will forever have a spot on the team. While Beverly was locked up, she met Sierra. Sierra held Beverly down in prison. For that she will forever have a spot on the team. Them being someone wife in the team. Has nothing to do with why they are a part of the team. It's the work they put in that got them on the team."

After hearing Supreme reason for agreeing with Solo. It made a lot of sense and he realized it wasn't anything personal against Erykah. Taking a seat once again. Jay now wanted to address the comment that Supreme mumbled earlier.

"What problem are you having with Uncle Solo?"

"That's none of your business Jay. What me and Solo are going through is between me and him."

"Oh it's like that Unc?"

"It's always going to be like that Jay."

Standing up Jay began walking towards the officer door to leave. Turning around he looked at Supreme. "You know Unc I feel like I'm out casted by you and Uncle Solo because my father is dead."

Turning around Jay grab the doorknob and open the door. Before Jay could get the door all the way open it was slammed back closed. "How dear you say some shit like that" Supreme roared. "Your father who was my brother, I would have giving my life to save him If I could have. Just like I would give my life If I had to save your life Jay. If you are feeling out casted by me and Solo. I'm sorry and so is Solo. In no way do we want you to feel that way." Supreme could see tears in Jay eyes as he spoke to him.

"Unc I miss my father" Jay said letting the tears fall down his face.

Grabbing a hold of Jay, Supreme wrapped his arm around him and held him tight. "I miss Gutta too. But know you didn't have one Father Jay, you had three and you still have two father's left. Me and Solo will always look at you Jay as our son. You got that?"

"Yeah" Jay said hugging Supreme back.

After Jay left the office Supreme sat back at his desk in deep thought. He had told Solo that he wanted out the drug game. But after talking to Jay. How the hell could he just up and leave the only brother he had left in the drug game by his self. Supreme mind was made up. He would stay in the drug game as long as his brother stayed in the drug game. But before he tell Solo, he was going to make him sweat just a little bit.

Hearing his desk phone ranging broke into Supreme thoughts.

"Hello" Supreme said picking up the phone.

"Supreme it's me Solo."

"No shit! You think I don't know my own damn brother voice? What do you want Solo?"

"What do I want" Solo repeated. "I see you still on your period talking to me like you want to get fucked up."

"The only fucking me up you gonna do Solo is in your dreams. Now what do you want?"

"I'll tell you what I want. I see Jay came to your club to talk to you."

"I'm sure you did see that since you track everybody movements."

"That's a very cute come back Supreme. I just hope you set Jay mind right."

"Yeah, I did, and do me a favor Solo."

"What?"

"Don't call me anymore."

"What! What the fuck do you mean don't call you anymore Supreme?" Hanging up the phone Supreme took his chain off his neck, placed it on his desk and left the club.

*****

Walking through Love it or Hate it like a mad man. Solo headed straight to Supreme back office. Opening the office door Solo was ready for war. To his surprise Supreme wasn't in his office. Pulling out his cell phone, Solo jumped on the internet, punched in his code, and pulled up Supreme chain tracker map. Supreme tracker map showed that he was in the club. Pulling out the tracker device, Solo put Supreme chain code in, and the tracker device began beeping like crazy in his hand. Looking at the device screen, it was pointing to Supreme desk.

"Mother fucker" Solo yelled seeing Supreme gold chain laying on the desk.

Picking the chain up Solo put it in his pocket. To say Solo was pissed off was a understatement. Hearing the desk phone ranging Solo picked it up.

"Love it or Hate it, how can I help you" Solo said answering the phone.

"You can help me by telling me why the hell you in my office Solo?"

"Supreme, you really playing yourself right now."

"Oh is little brother Solo mad at his big brother? Well since you seem to know everybody movements on the team. Why don't you tell me where I am right now Solo?"

"I can't because you know the rules, don't ever take off your chain. What If something…."

"Oh stop crying you big baby! I'm at home, so get over to my house because me and you need to talk about some serious shit."

Chapter 5

"Come in, everyone is in the living room" Tonya said letting Goody and Levi into the house.

Stepping in the living room, it was filled with men and women. None of whom Levi knew. As for Goody no one looked familiar to him except for one guy. He couldn't put a name on the guy, but he was sure he knew the guy from somewhere.

"Now that everyone is here let me introduce all of you to each other" Tonya said. "Cam, Mellow, China, Mike, Desean, and T.G." Tonya pointed to each one of them as she said their names. "This is my daughter Khia, her daughter Erykah, and her son Tymel. This is Nicole my late son Wayne's daughter. Goody, Levi, and Tameka. My stepchildren from my first marriage, Debra and Flaco. Last but not least my husband Trini."

"Oh hell no! I knew I knew him from somewhere. Years ago Trini was down with the Gibbs family. He's one of them" Goody said jumping up from the chair.

Walking up to Goody, Tonya pushed him back down in the chair. "Calm down Goody, I'm aware of that. Trini has not been down with the Gibbs family in over twenty years. When Joe Gibbs was murdered Trini walked away from the Gibbs crew and never looked back and been with me ever since."

"Now that we all know who's who. With me added to you all, it is a total of seventeen of us. When this meeting is over, I'm more then sure it will be less down with the Sams drug operation. It comes to my attention while my daughter Khia was running the Sams drug operation. A few of you in this room shitted on her. O know my daughter is tough as nails. Myself on the other hand I'm more like the hammer. Cross me one time, play me one time, and your life I will take without blanking an eye."

Tonya looked at everyone in the room while they all sat. Seeing that she still had everyone attention in the room she continued. "Mike the Sams family supply your drugs. Would you like to continue to run your own drug operation or join the Sams family?"

"With all due respect Tonya it's like I told Khia I'm good on my own and doing my own thing."

"I can respect that Mike; we will continue to supply you. Yet if you cross my crew in any way, I will take a hammer to your head. Are we clear Mike?"

"Crystal clear Tonya."

"Good, now get out." Standing up Mike walked out the house. "Desean and T.G, it comes to my understanding that you were both down with Mike team, but you two are no longer running with him. How do you feel about joining my crew T.G?"

"I'm down" T.G said without hesitation.

"How about you Desean?"

"I don't want any part in the drug game anymore. I been out the game for the past two months now and that's the way I want to keep it."

"I can't argue with that Desean. Have a nice day, you may leave."

Standing up Desean began walking towards the door to leave and Tonya called out to him. Turning around Desean looked at Tonya. "Desean what I told Mike it goes for you as well. Are we clear?"

"Very" Desean said walking out the door.

"Is there anyone else in this room that don't want to be down with the Sams crew?"

Erykah stood up. "Grandma with all due respect I am now married to a Gibbs. I don't know what you have planned, all I know is I don't want any part of it."

With a smile on her face Tonya walked up to Erykah. Getting close to Erykah ear Tonya began whispering. "You were born a Sams and you will die as a Sams. Go against your family for the Gibbs and you will die right alone with them. The choice is yours Erykah. Make your choice" Tonya said backing up from Erykah.

"I choose them" with that said Erykah walked out the house.

Tonya looked at those that were still sitting in the living room. "Well it looks like we have a crew of fourteen. Which is fine by me and more than enough for what I have planned. Our crew street drug name is, Sky-High. In the meantime everyone in here will take orders from Trini. But please don't forget you all work for me. For right now focus on getting this money and be ready for war when the time comes. And believe me when I tell you us going to war will be coming very soon."

"Tonya, I think me, and you need to have a private conversation" Trini said.

"Trini I really…." Hearing her cell phone ranging stopped Tonya in mid-sentence. Looking at her cell phone screen it was Gail calling her. Walking into the hallway Tonya answered her cell phone. "Hello."

"Tonya, I have Jo-Jo on his way to my house as we speak. I need you at my house as soon as possible."

"I'm on my way Gail." Hanging up the phone Tonya stepped back into the living room. "People I have to go. Trini will have that one on one conversation tonight when I get back home."

*****

When Tonya ended the meeting Trini headed back over to the store with Cam, Mellow, and T.G. As Trini held down the cash register. Cam, Mellow, and T.G held down the store back office. Fiend after fiend gave Trini their money and Trini gave them a blue ticket. Taking the ticket, the fiends walked out the store, walked around to the back of the store, and pick their drugs up at the store office window. In between fiends giving him their money. Trini mind kept going back to what Tonya had said in the meeting. To him it sound like Tonya plan was to go up against the Gibbs family. He agreed to come back to New York with Tonya to get the Sams drug operation popping in the streets again. In no way did he agree to join in on a war with the Gibbs family. Although he had let Joe get murdered over twenty years ago. His loyalty was still to the Gibbs family. Sometimes he wished he didn't let Joe get murdered. Joe was his best friend from childhood. Knowing he couldn't go back in time to undo things. He would be damn If he would have a hand in killing any of Joe children, grandchildren, or kill anyone down with the Gibbs drug operation. Standing at the cash register Trini went into deep thought. He was most definitely going to have a conversation with Tonya about what her true plan is for coming back to New York.

*****

It didn't take long for Solo to get to Supreme house. Taking a seat in the living room with Supreme. Supreme began telling Solo about the conversation he had with Jay in his office. After hearing everything Supreme said Solo began thinking to his self.

"Solo we have to do something to let Jay know…."

"I got a idea Supreme. I say me and you go pick up Jay and take us a road trip." Solo got up and walked out the house with Supreme following behind him.

*****

As Solo drove the car, Jay sat in the back seat behind Supreme. Not having a clue where Solo was taking them was killing Jay. Not able to take it anymore Jay sat up in his seat.

"Uncle Solo where are you taking us?"

"Were almost there" Solo said turning the corner.

Seeing what was up a head. Supreme and Jay looked at Solo like he was crazy. "Solo it's after 7 p.m. How the hell are we going to get inside of there" Supreme asked.

"Easy when you have a police detective on your payroll."

Pulling up to the cemetery Solo spotted detective Price standing at the gate. Getting out the car Jay followed behind Solo and Supreme with a smile on his face. Saying a few words to detective Price, detective Price told Solo they had one hour. Walking threw out the cemetery. The three of them found Gutta's head stone. Looking at the head stone it read:

Joe Gibbs Jr

A.K.A Gutta

R.I.P

The King Of Loyalty

Cracking a few jokes, shedding a few tears, and saying a few strong words. Solo and Supreme hugged Jay with all the love they had in them. Letting go of Jay, Solo and Supreme looked at each other.

"You ready little Bro" Supreme asked.

"Yeah, let's go see the old man." Walking through the cemetery Solo and Supreme stopped in front of their father head stone. The three of them looked at the head stone that read:

Joe Gibbs

A.K.A Pimp Daddy

R.I.P

The King Of The Team

Cracking a few more jokes Supreme looked at Solo.

"Daddy always said, mark my words Solo is gonna run the shit out of the drug game one day."

"Supreme, I miss the old man even though me and him always bumped heads when he was alive."

Supreme wrapped his arm around Solo shoulder. "That's because you two are so much alike. You both are good with the ladies and know how to lead a army that respect you."

*****

Many late nights Nancy got in her car and went for a drive. Somehow, she always found herself parking her car across the street from her late husband Joe old store. Joe store was left to Solo in Joe will. A store that Solo paid the taxes on very year but refused to reopen it. Parking her car Nancy held her set of the store keys in her hand. So badly she wanted to go in the store but could never bring herself to ever do it. Closing her eyes, Nancy opened her eyes and looked over at Joe store. Not believing what she was seeing Nancy blanked her eyes a few times. Yet she was still seeing the same thing. The gate to the store was up and the lights were on in the store.

Getting out the car Nancy walked across the street to the store. Walking up to the store she looked through the glass door. Nancy eyes grew large as she looked at the guy behind the cash register. Running back to her car, Nancy pulled out her cell phone and pulled off in her car.

*****

With his hand on his father head stone Solo looked at Supreme. "So what's it gonna be Supreme, you out the drug game or you gonna stay by my side" Solo asked.

Supreme placed his hand on Solo shoulder. "No way in the hell am I gonna leave my little brother in the drug game by his self. If you're staying in it, then so am I."

Smiling at Supreme Solo gave him the Gibbs million dollar smile and Supreme gave him the Gibbs million dollar smile right back. Taking his chain out of Solo hand. Supreme place his gold chain back around his neck.

"Well fellas let's get out of…." Hearing his cell phone ranging Supreme put his cell phone to his ear. "Yes Ma. What? Calm down Ma. What? Huh? Where are you? Ma are you sure you are okay? Okay, okay, Ma just try to calm down. I'm gonna go over there and check things out. I'll call you back later Ma." Hanging up the phone Supreme looked at Solo and Jay. Seeing the look on Supreme face Solo knew something was up.

"What's wrong big Bro?"

"Solo that was Mommy. She said, she was just by Dad old store, it was open, the lights were on and she saw Trini behind the cash register."

"What" Solo said confused out his mind.

"Who's Trini" Jay asked.

"Our father best friend that we wrote off as being dead over twenty years ago" Solo said still confused.

"Solo, I don't know If Mommy is bugging out, but I think we should go check out that store. Did you sell Dad store?"

"Hell no Supreme! And nobody better be in Dad store either."

"Let's roll over there" Supreme said leading the way out the cemetery.

Chapter 6

Stepping inside of Gail house nine women showed Tonya to the dining room where Gail was seated at the head of the table. Standing up Gail gave Tonya a hug and a kiss.

"Gail, I'm more than happy that you taught me as much as you did, otherwise I would be dead."

"Have a seats the nine women that showed Tonya into the house walked back into the dining room. "Gail, Jo-Jo is here, shall we let him in?"

"Yes ladies, let him in." One by one all nine women left the dining room. "Are you ready for this meeting Tonya?"

"Yes and no Gail. Yet I don't have a choice but to get ready."

"Have a seat Jo-Jo. Ladies you may leave us now" Gail said. All nine women made their exit out the dining room leaving them alone.

Taking a seat Jo-Jo looked at the women sitting across from him, then looked over at Gail. "Hello Gail, how have you been" Jo-Jo asked.

"Hello to you Jo-Jo, and I'm just fine. I'm sure you know why I called you to my house Jo-Jo."

"Not really."

"Jo-Jo it's about you holding the king of the Sams drug contract. It's that time you have to step down as the king of the Sams drug contract. This woman here is taking over the contract as the Queen of the Sams drug contract."

Looking at the woman sitting across from him Jo-Jo was confused. "Gail, I don't mean to be rude or question you. But the contract can only be taking away from me by the oldest Sams and that would be my sister Khia. This woman can't take my spot. Who the hell is she?"

Gail looked over at Tonya. Standing up Tonya walked over to Jo-Jo and placed a picture on the table in front of Jo-Jo. Looking down at the picture, Jo-Jo looked up at the woman standing over him. He then looked back down at the picture, then looked back at Tonya. The picture was of him at two years old sitting on a woman lap and them both smiling. Turning the picture over it read on the back:

Tonya Sams and Jo-Jo Sams

Mommy's Baby Boy

Turning the picture back up right Jo-Jo looked at his two year old self and the woman in the picture. He looked up at Tonya, then looked over at Gail. "Gail what the hell is going on here?"

"Jo-Jo this woman standing before you is Tonya, your mother."

"Gail, my mother died when I was three years old."

"Jo-Jo, I have never lied to you and I have no reason to lie to you now. This woman before you is your mother Tonya."

Pulling out his cell phone Jo-Jo dialed Khia cell phone number. "Hello, Khia this is Jo-Jo. I'm at Gail house right now and it's some woman here saying that she's Tonya our mother."

"It's true Jo-Jo. I found out that she was alive a month ago when she popped up at Nicole house in L.A. Let's just say I'm happy that's she's alive, but I'm not happy that she's taking over. But there's nothing I or you can do about it Jo-Jo. She's the real deal she's your mother."

Hanging up his phone Jo-Jo put his phone back in his pocket. "This is too much" Jo-Jo said standing up.

Standing face to face with Jo-Jo. Tonya didn't know If she should hug him or set him straight. "Jo-Jo, I'm sure this is a shock to you, but I'm sure in time…."

Jo-Jo held his hand up stopping Tonya in mid-sentence. "If the spot is what you want, it's what you now have. I'm leaving."

"Before you leave Jo-Jo me and you need to talk about a few things."

"Like what! You dropping off the face of the earth over twenty years ago! Save it because I don't want to hear it."

"That's fair, but I would like to talk to you about how you been working for both sides Jo-Jo. You need to choose what side you're going to be loyal to."

"I don't need to choose shit. I been doing just fine."

"Jo-Jo, you working for both sides will no longer work long as I'm on the scene. Either you are with your family the Sams or the enemy the Gibbs? Make your choice."

"I'm not making shit, but If I have to. I'm rolling with the Gibbs drug operation."

Leaning over Tonya got close to Jo-Jo ear. "Then you to can die with the Gibbs family."

"Your my mother and you will kill me?"

"Yes, I'm your mother, I love you, and I will kill you If you stand in my way Jo-Jo.":

"Well I guess there's nothing else to be said" Jo-Jo said walking out of Gail house.

Sitting back down Tonya looked over at Gail. "Tonya, I don't knock how you are running the Sams drug operation. If I was in your shoes, I would be running it the same way. But there's something I don't understand, and I want you to explain it to me Tonya. What's this beef with the Gibbs family that your family have against them?"

"Where do I start Gail? For one Joe Gibbs used me. He fucked me like crazy for over a year, and when his wife found out about us. Joe through me away like trash. On top of that Joe ordered Trini to murder me. My last conversation with Joe, I swore to him his whole family would all die at the hands of my family." Standing up Tonya looked at Gail. "I meant what I said then, and I still mean it today" Tonya said walking out of Gail house.

*****

Pulling up on the block of Joe old store. Solo, Supreme, and Jay looked across the street at the store. The gate to the store was down, there was no sign of the store being open at all.

"Supreme, I think our mother is losing her grip on reality" Solo said looking at Supreme.

"Solo, Mommy maybe getting a little older. But I don't think she's losing her mind. She sounded sure of what she saw Solo."

"Why don't we go inside the store. Look around and see If there are any signs of anyone being in the store" Jay said.

Getting out the car, Supreme, Solo, and Jay walked over to the store. Unlocking the gate to the store. Supreme and Jay helped Solo lift the gate to the store. Unlocking the door to the store. The three of them walked into the store and began looking around. Finding the light switch Jay turned on the light. Seeing the lights come on Supreme and Solo jumped, dropped to the floor, and pulled out their guns.

"What the hell is wrong with you two" Jay asked shocked at their reaction to him turning on the light.

"What the hell is the lights doing on?"

"Uncle Solo, I'm the one that just turned on the light. You two are being jumpy for no reason."

Standing back up straight Solo began looked around, Supreme walked over to Jay. "Jay, we know you just turned on the light. What shocked us is the lights actually working" Supreme said as he began looking around the store as well.

Jay still stood confused. "I don't understand what's the big deal about the lights working in this store?"

"Jay this store has been shut down for over twenty years. All I do is pay the taxes on the store, nothing more. In order for the lights to be working in this store. Someone had to pay to get the lights turned back on."

"Oh" Jay yelled fully understanding now that Solo explained to him.

"Supreme we haven't been in this store since Dad died. But it doesn't look like anything is out of place or missing. The only thing that seem strange is that somehow the lights work." Walking up behind Solo, Supreme slapped Solo in the back of his head. "Owww! What was that for?"

"Because you're not using your brain. Look around Solo! The lights working is not the only thing strange in here. We shut this store down 21 years ago and haven't open this store since then. Look at the floors! Look at the walls! Look at the cash register and the counter! There's a whole lot missing in here Solo. Dust! Where is the 21 years of dust at? This place has been clean from top to bottom. Mommy haven't lost her grip on reality. Someone paid to get the lights cut back on in this store. Someone also cleaned the hell out of this store. Mommy said, she saw Trini in this store when she looked through the glass door. I'm not sure If Trini is who she saw, but clearly she saw someone, because someone was in this store."

Rubbing the back of his head because he could still feel where Supreme hit him. Solo began thinking to his self. "Supreme what If Mommy did see Trini? It's not like we ever really found out If Trini was dead or alive."

"Well I tell you what Solo. If Trini is alive and back on the scene. He has a lot of explaining to do about where he been for the past 21 years."

"I got a idea to find out what's going on and who is coming into this store" Jay said. Supreme and Solo both looked at Jay. Seeing that he had their attention Jay continued. "Rome and Sierra both live right across the street from this store. I say we have them an eye out on this store."

"That's a good idea Jay. I'll tell Rome and sierra tomorrow to keep a eye out on this store. In the meantime let's lock this place up and get the hell out of here."

*****

Walking in the bedroom Trini noticed Tonya laying on the bed wearing nothing but a smile on her face. Nothing made Trini day like seeing Tonya in her birthday suit. Yet what Tonya had said at the Sams meeting earlier in the day. Was still weighting heavy on Trini mind.

"Tonya, we need to talk."

Looking at Trini, Tonya spread her legs wide as she could. Sticking two fingers into her wetness, Tonya began working her two fingers in and out of herself. "Trini do you want to talk, or would you like to have some fun?"

Snatching one of the covers off the bed, Trini through it over Tonya naked body. "I said we need to talk."

Feeling rejected Tonya tucked the cover under her arms and sat up in the bed. "So! You said we need to talk. Are you just gonna look at me or are you going to say what you need to say?"

"Tonya, I don't like the way you were talking in the meeting. I agreed to come back to New York with you. To make the Sams drug operation known again. But from your meeting it sounds like you are trying to go to war with the Gibbs family. That's something I can't allow you to do."

Letting the cover fall from her breast Tonya stood up in the bed. Still naked Tonya turned her back on Trini. "Trini, Trini, Trini, you can't allow me to do this, you can't allow me to do that. Can you at least allow yourself to please a woman that is hungry for that big dick of yours to be inside of me?"

"Tonya this serious!"

Dropping to her knees Tonya put her ass up in the air in a doggy style position. "I'm serious to Trini. I need that big dick of yours inside of me."

Although the conversation he wanted to have with Tonya was serious. It was hard for him to stay focus. Tonya was in her late 50's but still had the body of a twenty year old. Not able to take it any longer Trini got out of his clothes. Entering Tonya world of passion from behind. Trini began grinding his self slowly inside of her. Leaning over he began sucking on her neck giving her hickeys. Leaning back up right Trini grabbed a hold of Tonya hips. Pumping in and out of Tonya he held her in place so that she couldn't move. Each trust he gave her was hard and harder than the last. Trini strokes then became suddenly violent and uncontrollable.

"Shit, yes, oh my god, yes, fuck me" Tonya yelled catching her second orgasm.

*****

In Webster projects Brandy opened her apartment door. Seeing her boyfriend smoke, Brandy smiled as he gave her a kiss and a slap on her ass. Stepping aside Smoke walked inside the apartment. T.J followed inside the apartment behind his big homie. Behind T.J, Marty,

Kenny, Cancer, King, and Desean all walked in the apartment as well. Being the last one to walk inside the apartment. Desean winked at Brandy and ran his hand over her ass unnoticed to the rest of the blood members.

After Desean run in with the Gibbs family, and him shitting on Khia when she was running the Sams drug operation. Desean knew he had to find a real crew to have his back. Being down with Mike crew. Desean knew Mike crew was to weak, so he left Mike crew. The next best thing was to get down with the bloods meant a good form of protection. When it came to getting money being a blood member. Desean wasn't making nowhere near the money he was making when he was down with Mike crew or down with the Sams family. But for Desean it didn't matter because he saved his money well when he was eating off of Mike and Khia.

Smoke being the big homie of the blood set called, Red-Money. He appointed T.J the second homie in charge under him. The rest of the hats were called little homies. Except the homie named Cancer. Who was only fifteen years old. Smoke gave him the nick name baby homie because of his age. Although Cancer was the youngest in the set. Cancer name fit him because he was known for killing.

As everyone took a seat at the table in the kitchen. Brandy took her seat on top of Smoke lap. In the corner of Desean eye. He watched as Smoke rubbed on Brandy ass with his left hand. Brandy being the girlfriend of the big homie. Desean knew he would be crossing the line trying to get with Brandy. But being a butt man, and Brandy having a phat ass. No way in the hell could Desean see his self-pasting Brandy by without ripping the walls to her dark tunnel. For two months Desean had been down with Red-Money. For two months he had been doing his homework on Brandy. He found out Brandy loyalty was to a man that was in control and to money. Not only that Desean also found out that Brandy loved to be fucked in the ass. Fucking a female in the ass was Desean specialty. To his surprise Desean found out Brandy was doing her homework on him as well. Although Smoke was well respected throughout Webster projects. His money wasn't longer then Desean money roll. For the past two weeks they had been flirting with each other on the low. The other day Desean got a text message from Brandy that read:

"I'll give you the cakes, If you can keep it a secret and hit me with 500 dollars."

Texting back Desean wrote: *"Sounds good to me, just let me know when?"*

"Trust, you'll know when, just have those dollars" Brandy text back.

"Fellas, let's get this meeting started" Smoke said as he began rolling up some weed. "As you all know we sell weed, crack, and E-pills. It's come to my understanding that the crew that call their self, the team. Has set up a crack spot right here in my projects. That shit is disrespectful, and they have to be shut down. They run Soundview projects where they need to stay. Red-Money is the only niggas that eat in Webster projects. It also comes to my understanding that some new crew called, Sky-High. Is running drugs out a store on the same block Red-Money pump weight on the corner at. Where the fuck this crew Sky-High came from?

I don't know, don't care, but I do know they need to set up shop somewhere else. So yes, Sky-High needs to be shut down as well."

"Desean you been pumping weight for a while and in different places. Do you know anything about these two crews?"

"Yeah, the team, is run by the Gibbs family, with a guy name Solo running the show. Sky-High, is run by the Sams family, with a female by the name Tonya running the show. Right now both families are at war with each other. The Gibbs family think the war is over, but for the Sams family the war is only beginning."

"The Gibbs and the Sams families" Smoke said laughing. "Desean them names ranged bells in the streets of the Bronx when my grandfather was alive. Red-Money got the Bronx now. As a matter of fact. I say we shut these two new spots they just open down and then take over Soundview projects as well."

Taking a puff of the weed Smoke blew the smoke out his mouth, and past it to T.J. Taking a puff of the weed T.J past it to King.

"T.J what do you think?"

"Smoke, I say we send both of these crews a message."

"Good idea T.J, Cancer I want you…."

"Smoke, I don't think that's a good idea. Both of those crews are big timers in the drug game. Red-Money is small time players in the game."

"Move out the way baby girl" Smoke said pushing Brandy off his lap. "What the fuck is you talking about! Red-Money small time my ass!" Smoke yelled banging his fist on the table. "Niggas see the inside of body bags when Red-Money run down on niggas. We called Red-Money for a reason. We paint the Bronx with niggas blood, Red! We chase that green, Money! Red-Money nigga! The game done changed in these streets. It used to be, don't send a boy to do a man's job. Now it's, I'm a man and I can send a boy to do my job for me." Smoke looked over at Cancer. Baby homie, I want you to send those two crews a message from Red-Money."

Chapter 7

"Can I help you" Anton asked opening his house door.

"My name is Ruth Marshall and I'm here to take my son Jason Marshall home. Is he here in your house?"

"Yeah, but I don't…." Pushing Anton out the way Ruth walked into the house.

"Jason! Jason where are you. I'm here to take you home!" Coming out the bedroom Jason ware nothing but his birthday suit. "Oh my god!! Jason put on your clothes so we can leave."

"Mom what are you doing here?"

"Jason, please, put on your clothes."

Walking back in the room Jason began putting on his clothes. Going in her purse Ruth pulled out a bottle of pills.

"What are those" Anton asked looking at the pills in Ruth hand.

"None of your damn business! I know what's been going on between you and my son the shit stops today. My son is not gay and what you been doing with my son your gonna go to hell for it."

Anton grabbed his chest in shock as If he was having a heart attack. Walking out the bedroom Jason was fully dressed.

"Jason is this woman your mother?"

"Yeh, of course, who else would she be Anton?"

"Jason, I don't want to be disrespectful to her, but I want her out my house."

"Okay I can do that. Come on Mom your gonna have to leave" Jason said taking his mother by her arm.

Snatching her arm away Ruth tried to put a pill in Jason mouth. Turning his face Jason slapped the pill out his mother hand. "No more pills Mom. I'm done with taking pills."

"Nonsense Jason, you will feel better once you take one."

Ruth tried to put another pill to Jason mouth. Just like the other pill Jason slapped it out her hand. Running back in the bedroom Jason locked the door.

"Jason! Jason open this door!" Ruth yelled banging on the door.

As Ruth banging on the bedroom door. Jason walked over to the dresser, picked up a hairbrush and looked at his self in the mirror. The more Ruth banging on the door the more it sounded like music beats to Jason. Jumping up and down in front of the mirror, Jason held the brush to his mouth and began rapping:

"She tried to catch me slipping. Not me.

She tried to put a pill in my mouth. Not me.

She tried to change me back to the old me.

But I like the new me.

I'm getting bus and saying ooh weeeee.

She banging on the door.

But I'm trying to bang on the walls of the back door.

So phat, so sweet, so me.

How can I look back?

When I got this nigga looking back at me.

Saying hit it harder, just for me.

Bang, bang, yeah, I'm in it.

Bang, bang, I'm gonna stay in it. Catch me slipping. Not me.

Unless I'm slipping and sliding saying ooh weeeee."

Seeing that banging on the door was getting on where Ruth tuned to Anton. "My son is mentally ill, and he doesn't belong here. He takes medication, and he has not been taking his med's. On his med's he would never do such things with you."

"I'm not forcing him to do anything Ruth."

"I know that, but you can make him leave your home."

"Ruth I'm happy with Jason."

"This is not about you! Your being selfish! Can you not see he's ill!"

"You need to leave my house Ruth."

"Oh I'm gonna leave, but I'll be back." Placing her purse over her shoulder Ruth walked out the house.

*****

Walking in, Love it or Hate it. Tonya and Tameka took a seat at the bar.

"What can I get for you two beautiful ladies" Tank asked.

"Jobs but will settle for two beers" Tonya said.

Placing a beer in front of them both. Tank looked at Tonya and Tameka for a few seconds before speaking again.

"Ladies, I hope I'm not out of line by what I'm about to say. I think you two are very beautiful females. Here at Love it or Hate it, were not just a night club, were also a strip club for men and women. Were always looking for new strippers. If you ladies are interested. I'm sure the owner will higher you."

Like planned Tonya and Tameka looked at each other then back at Tank the bar tender.

"I'm interested" Tonya and Tameka both said. Picking up the phone Tank called Supreme to the front of the club.

"Ladies, Tank tells me that you two would like to become strippers here at the club" Supreme said.

"Yeah, are there any spots open" Tameka asked.

"Always, follow me ladies."

Walking behind Supreme, Tameka and Tonya followed him to the club back office. Stepping in the back office Tameka broke out in a sweat seeing Beverly and Solo sitting in the office. Noticing Tameka was getting nervous Tonya began to take control.

"So when can me and my home girl start?"

"Well first I have to make sure you both are over the age of 21 years old. So can I get your I.D's, so I can make a copy of them?" Pulling out there I.D's they both gave them to Supreme.

Although Solo and Beverly were both in a conversation among them self. They both kept cutting their eyes over at Tameka. Tameka could feel their eyes on her. Even though they kept looking over at Tameka they couldn't figure out where they knew her from, but they knew her from somewhere. Stepping back in the office Supreme handed Tonya and Tameka back their I.D's. Standing up Beverly grabbed Solo by his hand and began pulling him out the office.

"Will be back Supreme" Beverly said.

Not thinking anything was up Supreme got down to business. "Ladies you two are all set. You start tonight. I normally tell my strippers to come up with a stage name for their self. But to be honest with you. I think your giving names will do just fine. Tameka you go on stage at 8 p.m. When Tameka is done, Tonya you'll be going on stage right after her. Any questions ladies?"

"No."

"No."

"Good, well you two have a few hours before the strippers hit the stage."

Standing to her feet Tonya pulled Tameka up out of her chair as well. "That sounds perfect, will go buy us a few outfits and will be back."

Moving fast Tonya walked out the office with Tameka following quickly behind her. Outside in the club parking lot. Tonya and Tameka jumped in Tonya car.

"Now where are we going Tonya?" Pulling out a set of keys Tonya shook them in Tameka face. "First things first, were gonna make a copy of Supreme house keys."

"How did you get his house keys?"

"Girl stick with me and you will learn a few things. Today was your first lesson. Know that the hand is quicker than the eye. When we come back to the club tonight. I'll place his keys back in his desk, he'll never know they were gone."

Driving out the parking lot Tonya kept the conversation going with Tameka. "I have to move things faster than I thought."

"Why is that Tonya?"

"For the past week Trini has been on my back about my plan and how does the Gibbs family fit into it. Point blank Trini doesn't want any part in getting at the Gibbs family, and he doesn't want me going after the Gibbs family drug operation."

"So what do you plan on doing now?" Tonya looked over at Tameka like her question was like poison to her ears.

"Girl are you deaf? I just told you. I have to move things faster than I thought. Trini and nobody else is going to rain on my parade. Every time Trini try to talk to me about what my plan is. I lay this good pussy of mine on him and put his ass straight to sleep."

"Okay you seem to have Trini under control. But how are you going to get Erykah and Jo-Jo to become a part of your plan?"

"To tell you the truth Tameka I really don't need them when it comes to bringing down the Gibbs family. Yet them not joining their real family is a slap in the face to me. So it's only right that I hit back. I think it's about time someone let the Gibbs family know who Erykah and Jo-Jo are related to."

"Ooh! Tonya it sounds like a storm is about to come to the Bronx!"

"You better believe it Tameka" Tonya said giving Tameka a high five. "Tameka, hurricane Sandy ain't got shit on me. This is hurricane Tonya season, and mother fuckers better stay out my way."

*****

"Tank hit me with a apple martini" Beverly said sitting down at the bar.

"Tank hit me with a vodka without ice" Solo said sitting down beside Beverly. Turning to Beverly, Solo looked at her as If he was waiting for her to say something.

"Why are you looking at me like that?"

"Oh I don't know, maybe it has something to do with you pulling me out the office in a hurry. I'm more then sure it wasn't to come have a few drinks with you Bev."

"Well damn Solo let me get a drink in me first before I tell you why I dragged you out the office."

Tank walked back over to them and placed their drinks on front of them. Picking up the glass Beverly emptied the glass in one heads up. Slamming the glass down she told Tank to hit her with another one. Turning her attention to Solo, Beverly gave him a weird look.

"Solo, I saw you looking at that Tameka girl in the office. Have you put it together where you know her from yet?"

"Who said I knew her?"

"Oh you know her Solo, or should I say you know him."

"Him" Solo said confused.

"Yes him, do you remember Anton brother Eddie?"

"Yeah, but what does that…. No!!!!! Are you telling me Tameka is Eddie?"

"Yup!"

Placing his glass down Solo stood up. "Oh hell no! I'm telling Supreme! We not gonna be having no he she's stripping up in here."

Grabbing Solo arm Beverly pulled him back down. "Ms. Tameka is far from a he / she. Ms. Thing done had a full sex change. So there's no need to tell Supreme anything."

"How do you know he had a sex change?"

"Because Anton told me about it like three years ago."

Placing Beverly second drink in front of her. Tank leaned over the bar. "It's good that you two figured out who Tameka is. Yet I'm sure I know that Tonya girl from somewhere. But I can't for the likes of me figure out where I know her from. Do she look familiar to you two?"

Beverly and Solo shook their heads no. "Well I thought I would ask, but I'm sure it will come to me where I know that girl from."

*****

Coming in the house Jay found Erykah sleep in their bedroom. Walking over to her he could smell the alcohol on her. For the past week since Rome and her had that disagreement. Every night Jay came home he found Erykah past in the bed drunk. Tonight seem to be no different besides the fact that Jay was horny as hell. Seeing that he wasn't going to be getting any type of sex from Erykah. Jay headed out the room and into the living room. Booting up the computer Jay sat down and began to search porn web sites.

After searching the internet for a few minutes. Jay finally found a porn he could work with. Feeling the urge to release some of his creamy protein. Jay pulled out his penis and began stroking it back and forth. Normally when giving his self-pleasure he liked to use baby oil. Not wanting to go back in the bedroom. Jay felt the sweat from his hand would just have to do watching the porno Jay began working his penis like a jack hammer.

Walking in the living room Erykah saw that Jay was on the computer and walked up behind him. Seeing what was on the computer screen Erykah eyes grew triple their size.

"Are you fucking serious Jay" Erykah yelled.

Jumping Jay turned around. Looking down at Jay lap and seeing his penis in his hand Erykah flipped out even more. "Jacking your meat is better than fucking me!"

"You was sleep" Jay said placing his penis back in his pants.

"Jay you haven't touched me in over a week!"

"That's because you been knocked out drunk every night when I come home Erykah."

"Unbelievable! You rather watch an internet porno then to come in the room and fuck your wife! All this shit I been going through this past week!"

"Shit like what Erykah?"

"Unbelievable! Jacking it to an internet porno!"

It was becoming clear to Jay that Erykah wasn't hearing a thing he was saying. It was almost like she was in a drunken rage. Turning off the computer, Jay stood up and walked past Erykah. Looking back at Erykah. Jay saw that she was still yelling and going off staring at the computer chair.

"She want me to go against you Jay, but I won't! Then that asshole was here twice already wanting money!" Not understanding what Erykah was going on and on about. Jay grabbed his coat and walked out the house.

Chapter 8

Pit, Davon, Jo-Jo, and Lloyd sat in the living room of their Webster projects re-up apartment.

"Yo where the hell is Tone at" Lloyd asked.

"He went out to get that crackhead nigga Bill I was telling yawl about" Pit said. "I'm telling yawl, yawl got to see how this nigga Bill tweak out when he get high. It's like no shit I ever seen in my life."

Walking in the re-up apartment Tone walked Bill into the living room. Tone nodded at Pit to start the show for the fellas. On point Pit got straight to it.

"Ayo, what up Bill?"

"Ain't shit Pit, ain't shit."

"That's good Bill. I got one free one for you for bringing me mad customers this past week."

Throwing Bill a dime bag of crack and a crack pipe. Bill eyes lit up like a Christmas tree. "Go ahead and take a hit." Sitting down Bill began stuffing the crack pipe.

"Pit, you bugging my nigga, you gonna let this nigga smoke that shit right here" Jo-Jo asked.

Stopping Bill looked up at Pit for his response. "Go ahead Bill this is my spot I said it's cool." That's all Bill needed to hear. Putting the flame to the crack pipe. Bill put the pipe to his lips and sucked in. The five of them watch Bill close as he took a hit.

Hit after hit Bill took. Letting the smoke out his mouth Bill eyes got wide. Pit hit Tone to make sure he was watching Bill closely. Jumping up to his feet. Bill scared all five of them making them all jump back in their chairs. Running to the bathroom Bill locked his self in the bathroom.

"Man that nigga scared the shit out of me jumping up like that" Lloyd said holding his chest.

"Well hold on because that nigga Bill ain't done tripping out yet."

"What you mean by, he's not done tripping out yet?"

Before Pit could answer Bill ran back in the living room. "Where is my clothes" Bill yelled running over to Davon butt naked. Jumping up from the chair Davon picked the chair up and held it out between him and Bill. "Where the fuck is my clothes" Bill continued to yell at Davon.

"Yo, somebody get this crazy mother fucker! He got his Johnson hanging all out and shit!"

Tone, Pit, Lloyd, and jo-Jo, was laughing so hard tears were coming out their eyes.

"Yo, yawl fucking laughing! Get this crazy nigga!" Davon yelled trying to push Bill back with the chair. Reaching over the chair Bill tried to grab Davon shirt.

"Man fuck this shit" Davon yelled. Raising the chair in the air. Davon came down hard whacking Bill over the head with it. Falling to the floor Bill jumped up fast holding his head running at Davon again.

"Where is my clothes mother fucker!" Raising the chair again in the air. This time Davon whacked Bill over the head harder breaking the chair over his head.

Falling to the floor Bill was out cold. Dropping the rest of the chair Davon looked over at Pit.

"Man the next time you want to show me something. Put that shit on video. I don't ever want to see crack heads gone wild live again. I got to go get some air. When I get back make sure yawl have this crazy crack head the fuck outta here."

Leaving the re-up apartment Davon closed the door behind him. Walking down the hallway Davon watched as a young boy walked down the hallway towards him. "Yo, you Davon" the young boy asked.

"Yeah, what up little…."

"POP! POP!"

Two bullets to the face Davon body hit the floor as he died instantly. Jumping over Davon body Cancer ran over to the re-up apartment door and placed a paper on the door. Jumping over Davon body once again. Cancer ran down the hallway and down the stairs.

Hearing the gun shots, Lloyd, Tone and Jo-Jo ran out the apartment into the hallway. Seeing Davon laying on the floor with half of his face missing. Lloyd walked over to him and dropped to his knees. Looking down at his feet Pit saw a paper on the door. Snatching the paper off the door Pit read the letter. Folding the paper up Pit put it in his pocket.

*****

Taking a cigarette break Flaco and Cam stepped outside the store. As females walked by them. They did their best to get the females to give them their phone numbers. Yet each female that past them wasn't impressed with Flaco or Cam lamb come on lines.

"Man fuck these hoe's out here" Cam said putting out his cigarette as he walked back into the store. Walking across the street Cancer walked up to Flaco.

"Ayo you sell that Sky-High right" Cancer asked.

Looking at Cancer, Flaco thought to his self "this boy is too young to be smoking crack, but hey If he got the money, I'll sell it to him." "Yeah, youngen I sell that…."

"POP! POP!"

Stepping over Flaco body Cancer spit on the store door and slammed a paper over the spit. Running down the block Cancer turned the corner and continued to run.

*****

Seeing Beverly sitting at the bar. Trina placed her purse on the bar and took a seat next to Beverly.

"What you doing here Cuz?"

"Bev, I was bored just sitting at home. So I decided to come down to the club and chill out. I'm happy to see you here, at least I won't be here by myself."

"Tank hit us with two apple martinis" Beverly yelled out.

Picking up her purse Trina hit Beverly with it in her arm. "You know damn well I'm pregnant and I can't drink."

"I know, that's why I'm gonna drink for the both of us."

Busting out laughing Trini hit Beverly with her purse again. "Where are our kings at?"

"In the back office. Solo left me here drinking at the bar like three hours ago. So he could go to the back office to go chill with Supreme."

"Three hours ago! Girl you been sitting at this bar drinking for that long?"

"Yeah, and what is it to you bitch?"

"Oh see now I know you drunk calling me a bitch. Tank!"

"What's up Trina" Tank asked walking over to them.

"Tank, no more drinks for this bitch she's drunk."

"Your wish is my command" Tank said.

Trying to stand up Beverly fell back down on the bar stool. "Hey" Beverly yelled slamming her fist on the bar. "You better deny this bitch wish, and don't forget my husband own this club."

"Sorry Trina your wish has been denied" Tank said laughing as he walked off to serve another customer.

Walking in the club Jay took a seat in front of the stage. His wife was drunk, he couldn't watch porn at home. The next best thing was to come down to Love it or Hate it, and at least get a lap dance.

Beating on the mic DJ L-Boogie got on the mic. "Party people we have a newcomer coming to the stage! Give it up for Tameka!"

Hearing the name Tameka, Beverly turned around in her bar stool to face the stage. Seeing Tameka walk on the stage Jay penis immediately got hard.

Walking up to Beverly, Supreme gave her a kiss on the cheek. "Sweet lady your man is tired and I'm going home. Solo is going to hold down the club tonight" Supreme said walking out the club.

Working the pole like a pro. All eyes watched as Tameka went up on the pole and came down in a full split. Stepping off the stage Tameka hand was grabbed by Jay. Pulling her closer to him Jay began whispering in her ear. "Here's my number. Let's say me and you get out of here and hit the hotel. How does two thousand dollars sound for the whole night?"

"Like music to my ears, let me just go get my clothes out my locker and I'll be right back."

"Cool, I'll be in the parking lot waiting for you."

Taking the piece of paper from Jay. Tameka went straight down the stairs to the strippers locker room. Standing up Jay walked out the club.

"Did you just see that Beverly" Trina asked.

"Yeah" Beverly said with attitude as she picked up her glass.

"Beverly, I haven't seen a bitch work the pole like that since me and you were strippers."

Taking the glass to the head Beverly slammed the glass down on the bar. "Fuck that bitch working a pole! Did you see what I just saw Trina? That bitch think she going to lay up with our nephew Trina."

"Yeah, it look like they just made plans to hook up outside the club Bev. Jay know he's wrong when he is married."

"No he ain't wrong, that bitch is wrong knowing what she is" Beverly yelled standing up. Almost falling back down Beverly caught herself on the bar and stood up straight. Walking towards the steps Beverly tripped a few times.

"Where are you going?"

"To check that bitch" Beverly yelled over her shoulder, walking down the stairs to the locker room.

Hearing what Beverly said Tonya pulled out her cell phone and called the police. Hanging up, instead of going on stage, Tonya left the club and got in her car.

"Hey" Beverly yelled walking over to Tameka locker. Tameka pointed to herself not sure If Beverly was talking to her. "Yeah, you Eddie!"

"Please don't call me that, I go by the name Tameka now."

"I don't give two fucks what you go by now! O know damn well you remember me and know Jay is my nephew. Whatever you two just planned is dead. Stay your he she ass away from my nephew."

"Listen Beverly, I'm grown, and I can do whatever I want. With whoever I want to do it with."

"This is just how bitches get fucked up because they don't listen" Beverly said taking her earrings out her ears.

"You beat my ass, bitch please! Beverly who the fuck do you think you talking too?"

Beverly looked around the empty locker room then looked back at Tameka. "I must be talking to you Eddie, because ain't nobody else up in this mother fucker."

Slamming the locker closed Tameka turned around punching Beverly in her face. Not seeing the punch coming and being so drunk Beverly landed flat on her back. "Bitch didn't I tell you don't call me that name again!"

Standing to her feet Beverly looked at Tameka like she had lost her mind. Ramming Tameka into the lockers. Beverly grabbed Tameka by her hair and began punching her in her face. Not backing down Tameka grabbed a hand full of Beverly hair and went for what she knew punching Beverly back in her face.

Checking his watch Tank walked over to Trina who was still sitting at the bar. "Trina, you might want to go down to that locker room and check on things down there."

"Why you say that Tank?"

"Well for two reasons, Beverly said, she was going down there to check a bitch. Plus she been down there for a while now. You know how your cousin get."

"You right about that Tank" Trina said jumping up from the bar stool.

Stepping in the locker room Trina saw Tameka and Beverly rolling around on the floor going blow for blow. Although Beverly wasn't getting beat up. Trina could tell Beverly wasn't giving it her all in the fight due to her being drunk. Pregnant or not no way in the hell was Trina going to let anyone try to take advantage of her cousin because she was drunk. Grabbing Tameka by her hair Trina started kicking Tameka in her head. Jumping up to her feet Beverly pushed Trina out the way. Grabbing Tameka by her hair Beverly began punching Tameka in her face again. Trina blood was still boiling, and she still wanted some more action. Grabbing Tameka by her shirt Trina started punching Tameka in her back. Not giving up Tameka fought back like a wild animal punching everything she could catch.

"Officers I don't know who called you but there's no problem in this club" Tank said to two officers.

"Sir we got a call that a woman is being attacked in the locker room here. Please step out the way."

Having no choice Tank moved to the side and let two officers past by him. Seeing three girls fighting both officers placed all three of them in handcuffs. Waiting for Tameka to come out to his car Jay had fell asleep inside of his car. Placing Trina, Beverly, and Tameka, in separate police cars. They were arrested and taking to the police station. Calling Solo to the front of the club. Tank told him what had just happen. Solo told Tank, "to hold down the club" and ran out the club. Jumping in his car Solo followed the police cars to the police station.

*****

Asleep Supreme woke up to his penis getting the full attention of a warm hot mouth. He was hard, he was ready to let loose, but didn't want to because the blow job was feeling so good. Sex with Beverly was good but even greater when she was drunk. Before he left the club, he could see that Beverly was drunk. He knew when she came home, she was going to bless him with some great sex. The darkness in the room and just waking up made it impossible for Supreme to see the treatment his penis was getting, but he could damn sure feel it. Feeling a condom being rolled down his penis. Supreme then felt her get on top of him and began riding him slow. Her pussy walls felt tight, tighter then they had ever felt before.

For the first time in his life, he could hear his self-moaning out loud the faster she rode his penis. Faster and faster she rode his penis. Supreme felt like his penis was growing an extra inch every time she went down on his penis. Grabbing a hold of her ass cheeks, Supreme had to admit to his self that Beverly ass cheeks even felt softer then they had ever been. Although she was on top of him and was supposed to be in control. Supreme began pumping back hard underneath her. The rhythm between them was beyond perfect. Feeling his penis swelling inside of her, she jumped up, snatched the condom off, jerked his penis and let Supreme shoot his thick cum in her mouth. Spitting his cum out her mouth onto his penis, she took his penis into her mouth. Working Supreme penis, she took his penis into her mouth. Working Supreme penis into overtime with her jaw muscles. She lifted her head up just in time with her jaw muscles. She lifted her head up just in time as Supreme shot his second nut straight up in the air. Laying his head back on the pillow Supreme tried to catch his breath. Standing up from the bed she turned on the bedroom light. Opening his eyes Supreme felt like he was going to pass out seeing Tonya getting dressed.

"What the fuck" Supreme yelled.

Turning around Tonya looked at Supreme as she put the video camera in her bag. "I'm so glad I brought the camera that can video tape in the dark. Supreme I must say your dick game is way better than your father dick game."

Trying to get up from the bed Supreme realized both of his feet was tied down to the bed. "You fucking bitch I'm gonna kill you."

Running out the room, Tonya ran out the house to her car. With two free hands Supreme untied his feet. By the time Supreme got downstairs in his house Tonya had pulled off in her car.

"Fuck" Supreme yelled punching his house door. "How the fuck am I gonna explain this shit to Beverly" Supreme yelled slamming his house door closed.

Chapter 9

Five hours had passed since Beverly, Tameka, and Trina were arrested. Within the first hour of them being placed in separate bull pins, they laid out on a bench and fell asleep. Tonya and Tameka lucked up and was placed in empty bull pens. Beverly on the other hand had to share a bull pen with another woman. A woman that Beverly was sure was a crack head.

Waking up Beverly felt rebooted, full of energy and no longer drunk. Looked over at the other bench in the bull pen. Seeing the female crack head sitting on the bench. Beverly rolled her eyes and stood up. Walking over to the bull pen bars. Beverly knew Tameka was in the bull pen on her left, and Trina was in the bull pen on her right. Although she couldn't see them, she knew they were there. Walking to the left wall of the bull pen Beverly banged on the wall a few times.

"Tameka!" Not hearing a response Beverly banged on the wall again. "Bitch, I know you hear me over there! This shit between me and you is not over."

Truth be told Tameka didn't hear a word Beverly was saying. Tameka was in a deep sleep and down for the count with a hell of a headache. Although Tameka wasn't responding Beverly continued to yell. "Tameka soon as we get out of here, we gonna get it popping again! You hear me bitch!!!"

"Yeah, I hear you" the crack head lady said. Turning around Beverly looked at the lady in disgust.

"Bitch do I look like I'm talking to you?"

"I'm the only one in this…."

"Well I'm not talking to you!"

Waiving Beverly off the female looked at the wall. Walking over to the right wall of the bull pen Beverly banged on the wall.

"Trina!!"

"Yeah Cuz" Trina answered waking up. "Bev you know I got your back no matter what. But what the hell happen? How did you and Tameka get into a fight?"

"Trina that bitch punched me in my face, and it was on and popping from there."

"Bev, I still think you were tripping first. What's the big deal If Tameka and Jay would have had sex? Like damn, why are you hating on that girl so much? Is it because she may have worked that strip pole better then you Bev?"

"Trina, I may have retired from stripping, but can't no bitch work a pole better than me. And this is not about Tameka working a damn pole. I find it funny how you keep calling Tameka a, she."

"What you mean by that Beverly?"

"Trina do you remember Anton older brother Eddie?"

"Yeah, but what does he have to do with what we're talking about?"

"It has a lot to do with what we're talking about Trina. Because Tameka is Eddie."

"What! Huh? What are you talking about Beverly?"

"I'm talking about Eddie having sex reassignment surgery."

"What!!!"

"Trina and now that I'm not drunk. Your right, Trina it's not a big deal If Tameka and Jay have sex. By law that bitch is a woman, so I'm over that now. What I'm not over is that bitch popping on me in that locker room. That bitch popping on me while I was drunk."

"Bev, drunk or not, Tameka didn't beat you up."

"Oh I know that! But ain't no way a bitch gonna get a piece of me while I'm drunk and not get a piece of me sober."

"I know that's right" the crack head female yelled.

"Do you mind" Beverly said looking at the female. Waiving Beverly off once again the crack head fiend rolled her eyes and looked at the wall.

"Who is that" Trina asked hearing another female voice.

"Some damn crack head fiend."

"I got your crack head" the lady said.

Turning around Beverly looked at the female. "Bitch do you want to take the ass whooping that Tameka is gonna get?"

Looking at Beverly the lady eyes almost popped out her head. "Hell no! What I look like taking an ass whooping meant for somebody else."

Rolling her eyes Beverly turned back towards the bull pen bars. "Trina!"

"Yeah Bev, please try to be easy over there."

"I'm trying If this crack head fiend bitch stay out my business."

"Listen here girl I'm not gonna be to many more of your damn crack heads."

Turning around again Beverly was ready to go to war. "What you say?" Waiving Beverly off once again the female turned her head towards the wall once again.

Trina, I swear to god. Soon as we get out of here. I'm getting locked right back up. Soon as I see Tameka, I'm gonna beat her the fuck up."

"You mean you gonna fuck him up" the crack head fiend lady said.

"Bitch! What is your problem" Beverly asked turning around again.

"I'll tell you what my damn problem is. You up in here talking to people your ass can't see, and I'm sitting right here in your face, and you act like you don't even see me. That's my damn problem!"

Looking at the lady Beverly grabbed her mouth in shock. Running over to the lady Beverly gave the lady a hug. "Oh my god, I'm so damn pissed off I didn't even realize that was you sitting there Ms. Renee. I'm up here talking about how I'm gonna beat one of your kids up right in front of you."

"Beverly please, Eddie maybe one of my kids, but you know me, and that boy never got along. I can give two shits If somebody beat his ass. I wrote him off as my kid when he had that damn sex change. Now Anton, although he get on my damn nerves, that's my heart. Long as you ain't talking about hurting my Anton I don't care. Now sit down and let me put a bug in your ear Beverly."

Taking a sit next to Renee told Beverly everything she knew about Tameka dealing with a female named Tonya. Renee then ended the conversation with Tonya being Khia mother and Khia is still alive. Trina held her ear to the bull pen bars listening to every word.

"Tell me you are joking Ms. Renee" Beverly said standing up.

"Beverly when the hell have you ever known me to joke around? What I just told you is true girl." Beverly looked at the left wall in the bull pen. "Oh don't worry about Eddie over there. He didn't hear a thing." Beverly could hear Tameka snoring. "Beverly a damn train can run through this jail and that shit wouldn't wake that damn boy."

Beverly sat back down on the bench. "I can't believe this shit. Wait until I tell Solo this shit. He's gonna flip when he hear this shit."

*****

Six hours had passed since Beverly and Trina were arrested. They bail had been set at two thousand dollars each. A bail that Solo had paid in full for Trina and Beverly. Yet the jail told Solo, "it could take up to eight hours before they would be released, due to the paperwork." For six hours Solo had been sitting in the jail parking lot waiting for them to be released. By the forth hour he got bored and called Rome and told him what happen. Without a question Rome and Sierra made their way down to the jail. Parking their car beside Solo car the three of them spoke to each other out the car windows.

While talking to Rome, Solo cell phone started beeping off the hook letting him know he was receiving text messages. Pulling out his cell phone he began reading the text messages. He had three, the first one was from Supreme:

"Meet me at the club I just got myself into some serious shit."

The second text message was from Pit:

"Death in the fam, meet me at the club."

The third text message was from detective Price:

"We need to talk, meet me at your brothers club."

Seeing three serious text messages Solo knew what he was about to find out wasn't going to be good. Not wanting to leave the jail without Trina and Beverly. Solo knew he had to go see what was going on.

"Rome some shit is going on. I have to go to the club. If you and your wife can't handle shit when Trina and Beverly get out call me."

"We can held things Unc, when they get released will all head over to the club and meet up with you."

*****

"Who is it" Jo-Jo yelled.

"Your sister, now open the door boy."

Not knowing why Khia was at his house. Jo-Jo ran back to his living room, pressed a few buttons on his entertainment system, Jo-Jo then walked back to his front door. Opening his house door Jo-Jo nerves began to jump. Although Khia was his sister. She was still somewhat of an enemy to him since he was down with the Gibbs family.

"Khia what do you want?"

"You know Jo-Jo talking to me like that has never gotta you anywhere with me. We maybe on other sides at the moment. But keep in mind that we are still blood related and blood is thicker than water. I have always had your back, and If I wanted you dead. I would have been made that happen. Now are you gonna let me in or should I really write you off as being my baby brother?"

Jo-Jo knew Khia was right. If she wanted him dead, she could have been had it done a long time ago. Stepping to the side Jo-Jo allowed Khia to walk into his house.

"So are you going to tell me why you at my house" Jo-Jo asked as they both took a seat in his living room.

"Listen Jo-Jo, I need your help."

"Khia, I told you and that woman Tonya I'm not going against the Gibbs family."

"First off that woman Tonya is your mother. Second, I don't want you to help me go against the Gibbs family. I need your help to go against our mother. And I also need your help to end the beef between me and Solo."

Jo-Jo looked at Khia for a few seconds before he spoke. Khia I don't know what type of games your trying to play but count me out. Jo-Jo please I'm begging you. Jo-Jo knew his sister and he knew her well. He could see in her eyes that she was serious.

"Khia although I was too young to remember our mother before she went into hiding. I heard many stories about how heartless she could be and going up against her was a fast trip to the cemetery. When it comes to getting you in good with Solo. That would mean I would have to tell him how I'm related to you and the Sams family. Which would mean my life might be on the line Khia."

"Jo-Jo, I thought about all of that already. I been thinking long and hard about how to fix all of this. I know Trini don't want to go up against the Gibbs family. If I can get Trini to flip on our mother. Tonya will lose the power she hold and all she will be left with is just her words."

"Khia how do you plan to get Trini to flip on our mother?"

"Jo-Jo by taking Mommy words literally. She once told me years ago; *your pussy has power. Keep it clean, keep it tight and know how to work it and work it good. With good pussy you can get anything, and you can make men do anything you want.*"

"Okay Khia lets say your plan with Trini works out. How are we gonna get you back in good with Solo, and how will he know this is not a trick?"

"Jo-Jo the only reason why I was beefing with the Gibbs family and wanted them all dead. Was because I thought Joe murdered our mother all those years ago. But me knowing now that wasn't the case. I don't have beef with them anymore. All those years our father Carlos lied to us about Joe murdering our mother. When the damn truth was, she was in hiding from him all these years."

"Khia it seem like you settled any future beef between you and Solo. But how can you make it right to him and his family, for all you already did to him while you were beefing with him and his family?"

"Remember when I told you a long time ago that I have two children?"

"Yeah."

"Well their names are Erykah and Tymel."

"Erykah, Erykah as in Jay wife Erykah?"

"Yeah Jo-Jo."

"Khia! Are you telling me Erykah is down with the plan to bring down the Gibbs family!"

"No she's not down with any such thing."

"Good…. Wait a minute Tymel! Tymel as in the Tymel that's living in your house, that came to town with our mother is your son?"

"Yeah."

"Khia this all sounds crazy."

"Jo-Jo it gets more crazier but listen. I already spoke to Erykah and Tymel. Erykah as we all know don't want any part in getting at the Gibbs family. And to my surprise Tymel doesn't really want any problem with the Gibbs family either. It's more so of our mother raising him all these years that got him thinking there's a beef when it's not. After I sat Tymel down and had a one on one with him and explained everything to him. He now no longer want in on our mother plan. Now remember Jo-Jo when I just said, it gets more crazier."

"Yeah" Jo-Jo said real slow not sure If he wanted to hear what was coming next out of Khia mouth.

"Jo-Jo although I told you about me having two children. I never told you about who their father is."

"Who's their father?"

"Solo is the father of both of my children." Jo-Jo looked at Khia in shock. "They don't know, and Solo doesn't know. Well I mean they didn't know until yesterday when I told them both, but Solo still doesn't know. The way I see things Jo-Jo. Once Solo find out that he's the father of my two children. How can he still want the mother of his two children dead?"

"Khia I'm willing to help you. But you have to promise me this beef thing between you and Solo is over."

"You have my word Jo-Jo. I'm done with beefing with Solo and the Gibbs family."

*****

"Solo what the hell am I going to do? Should I tell Beverly what happen between me and Tonya or not?"

"Supreme for right now I think you should keep what happen between you and Tonya to yourself."

"Solo she has it on video tape. What If Beverly see that tape before I explain things to her? Beverly is going to flip the hell out and you know that Solo."

"Supreme it will all work out and I'll back you up If Beverly get wind of this. But Supreme you have to do a favor for me."

"A favor such as what? Well let's just say that Beverly has a big secret to tell you. When that secret come out. I want you to be understanding Supreme and look past it."

"Your saying not hold it against her?"

"Exactly. Solo what secret is she holding from me?"

"That I'm not gonna tell you. Now listen Supreme, Rome called me a few minutes ago and told me, Tameka was released first about an hour ago, they just released Beverly and Trina a few minutes ago, and their all on their way to the club. So let's go see what Pit and detective Price want to talk to us about."

Walking out the club back office. Supreme and Solo walked up to the front of the club where Pit and Price was waiting for them at.

"Detective Price you said that we need to talk. What's up?"

"Solo it's been a murder at the store you own. Not in the store, but in front of the store. Do the name Flaco Sams rang a bell?"

Solo and Supreme looked at each other. Flaco they knew, but him being a Sams they didn't know. The same thing began running through their minds. "If Flaco was a Sams then so is his sister Debra. Which meant Debra had part in their home so is his sister Debra. Which meant

Debra had part in their home boy Bullet murder." For sure Debra would have to be dealt with, they both thought.

"You not saying anything, tells me that you know this guy Flaco that was murdered. Do you know that a crew by the name Sky-High has been selling drugs out that store that you own?"

"No I didn't know that" Solo said.

"Solo Sky-High is run by a woman by the name of Tonya, Tonya what, we don't know yet."

Standing up Supreme ran to the back office and came back to the group with a paper in his hand. The paper was the copy he made of Tonya I.D.

"Fuck" Supreme yelled slamming the paper down on the table in front of everybody.

"What's wrong big Bro?"

"Tonya Sams is what's wrong with me Solo. That bitch tricked me and she's one of them damn Sams!"

Picking up the paper Solo saw it in black and white, the name, Tonya Sams. Placing the paper back down on the table Solo shook his head.

"Detective Price none of this makes any sense. If Flaco is a Sams, then why would Tonya have him murdered?"

"She didn't Solo, a blood gang that go by the name Red-Money is who murdered Flaco in front of that store."

"How do you know this Price?"

"Because they left this paper at the scene."

Taking the paper from detective Price, Solo read it out loud: *"Bloods rule, and Red-Money is king. You are selling drugs where Red-Money sell drugs at. Pack up and move out, or Red-Money will paint the block with the blood of the, Sky-High members. One love, Red-Money."*

Giving the paper back to detective Price, Solo turned towards Pit. "Pit I got your text message. Fill me in because…."

"Davon is dead."

"What? How?"

"He was murdered in front of the door of our re-up apartment in Webster projects. This was left on the door."

Taking the paper from Pit, Solo read the note out loud: *"Bloods rule, and Red-Money is king. You are selling drugs where Red-Money sell drugs at. Webster projects belong to Red-Money. Pack up and move out, or Red-Money will paint Webster projects with the blood of your team members. One love, Red-Money."* Placing the note on the table Solo shook his head once again.

"Price you police, what do you know about these Red-Money bloods?"

"All I know is they have been making a name for their self for the past five years. How many members, I don't know. What are their names, I don't know is they have a drug spot in Webster projects, and they sell drugs on the block where your store is."

Walking in Love it or Hate it. Beverly, Trina, Rome, and Sierra walked up to Supreme, Solo, Price, and Pit. After Solo told them all what they had missed. Beverly began explaining everything that Ms. Renee had told her in the jail bull pen. What hit Solo nerve the most was hearing that Khia was still alive, when he thought he had killed her.

"Listen it's been a long night and a long morning. I say we all go home and get some sleep."

Chapter 10

With the fellas of Red-Money going to get their re-up of E-pills. Brandy took advantage of the free time and the empty apartment to the heart and called Desean over to her apartment. Knowing that they didn't have much time before everybody came back to Brandy apartment. Soon as Desean stepped inside of Brandy apartment. It wasn't long before Desean dropped his pants and boxers and exposed the biggest penis Brandy had ever seen in her life. Brandy had fucked many guys since she had been sexually active. But none of the men she had been with was ever blessed like what she was seeing before her. Her mouth began to water while her pussy began to throb instantly.

As Brandy dropped to her knees in front of Desean. She took his penis into her mouth. Although Brandy was a pro at giving blow jobs. Desean had never been big on getting a blow job. What gave Desean pleasure was a phat ass that he could fuck straight up the shit hole. A female offering him a blow job or pussy. Was a female offering him nothing at all. Yet a female offering him a tight asshole to fuck, was like offering him the world down a dark warm tunnel. Gently grabbing Brandy by her hair Desean pulled her head back from his penis.

"Yo you know we don't got a lot of time before the fellas get back here. I told you before I came over here, I want to fuck you in that phat ass of yours. You ready for this to go up in you or what?"

"Ooh I love a man that got a big dick and like to talk dirty to me."

"Word, well I like a bitch to shit on my dick. So what's up we wasting time?"

Standing up Brandy leaned over the arm of her couch with her ass sticking up in the air. Multiple thoughts were running through Brandy mind. "I like to get fucked in my ass, but this damn boy got at least 13 inches of dick. My asshole is gonna hurt like hell taking all that dick.

Brandy just do this and hope he's a minute man, so this can be over fast. His paper is long, and it's time I drop Smoke and upgrade and get with a nigga like Desean."

Positioning his self behind Brandy, Desean spread her phat ass cheeks.

"Aren't you forgetting something" Brandy said slapping Desean hands off of her.

"My bad" Desean said reaching over to his pants pulling out a condom.

Rolling the condom down the length of his penis he got back into position behind Brandy. Turning around Brandy looked at Desean.

"I was talking about that 500 dollars you suppose to give me" Brandy said holding out her hand.

Smiling at Brandy, he reached over into his pants once again. Handing Brandy the 500 dollars he had promised her. Brandy stuffed the money inside her bra. Desean smiled to his self. He was most deafly going to enjoy making Brandy gold digging ass shit on his dick.

Once again Desean positioned his self behind Brandy. Spreading her ass cheeks, he spit in the crack of her ass. With his penis at the door of her dark tunnel. Desean made sure he had a tight grip on Brandy waist and made sure there was no way Brandy could get up. Smiling Desean rammed his 13 inches of dick inside of Brandy.

"Ooooooh" Brandy yelled out in pain.

Pumping inside of Brandy. Each long stroke he gave her, he could feel things ripping inside of her with every pump. He could feel things ripping inside against his thighs. With every pump inside of her, Brandy felt like a knife was being stuck inside of her. Sharp pains were shooting up and down Brandy spin.

"Shit bitch, shit on my dick bitch" Desean yelled pumping in and out of Brandy like a mad man.

Grabbing a hold of one of her couch pillows. Brandy put the pillow in her mouth and bit down hard. Slapping Brandy hard on her ass Desean pounded even harder at her dark walls.

"Shit bitch, shit on this big dick" Desean yelled.

Taking the pain she was being giving. Brandy growled like a dog as she bit down on the pillow that was in her mouth. Pulling his penis out of Brandy, Desean snatched the condom of his penis and rammed it back inside of Brandy. Just when Brandy thought it was over. Desean pumped at her hole with vengeance. Going in as deep as his penis would go. Desean let loose his thick load inside of Brandy dark tunnel.

"Aww" Brandy yelled feeling Desean semen shooting up inside of her like a hot rocket.

Pulling out of Brandy once again. Desean smiled when he looked down at his penis and saw shit all over his penis. Walking to the kitchen Desean washed his penis off in the sink. Still in pain Brandy pulled herself together, got up and went straight to her bathroom to wash herself up. Coming out the bathroom Brandy was ready to complete her plan. Walking back into her living room Desean was fully dressed and sitting on the couch. Fully dressed as well, Brandy sat down next to Desean.

"I been doing some thinking Desean."

"About what?"

"About me, Smoke and you. Listen getting tired of being with Smoke. I think me and you should get together Desean." Hearing Brandy last statement Desean bust out laughing. "What's so funny?"

"You."

"Desean I'm serious. I'm willing right here and now to drop Smoke and get into a relationship with you. I think me and you make a cute couple."

"Me cute, okay, but your ugly as hell Brandy. Granted you have a nice phat ass, but your face is jacked."

Jumping up from the couch Brandy felt rage building inside of her. Not only was her asshole hurting, now her feelings were now hurt.

"Who the fuck are you calling ugly Desean!"

Still sitting on the couch Desean looked around the living room, as If he was looking for someone, then looked back at Brandy.

"You bitch! You the only one in this apartment besides me. I'm calling your ugly as ugly!"

"Don't be trying to play me Desean. Mad niggas in these PJ's want to get with me. I give good head, I got some good pussy, and I take it in the butt."

"Do you hear yourself Brandy? You give this, you got that you take this. What the hell does that have to do with how your face look? Check it If you suck dick so good. Why don't you go slob on a knob and get back at me when your money is up to mine."

With an evil look on her face Brandy wanted Desean to drop dead right then and there. Seeing the look on Brandy face he knew he had hit a nerve. Not stopping there Desean continued. "Brandy you are a gold digger. You want me for what I can do for you."

Although it was clear that Desean had played her, she wasn't going to let him think that she didn't have fire to spit back at him. "Call me what you want, but know I already got 500 dollars out your sorry ass."

"Yeah, you got that, but that's nothing to a boss like me. But tell me this, how do your asshole feel right now bitch?"

"Fuck you, you fucking bastard!"

"I don't know who you getting loud with, or who you talking to. With that Mr. Ed's tail swinging from the back of your head. You better take it down a few levels."

With fire in her eyes Brandy snatched the fake pony tail out her hair and ripped the front of her shirt. Desean looked at Brandy like she had just lost her mind.

"What the hell was that all about?"

"You raped me Desean!"

"What" Desean yelled jumping up from the couch.

"I'm gonna tell Smoke that you raped me. Believe me when I tell Smoke you raped me. You, dead, because Smoke is gonna kill your ass." Walking over to Brandy, Desean stood face to face with her.

"Bitch it will be a cold day in hell before I let a gold digging bitch like you, put a death sentence on my head. I always keep a wild card in my pocket to get me out of death sentences. Your man Smoke will see death before I do thinks to you. When it's all said and done. I bet you'll shit on my dick again."

"I will never let you fuck me again."

"Talk is cheap bitch I can show you better than I can tell you" Desean said walking out of Brandy apartment.

Running over to the door Brandy stuck her head out the door. "Enjoy your life while you still got it because I'm gonna make sure Smoke take it from you" Brandy yelled slamming her door closed.

*****

Sitting at the bar, Solo, Beverly, and Supreme gave out orders, as they tried to come up with a plan to get their drug operation back in order. Solo sent Tone, Pit, Corey, and Lloyd, back over to Webster projects to pump weight. But told them to keep their eyes open. Beverly sent Sierra, Rome, and Trina, to pump weight in Soundview projects. As for Jay and Jo-Jo for some reason they both wasn't answering their cell phones. Doing what Solo did best. Solo looked up their chain trackers and knew they were fine and just not answering their cell phones. Being that Jo-Jo and Jay were both close to Davon. Supreme and Solo felt they may be taking Davon death hard and chose to give them a little bit of space.

"Tank what do you think about this crew called Red-Money" Supreme asked.

"Supreme all I can say is the drug game somewhat changes every decade. The sixties was heroin, the seventies was cocaine. Then came the eighties with crack. The 90's was weed. Here we are in the 2000's. The 2000's is changing the whole game with pills, and every other thing else these crazy ass kids chose to get high off of. I been around a long time to know two things."

"And what's that Tank" Beverly asked.

"Well one, drugs will always be on this earth. And two, sometimes the old have to teach the young how to act. Whether it be talking to them, beating them, or even killing them. I'll tell you something else. I knew I knew Tonya from somewhere. Yesterday when yawl put it all together. It all came back to me. Tonya use to run drugs in here to Pop when he used to own this here strip club. That woman Tonya is used to own this here strip club. That woman Tonya is one wicked woman. The fight in that woman is strong. My advice to you three is this. Don't for a minute underestimate Tonya. When you think you've won and beat her. She'll be back and stronger than before. As for the Red-Money crew. Their young, dumb, and want to be legends. Each new crew always think they are taking the drug game to the next level. But the drug game don't really change. The only thing that does change is the faces in the game. In the drug world you have smart drug dealers, and you have stupid drug dealers. As you three know, only the smart will survive."

Walking away to serve a customer Tank left them with all he had just said. Standing up from the bar Solo looked at Beverly and Supreme.

"Well you two heard Tank. We have to play this game smart."

Supreme stood to his feet. "Yeah, we do have to play our situation smart Solo. That's why me and you are going over to Dad old store. We gonna go lay low in that store, until someone walk in it. Right now no one is in it, but tomorrow were sure someone will pop up. As for you Bev, go to Soundview and run your spot."

Standing up Beverly looked at Supreme and Solo. "Do you two really think Trini is still alive and trying to run Joe old store?"

"Bev, Mommy said, she saw Trini in that store. It's only one way to find out the truth."

"Lay low and wait" Solo added in.

"Okay, well when you two are done at the store tomorrow. Please head over to Webster projects. I don't want anyone else to die."

"Will do, will see you tomorrow" Supreme said kissing Beverly on her forehead.

*****

After dropping Tameka off at her house. Tonya headed back to Khia house. Walking in the house Tonya walked up to her bedroom door. Hearing sex coming out her bedroom. Tonya broke out in a cold sweat. She could hear Trini moaning, moans that she knew well for the past 23 years. The female moaning Tonya was hearing. It wasn't a doubt in Tonya mind that it was Khia. Tonya knew and felt on the plane ride to New York. That Khia felt some type of way about her taking the spot as the queen of the Sams drug operation. Tonya laughing to herself, "If this bitch think her pussy is more powerful than my pussy, this bitch got another thing coming to her."

Go up and down with her hands on Trini chest. Khia looked into his eyes as she rode his dick. Tightening her pussy walls around his penis Khia began riding Trini penis even faster. Trini eyes began rolling back into his head in pleasure. What started off earlier in the day as a onetime creep with Khia. Was now turning into a commitment. As bad as he wanted to let loose, he felt he had to hold out until she got off first. Grinding herself on top of Trini. Trini could feel Khia pussy muscles contracting letting him know that she was climaxing. Opening his eyes Trini pumped back underneath Khia finally releasing his load. Still on top of Trini, Khia laid her head on his chest.

"Trini please give some thought to what I said."

"I will, I got that address you gave me" Trini said between heavy breathing.

After getting dressed Khia gave Trini a kiss on the lips. Opening the bedroom door Khia stood face to face with Tonya. Tonya looked in Khia face with a deranged expression on her face. Lifting her French manicured nails in the air, Tonya smacked the shit out of Khia. Immediately Khia pushed past Tonya and walked out the room holding her face.

"Your pussy got power but not against the pussy that birth you" Tonya yelled at Khia back side. Turning her attention to Trini. Tonya walked into her bedroom and slammed her door closed. "How dear you scoop so low as to sleep with my daughter?"

"Tonya it's not what you…."

"Don't you dear try to play me like I'm stupid Trini! Don't forget who run this show. I own your ass! And I've own you for the past 21 years."

"Own me?"

"Yeah! I own you Trini! I make the damn rules and you follow them."

"Is that right Tonya?"

"Damn right, now here is how things are going to play from here on out. Make that your last time having sex with my daughter. You want to know my plan? Well here it is! I plan on bringing down the Gibbs family and your gonna help me do it."

"Tonya your so hooked on yourself that you don't even know what happen two days ago. Do you know Flaco was murdered in front of our drug spot, while you were out all day and night trying to get back at the Gibbs family?"

Shock ran across Tonya face hearing Flaco was dead. "They found out that were running drugs out of…."

"He wasn't murdered by anyone in the Gibbs family. It seems like we now have beef with a blood crew called Red-Money."

"Red-Money" Tonya repeated to herself. The name wasn't ranging a bell in her head at all. "Is Red-Money down with the Gibbs family?"

"No!!!!! Everything is not about the Gibbs family Tonya!"

"Well then who is this Red-Money crew Trini?"

"I don't know, all I know is they murdered one of ours and they murdered one of the Gibbs members."

"You don't know, and I guess you just shut down our spot, right? Sams don't fold Trini! I want you to go back to that store and get some answers about this Red-Money crew. When you get some answers about this Red-Money crew. When you get some information on them, then we can open shop back up. We are losing money right now by the store being closed, and you're the cause of it."

"Me?"

"Yeah you! Now get the fuck out my face."

With a heavy mind Trini walked out the bedroom and out the house. Walking in Khia bedroom. Tonya walked straight up to Khia face. "Whatever you think you have planned you better knock it off. You may be grown now, but don't forget I'm the woman that taught you everything you know. Cross me Khia and I swear to god I'll smash your head right against the ground." Before Khia could get a word out Tonya made her exit out the room. Picking up her cell phone Khia called Jo-Jo.

Chapter 11

Inside the store Trini sat behind the cash register. Thinking to his self he held the piece of paper with the address that Khia gave to him. The address he held in his hand. All he had to do was go to it and that would stop Tonya madness. Yet he also knew If he did that. Tonya would for sure flip out and may even try to murder him. But If he did nothing for sure Tonya would make good on her promise and murder Solo and Supreme. He let Joe die, something he wished he could take back. In no way did he want to sit back this time around and let another Gibbs die. Then there was that comment Tonya kept repeating to him that he couldn't shake, "I own your ass." More and more Trini thought to his self. If he chose to go to the address Khia gave him. What would he be up against? Making up his mind he had to stop Tonya plan. The only way to do that he had to go to the address Khia gave him. But first he needed some protection just in case. Stepping in the back office of the store. Trini closed the door and turned on the office light.

"Looking for this Trini" Supreme said holding up the gun he found in the back draw.

Jumping in shock at the sight of Solo and Supreme sitting in the office. Trini fell into the office door. Solo stood up and walked over to Trini.

"You look shocked to see us. When we should be the ones shocked to see you. Especially since you knew we were a live and we thought you were dead for the past 21 years."

"I...."

"Sit your ass down" Solo yelled pushing Trini down in the desk chair. Still holding Trini gun in his hand Supreme got up and walked over to Trini.

"Get to explaining and start from the beginning" Supreme said rubbing his gun against the top of Trini head.

After telling Solo and Supreme everything. Trini sat with his head down. Not because he was scared, but because he was ashamed of his self. A shame for letting their father be murdered who was his best friend. Solo and Supreme looked at each other. It was something they did almost as If they could see what the other was thinking. Looking at Trini neither one of them wanted to kill him, but they wouldn't hesitate to kill him If they had to. Trini was more than just their father best friend. He was also like a uncle to them.

"Do you really think you can make this all right again" Supreme asked.

"Yeah…."

"Then go make it right" Supreme said throwing the gun on Trini lap.

"If you can't make it right watch your back. If you do make it right your down with the Gibbs family where you belong" Solo added in. "Don't come back to this store. You know where to find us."

Opening the door Trini left store. Once Trini was out the store. Solo and Supreme began changing all the locks on their father store.

"Solo what you think about all of this that we been finding out these past few weeks?"

"Supreme all I know is my name is not Any, Many, Mindy or fucking Moe. And I will be damn If I just let somebody put a fucking toe tag on my foot or yours. If Red-Money want war, then they can get it. If Tonya want to follow her ex-husband Carlos to the cemetery. I'll be more then glad to drive her ass there personally."

Feeling his cell phone vibrating on his hip. Solo pulled it out and looked at the screen and saw that it was Jo-Jo calling him. "Hello."

"Solo, I need you to come to my house right now it's important."

"I'm on my way." Hanging up Solo put his phone back in his pocket. "Big Bro that was Jo-Jo. He want me to go over to his house. When I'm finish over there, I'll meet you over in Webster projects."

"Be safe" Supreme said Solo a pound.

"Same to you big Bro" Solo said jumping in his car.

*****

After Tonya dropped Tameka off at home. Tameka remembered that Jay gave her his number the other night. Calling him, Tameka told him to come over to her house, and she gave him her address. Seeing life differently Jay never did go home from the strip club the other night. With Rome owning the Bank's hotel. He checked his self into the hotel. When he got Tameka call, he told her, "he would be at her house in less than ten minutes."

Although Jay and Tameka agreed on him paying her two thousand dollars to sleep with her. Once Jay got to Tameka house. Tameka told Jay to keep his money. Tameka thought Jay looked good in the dark strip club. But seeing him in the light in her house. She thought he was fine as hell and couldn't bring herself to take his money. Tameka refusing to take his money made Jay think even harder to his self. He loved Erykah, but her past two weeks getting drunk and passing out. Was something he wasn't feeling at all. Erykah had showed him a side of her that was a deal breaker. In Jay case it was more like he was getting a divorce from Erykah as soon as possible.

Inside of Tameka bedroom she was working Jay body as well as his mind. Even though Tameka knew Jay had come already. She continued to ride him keeping his dick hard as a rock. The more Tameka road his dick. The more Jay was replacing Erykah with Tameka as the one winning his heart.

"Damn girl when was the last time you had sex? Your pussy is so tight, so good" Jay moaned." Flipping Tameka off him, Jay got behind her.

Catching the rhythm Jay pounded away at Tameka hot hole. No matter how hard he tried to give her all of his dick, he could only go but so far inside of her. Her walls were tight, turning Jay on even more. Her hot hole was only letting 75 percent of his dick enter her world of bliss. So badly Jay wanted to give her the extra 25 percent of his dick that she was missing. Harder and harder he pounded away at her hot hole.

*****

"Okay you got me at your house Jo-Jo. What's so important that you needed me to come over here?" Looking at Solo sitting on his couch. Jo-Jo didn't know If he should talk to Solo first or show him the video of him and Khia talking in his living room the day before. "Jo-Jo" Solo yelled seeing that Jo-Jo was lost in his thoughts.

"Solo let me first say from day one I been loyal to you."

"I know that Jo-Jo."

"Solo but there's a secret I been holding from you since day one of us meeting."

"Jo-Jo do I need to pull out my gun?"

"I hope not because my loyalty is still to you."

"A secret such as what Jo-Jo?"

"My name is Jo-Jo Sams, Khia is my sister and Tonya is my mother." Solo looked at Jo-Jo without saying a word. "Say something Solo."

"That's why you gave your word to Gail to get me a drug family contract with her. Your brother Wayne had my wife violated. You were there when my team murdered Wayne. Me and my brother Supreme look at you like a little brother Jo-Jo. Time and time again you showed your loyalty to my family Jo-Jo." Solo stood up, "Jo-Jo your secret is for giving."

"Solo you might want to sit back down there's more."

"More like what Jo-Jo?"

"I was talking to Khia and she want the beef to end between you two."

"Jo-Jo your sister is as good as dead when I catch her."

"You might rethink that after you see this."

"See what?"

"This" Jo-Jo said pressing play on his DVD player.

After seeing the video of Jo-Jo and Khia having a conversation. Solo continued to look at the T.V screen in a daze. "Solo say something." Solo continued to look at the T.V screen in a daze.

Leaving Solo in the living room by his self. Jo-Jo went to his bedroom. A minute later Jo-Jo walked back into the living room with Khia in front of him. Looking over at Khia, Solo had a blank expression on his face. Walking over to Solo, Khia placed two D.N.A test results, and two pictures on his lap. One picture of Erykah and the other of Tymel. Solo looked over the D.N.A test results and looked at both pictures. He wanted to ask Khia, how did she get his D.N.A to get the two test done. But he was sure she didn't have a hard time getting his D.N.A. Especially since they had sex many times back in the day.

Erykah and Tymel were both smiling in the pictures. They both had the Gibbs signature smile. Folding up the two pictures and two papers. Solo put them in his pocket. Standing up he looked Khia straight in her face.

"How could you do this to me? How could you not tell me we had two children together?" About to speak, Solo stopped Khia by smacking fire out of her across her face. Khia saw stars as she flew across the living room. "When I call you in a few days or weeks. Make sure you bring my damn kids with you." Walking out Jo-Jo house Solo slammed the door behind him.

Helping Khia up off the floor. Jo-Jo sat Khia down on his couch. "Jo-Jo what do Solo mean by that? Is our beef over or is he going to try to kill me and my two kids?"

"I believe that was his way of saying you and his beef is over Khia."

*****

"ladies you may leave us" Gail said. One by one all nine women that showed Trini into the house, made their exit out the dining room. Taking a seat across from Gail, Trini tried to find his words. This was the first time in his life he was scared to talk to a female. There was something about Gail that screamed, you better respect me or face death.

"Your mighty quiet I'm sure you didn't come to my house to just look me in my face. What can I do for you Trini?"

Trini looked at Gail in shock. "How do you know my name?"

"Trini there are many things I know. Just like I know why you are here to see me. But I'm not into telling people what road to go down. I rather see where their mind is at. So! What can I do for you Trini?"

"Gail, I'm aware that Tonya holds the Sams drug contract with you." Gail nodded her head at Trini. "I'm more than sure you know me, and Tonya got married a few years ago."

"So I heard, but what are you getting at Trini?"

"I took Tonya last name which makes me a Sams as well."

"That it does Trini."

"I'm two years older than Tonya." Trini slid his I.D across the table at Gail. Catching the I.D Gail slid it back across the table to Trini.

"I don't need to see that. I know your age, as well as I know Tonya age."

"Gail, I'm gonna get straight to the point of why I'm here."

"I truly wish you would Trini."

"Gail, me being the oldest Sams. I want to be the king of the Sams drug contract."

"Good move Trini, very good move on your behalf. Due to you being the oldest Sams the contract is now yours Trini. I'll do the pleasure of telling Tonya her spot has been taking."

"Another thing Gail, I would like you to add two lines in my contract."

"Oh really, this sounds like it's gonna be good Trini. What would you like to add in your contract?"

"This" Trini said sliding a piece of paper across the table. Opening the paper Gail read the two lines. Laughing Gail folded the paper.

"So order Trini, I will place these two lines into your contract." Sliding a business card cross the table at Trini, Trini caught it and picked it up. "That's all you need to know to get a re-up of drugs from me. Ladies! Please show Trini to the door!" The same nine women that showed Trini into the house, showed Trini to the door.

*****

"Brandy what the fuck do you mean he raped you!"

"Smoke, Desean came to the house after you all left the other day. I told him you wasn't here, and he said, he would wait for you to come back. I didn't think anything of it. Because I thought yawl were coming back, but yawl didn't. A few minutes later he jumped on me. He ripped my shirt, pulled down my pants and forced his self-inside of me. I tried to fight him off me and he pulled my pony tail off. I'm scared Smoke. After he was done, he just left nothing happen."

Brandy began sobbing uncontrollably, holding Brandy in his arms Smoke wanted Desean head. Not just for violating Brandy, but for violating him as the big homie of the Red-Money crew. Kenny, Marty, TJ, King, and Cancer, all looked at Smoke as he held Brandy in his arms. In no way did they believe Brandy story. They knew Brandy was a whore, because they had all ran threw her at one point or another behind Smoke back.

"Yo King, take Brandy in the back room while I make a phone call." Doing as Smoke said King walked Brandy towards her bedroom. Pulling out his cell phone Smoke dialed Desean number.

"Hello."

"Yo, you already know who this is Desean. Is you serious my nigga!"

"Serious about what Smoke?"

"Nigga serious about rapping mine and thinking I'm not gonna get at you blood?"

"Listen Smoke…."

"No blood you listen! Blood in, blood out nigga. When I see you, blood on my hands. Because I'm gonna make your ass lean." Hanging up the phone Smoke cocked his gun.

Although Smoke had hung up the phone. Desean continued to hold the phone in his hand. Sweat began to pour from Desean forehead. He knew Smoke long enough to know Smoke meant every word that had just came out his mouth. Placing the phone on the receiver Desean began thinking to his self. "Where there's smoke, there's fire, and I'm about to make a blood feel it" Desean said to his self-picking his phone back up. It was time he pulled out his wild card and used it.

"Yo, who this?"

"Solo it's me Desean."

"Desean…. Nigga what are you calling my phone for?"

"I got some information you might want to hear."

"Listen Desean good looking on that last info you hit me with a while back. But right now I think I heard more than enough info for today. Call me back tomorrow…."

"I know who murdered Davon."

"Who!"

"A nigga name Cancer, who got the order from the big homie Smoke."

"How do you know this Desean?"

"I was down with Red-Money."

"Was?"

"Yeah was, until I got this info. I heard the nigga Smoke had ordered one of your niggas to be murdered, and I hung my red flag up. I don't want you to think I had anything to do with one of your people being murdered Solo. I also know that Smoke is planning to send out another hit on your crew."

"Let me ask you something Desean. Did you tell this Smoke guy you not rolling with his crew anymore?"

"Nah, I just haven't answered my phone for him in the past few days."

"Good, you know all the info about where I can catch up with this nigga Smoke?"

"Yeah, I know his drug spot in Webster projects."

"My man! Check it Desean, keep not answering your phone for this Smoke guy. I'm gonna need your help to get at this nigga. I'll be in touch."

*****

"How can I help you Sir" the hotel desk clerk asked.

"I need a room for one."

"What's your name Sir, and how long will you be staying with us?"

"Trini Sams, and I'm not really sure. Just charge me by the day."

"Will do Sir, here's your room key."

Taking the room key from the desk clerk. Trini went up to his room. There was no telling when Gail would give Tonya the bad news. When she did Trini didn't want to be anywhere near Tonya, when she got the news that she was no longer holding the Sams drug contract.

*****

Parking his car in front of Webster projects. Solo sat in his car thinking to his self. All together he now had five children. Erykah, Jay, Rome, Tymel, and Quinn. He would soon have six children when Trina give birth in a few months. The only children that didn't know he was their father now was Jay and Rome. No matter who it may hurt. Beverly was right, he needed to tell Rome and Jay that he's their real father. Punching the dashboard reality set into Solo. With Erykah being his daughter. That meant Jay married his sister and had been having sex with his own sister.

Holding the cross to his chain in his hand Solo began to pray. "Dad, I know you are up there chilling with Jesus, but please listen to me for just a few minutes. I need your help Dad. Please help me keep the family together. And help them all understand and help them move past this drama that will be coming their way. I miss you Dad, tell Gutta I miss him too. In Jesus name, Amen."

Walking in the re-up apartment. Solo took Supreme to the back private room of the apartment.

"Big Bro I have a lot of things I need to tell you. I have something to tell you to Solo. Trini called me a few minutes ago and told me, his business deal with Gail went well and Tonya is out."

"Supreme, I just found out that Khia had two kids by me. Jay wife Erykah is Khia daughter and my daughter. Me and Khia also have a son by the name of Tymel."

Solo handed the picture of Tymel over to Supreme. Looking at the picture Supreme smiled. "Damn little Bro you got some strong jeans. All your kids look alike. Solo I have to say, Erykah and this Tymel guy, I didn't see it coming."

"There's more Supreme. Jay and Rome are also my sons."

"Well about damn time you finally came out and said it Solo! If Gutta was a live I would owe him a thousand dollars, because I just lost the bet me and him had. Gutta said, you would wait until Jay and Rome are in their 20's to tell them that you are their father. I told Gutta, you would wait until they were in their 30's to tell them that you're their father."

"Gutta, you, yawl knew I was Rome and Jay real father?"

"Boy you not the only one in the family with a brain. Of course me and gutta knew. For one me and gutta never ran up in a female without a condom. Even with a condom on we would still pull out before we bust our nut off. We knew Monique and Beverly didn't get pregnant by us. But we said fuck it and went along with it because we were feeling them. Yet the day Beverly and Monique went into labor. Seeing what Rome and Jay looked like fucked our heads up. We knew we were not their fathers, but they both had the Gibbs million dollar smile. Then you came up to the hospital to see Jay and Rome. And that's when me and gutta put the pieces together. Your hoe ass fucked them both at that graduation party. Then the look on your face when you saw them. That made it clear to me and gutta you were they father."

"I can't believe you knew all these years Supreme that I was Jay and Rome father."

"You was scared out your mind to tell me wasn't you little Bro?"

"Hell yeah, I'm not gonna lie. Now all I have to do is tell Rome and Jay that I'm their father."

"Breathe easy little Bro. Me and Gutta told Rome and Jay you were their father when they were fifteen years old. But it would be nice for them to finally hear it come out your mouth Solo." Solo sat down on the chair. "You all right little Bro?"

"Supreme, I don't know If I shitted on myself, If I need to shit, or If I will ever shit again."

Supreme bust out laughing. "Damn little Bro your nerves are doing flips like that? You was that scared to tell me?"

"Hell yeah! I thought you was going to take my head off my shoulders for sleeping with Beverly and Rome being my son."

"Solo that all happen before me and Beverly got together. Although you knocked her up and I got with her the same day. You and her, were respectful and never slept together again. Even though I know you want to fuck Beverly again. But your ass better not ever try it because I'll put a bullet right in your ass."

Solo closed his eyes. "Can you please not talk about bullets. I been having flashes of you shooting me since I walked in this re-up apartment."

Looking at Solo, Supreme could see that Solo was shaking a little bit. Supreme wrapped his arms around Solo. "It's all good little Bro we cool. Grabbing the cross around his neck Solo said in his head, "thanks Dad."

*****

"king on the real that nigga Desean still got my vein" Smoke said.

"So what you want to do about it Smoke?"

"Desean is a done deal when I catch up to him. For right now I feel like running down on a few niggas and making it clap."

"I'm down with that. Who you got in mind Smoke?"

"King, I say we go see these niggas that think it's cool to sell drugs in our projects." TJ, Marty, King, Kenny, and Cancer all stood up and followed Smoke out their re-up apartment.

Hearing a knock on the re-up down. Tone open the door to see a little boy standing before him.

"What up little man, what can I do for you?"

Pushing Cancer out the way Smoke, King, TJ, Kenny, and Marty, ran up in the apartment knocking Tone to the floor with their guns out. The ambush happen so fast, Tone, Pit, Corey, and Lloyd, didn't have a chance to react. Four of them and they had six guns in their face. Cancer held out a bag while the Red-Money crew stripped Tone, Pit, Corey, and Lloyd of their guns, jewelry, and wallets. Taking the bag from Cancer, Smoke told Cancer to stand outside the apartment door.

Making Pit, Tone, Corey, and Lloyd, line up. The Red-Money crew walked them to the back room of the apartment. Opening the room door the Red-Money crew was surprised to see Solo and Supreme in the room, but not as surprised as Solo and Supreme was seeing them. Moving fast the Red-Money crew pushed Pit, Lloyd, Corey, and Tone, down on the floor in the room. They then pointed their five guns at Solo and Supreme. The two movements happen so fast Solo and Supreme were court off guard. Marty and Kenny held the others on the floor at gun point. While King and TJ held their guns on Solo and Supreme. Walking over to them Smoke held the bag open.

"You two niggas know what this is. Guns, jewelry and wallets in the bag now!" Doing as they were told they were also pushed down on the floor.

"Listen up fellas! One by one three of my people are gonna take you over to my re-up spot. If one of you buck, you will die. If one of you talk, you will die."

"This is some foul shit" Corey yelled.

Walking up behind Corey as he laid on the floor Smoke looked down at him. "Hard of hearing, huh? Well let's see if all of you can hear this."

"POP!" The bullet ripped through the back of Corey skull killing him instantly.

"Now like I was saying. You six, I mean the five of you now that one of you are already dead. While you five are being taking over to my re-up spot. No talking, no bucking, or you will meet your boy here in death. For those of you in this room that don't know my crew. We go by Red-Money and I'm Smoke the big homie of the crew. Let's get to moving these lamb as niggas."

Chapter 12

In Soundview projects Beverly kept checking her watch. A whole day had passed since she saw Solo and Supreme at the bar. For the last hours she had been calling both of their phones, but they wasn't answering their phone. Two hours ago now Trina was also beginning to get worried as well. Beverly began walking back and forth in the living room.

"Bev something is not right. Solo and Supreme told you, after they check Webster spot out today, they was coming over here. They haven't been answering their phones, and they haven't called us back. I think something is wrong Bev."

"I'll be right back" Beverly said running to the back private room.

Closing the door Beverly locked it. Turning on the computer Beverly pulled up Solo and Supreme chain tracker maps. Their maps showed that they were in Webster projects. Yet they were not in their re-up apartment, but in another apartment in Webster projects. Looking at the computer screen closer Beverly felt it look weird. They were side by side and not moving. Going back an hour on both of their tracker maps, they had both been in the same position. Beverly hands began to shake. Solo and Supreme chains were to close together on the screen. Pulling up Corey, Lloyd, Pit, and Tone chain trackers. Beverly whole body began to shake in fear. All six of their chains were all on top of each other. For the past two hours there were no movements on the chains. "All of them are dead in this apartment" Beverly said in her head. "No this can't be" Beverly said writing down the apartment number the chains put them all at. Walking back into the living room Beverly eyes were blood shot red.

"Ma, you okay" Rome asked.

"Rome hold down the spot. Trina, Sierra, let's roll!"

Jumping up Trina and Sierra was on Beverly back as she walked out the apartment. Looking out the window Rome saw Beverly through Trina and Sierra a gun, and the three of them in Beverly car and speeded off. Not wanting to disobey his mother. Rome couldn't take it; he knew something had to happen in Webster projects and they were on their way over there. Running out the apartment, Rome jumped in his car. Speeding like a bat out of hell. Rome spotted Beverly car turning on Webster avenue towards Webster projects. Not wanting to be spotted Rome fell back four cars behind Beverly car. When Beverly parked her car, Rome parked his car on the corner. Seeing the three of them going into one of the building in Webster projects. Rome ran like a track star to the same building. Making it to the building just in time to see them get in the elevator. Rome stood in front of the elevator and watched as the elevator came to a stop on the fifth floor. Running up the stairs, Rome stood inside the fifth floor staircase. He could hear Beverly talking to Trina and Sierra. Looking through the window of the staircase door. Rome saw what apartment they were focused on. Sitting on the stairs Rome sat and listened as Beverly laid her plan out to Trina and Sierra.

*****

"Hello."

"Hey Gail, this is Tonya. How are you?"

"I'm just fine. I'm glad you called me Tonya. I was planning to call you a little bit later in the day."

"I guess great minds think a like Gail. Well I don't want to hold you too long. I know you are a businesswoman Gail. I just called to let you know that I need a new re-up supplier."

"Tonya, I'm sure you do, but I can't help you with a re-up."

"Did the ship not come in yet?"

"My shipment always come to me on time Tonya. I can't help you because your no longer the queen of the Sams drug contract."

"Excuse me, Gail what are you talking about?"

"I'm talking about Trini coming to see me, and he is now the king of the Sams drug contract."

"Gail! Gail how could you do this to me and allow him to do this?"

"Tonya, you might want to correct your words. It's not what I did, it's what you did. You married Trini, you gave him your last name, you knew he was older then you. The Sams contract clearly states when you were the holder. The oldest Sams must be the holder of the contract. Tonya, I thought I taught you well. Yet this was a very stupid move on your behalf. You no longer holding the Sams contract there's no need for us to talk any longer."

"Gail…." Gail hung up the phone without saying another word.

Getting off the phone with Gail, Tonya was beyond pissed off. There wasn't a doubt in her mind that Khia was the reason Trini had crossed her. Standing up Tonya walked out her bedroom and headed down to the living room. Walking into the living room Tonya shot fire out her eyes at all that was sitting in the living room. Khia, Jo-Jo, Cam Debra, Mellow, China, TG, Nicole, Goody, Levi, Tymel, and Erykah. All of them sat in the living room talking like they didn't have a care in the world. While Tonya felt like her head was about to explode. Seeing Erykah and Jo-Jo sitting in the living room made Tonya blood pressure go up even higher. Seeing as they told her they wanted no part in getting at the Gibbs family.

"Khia put this all together, that's why they are here, my own damn daughter crossed me" Tonya said in her head. Like lighten Tonya strike. Running over to Khia, Tonya wrapped her hands around Khia neck.

"You fucking bitch, I birthed you, and you cross me" Tonya yelled squeezing her hands even tighter around Khia neck.

Jumping to their feet Jo-Jo, Tymel, and Erykah, pulled Tonya off of Khia. Falling to the floor Khia gasped for air holding her neck.

"Let me go, I'm gonna kill that bitch" Tonya yelled trying to break free from them holding her back.

"What the hell is going on" Nicole asked still shocked from the whole scene.

"I'll tell you what's going on! Khia crossed us! And so did Trini! I'm not the Sams drug queen anymore. Trini is now the king of the Sams drug operation. And that bitch helped him do it!"

Nicole, Cam, Mellow, Debra, Goody, China, TG, and Levi, all looked at Khia in shock. Standing to her feet Khia looked them all back in their face. Khia then looked over at Tonya.

"You damn right I crossed you. Take whoever is still rolling with you and get the fuck out my house."

Trying to break free, Jo-Jo, Erykah, and Tymel, continued to hold Tonya back from Khia.

"Khia, I warned you what would happen to you If you crossed me." If Khia had forget what Tonya had told her. Tonya repeated her warning to Khia once again. You may be grown now Khia, but never forget I'm the woman that taught you everything you know. You crossed me, and as god is my witness. I'm gonna smash your fucking head against the ground when I get my hands on you." Breaking free Tonya headed towards the front door. Turning around Tonya looked at Khia once again. "Watch your back bitch because I'm gonna get you. Let's roll" Tonya yelled walking out of Khia house.

One by one Nicole, Debra, Cam, Mellow, Goody, TG, China, and Levi, followed Tonya out the house. Getting in Tonya car Tonya speeded off down the street.

*****

Reaching in her bra Beverly pulled out three silencers. Passing one to Trina, she passed one to Sierra. The three of them screwed the silencers on their gun. Beverly and Sierra tucked their guns under their shirts. Trina being five months pregnant now, and her stomach showing just a little. Tucking the gun under her shirt wasn't a option for her. Holding the gun behind her back. Trina stood behind Beverly and Sierra as they knocked on the door.

"Who" Smoke yelled on the other side of the door.

"Destiny" Beverly said using her old stripper name.

Opening the door just a little bit and seeing three females. Smoke tucked his gun in the back of his pants and open the apartment door all the way.

"What can I do for you three beautiful ladies?"

"We came to buy some E-pills and some weed" Sierra said with a smile.

"How much yawl trying to spend?"

"Two" Trina said over Beverly shoulder.

"Two what?"

Reaching over Beverly shoulder Trina shot Smoke in his head twice.

"Two bullets nigga" Trina said following Beverly and Sierra into the apartment. Stepping over Smoke body Beverly did a quick scan of the apartment with her eyes. Hearing voices coming from the back of the apartment. Beverly lead the way to the back of the apartment.

In the back room of Smoke re-up spot. Supreme, Solo, Tone, Lloyd, and Pit, all sat gagged and tied down to chairs. TJ, King, Marty, and Kenny, sat in the room with them, with their guns tucked in their pants. Standing up King walked around those that were tied up in the chairs. Slapping each one of them in the back of their heads. King began speaking.

"Fellas right now Cancer is over at your drug spot in these projects. Your money and drugs over there he's collecting all of it. When he's done, he'll be back. When Smoke come back in this room. He's gonna shoot each one of you in the head one by one."

"Fellas I do have one question for you. Which one of you want to die first" King asked laughing.

"Can us girls join the all-boys party" Beverly, Trina and Sierra yelled busting into the room.

Dropping to the floor, Beverly leaned to the left letting off a shot, hitting Kenny threw his right eye. Sierra did the same leaning to the right, shooting TJ in his nose. Still standing Trina let off a shot hitting King in the middle of his forehead. Marty being the last man standing and alive.

Moving fast Marty knocked Beverly and Sierra to the floor. Jumping over them Marty rammed Trina into the hallway against the wall. Kneeing Marty in his balls, Trina whacked him in the top of his head with the butt of her gun. Falling backwards back into the room Marty hit the floor in pain. Grabbing Marty by the collar of his shirt Beverly let off two shots to his head.

Running out the room Beverly went to check on Trina. Seeing that Trina was fine they both walked back into the room. Untying the guys, Supreme jumped up grabbing Beverly up in a bear hug.

"Damn girl you the best" Supreme said holding Beverly even tighter.

"I can't breathe Supreme."

 Rubbing Trina stomach Solo looked up at her. "You all right baby girl?"

"Yes, and so is the baby."

Pulling away from Supreme, Beverly looked at Supreme, then walked out the room. Knowing that look Supreme followed Beverly out the room. Walking in the kitchen Beverly walked over to the kitchen table. With a gun in one hand, Beverly grabbed the table with the other hand and flipped it over. Brandy looked up at Beverly like a deer look into headlights with fear.

"You got to be the stupidest bitch I know! You think I didn't see you when we came in this apartment? I saw you, just like I saw you dive under the table. Common since would have told your stupid ass to run out the apartment when you saw us go to the back room. But no your stupid ass stayed under the table. Let this be a lesson to you."

Beverly let off a shot hitting Brandy in her left leg. Brandy yelled out in pain as she held her leg. "Next time run out the apartment! Tell the police you saw us, and we will back. And the next time were not gonna leave your ass alive. You understand me!"

Brandy shock her head up and down still holding onto her left leg. Beverly sat in the kitchen with Brandy, while the rest of the team got all their belongs that the Red-Money crew took from them.

With three duffle bags full of drugs and money from Solo drug spot. Cancer got off the elevator and began walking towards the Red-Money re-up apartment. Getting closer to the door. Cancer noticed the apartment door was wide open. Dropping the duffle bags, he pulled out his gun and peeked his head inside the apartment. Seeing Smoke laid out on the floor dead. Cancer looked to the left side of the apartment, saw Beverly and Beverly saw him. Locking eyes on each other, Beverly jumped up and Cancer jumped back. Running down the building hallway, Beverly ran out the kitchen trying to catch him. Making it to the staircase Cancer bust threw the staircase door.

"POP!"

Hearing a gunshot Beverly stopped in mid run. A bullet to the head Cancer body flew back into the hallway landing on the floor. Seeing Cancer body it the floor. Beverly jumped in shock not knowing how the boy got shot.

"I got him" Rome said stepping out the staircase into the hallway.

Picking up the three duffle bags that Cancer dropped. Supreme, Solo, Tone, Pit, Sierra, Lloyd, and Trina, all walked down the hallway. Beverly continued to look at Rome in shock. This was the first time she had ever seen Rome kill someone.

"We got everything, let's get the hell out of here" Supreme said holding the elevator doors open.

Chapter 13

A Month Later

Giving Jay a divorce Erykah moved in with Khia. Head over heels with Tameka; Jay married her the day after divorcing Erykah. Driving to the club Jay looked over at Tameka.

"You look nerves sweet thing."

"Jay, I think this is a bad idea with me going to your Uncle club. On top of that me and Beverly had that fight. I think I should fall back…."

"You're not falling back Tameka unless you're on your back, with your legs over my shoulders, and feeling my ambition in your stomach."

"Jay, you are so damn nasty. Fine, I'll go to the club with you."

*****

Opening the house door Erykah looked at Henry in disgust.

"Why are you here?"

"Why am I here! Bitch did you forget the deal me and you have every Friday?"

"No I didn't, because we no longer have a deal Henry."

"Bitch, you think you can play musical houses and think I wouldn't find you? You owe me four Fridays of blackmail money. You got my four thousand dollars, or would you like for me to tell your secret to Jay?"

"Henry do whatever makes you happy. Me and jay are divorced, the Gibbs family already know I'm a Sams. Your pay day is over. If you would excuse me, I have to get ready. Me, my Uncle, my mother, and brother are going to my uncle Supreme club tonight."

Henry looked at Erykah confused. Not having anything else to say to Henry. Erykah slammed the door in his face. Lashing out in anger Henry kicked the door.

"Bitch you better get back out here and give me my four thousand dollars" Henry yelled kicking the door again.

Opening the door Jo-Jo and Tymel looked at Henry up and down.

"Nigga If you don't get the fuck from around here you gonna be a body on the ground" Jo-Jo said looking at Henry.

"Move on with your life or be a body on the ground like my uncle said" Tymel said cocking and pointing his gun at Henry head.

Finally sinking in that his come up, was now a come down. With his head held low Henry turned around and walked away from the house.

*****

"How can I help you miss" the hotel desk clerk asked.

"My husband is expecting me."

"How nice, what's your name and your husband's name?"

"My name is Khia Sams and my husband name is Trini Sams." Pressing a few buttons on the keyboard, the clerk looked at the computer screen.

"Yup, we have a Trini Sams. Here's your key Ms. Sams, he's in room 21, on the third floor."

"That's so nice because me and him been together for 21 years."

"Enjoy yourself Ms. Khia Sams."

"I will" Tonya said stepping into the elevator.

Using Khia name for the set up Tonya smiled to herself as she road on the elevator. For the past month Tonya had been looking high and low for Trini. She couldn't find him anywhere. Then she remembered they shared a cell phone plan. Looking up the G.P.S on his cell phone. His cell phone put him at the address of the Bank's hotel. Stepping out the elevator, Tonya used the hotel room key to let herself into Trini hotel room. Walking in the room Trini was sound asleep in the bed. Coming down hard on Trini stomach with the butt of her gun. Trini sat up fast in pain. Seeing Tonya face, Trini eyes grew large.

"Cross me huh" Tonya said shooting Trini in his face. Looking at the pieces of Trini brain on the wall Tonya laughed. "I guess this makes me the queen of the Sams drug contract again." Laughing again Tonya tucked her gun in her pants and left the hotel.

*****

In Love it or Hate it. Seeing everyone was finally all at the club. Solo began to make his way to the stage. Beverly walked over to Jay and pulled him to the side of the room.

"Jay it looks like your happy with Tameka."

"I am Aunt Bev."

"How you take what I'm about to say to you. Is up to you, but I feel you should know."

"Know what aunt Bev?"

"Jay, Tameka wasn't born a woman. Tameka was once known as Eddie and had a sex change and became Tameka."

Looking over at Tameka sitting down Jay began thinking to his self. "Is that why her pussy is always so tight, and I can't go but so deep inside of her?" Jay stared at Tameka trying to find some male features. In no way did he see any male features in Tameka. Beverly placed her hand on Jay shoulder.

"Legally Tameka is now a full woman and should be treated as such. I just felt you should know."

"Aunt Bev is your beef with Tameka over?"

"Yeah, that's water under the bridge, that bitch don't want no more of me."

"Aunt Bev I'm gonna keep rocking with Tameka. But thinks for telling me."

"Sounds good to me, go over there and be with your wife."

Giving Beverly a kiss on her cheek. Jay headed back over to Tameka, gave her a kiss, and sat down beside her. Beating on the mic Solo got everyone's attention in the club.

"To the Gibbs family and to the Gibbs drug family" Solo yelled. All in the club raised their glasses in the air with pride.

Solo continued to speak into the mic. "People we have had one hell of a year. We lost some, and we gained a few new faces. R.I.P to Davon and Corey."

"Rest in peace" everyone in the club yelled out. Feeling the loss of Davon, Rihanna his girlfriend lifted her glass in the air.

"I have a total of five children with one on the way. Three of whom have always been in my life. Jay and Rome always know love is love, and can't no body take that away from us."

Rome and Jay raised their glasses in the air at Solo.

"Then there are two of my children I knew nothing about. Erykah and Tymel, know that I'm your Dad and I will always be here for you long as I'm alive." Smiling at Solo they raised their glasses in the air.

"Beverly my sister in law. We almost lost you this year. I'm glad we didn't. All I can say to you Bev, is this. What the hell would we do without you?"

Tone, Pit, Lloyd, and Supreme stood to their feet. "Beverly! Beverly! Beverly!" they all yelled.

"To my two newfound children here's my gift to you. Pulling two gold chains with iced out crosses on them out his pocket. Solo put one on Erykah neck and the other one on Tymel neck. "Never take those chains off not even to wish your ass. Take them off and a enemy to me you will be."

*****

In the parking lot of, Love it or Hate it. Tonya sat in her car watching as people left the club to go home. After sitting in her car for over two hours. Tonya finally spotted Khia walking out the club. Seeing Khia walking to her car alone. The timing couldn't have been more perfect. Getting out her car Tonya walked behind Khia while ducking behind a few cars until she was close enough to Khia. Standing up straight Tonya walked up behind Khia. Jumping on Khia back Tonya took Khia down to the ground. On Khia back Tonya grabbed Khia by her hair and began slamming Khia head on the ground.

"Bitch, I told you If you cross me. I was gonna smash your fucking head against the ground."

In a rage Tonya began slamming Khia head on the ground even harder. Satisfied that she made good on her promise. Tonya stood to her feet and got back in her car. Leaving Khia on the ground unconscious Tonya speeded off in her car.

*****

Finding Khia unconscious in the club parking lot. Solo, Erykah, Jo-Jo, and Tymel, rushed her to the hospital. After waiting in the hospital waiting area for over two hours. A doctor finally came out to speak to them.

"Doctor, how is my sister" Jo-Jo asked.

"Well she took one hell of a beating to the head, but she's a fighter, she'll be fine. Due to her pain we thought it would be best to put her in a medical coma."

"Coma" Jo-Jo repeated.

"Son, it's not as bad as it sounds. She didn't fall into a coma. We put her in a coma, so she won't suffer in pain while she heal. When we feel she healed enough. We will medically bring her out the coma that we put her in. In about a week or so she will be able to deal with the pain of her injuries on her own. We should be able to bring her out the coma then." Saying all he need to say the doctor walked away.

Not knowing who attacked Khia. Jo-Jo thought it would be best that she had round the clock security at her hospital to place two security guards at Khia hospital door. Jo-Jo gave them a list of the only people that were allowed to visit Khia. A list of four names his self, Erykah, Tymel, and Solo.

<u>The Next day</u>

Driving to Jersey to see Gail, Tonya felt better then she had in years. Goody, Mellow, China, Cam, TG, Debra, Levi, and Nicole, all sat in the car with Tonya. Parking her car in front of Gail house. Tonya told them all, "to wait in the car."

"Have a seat Tonya" Gail said. Taking a seat across from Gail.

Tonya looked over at the nine women that showed her into the house. Normally Gail would send them away for privacy. Yet there they stood all of their eyes on her.

"Tonya if you're wondering why my ladies are still standing there. It's because you won't be here that long."

"Gail, Trini is dead as of last night."

"I'm aware of that Tonya, and I know you're the one that murdered him."

"Well Gail with Trini being dead he's no longer the king of the Sams drug contract."

"I'm aware of that as well Tonya."

"Gail with Trini being dead that puts me back in my spot as the queen of the Sams drug contract."

Looking down at her fingernails Gail then looked over at Tonya. "Tonya with Trini being dead, that doesn't make you the queen of the Sams drug contract."

"I'm the oldest Sams. Why doesn't it?"

"Tonya in that short time of Trini being the holder of the Sams contract. He had two lines added into Sams contract." Gail pulled out the Sams drug contract. "The two lines added into the Sams contract is as followed; Upon my death as the holder of the Sams drug contract. The contract is to go to the second oldest Sams and not the oldest Sams."

Just hearing Gail read the new two lines that Trini added into the Sams contract. Tonya head began to hurt. "Gail, those two new lines, what does this mean?"

"It means that the Sams drug contract goes to Khia. Khia is now the queen of the Sams drug contract."

"Not for long" Tonya said standing up.

Chapter 14

Parking her car in Kings county hospital parking lot. Tonya tucked her gun under her shirt, then checked her makeup out in the car mirror. Seeing that she looked good as always Tonya looked around her car. Sitting in Tonya car, Goody, Mellow, China, Cam, TG, Debra, Levi, and Nicole, all kept their eyes on her every move. Getting out the car Tonya left them all sitting in the car as she walked inside the hospital.

It had been two weeks that Khia had been in the hospital. Tonya felt it was about time that she paid her daughter Khia a see you in hell visit. Gail made it clear that Khia was the holder of the Sams drug contract. The only way Tonya saw herself being the queen of the Sams drug contract again. Is If Khia turned the contract over to her or If Khia was dead. Either way didn't make a difference to Tonya. Because she had a mouth to ask Khia to turn over the contract. She also had a gun If Khia said no, so she could kill Khia and take the drug contract back. Walking up to the hospital front desk. Tonya gave the receptionist a warm and inviting smile.

"Hello, I'm here to see my daughter."

"What's your name and your daughter name miss?"

"My name is Tonya Sams, and my daughter name is Khia Sams."

"One minute Ma'ma" the receptionist said pulling Khia name up on her computer screen. Looking at the screen the receptionist looked back at Tonya.

"Ma'ma, there's a strict order that have been placed on Khia Sams."

"What type of strict order?"

"Well her next of kin placed a visiting order on who is allowed to visit with Khia Sams and you're not on it. Which means I can't give you a pass to go up to her room to see her."

Taking a deep breath Tonya tried her best to stay calm. "Miss I'm her mother."

"I understand that Ma'ma, but she doesn't have you down as her next of kin. Her next of kin is who placed this strict visiting order."

"Fine, just call up to my daughter room and tell her I want to see her."

"I wish I could Ma'ma. But at this time Ms. Khia Sams is in no way able to make any choices."

Tonya notice being nice wasn't working with the receptionist. "Bitch did I just not say I'm her mother! I don't give a flying fuck about no damn strict visiting order! Give me a damn so I can go see my daughter!"

Looking at Tonya the receptionist kept her cool. On a everyday basis she dealt with rude visitors. "Ma'ma, you can get mad, you can yell, you can even offer me money. Yet none of that is going to get you upstairs to your daughter room. You can even try to pull a magic trick and get up to her room. But you would be wasting your time because she has two security guards outside her hospital room. The same strict visiting order I have here at this desk. Is the same strict visiting order the two security guards have upstairs. Do yourself a favor and take your self-home."

Getting closer to the receptionist Tonya spoke in a low tone. "Who put this strict visiting order on my daughter room?"

"Ma'ma that's personal business that I'm not allowed to tell you. Now like I said…."

Tonya pulled her gun out and put it on the desk in front of the receptionist. "Maybe you didn't hear me. Who put this strict visiting order on my daughter room?"

Looking at the computer screen quickly the receptionist looked back at Tonya. "A Jo-Jo Sams."

Seeing Tonya snatch the gun off the desk the receptionist dropped to the floor. Tucking the gun back in her pants Tonya walked out the hospital. Clearly that was all the information Tonya was going to get. The only way Tonya could see herself getting up with Khia is when Khia get released. Getting her title back as the queen of the Sams drug contract would have to wait. In the meantime she had many moves she needed to make, to bring down the Gibbs drug team family.

*****

In Soundview projects the whole Gibbs team sat in the living room of their private drug apartment. Standing up Solo looked at each person sitting in the living room. Supreme, Beverly, Lloyd, Tone, Pit, Rome, Jay, Sierra, Tameka, Trina, Tymel, Erykah, and Jo-Jo. Going in his pocket Solo pulled out a gold chain and through it at Tameka.

"I don't think I need to tell you what that chain mean, just make sure you wear it at all times. Let's get this meeting started. Me both agreed to re-open our father store and make that our third drug spot. Which mean a few things will have to change in order to run a third drug spot. Beverly being the queen of our drug operation will still run this Soundview drug spot. Jay, Sierra, Lloyd, you three will help Bev run this spot."

"I will be running our Webster projects drug spot. Tone, Pit, you two will help me run that spot. Joe's store, which is named after my father. Tymel, Erykah, you two will be helping Khia run Joe's store. As we all know Khia is in the hospital. But when she's back up and running Khia will be running our third drug spot."

"Rome, you and Tameka need to take a step back from the drug game and focus on running the Bank's hotel. Rome you own the Bank's hotel, and you need to get it in order. Supreme and own that strip club slash night club. It's no secret that we have closed down that club more times than I can count. Every time we close it down, we lose money. If you don't know I'll tell you. The strip club Love it or Hate it is very important to our drug operation. Our drug money get washed in that club and come out legal. Legally we are all employees of Love it or Hate it in the eyes of the I.R.S."

"Last but the most important person here. Jo-Jo you are the running man for the Gibbs drug team. Jo-Jo dirt house is where we will store all of our drugs at. When a spot need a re-up, call Jo-Jo and he will bring it to you. He will also be collecting the money from the drug spots and dropping it off at the club to Trina."

Ending the Gibbs team meeting, the whole team departed going their way. Having a lot on his mind Solo headed to the one place that always cleared his mind. Hearing movement downstairs in her house. Nancy made her way downstairs. Turning on the kitchen light Nancy jumped in shock seeing Solo sitting down at the table.

"Boy, you damn kids ain't gonna be satisfied until one of you give me a damn heart attack."

"Sorry Ma, I didn't mean to scare you."

Taking a seat across from Solo at the table. Nancy looked at her youngest son.

"So what's on your mind?"

"Who said something is on my mind Ma?"

"Jayquan Gibbs it's late at night and I'm in no mood to play the question game. I ask you a question and you answer me back with a question. Every time one of you kids are going through something or have a lot on your mind. All yawl use your key to get in my house. Go to my kitchen and sit in the dark. Spill it boy!"

"Ma, I have five children with one on the way."

"And your point is Jayquan?"

"Ma, I came over here for some advice and you being mad rude."

"You know Jayquan you boys are real tough in those streets, but when you having a one on one with me. Yawl all get real soft."

"Ma what do you want me to do? You want me to pull out my gun and shoot you in your face? Because that's what happen to people that talk shit to me like you're doing now. You gave me life of course I'm going to be soft around you."

"Jayquan four of your children are grown. Your fifth child is now five years old and is in school now. Money is not an issue for you, your children all love you. So spill it Jayquan because your children is not why you are here."

"Fine Ma! I'm here because I'm unsure about Khia."

"Unsure how?"

"Ma, Khia has been trying to get at our family for years. Hell I even thought I had murdered her a few years ago. Although me and Khia both agreed to put our beef to rest a few months ago. I don't know If I believe her."

"Jayquan that all sounded real nice, but we both know that's not the reason why you are here. One thing about my three children you have always been a good judge of character. You know If you can trust Khia or not. The real reason why you're here is because you still have strong feeling for Khia, and you're unsure of what to do with your feelings because you are married to Trina."

"Ma how do you know that?"

"Because Jayquan with age comes wisdom. Plus I also know my children. Yeah, you always liked Trina, yet you also liked Khia. I used to hear when you was on the phone with Khia when you were younger. That was puppy love for real. Then she up and disappeared for years. In that time your feelings grew stronger for Trina. Here we are now, and you are unsure on who you love more, Trina or Khia?"

Solo lowered his head. "Ma, I cheated on Trina a few years ago with Khia."

"I heard about that, and If my memory serves me right. Trina found out about that and she forgave you. Jayquan, you can't plan your life, only god can plan a person life."

"Ma what is that supposed to mean?"

"That means whoever you are supposed to be with, you will be with. Whether you be with Trina, Khia, or neither. The only advice I can give you is, live your life and let god do the rest."

Standing up from the kitchen table Nancy walked over to the kitchen counter. Looking at the stack of bills on the counter. Nancy picked up the envelope that contained her phone bill.

"Is that the phone bill Ma?"

Tuning around Nancy looked at Solo. "Yeah, it is, why you want to know? You got something you want to tell me Jayquan Gibbs?"

"I hate when you say my full government Ma."

"Oh excuse me let me get down with the get down. Jayquan, I mean Solo, yes this is my phone bill. Is there something you want to tell me Solo?"

"No, but If you need me to pay it…."

"Oh really? The last time you asked me about the phone bill in my house. I received a phone bill a week later for nine hundred dollars' worth of calls to some phone sex line number."

"Ma that was when I was like twelve years old. I'm 39 years old now."

"So! What does that mean?"

"Ma that mean I don't need to call a sex line to get off. When I can get the real thing. Plus I don't live in your house anymore, and I got my own phone. Now do you need me to pay…."

"No, I don't need you to pay any bills in my house. But thank you for offering." Nancy sat back down at the table with Solo.

"Ma, I don't know If I agree with you, about god plan our life."

"You don't agree, well let me tell you a bedtime story."

"Ma…."

"Shut up. Now like I was saying, we don't plan our life, god plan our life. Let me tell you the plan I had for my life. I planned to grow old with my husband. When I die the plan was for all three of my sons to put me in the ground. But guess what? God laughed at my plans and started showing me his plan. My husband died over twenty years ago. Growing old with him didn't and will never happen. My oldest son I put in the ground not once, but twice. So I guess the plan for all three of my sons to put me in the ground is out. Now like I said, live your life and let god do the rest. With god plan we may not see the point, but in the end it all makes sense. You then realize what you wanted in the beginning; you'll have it in the end."

Chapter 15

Opening the door and seeing Renee, Anton smiled at his mother. Normally when Renee popped up at his house his blood pressure would hit the roof. But being dick down real good by Jason just a few minutes ago. Had Anton feeling like he was walking on cloud nine.

"Ma what can I do for you?"

"Anton my welfare check was supposed to come today, and it didn't. Can you spot me twenty dollars?"

"Off the back Anton knew Renee was lying, because today was Sunday, and mail never get delivered on Sundays. But lying was his mother way of trying to game a person out of money. So she could go get herself a hit of crack. Going in his pocket Anton pulled out a twenty dollar bill and gave it to Renee. Normally Anton wouldn't give his mother money because he knew she would spend it on crack. But still feeling good from the sex he had just had with Jason. Anton was in a good mood.

Holding the twenty dollars in her hand Renee looked at Anton. For sure she knew Anton wouldn't give her the twenty dollars. Him giving it to her she was shocked.

"Boy you feeling all right?"

"Yeah."

"Boy this is the first time you ever gave me money since I been on drugs. You must got yourself a man living up in this house giving it to you good. Don't you?"

Before Anton could answer his mother question. A car came speeding up the block stopping with a jerk in front of his house. Jumping out the car Ruth made her way up to Anton door like a raging bull. Following behind her a man got out the car and slowly walked over to the house behind Ruth.

"I came for my son! Jason get out here right now!" Ruth yelled at the top of her lungs.

"Ms. Marshall, Jason told you the last time you were here, that he wasn't going anywhere. Now please stop making a scene in front of my house. Paying Anton no mind Ruth continued to yell. "Jason! Jason get your things! Me and your father are here to take you home!"

"Hey Ma, hey Dad" Jason said coming to the door with a robe on.

"Jason get dressed, get your things, and lets go."

Walking up to Ruth, Jason looked his mother straight in her face. "Ma do you know what I been doing at this house?"

"Jason we will talk about all of that at another time. In the meantime just get…."

"I'll tell you Ma what I been doing here. I been getting my dick sucked every time it get hard. I been fucking a tight phat butt." Ruth grabbed at her chest at what her son had just said to her. "Look Ma" Jason said opening his robe showing his naked body. "Look Ma, my dick is soft because I just bust a nut a few minutes ago."

Grabbing at Jason robe Ruth tried to close it. Snatching the robe off Jason ran around the yard, then ran back into the house. Renee looked in shock at the whole scene.

"Dennis don't just stand there! Get our son so we can go" Ruth said. Shaking his head in disbelief Dennis walked in Anton house after Jason. Although Ruth didn't Know Renee, she felt like she had to explain her son actions.

"Miss please don't think of my son as If he's crazy."

"Why the hell not, he just ran around the yard butt naked" Renee said.

"My son is mentally ill from being attacked some years ago. He take site medication and he haven't took his medication in a year. In his right state of mind, he wouldn't have done what he just did. And he damn sure wouldn't be having sex with another man."

Just the thought of her son having sex with a man put Ruth in a rage. Walking over to Anton, Ruth pointed her finger in Anton face.

"You are taking advantage of my son! He is ill! This between you two have to stop! I will kill you before I let you send my son to hell for being a homo!"

"Listen here, get out my damn son face talking like that. Ill or not, my son is not making your son do a damn thing" Renee yelled jumping in Ruth face.

Although Anton was surprised that his mother jumped to defend him. He didn't want his mother to get involved in the nonsense. "Ma, I will handle this."

"Anton you may be grown, but I'm still your mother. And I will be damn If I let another parent judge my damn child. Only I can do that." Turning back around Renee got back in Ruth face. "Face it bitch, your son is a fagget just like my son is."

"My son is mentally ill."

"Girl, your son is a fagget!!"

Having enough of the whole scene. Anton left Ruth and Renee outside and walked in his house to call the police.

"Jason open this door" Dennis yelled banging on the bedroom door he followed Jason to.

With the bedroom door locked and hearing he father banging on the door. Jason felt like he was in a concert. His father banging on the door sounded like music beats in his head. Still butt naked, Jason grabbed the brush off the dresser, looked at his self in the mirror, and started raping:

"Keep making that beat.

So I can spit this heat.

I'm ready to rock this flow.

So I can get this, Doe.

Ooh, I can make the city mine.

If I keep busting nuts, like I bust my gun.

Can't no body fuck'em better than I can.

My mother and father, keep trying to rain on my parade.

But I keep telling them.

I fuck niggas in the mouth and butt.

Because it makes me nut.

Fuck the pills when I can get in for real.

Hold up, hold up! My dick is sticking straight up.

It's time for me to bust that nut."

Seeing that he was getting nowhere with Jason. Dennis went back outside with Ruth.

"Dennis where is Jason?"

"Ruth this is pointless, the boy has made up his mind."

"Dennis our son don't have a mind without taking his medication."

"Ruth, Jason is a grown man and it's time that you let him live his life."

"You think him fucking another man is him living his life Dennis?" Seeing a police car coming up the block. Dennis grabbed a hold of Ruth arm, and got her in the car. "This is not over; I will be back" Ruth yelled out the car window as Dennis drove off.

*****

Picking up her phone book Brandy through it across her living room in a rage. Every guy that she had sex within her phone book she had just called. She got nowhere with any of them. Some of the guys had changed their number. Some of them were in a relationship, and they refused to jeopardize their relationship to mess around with her again. The others she called flat out told her, "they were not fucking with her, because word around Webster projects is that she set up the whole Red-Money blood set to be murdered." Which was a lie. All she had did was tell her boyfriend Smoke, the big homie of the Red-Money crew, that Desean a Red-Money member had raped her. Which was a lie. Yet she wanted pay back on Desean for trying to play her after she had sex with him. Instead of Smoke getting at Desean. Smoke decided to go up against the Gibbs family first before he went after Desean. Smoke, TJ, Marty, Kenny, King, and Cancer, were all murdered by the Gibbs family. Leaving Desean still alive.

Brandy continued to sit in her living room trying to think to herself what would be her next move. She was facing a eviction notice for months of unpaid rent. She was a gold digger without a job that didn't have anyone to dig off of. Although Smoke was her man. Behind Smoke back Brandy was having sex with every member of the Red-Money crew. In return for having sex with them they gave her money. Money that paid her rent, bills, put food in her apartment, and money in her pockets. Smoke and his crew had been dead for a few months. And Brandy was just feeling the lost for them all. Not because they were all dead, but because she could no longer get any money from them.

Standing up from the couch Brandy picked up her phone book. The only guy she had not call was Desean. Sitting back down on her couch Brandy mind flashed back to her last encounter with Desean:

Dropping to her knees in front of Desean. She took his penis into her mouth. Gently grabbing Brandy by her hair Desean pulled her head back from his penis. "Yo you know we don't got a lot of time before the fellas get back here. I told you before I came over here, I want to fuck you in that phat ass of yours. You ready for this to go up in you or what?"

Ooh I love a man that got a big dick and like to talk dirty to me."

"Word, well I like a bitch to shit on my dick. So what's up we wasting time?" Standing up Brandy leaned over the arm of her couch with her ass sticking up in the air. Multiple thoughts were running through Brandy mind. "I like to get fucked in my ass, but this damn boy got at least 13 inches of dick. My asshole is gonna hurt like hell taking all that dick. Brandy just do this and

hope he's a minute man, so this can be over fast. His paper is long, and it's time I drop Smoke and upgrade and get with a nigga like Desean."

Positioning his self behind Brandy, Desean spread her phat ass cheeks. "Aren't you forgetting something" Brandy said slapping Desean hand off of her.

"My bad" Desean said reaching over to his pants pulling out a condom. Rolling the condom down the length of his penis he got back into position behind Brandy.

Turning around Brandy looked at Desean. "I was talking about that 500 dollars you supposed to be giving me" Brandy said holding out her hand.

Looking up Desean phone number in her phone book. Brandy picked up her phone and dialed Desean cell phone number. Hearing the phone rang once Brandy hung up remembering what else happen that last encounter with Desean:

Smiling Desean rammed his 13 inches of dick inside of Brandy. "Ooh" Brandy yelled out in pain. With every pump inside of her, Brandy felt like a knife was being stuck inside of her. Sharp pains were shooting up and down Brandy spin.

"Shit bitch, shit on my dick bitch" Desean yelled pumping in and out of Brandy like a mad man. Grabbing a hold of one of her couch pillows. Brandy put the pillow in her mouth and bit down hard. Taking the pain she was being giving. Brandy growled like a dog as she bit down on the pillow that was in her mouth. Pulling his penis out of Brandy, Desean snatched the condom off his penis and rammed it back inside of Brandy. Just when Brandy thought it was over. Desean pumped at her hole with vengeance. Going in as deep as his penis would go. Desean let loose his thick load deep inside of Brandy dark tunnel.

"Ooh" Brandy yelled feeling Desean semen shooting up inside of her like a hot rocket.

Brandy sat with her phone book on her lap as she began thinking to herself. "Is going through the pain of having sex with Desean worth the money she could get from him.?"

Driving Desean pulled out his cell phone to make a phone call. Looking at his cell phone he noticed he had a miss call from Brandy. Pulling over he checked his messages and notice Brandy didn't leave a message. Holding his cell phone in his hand Desean began thinking hard to his self. "Although Brandy was ugly, she did have a phat ass, a asshole that felt good around his dick." He loved nothing more than fucking females in their butt. Months ago he had to sex Brandy on the low because she was with Smoke. With Smoke being dead he didn't have to smash Brandy on the low. He could now smash, give her a few dollars, and send her on her way. She made threats on his life, that no longer had power towards him with Smoke being dead. Dialing Brandy number Desean put his cell phone to his ear.

"Hello" Brandy said answering her phone.

"Yo, you called me?"

"Yeah, it was by a mistake."

"Sure it was shorty, check it though, your man Smoke is resting in peace. You want to get up with a real nigga right about now?"

"Please boy, what happen to me being so ugly?"

"Kill all that Brandy, you tried to play me, and I played you right back. Now what up? I can be in your area in a few minutes. I want to take you somewhere. And not to worry I'll put some money in your pockets. I know you hurting for some cash seeing how Smoke and the boys are all dead."

"I'm not hurting for shit" Brandy yelled knowing she was.

"Brandy I'm not gonna go back and forth with you. You trying to get up with me or not?"

"Yeah."

"Good, be in front of your building in five minutes."

Pulling up in front of Brandy building. Desean looked at Brandy and couldn't help but to say to his self. "She is so damn ugly, but she got a nice phat ass." Getting in the car with Desean, Desean pulled off.

"So, where are we going?"

"Why you got a curfew" Desean snapped.

"No, but I would like to know where you taking me to." Stopping at the red light Desean looked over at Brandy.

"That's how you talk to a person that want to take you somewhere? You start fucking questioning them!"

"I'm just…."

"I got a few questions for you Brandy. You told me before that you want to fuck with me, right?"

"Yeah."

"Are you gonna let me fuck you in that good ass you got?"

"Yeah, If you serious about being my man this time?"

"That's all I wanted to hear" Desean said pulling down a dark alley.

Getting out the car Desean got in the back seat and told Brandy to do the same. Getting in the back seat with Desean. Brandy knew exactly what he wanted with no panties on Brandy bent over the front seat. Remembering the pain she went through the last time she let Desean fuck her in her ass. Brandy was prepared this time. Before she left her apartment, she squeezed a half bottle of lubrication inside of her butthole. Getting on top of Brandy, Desean went to work. Balls deep Desean rammed his penis in and out of Brandy dark tunnel. Even a half bottle of lubrication inside her dark tunnel. Brandy still felt like Desean was ripping her asshole apart. Biting down on the car seat. Brandy did her best to indoor the pain of a 13 inch dick inside her asshole. With no remorse Desean pounded away at Brandy hole as he yelled in her ear.

"I told you talk is cheap bitch! Now shit on my dick bitch! Shit bitch!"

Brandy wanted to scream, "Get off me." But she refused to let go of the last cash cow she had left. Going in deep as his penis would go Desean let loose his thick load inside Brandy. Pulling his penis out of her it was painted with shit all over it. Taking his T-shirt off he wiped his penis off. Throwing the T-shirt on the ground Desean got back in the driver seat. Weak and in pain Brandy slowly made her way out the back seat. Walking around the car to the passenger seat, Desean stuck his head out the car window.

"Yo I just wanted to make good on my words, that I would make you shit on my dick again. Bitch I still don't want to be with your ugly ass. I'll call you when I want to fuck you in your ass again. Peace out bitch" Desean yelled throwing ten hundred dollar bills At Brandy. Driving off Desean burned rubber as he speeded out the alley.

"You fucking bastard! I swear on everything I love! You will never fuck me again! This time you gonna wish you never played me" Brandy yelled as she picked the thousand dollars up off the ground. Walking two blocks down from the dark alley. Brandy walked into the police station.

"Can I help you Ma'ma" the desk sergeant asked.

"Yes, my name is Brandy Cooper, and I was just raped."

"Do you know who your attacker was Ms. Cooper?"

"Yes, his name is Desean Evans."

Chapter 16

In Kings county hospital doctors stood around Khia hospital bed. A few weeks ago they had placed her in a medical coma due to her injuries. Feeling like she would be able to deal with her injuries. Doctors had just reversed her medical coma and was now waiting for her to wake up. Seeing that Khia was waking up two of the doctors stepped out of the room. One to call her next of kin Jo-Jo. The other to respect the order to contact the police department when she wake up.

"Where am I" Khia asked still a little out of it.

"You're in a hospital Ms. Sams" Dr. Owens said. "Do you remember what happen to you Ms. Sams?"

Khia looked at the doctor confused for a few minutes. "The last thing I remember was coming out the club and walking to my car in the parking lot." Grabbing her mouth in shock as she remembered her mother jumping on her back.

"I take it you remember who attacked you Ms. Sams?"

"It was my…." Stopping in mid-sentence Khia watched as two police officers walked in the hospital room. Following behind them was a guy that Khia was sure to be a police detective.

"I'm detective Price…."

"I know who you are. I remember you from a few years back. I take it that you're here to take my statement, on what happen to me the night I was attacked?"

"Yes, and your statement on what you did earlier that day before you were attacked."

"My mother Tonya Sams was the person that attacked me."

"I see, do the name Trini Sams mean anything to you Ms. Sams?"

"Yeah, that's my mother husband."

"Ms. Sams, I have a hotel clerk that names you as the woman that went up to Mr. Trini Sams hotel room and murdered him."

"What!!!!! He's dead? I didn't murder anyone!"

"Well as of right now your under arrest Ms. Sams for the murder of Trini Sams."

Handcuffing Khia left hand to the hospital bed. Following Price out the room, both officers sat down outside of Khia hospital room. Outside the hospital room Price began whispering to the two officers he brought with him.

"Fellas stand guard. I have to go show her picture in a six female paper line up to that hotel clerk. When the clerk point her out. We can transfer Khia to the jail for booking. I'll be back in a hour."

A few minutes after Price left the hospital room. Khia began to hear commotion outside of her hospital room. It didn't take long for Khia to realize her brother Jo-Jo was arguing with the officers outside of her door. A few minutes of going back and forth. Jo-Jo walked in the room and closed the door behind him.

"Khia two officers are outside your door saying you under arrest."

"I'm aware of that" Khia said raising her left hand showing that she was handcuffed to the bed.

"You were attacked, why are you being arrested?"

"Their saying I murdered Trini in his hotel room the day I was attacked."

"Trini is dead?"

"Yes Jo-Jo! Or did you not just hear me?"

"Okay, okay, let me think Khia. Ummm, I'll call Solo and tell him you need a lawyer. In the meantime did they find out who attacked you?"

"I remembered who attacked me and I told them."

"Who?"

"Our mother attacked me Jo-Jo. I told detective Price and he didn't seem to care at all. Jo-Jo with Trini being dead that makes our mother the queen of the Sams drug contract."

"Khia, I got a call from Gail the day you were attacked. She told me that you need to call her." Picking up the phone beside the hospital bed. Khia called Gail.

"Hello, how may I help you" Gail said answering the phone.

"Gail it's me, Khia."

"Khia I really don't like to talk over the phone. So I will make this fast with what I have to tell you. You are the Queen, not your mother, that case against you will be over within hours, come see me when you are released."

Saying all she needed to say Gail hung the phone up. Hanging up the phone Khia looked over at Jo-Jo.

"What did she said?"

"She said, I'm the queen of the Sams drug contract not our mother. The case against me will be dropped in a few hours. When I get released come and see her. Jo-Jo I don't know how I'm queen. I don't know how Gail know I was arrested. I guess I will find out everything when I go see her."

*****

"Ma'ma here's a six female paper line up. I just need you to point out Khia Sams. So I can send word to the two officers I have sitting outside her hospital room to take her over to the jail."

Looking at the six females on the paper, the hotel clerk then looked back at detective Price. "The woman that came in here that night saying that she was Khia Sams, is not in this paper line up."

"Are you sure? Maybe you should have another look."

"I don't need to I'm telling you she's not in this line up."

"Damn it" Price yelled banging his fist on the hotel counter. Pulling out his cell phone Price called the two officers sitting outside of Khia hospital room. "Cut her loose, were not arresting her" Price said into the phone.

Walking in the hospital room. Both officers notice that Khia was holding her hand up with the handcuff on it.

"It took you boys long enough. Can you please uncuff me" Khia said with a evil smile on her face.

"It's been a misunderstanding Ms. Khia Sams, the charge have been dropped" the officer said unhandcuffing her.

Once both officers were out the room Khia turned to Jo-Jo.

"Jo-Jo go get a doctor and tell them to bring me my release papers."

"Khia, you just came out a coma. I don't think it's such a good idea for you…."

"Jo-Jo they put me in a coma, I didn't fall into a coma. I feel fine and I'm ready to get the hell out of here."

Getting out the bed Khia began getting dressed. Seeing Khia moving around the hospital room just fine. Jo-Jo walked out the room in search of a doctor.

*****

Pulling the mail out the mailbox, Beverly went through the mail in her hand as she walked into her house. Coming across a big yellow envelope. Beverly notice the envelope didn't have a post mark stamp on it. Which meant it had been hand delivered by someone that wasn't the mail man. Opening the envelope Beverly pulled out a video tape and a paper. Opening the paper Beverly began reading the letter:

"Girl, me and your husband have been fucking for a while. We even fucked in your bed. Have a look for yourself. I recorded one of our nights together just for you.

Love always,

Your husband, got some good dick!"

Holding the video tape in her hand Beverly spoke to herself out loud. "Supreme, I swear to god you better not be on this tape having sex. Because If you are all hell is going to break loose." Popping the video tape in, Beverly turned on her T.V, and press play on her remote. Seeing Tonya giving Supreme a blow job in the bed they share. Beverly eye's grew wide in shock looking at the T.V screen. As the sex video went on. Tonya began riding Supreme dick. Beverly could hear Supreme moaning on the tape in pleasure. With the T.V remote in her hand. Beverly through it at the T.V screen, making the T.V tube explode. Snatching the tape out, Beverly headed out her house and back to her car.

*****

In Love it or Hate it. Supreme sat in the back office with Trina and his mother.

"Jerome, I must say your income record books of the club are in good shape. You shouldn't have any problems come tax time."

"Ma, that's why I wanted you to look over the books to make sure."

"Boy, you could have brought them to my house for me to look over them. Instead of making me drive over here while you got these men and women butt naked in this club."

"Ma, you act like you have never been in this club before."

"I have times, but never when you had people taking their damn clothes off in here."

Walking in Love it or Hate it. Beverly looked like Satan in a dress. Seeing the evil look on Beverly face from behind the bar. Tank the bartender could tell Beverly was there to go off on somebody. Without a hello Beverly walked pass the bar straight to the club back office. Walking in the office Beverly slammed the door close behind her. Surprised Supreme, Nancy, and Trina, all jumped.

"Nancy, I know me, and you haven't been that close when I first got in your family. But these past years me and you have got real close. Out of respect for you I think you should leave while I have a talk with your son."

"Beverly I'm sure whatever you have to say to Jerome won't disrespect me. Go ahead and talk to him." Without hesitation Beverly turned her attention to Supreme. Being with Beverly over 25 years. Supreme could tell the look on Beverly face meant she pissed off.

"Supreme sense me and you got back together. I have not slept with another man. Yet you cheated on me with that girl Candy and I forgave you. But you cheating on me with this bitch. I'm not forgiving you."

"Bev, I don't know what you talking about. I haven't cheated on you with you any one since Candy."

"Oh really" Beverly said walking over to the T.V in the office.

Popping the tape in Beverly turned up the volume on the T.V. Looking at the T.V screen Trina held her mouth in shock, seeing Tonya riding Supreme dick. Seeing the woman that was having sex with Supreme on the T.V. Nancy stood to her feet pissed off.

"Bev, I can explain…." Slapping Supreme with all her might. Supreme fell back tripping over the chair onto the floor.

"What the fuck is there to explain Supreme! You're on tape having sex with that bitch!"

Just as mad as Beverly, Nancy pushed Beverly out the way and stood over Supreme. With a strong right hand Nancy slapped Supreme across his face as he laid on the floor. "Boy are you out of your damn mind! Do you have any idea who that woman is Jerome? How could you be so stupid to cheat on Beverly with that Tonya girl?"

"Ma, how do you know Tonya?"

"How do I know Tonya" Nancy repeated getting even more angry. "I know that slut because your father Joe cheated on me with that bitch, and I caught them. Not only did I catch them, but I also went upside that bitch head for it to. Now here it is years later, and she fuck one of my own damn kids to. I swear you men always think with the head in your pants and not with the one on your shoulder. I told that Tonya girl If I ever see her again. I would beat dog shit out of her. Wow!!!! I can't wait to cross paths with that bitch. I swear I'm gonna stump her a new asshole!"

Snatching her purse off the desk Nancy walked out the office. Walking back over to Supreme Beverly looked down at him.

"I'm want a divorce, you hear me, a fucking divorce!"

"Bev let me explain, please."

"You don't have shit to explain to me Supreme. Not only are you a cheater, you are two faced. You been fucking the damn enemy! Don't bring your ass home because you no longer live there."

Just fast as Beverly had walked into the office, Beverly left the office the same way. Getting up off the floor Supreme took the tape out the player. Turning around Trina was looking at him with a disappointed look on her face.

"Trina this tape is not what it looks like. I didn't cheat on Bev Knowingly. I have to go fix this."

"Where are you going Supreme?"

"I have to go talk to Solo. Can you hold down the club and lock it up when it close?"

"Just because I'm six months pregnant don't mean I can't handle things. You just go and make shit right with my cousin Bev before she hill your ass."

*****

"Tonya are you sure were not waiting out here in this parking lot for our health?"

"Goody when have I ever done anything for my down health? Everything I do is for a reason. Now I have a good friend that work at the Bank's hotel. From what my friend told me. Their putting Henry out the hotel today."

"Tonya who is Henry and why are they going to put him out?"

"Henry is Erykah ex-boyfriend. He's been living in this hotel ever since Erykah and him broke up. My friend told me, he has no job, he has no money, and he can't pay the hotel bill anymore."

"Tonya that all sound real fucked up, but what does this Henry guy have to do with us?"

"Goody clearly you been out the game to long. Goody desperate people do desperate things. Putting a desperate person down on my team is always a good thing. Because they will do anything, I ask them to do."

"Tonya this guy Henry maybe down on his luck. But how do you know he will agree to join the Sams team?"

"There's only one way to find out Goody, and there he go. Show time!"

Getting out the car Tonya walked up to Henry as he dragged a suitcase. Henry looked at Tonya with a confused look on his face. He knew he knew her but couldn't remember where he knew her from.

"Don't tell me you don't remember me. I'm Tonya, Erykah grandmother."

"Oh, hello Ms. Sams. I don't mean to be rude, but me and Erykah are no longer together. And right about now I'm going through a few problems of my own. So If you don't mind, I have to…."

"Henry, I'm sure you haven't heard that me and Erykah no longer talk anymore. To be honest with you I'm glad that I ran into you."

"Why is that Ms. Sams?"

"Well you see I really want to teach Erykah a lesson about respect and loyalty. Her dealing with that Gibbs family is a total slap in my face."

"Ms. Sams with all due respect. I don't know what you have plan for Erykah. Me on the other hand I want to put hands and feet on her. She dropped me for that nigga Jay like I was a no body."

"Henry beating Erykah ass or putting her in a body bag it really don't make a difference to me. Far as I'm concern Erykah is no longer my family."

Goody watched from the car window as Tonya spoke to Henry. The conversation to him looked a little bit shaky at first, but it was now looking like Tonya was getting into his head. Seeing Tonya and Henry walking together towards the car. Goody shook his head in disbelief. Tonya had been out the game for over twenty years. Yet she still had the power to make a man do anything she wanted them to do. Getting in the car Tonya tapped Goody on his shoulder.

"Goody this is Henry, Henry this is Goody."

"What up" Henry said giving Goody a pound with his fist.

"I hope you get heart and you're not a pussy. Because what your about to get into is some real shit" Goody said back to Henry.

"My brother I'm far from a pussy. Nothing would make me more happy then getting back at Erykah."

Hearing all he needed to hear. Goody started up the car and drove out the parking lot.

Chapter 17

Stepping inside Gail house. Nine women showed Khia to the dining room where Gail was seated at the head of the table.

Have a seat so we can discuss a few things Khia." Once Khia was seated the nine women that showed Khia into the house departed from the dining room.

"Gail how have you been?"

"Khia life is life and within the hour I will truly know how I'm doing. But enough about me. You just got out the hospital the other day. How are you doing?"

"I'm fine Gail, I'm just a little bit confused by our last conversation. If Trini is dead…."

"Khia, you are more like your mother then you know. That was a good move you did by getting Trini to take over the Sams drug contract. Although Trini only had the Sams drug contract for a day and a half. In that short time he made a big change in the Sams drug contract."

Gail pulled out the Sams drug contract. "The two lines Trini placed in the contract is as followed; *Upon my death as the holder of the Sams drug contract. The contract is to go to the second oldest Sams and not the oldest Sams.* What that mean is that your mother Tonya is skipped, and you become the queen of the Sams drug contract, as the second oldest Sams."

"Gail that explains how I'm now the holder of the Sams contract. Yet that doesn't explain how you knew I was arrested, and the charges would be dropped."

"Khia your mother set you up to slow you down so she could think. Yet at the same time she knew you wouldn't take the fall for Trini murder. Because she knew there wasn't any proof that you murdered him. Khia I don't think I need to tell you that your mother is a very smart woman. But If I have to, let me just say I taught her a lot. Yet I didn't teach her everything I know. A good teach will never teach you everything they know. You are a smart girl as well, and that's because your mother taught you well. But keep in mind she didn't teach you everything she know. With that said, you are the new holder of the Sams drug contract. My advice to you would be make a change to the contract right now while you have it. So Tonya won't get the contract again."

Khia began thinking to herself. "You know what Gail; I think I will leave the contract as it is. Because god forbid If I die the contract will still not go to Tonya. It would go to the second oldest Sams which would be my little brother Jo-Jo."

"That's true Khia but always remember where there's a will there's always a way to get around things. So If you change your mind about making a change in the contract while you're the holder. Just let me know."

The nine women that showed Khia into the house appeared back into the dining room. "Gail your doctor is here to see you" One of the women said.

Gail turned her attention back to Khia. "Well Khia it seems that me and you have discuss all that we needed to discuss. Let me say these last words to you Khia. Your mother Tonya will not stop until she get the Sams contract back or figure out a way to get a contract from me. Ladies, show Khia to the door and show my doctor in."

Within minutes Khia was out the house and Gail doctor was seated before her. "Doctor, I assume you're here because you got my test results back?"

"Indeed I did Gail."

"I also assume my test results are bad? Otherwise you would have called me on the phone to give me my results."

"Gail there bad, but not as bad as you think. With strong treatment you will be as good as new."

Gail took a deep breath and let out slow. "When can we start my treatments?"

"Well I can move a few things around and in a week or so we can began."

"How long will these treatments take?"

"Within one month your treatments will be complete."

Reaching under the dining room table. Gail through two stacks of money across the table at the doctor. "A week or so my ass. Fit me in your schedule within a few days." Standing up the doctor placed the two stacks of money in his briefcase.

"You have my word you will be in my schedule within a few days.

"I better because it's either your words or your life I will have. Ladies!" Nine women appeared in the dining room within seconds. "Ladies, please show my doctor to the door."

*****

Hearing the doorbell Beverly swung her house door open with evil written all over her face. A look that Solo knew very well. A look that meant I'm not in the fucking mood at all.

"What can I do for you Solo?"

"I was hoping to have a few words with my sister in law."

"Oh you must not have heard. Me and your brother Supreme are getting a divorce. So me being your sister in law won't be for too long. As a matter of fact. Why don't you come in so I can give you my divorce papers. So you can serve them to your brother."

Walking away from the door Beverly headed to her kitchen. Closing the door Solo following behind her and took a seat at the kitchen table. Pulling out the divorce papers. Beverly placed them on the table in front of Solo. Looking at the papers a flash of fire outside the kitchen window caught Solo eye. Standing up Solo walked over to the kitchen window.

"Holy shit! Bev, there's a big ass fire in your back yard!"

"No shit Solo" Beverly said taking a seat at the table. "When you give your brother those divorce papers. Make sure you tell him, he has nothing left in this house, so there's no need for him to come pick anything up."

"Damn I wish I would have come over here yesterday before you, waiting to exhaled, his shit."

"Solo you coming to speak to me yesterday would have not changed shit. Like it's not going to change shit today. Your brother cheated on me again. Not only did he cheat on me. He cheated on me with that bitch Tonya. Not only should I be mad at Supreme, you should be mad with him to. Tonya is trying to bring down our drug operation."

Taking a seat next to Beverly, Solo looked into her eyes. He could tell she was hurt. He could see the tears in her eyes. Not wanting to cry in front of Solo. Beverly turned her face and wiped at her eyes. Solo turned her face back towards him.

"Bev, Supreme didn't cheat on you."

"Solo, I saw the fucking tape!"

"I know you saw the tape Bev. But I'm more then sure you didn't see the ending of that tape."

"Oh I saw enough Solo believe that."

"Bev, Supreme thought he was having sex with you."

"How the fuck did he think he was having sex with me? When clearly on the tape he's having sex with Tonya."

"Bev, Supreme told me about how Tonya tricked him into having sex that same day. I told him not to tell you."

"You fucking knew he cheated on me?"

"Bev, let me show you the ending of the tape."

"Solo, I don't want…."

"For me Bev. I'm asking as a favor to me that you take another look at the tape."

Getting up Beverly followed Solo into her living room. Placing the tape in, Solo press play, and turned the volume up.

"Solo, I do not want to see this!"

"Bev don't look at them having sex. Look at the left corner of the screen. It says dark lighting. That means Tonya programmed the camera to see in the dark. Supreme couldn't see who he was having sex with. Now close your eyes Bev and listen to Supreme moaning."

Doing as she was told Beverly could hear Supreme moaning the name, Bev.

"Do you hear it sis, he's moaning your name not Tonya name. Think about it Bev. What bitch is going to let you moan another female name while she's having sex with you? Now open your eyes and see Supreme reaction when Tonya turn on the light."

Beverly watched as Supreme eyes almost popped out his head looking at Tonya when she turned on the light.

"Look Bev, Supreme is tied down to the bed. Now see how the video go total dark. She put the camera in her bag, but it's still recording. Come to the T.V and listen closely to what their saying to each other."

Getting up Beverly put her ear to the T.V speaker; *What the fuck" Supreme yelled.*

"I'm so glad I brought the camera that can video tape in the dark. Supreme I must say your dick game is way better than your father dick game."

"You fucking bitch I'm gonna kill you."

Beverly continued to listen with her ear to the T.V speaker. She could hear someone running, then she heard a car door slam, then a car start up. Then she began to hear Tonya talking again; *"Damn I'm good, that damn boy had no idea he was fucking me and not Beverly. I can't wait to mail this tape to that bitch."*

Beverly pulled her ear back from the T.V speaker when she heard the tape cut off. Looking over at Solo, Beverly looked even more pissed off then when he first got to her house.

"Solo I'm gonna beat fire out that bitch when I catch her. She broke into my house, tricked my damn husband into having sex with her when he was half asleep. She made me set all Supreme shit on fire in my back yard." Standing up Beverly grabbed her car keys.

"Where are you going Bev?"

"To go kiss Supreme ass and hope that he forgive me for burning up all his shit" Beverly said walking out the house.

*****

In Manhattan Tonya walked into her hotel suite in the Trump hotel. Goody and Henry followed close behind her. Walking into the hotel living room. Nicole, Mellow, China, Cam, Debra, Levi, and TG, were all sitting and waiting.

"Everyone this is Henry. Henry is Erykah ex-boyfriend and he is now a part of our team."

After Tonya introduced everyone to Henry. Tonya sat down and kicked her heals off.

"I think we should all be on the same page. Because I don't want any mistakes tomorrow when we move on the Gibbs drug family. Tomorrow were gonna hit them and were going to hit them hard. Were gonna kill two of them, three If we're lucky. We're going to get Nicole son Little Supreme back. We are also going to send four of them to jail."

"How are we gonna get four of them locked up" Nicole asked.

"Now when we were living in Khia house. I ran across a tape. She has Albert being murdered in Mike apartment on tape. Seeing what was on the tape and who was involved. I stole the tape from Khia house and put it in the trunk of my car. When I turn that tape over to the police. Everyone on that tape will be arrested for Albert murder."

Tonya looked over at Mellow. "Your finally gonna get some justice for your brother Albert being murdered. When we are all done with that. We are leaving New York tomorrow and going back to L.A. When the dust settle. We will come back to New York to deal with Khia and I will take my spot back as the queen of the Sams drug contract."

Putting her heels back on her feet Tonya stood up. "I'll let all of you think about what I just said. If you're not down with everything I just said. Make sure you're not here when me and Goody get back."

As Tonya walked towards the door, Goody asked. "Where are we going now?"

"First me and you are going to go catch a courthouse before they close."

"Why?"

"Because stupid, me and you are getting married. Then me and you are going to meet up with my good friend. To make sure there on the same page for tomorrow. Because when I pick up the phone tomorrow and call them. They better be ready to pull that trigger."

Grabbing Tonya by her hand Goody pulled her towards him for a kiss. Yet instead of a kiss he received a slap to his face.

"Boy don't be stupid; this is about business. If I wanted to get with you. I would have got with you years ago. And If I wanted some dick from you. I sure as hell don't need to marry you to get it."

"Listen here Tonya I'm not your damn toy. You want a favor from me, you have to do a favor for me. You needing to marry me is business. Well me marrying you is business for me to. Sexual business! So make sure I get to tear that pretty little ass of yours up tonight. Because If I don't, come tomorrow morning a divorce we will be getting." Slapping Tonya on her ass Goody looked in Tonya face. "Do we have a understanding?"

"We do, and just to let you know Goody. If you didn't still look good. I wouldn't dear agree to let you fuck me. Now let's get going before we miss the courthouse."

Hearing Tonya and Goody finally leave the hotel sweet. Debra got on the phone and called room service. So they could send some food up to the room. Nicole turned the music on and turned it up. Mellow and Cam pulled a few bottles of liquor out. Levi started passing plastic cups out. Taking the cup from Levi, Henry looked at him confused by the way they were acting.

"Lighting up playboy. This is what we do when the boss lady Tonya leave. We party, get drunk, and fuck" TG said to Henry.

Dancing to the music, Nicole, Debra, and China, began taking off their clothes. Seeing their clothes coming off Henry eyes grew wide, as his penis got hard. Walking over to Henry, Debra dropped to her knees between his legs. Undoing Henry pants Debra took Henry penis into her mouth. Walking up behind Debra, Levi dropped his pants, slid his penis inside Debra sweet box and began pumping away on her back. Sitting on the couch beside Henry, Mellow pulled his dick out, Nicole sat down on it, and began bouncing up and down on it. Standing in front of Nicole, TG dropped his pants, grabbed Nicole head, and stuck his penis in her mouth. Bending China over the arm of the chair Cam began working her pussy walls with his dick doggy style.

*****

Walking in Love it or Hate it. Beverly waived hello to Tank and headed to the club private back office. Opening the door Beverly saw that Supreme was in the office by his self-working on the computer. Closing the office door Beverly locked it and walked over to Supreme. Looking up from the computer screen. Supreme looked at Beverly then back at the computer.

"Should I duck now or close my eyes and just let you shoot me in my head Bev?"

"I come in peace today Supreme. Can we talk?"

"No."

"Come on Supreme…."

"Bev there's no need to talk about it. You saw, you flipped, I understand, Solo showed you the truth, your sorry. I just hope the next time if something like this happen. You let me explain before you walk out on me and say we are done."

"I promise I'll let you explain the next time."

"Sure you right, your ass is going to flip out again. To be honest with you Bev. That shit just shows me how much you really love the hell out of me. And I love the hell out of you to baby girl."

Taking a seat on Supreme lap Beverly looked into Supreme eyes.

"I hope you feel the same way after I tell you what I'm about to tell you."

"Tell me what?"

"I took all your clothes, coats, and footwear to the back yard and set it all on fire."

Shaking his head Supreme laughed. Wrapping his arms around Beverly Supreme buried his face into her breast. "Those are materialistic things that can be replaced baby girl. Long as I still have you by my side, I can always face another day. Tomorrow me and you will hit the stores and replace everything. In the meantime on more black movies for you. Where females go off on their husband."

"Fuck you Supreme" Beverly said with a laugh.

"Fuck you Bev, burning all my shit up like home girl did to her husband in that movie, waiting to exhale. I should fuck you up."

"Supreme how about you just fuck me instead."

Standing up together Beverly pulled her dress off over her head. Undoing his pants Supreme let them fall to the floor with his boxers. Sitting back in the office chair Beverly climbed onto of him. Riding Supreme nice and slow. Beverly picked up her speed and began bucking like a true bull rider.

*****

Seeing flashing cop lights behind his car. Desean pulled over to the side of the road and rolled down his car window.

"Sir, do you have I.D on you" the officer asked walking up to Desean car window.

"Sure do" Desean said handing his I.D to the officer. Handing the I.D back to Desean the officer opened Desean car door.

"Step out the car Sir."

"Why? All my shit is legal."

"I said step the fuck out the car Sir!" Stepping out the car, the officer pushed Desean up against the car, and placed him in handcuffs. "Desean Evans your under arrest for the rape of Brandy Cooper."

"Rope! I didn't rape that bitch!"

"You can say all of that in a court of law. In the meantime it's a warrant out for your arrest and I have to take you in."

Chapter 18

Walking around in the bull pin. Desean didn't have a clue how he was going to get his self out of the situation he was in. He had just saw the judge and was giving a twenty thousand dollar bail. He had the money stashed to pay his own bail. Yet he had no one in the street he could trust to go into his stash. On top of that he had no living family members he could call. His two best friends Albert and Gregg were both dead. He knew he could count on Albert little brother Mellow. Yet he didn't have a number to reach Mellow. The only other person he could think of was to call Solo. Him and Solo wasn't friends, yet they were not enemies either. Many times Desean had called Solo to give him a heads up on someone trying to get at him or the Gibbs family. Dialing Solo cell number. Desean hoped like hell he could count on Solo for a favor now.

"Hello" Solo said half sleep.

"Solo it's me Desean. I need a big favor."

"Yo, it's like six in the morning nigga."

"I know, and I'm sorry for calling you so early in the morning. But I really need your help and I don't have anyone else to call."

"What's the problem Desean?"

"I'm locked up."

"You need a lawyer?"

"Nah, I got one of those. I need someone to post my bail and I can handle the rest of this shit from there."

"How much is your bail?"

"Twenty thousand, and I will give you the twenty thousand back today. I got the cash, but I don't trust a nigga to go in my stash."

"Where you jailed at?"

"I'm in Manhattan Tomus. If you can, can you post my bail, drive me home, and I'll give you the money when we get to my house."

"Nigga you better be lucky you fed me good information throughout the years. I'm on my way sit tight nigga."

*****

After posting Desean bail Solo sat in his car outside of Manhattan Tomus. Two hours later Solo watched as Desean made his way over to his car. Getting in the car Desean gave Solo a pound with his fist.

"Solo, I can't tell you enough how much I appreciate you doing this favor for me."

"When I get my twenty stacks back, then I'll know how much you appreciate me doing this favor for you."

Telling Solo his home address Solo began driving Solo cut his eye over at Desean.

"Spill it nigga, what you got popped for?"

"Solo do you remember Smoke girlfriend Brandy?"

"Yeah, my sister in law Bev shot shorty in the leg. What about her?"

"Well I smashed her a few days ago and through her out my car. Long story short, that bitch went to the police and said I raped her."

"Damn son, I feel for you."

"You feel for me, shit I feel for myself. I got to get this bitch the wall. I want to kill that bitch but that's not gonna help me. She already gave the police a statement and they found my D.N.A in her crack. So even If I kill that bitch. The state can still send me up north with the evidence they have."

"So in other words you have to get Brandy to drop the charges on you."

"Pretty much, otherwise prison here I come. I'm not really sweating it. Brandy is a gold digging bitch. I'm gonna through some money her way and she'll drop the charge."

"Desean you sound like you have a lot to learn when it comes to a gold digging female. The best way to deal with one is to check they ass. Giving her money in this type of situation. Is like giving her control over you."

"So how do you think I should handle Brandy?"

"Well since she like getting the police involved in things. Use the law against her ass. See how she like being locked up."

"How can I get her locked up?"

"Easy, do you have video recording on your cell phone?"

"Yeah."

"Perfect, get her to admit she lied about you raping her on tape. Then have sex with her. Then take the video to your lawyer and have your lawyer bring her up on charges. The judge will drop the charge on you and look her up for making a false report. She'll sit in jail for a few day. And most likely the judge will give her probation. After that, that bitch words will mean nothing in a court of law. From then on you can run through her like a car run through a tunnel."

Pulling up to Desean building, Desean jumped out the car and ran into his building. Five minutes later Desean was getting back in Solo car with a book bag.

"Here's your twenty stacks plus ten stacks for looking out for me."

Passing the book bag to Solo, Solo open the book bag, looked inside it, closed it, and gave the book bag back to Desean. Holding the book bag in his hands Desean looked at Solo confused.

"Why you giving it back to me? That's yours."

"Desean sometimes there are better things in this world then money. You being a man of your word is enough payment for me doing you this favor."

"Solo, I'm not gonna feel right If you don't take this money."

"Good, now you know how I felt when I didn't murder you for what you did to my wife a few years back. Yet my wife got her pay back on you. So I was able to let things go between me and you. Now keep that money and get your pay back on that bitch that's trying to take your freedom from you."

Getting out the car Solo stopped him. "Another thing Desean, don't ever think for a minute that I'm stupid. I know the games you be playing. You get into shit, and when it get to deep, you always call me to clean up your mess. Every time you ever called me to give me a heads up. I always knew you were involved. From the Wayne shit, from the Mike shit, to the Khia shit, and that Red-Money crew shit. Yet you always gave me the heads up before any of them could make their move on me. Smart man Desean. You stack your paper with them, then sale they as out to me. I'm not mad at you though, seeing as that's your hustle. Just remember everyone in the game always need one true friend. Keep being my friend and I'll keep being your friend. When you call, I'm always there. When I call on you, you better be there."

"You got my word I'll be there for you when you call me." Giving Solo a pound Desean get out the car.

*****

Hearing a knock on her apartment door. Brandy open the door without asking who it was. Seeing Desean, Brandy tried to close the door back. Stopping the door from closing Desean stuck his foot in it.

"If you don't get away from my door. I'm gonna call the police!"

"Brandy, I just came to talk to you, not on no beef shit, but on some one on one shit." Brandy continued to hold all her weight against the door.

"Desean I'm not stupid. If I let you in, you gonna try to do something to me."

"Not at all, you got my word I won't do anything to you."

Thinking to herself for a few seconds. Brandy let the door open all the way and let Desean into her apartment. She was nerves, yet if he wanted to kill her. All he had to do was just stick his gun in the small space in the door and shoot. Walking in the kitchen Brandy kept her eyes on both of Desean hands. Pulling out his cell phone Desean put it on the kitchen table. Not wasting any time Desean got straight to the point. "Brandy, you know I didn't rape you. Why did you go to the police and say that I did?"

"Because I let you have sex with me and then you tried to play me Desean."

"So that mean go to the police and say I raped you, that's foul Brandy."

"It's not as foul as you fucking me and just leaving me there looking stupid. You didn't rape me Desean. But me lying to the police saying you did, was my way of getting back at you."

"Brandy listen I do want to be in a relationship with you. Me having sex with you and riding off on you. That was my way of seeing how you really felt about me. If you would have called me back on the phone after I drove off. I would have come back and got you. Because I would have felt you was serious about being with me. But you going to the police and lying and saying I raped you. I don't think I can be with a person like that."

"Desean, I thought you were trying to play me again. So that's why I lied to the police. Tomorrow morning I'll go to the D.A that got your case. I'll tell him I lied and to drop the charges on you."

"Will I be able to trust you after you drop the charges?"

"Yes, I swear."

"Cool, in the meantime can I get some pussy."

Without a hesitation Brandy got out of her clothes. Undoing Desean pants, she pulled his penis threw the slit of his boxers. Pushing Desean down in the kitchen chair. Brandy got on top of him, wrapping her legs around him, she began riding him.

*****

After having sex with Brandy, Desean put his cell phone back in his pocket.

"Yo, Brandy I have to go handle some business. First thing in the morning go see that D.A. In the afternoon tomorrow I'm gonna swing by and pick you up. We gonna hit a few clothes stores, catch a movie, and go out to eat. So make sure your dressed and ready to go when I call you tomorrow."

"A'ight? I will."

Giving Brandy a kiss on the cheek Desean left her apartment. Soon as Desean got in the hallway. He e-mailed the video of him and Brandy on his phone to his lawyer.

Driving home Desean had a big smile on his face. Traffic was backed up on the highway. Pulling up to his building he looked at his watch. It had taking him two hours to get home from Brandy place. Pulling out his cell phone he called his lawyer.

"Sammy it's me, Desean Evens. Did you get the e-mail that I sent to you?"

"I did, good work, I made a copy and sent it to the judge. The judge was so piss when she saw the video. She issued a warrant out for Ms. Cooper arrest, for filing a false police report. I'm just glad that you sent me that video at 1 p.m. It was more than enough time to make the copy and get it to the judge. As for the rape charge on you Desean. The judge dropped the charge immediately once she saw that video. The only issue now is what time and place are they going to arrest Ms. Cooper."

"Not to worry about that Sammy. Brandy Cooper will be in the D.A office first thing in the morning. She's going to the D.A to drop the rape charge on me."

"Oh that's perfect they can arrest her there. Well good luck to you Desean. As for me, I'm gonna give the D.A a call. I'm gonna give him the heads up that Ms. Cooper will be in his office tomorrow morning to see him."

*****

Walking in Joe's store Solo greeted his two kids, Tymel and Erykah at the cash register.

"Where your mother at?"

"In the back office" Tymel said.

Walking in the store back office Solo closed the door behind him. Seeing Khia sitting behind the desk Solo let out a hard laugh.

"What's so funny?"

"You, look at you sitting behind that desk looking all professional."

"I am always professional, or did you forget that Solo?"

"You ain't never lied Khia. From the first day I met you, you were very professional."

Remembering back to when they first met. Khia gave Solo the middle finger knowing that he was trying to be a smart ass. "When we first met you pulled out your dick, put me on your lap, and I bounced up and down on it."

"You sure did, just like a professional."

"Did you come here to go down memory lane or for something else?"

"I came by to see how things are going here at the store."

"In that case I'm glad you're here. Sit down so we can talk business Solo."

Taking a seat in the chair that was in front of the desk. Solo crossed his legs, crossed his arms, then looked at Khia. "Talk."

"Well I had a meeting with Gail a few days ago. Long story short, Trini dying didn't make my mother the head of the Sams drug contract. Upon Trini death he made sure that the contract would go to me. So I'm the queen of the Sams drug contract."

"With that said I guess you don't work for me anymore.

"No, but I hope that If I need a job that you will hold a spot for me on the Gibbs team."

"You pushed two of my children out. Of course I will always have a spot for you Khia."

"That's good to hear, now down to business. I want the Joe's store to be the Sams drug spot and not the Gibbs drug spot. In return I will pay you a fee for renting this store from you. So what do you say?"

"That's cool, I really didn't want to run three drug spots any way. Two is more than enough for me. I take it that you want to pull Tymel and Erykah off the Gibbs team and put them on the Sams team with you?"

"Yes indeed, is that all right with you?"

"Yeah, that's cool. Hey If, you got the Sams drug contract. That mean that nigga Mike works for you, now right?"

"Yeah, why?"

"No reason I just like to keep myself in the loop of things."

"Well in that case Solo. Yes, I'm now Mike drug connect. And yes, Mike still runs Courtlandt projects."

Standing up Solo looked at Khia. "Damn you still look so damn good" Solo said to his self.

"Why you looking at me with that weird look on your face?"

"Because I was just thinking to myself. I come over here to check on things. Yet somehow, I lost my third drug spot and lost three of my drug team members. I'm just wondering how I didn't get anything out of this business discussion we just had? Girl your game is tight."

"You trying to say I gamed you just now?"

"No, I'm wondering what you're going to want from me next?"

"Your heart" Khia mumbled.

Although she said it low Solo still heard what she said. Clearly, she still had feelings for him just like he still had feelings for her. Sitting back down in the chair they both locked eyes on each other.

"You are married, and you swore to Trina you wouldn't ever cheat on her again" Solo said to his self in his head. Not wanting to get his self into trouble. Solo know he had to think of a way to change the subject. "Ummm, how is your mother Tonya taking the news that you got the spot, and she didn't?"

"I don't know. I haven't seen her since she put me in the hospital. Yet I'm sure that a storm is coming my way. I hope you know she's not gonna stop trying to get even with the Gibbs family. So believe me when I tell you a storm will be coming your way to. And just like the weather people name their storms. Let's just name our soon to come storm, Tonya."

*****

In the Trump hotel Tonya walked into her hotel living room sweet. Standing in the middle of the living room floor. Tonya dropped a duffle bag on the floor. Nicole, Mellow, Cam, China, TG, Levi, Henry, and Goody, all sat in the living room.

"Like I told all of you yesterday. Today we are gonna hit the Gibbs family, and were gonna hit them hard." Opening the duffle bag Tonya gave Nicole an envelope. "That's your son birth certificate and the address to his day care where he's at. You and China go pull him out of day care." Going back in the bag Tonya pulled out a video tape. "Mellow, Cam, you two take this tape over to the police station. Reaching back in the bag. Tonya pulled out a piece of paper. "These are the names of all the people that's in that video." Going back in the duffle bag Tonya pulled out two guns. Handing one to Henry, she handed the other to Levi. She then gave them a address. "I want you two to go to that address. Make sure my good friend kill the person that their supposed to kill. If not, you two do it and kill that good friend of mine as well. TG, you stay here and pack up all of our things. In one hour we will all meet back up here and leave and head to L.A. As for me and Goody. We are going to go rock us a Gibbs to sleep. If we're lucky we just might catch us two Gibbs." Clapping her hands in the air. Everyone in the living room started walking towards the door of the hotel room.

Chapter 19

Receiving a text message from Levi. That him and Henry, were parked in front of the address they were giving. Tonya dialed her good friend number. Seeing Tonya cell number pop up on her cell phone screen. Tameka took her phone to the living room for privacy. "Hello" Tameka said whispering into her phone.

"Tameka today is the day. You need to make that move."

"Tonya can I just get a few more months with Jay" Tameka whispered.

"Bitch your time is up I have two shooters outside your house. Either kill Jay or both of you can die together."

Not waiting for a response Tonya hung up on Tameka. Holding her cell phone in her hand Tameka took a deep breath. At the beginning getting with Jay was all part of a plan. Get his trust and murdering him without him seeing it coming. Yet for the past few months being with Jay. She had falling in love with him, Not only that, she could tell Jay truly loved her for her. Since they had got together Jay had been treating her like a queen. They were married. Any and everything she wanted Jay made sure she had it. In no way did she want to give up what she had going with Jay. Yet she had agreed to the plan with Tonya that she would murder Jay. Now here she was facing the big question. Is a plan a plan or is love worth dying for?

Walking out the bathroom Tameka got her gun out the nightstand. Walking in the living room Tameka looked out the living room window. Sitting right across the street in a car Tameka saw Levi, and a guy sitting in the passenger seat she didn't know. Walking up behind Tameka, Jay looked over her shoulder out the window. Seeing the car across the street from his house. Jay spotted Henry sitting in the passenger seat.

"I know this nigga done fell and bumped his head coming around where I live at" Jay said walking away from the window.

On his way back upstairs to get his gun.

Tameka called out his name stopping him before he got to the stairs. "Jay, the two guys in that car is not who you should be worried about."

"That nigga come around my house and he brought some other nigga with him. If I shouldn't be worried about them. Then who should I be worried about?"

"Me" Tameka said turning around letting off two gun shots.

Levi and Henry watched Tameka and Jay watching them from her living room window. Seeing the living room curtain close, a minute later they heard two gun shots go off. Fifteen minutes later they watched as Tameka walked out the house like she didn't have a care in the world. Walking over to the car Tameka dropped the gun on Levi lap.

"Get rid of that gun for me. I have to go to work at the Bank's hotel to create an alibi for myself."

Not waiting for them to respond Tameka walked away, got in her car, and speeded off. Levi and Henry looked at each other. The same thing popped in both of their heads and they both said it out loud to each other. "That's a cold hearted bitch." Started up the car Levi pulled off heading back to the Trump hotel.

*****

Placing Little Supreme in the back seat of the car. Nicole put his seatbelt on him. Getting in the driver seat Nicole looked in the back seat at her sleeping son and smiled. Three years she had missed out on his life. He was now four years old. Looking over at China in the passenger seat. Nicole started up the car and headed for the Trump hotel. Driving away from the day care Nicole saw Sierra pulling up to the day care.

Walking inside the day care Sierra had a big smile on her face. Five minutes later walking out the day care Sierra look like she was going to have a nerves break down. Her hands shake as she placed her one year daughter Lisa in her car seat. Pulling out her cell phone she dialed Rome cell phone number.

"What can I do for my beautiful wife" Rome asked answering his phone.

"Rome, she took Little Supreme! I got Lisa, but she took Little Supreme from the day care."

"Who?"

"The supervisor of the day care center said, Nicole came with his birth certificate and her I.D proving that she was his mother. And they gave him to her."

"Sierra please tell me you are joking!"

"Rome I'm serious." Hanging up on Sierra, Rome called his grandmother Nancy.

*****

"We don't have all day, hurry up" Tonya whispered kicking Goody in his back.

Turning around on his knees Goody shot Tonya a dirty look. Turning around on his knees Goody continued to work on Solo house door trying to pick the locks.

"Got it."

Pushing Goody out the way Goody fell on the ground. Pulling out her gun Tonya walked in the house. With light steps Tonya walked around the house on the dark. Hearing the sound of a T.V coming from upstairs. Tonya made her way up the stairs. Walking in the room Tonya closed the door behind her and turned on the light. Looking up from the T.V Trina was expecting to see Solo. Yet was face to face with Tonya. Looking at each other no words were spoken. Tonya held her gun in her hand pointing it at Trina. Trina knew her life was on the line. Not only was her life on the line. She was six months pregnant, and her five year old son Quinn was asleep two rooms away.

The only chance Trina saw at staying alive was stripping Tonya of her gun. In rage Trina jumped up from the bed. As she jumping on Tonya, they both fell to the floor.

"Pop" the gun sounded.

To be six months pregnant Trina moved so fast Tonya didn't have a chance to react. Although the gun went off, she didn't feel any pain. Opening her eyes slowly she saw blood all over her. Pushing Trina off of her Tonya stood up. All the blood on her was Trina blood. Looking on the floor Trina laid motionless. Seeing Trina shirt soaked in blood Tonya knew the bullet had hit Trina in her stomach. Trina eyes was staring up at the ceiling. Tucking the gun in her pants Tonya moved fast running out the house. The sound of a car speeding off, weak but still a live Trina stood on her feet. She knew she had to play dead in order to survive. Pressing tightly on her stomach where she was shot. Picking up the phone she dialed 9-1-1. Hanging up with 9-1-1 she called Solo. Telling him who shot her, Trina hung up not waiting for him to respond. Checking on her son, Quinn was sound asleep. Walking down the stairs in her house, Trina opened her house door, and collapsed.

*****

Walking in the district attorney. Brandy placed her name on the waiting list to meet with the D.A in her rape case. After placing her name on the list she took a seat in the waiting area. Twenty minutes of waiting she was told to step in Jack office.

"Have a seat Ms. Cooper."

"Mr. Murray…."

"Oh no need to be professional Brandy. Just call me Jack. Seeing as after the tape I've seen of you. Clearly you don't have a professional bone in your body."

Not understanding what Jack was talking about. Brandy paid his commits no mind. "Jack, I have thought long and hard and I no longer want to continue my rape case against Desean Evans. I would like to drop the rape charge against him."

"Brandy the rape charge against Mr. Cooper Evans was dropped yesterday."

"Oh that's good, well ummm, I guess I'll be going now."

"Oh you'll be going all right, going straight to jail."

"Excuse me, going to jail for what" Brandy yelled standing up.

Standing up as well Jack press two buttons on his desk phone. Within seconds two police officers appeared in Jack office. "Officers please place Ms. Brandy Cooper under arrest. Charge her with filing a false rape charge and obstruction of justice."

Reading Brandy her Miranda rights both officers tried to place her in handcuffs. Not understanding what was going on and not wanting to be arrested. Although Brandy knew she had nowhere to run. Pulling away from the officers Brandy tried to run to the door of the office. Fighting with Brandy both officers took her down to the floor and placed her in handcuffs.

"Officers also add resisting arrest to her charges" Tack yelled as the officers dragged Brandy out of his office.

*****

In the hospital waiting area Solo walked back and forth trying to get his thoughts together. One by one Supreme, Beverly, Tone, Pit, Rome, Jo-Jo, Vera, Lloyd, and Nancy, all walked into the waiting area.

"How is my cousin" Beverly asked with tears in her eyes.

"She's been in surgery for the past twelve hours. They haven't come out here to give me a update."

"Solo I dropped Quinn off at Sierra house." Walking over to Solo, Nancy placed her hand on his shoulder. "Jayquan we have some serious problems going on here."

"Ma, I'm aware of that, my wife is in surgery."

"Jayquan your wife being shot is not the only thing that happen last night. Jay was murdered in his house last night. Tameka found his body when she came home from work. On top of that Nicole kidnapped Little Supreme from the day care center yesterday. Police have put out a Amber Alter to find Little Supreme."

Solo looked at his mother with wide eyes not believing what she had just said to him. Nancy held Solo face in her hands.

"Listen to me, there's nothing we can do for Jay now, he's safe. There's nothing we can do for Trina; her life is in the doctors hands. Our focus need to be on getting Little Supreme back."

Solo turned his head towards Supreme. Nancy turned his face back towards her. His mother statement didn't make sense to him, "there's nothing we can do for Jay now, he's safe." Yet just seeing the look on Supreme face it was a calm look. Seeing that look on Supreme fuck his mother statement now made sense to him. "He safe" Solo repeated to his self in his head.

While Nancy continued to talk to Solo. Beverly looked over at Vera. Although Vera was sitting down, she looked as If she was going to fall over. Walking over to Vera, Beverly sat down beside her.

"You okay aunt Vera?"

"Beverly, my daughter is in this hospital fighting for her life. I just got back into Trina life a few years ago. I can't lose my daughter."

Walking in the waiting area Stephanie spotted her sister Vera and her daughter Beverly talking. Seeing Stephanie Vera ran over to Stephanie, and Stephanie wrapped her arms around her.

"How is Trina?"

"She's still in surgery Stephanie."

Seeing Rome staring at the wall. Solo walked over to him and took a seat beside him. Pulling out his cell phone, Solo put his cell phone in Rome face, and began whispering in his ear. Solo began breaking down to Rome about the tracking devices he has in everyone cross on their gold chains. He also told him about the tracking devices he has in the iced out cross earrings all the little kids in the family wear. Solo then showed Rome how to go on the internet and look up the trackers and find out where a person is located. Holding the cross that was on his chain that was around his neck. Rome looked at Solo in shock.

"Uncle Solo, you gave Little Supreme one earring cross for his ear, and one gold chain with a cross. That means he has two trackers that he's wearing?"

"Yeah, and here's the address Nicole have him at right now" Solo said pointing to the cell phone in his hand.

Looking at Solo cell phone screen Rome was confused. "Unc, both of Little Supreme trackers put him at an address in L.A."

"Listen Rome, Nicole is not gonna hurt Little Supreme. You can breathe easy now that you know how to find your son."

"Unc, is this how you found my son the first time Nicole had him kidnapped?"

"Yeah."

"Thanks, Dad, for always looking out for all of us" Rome said giving Solo a hug.

Hearing Rome call him Dad for the first time Solo eyes watered up a bit. Seeing a doctor walk into the waiting area. Solo jumped up to his feet and ran over to the doctor.

"Doc tell me something, how is Trina and the baby?" Vera ran over to them so she could also find out about her daughter.

"Are you the husband and mother of Trina Gibbs?"

"Yes."

"Yes."

"Well you both already know she was six months pregnant and she was also shot in her stomach. What you didn't know because it didn't show up in the sonogram, she had done two weeks ago. Is that she was pregnant with twins. She was pregnant with a boy and a girl. We had to deliver both babies. I'm sorry to tell you this. But the baby boy didn't make it. Yet the baby girl did make it. She's five pounds even."

Although Solo and Vera was happy to hear the good news about the baby. They both truly wanted to know how Trina was doing?

"Doc how is my wife?"

"Mr. Gibbs, I'm sorry to…." The Doctor stopped in mid-sentence seeing a group of officers walk into the waiting room.

Seeing the weird look on the doctor face. Solo and Vera turned around to see what was behind them that the doctor was looking at. With handcuffs and guns out the officers began surrounding all that was in the waiting area. Walking up to Pit the officer looked at the photo in his hand.

"Daniel Dawson" the officer said looking at Pit.

"Yeah" Pit said confused to why the officer was saying his government name.

"Daniel Dawson, Jayquan Gibbs, Jerome Gibbs, Vera Bookman. You four are under arrest for murder" the officer in charge yelled. Without hesitation officers placed them in handcuffs.

"Officers I'm the lawyer of the four people that you are arresting. Why are they being arrested for murder, and who has been murdered" Nancy asked pulling out her badge to practice lawyer.

"Ms. Nancy Gibbs their being arrested for the murder of Albert Simmons. You can meet us down at the police station."

As the police officers placed Pit, Vera, Supreme, and Solo, in police cars. Nancy jumped in her car following behind the police cars to the police station.

Beverly and Rome walked over to the doctor who was still looking in shock.

"Doctor how is my cousin Trina?"

"Ma'ma unfortunately I can't discuss Trina condition with you. I'm only allow to discuss her condition with her next of kin, which is her husband."

"Can I see her?"

"Not at this time" the doctor said walking away.

Chapter 20

In Manhattan Supreme court Nancy walked through the courthouse hallways to the court room she needed to be in.

"Ms. Gibbs, Ms. Gibbs" Nancy heard someone yelling from behind her. Turning around to see who it was. Nancy face turned up as If she smelled something foul seeing Jack Murray.

"I have to be in court in a few minutes. What can I do for you Mr. Murray?"

"I just wanted to let you know I'm the D.A trying your four client case. I'm gonna enjoy wiping the floor with you in court. You got your son off that other case years ago when I was a new D.A. Now look a here years later we meet again going up against each other."

"Mr. Murray it's sad that after all this time you are still upset that I beat you in court. That was over twenty something years ago. I think you should get over it."

"Twenty something, twenty something years is exactly the years I'm gonna give each one of your clients."

Walking around Jack, Nancy walked into the court room with Jack following close behind her.

Taking the bench the judge sat down. "You may all take your seats."

Sitting down Solo spotted detective Price in the court room. Looking back at Solo, Price gave him two thumbs up. Detective Price could only mean one thing. The evidence against them found its way in the river somewhere. Leaning over Solo whispered in his mother ear.

"Ma, detective Price is here. He Just gave me a signal the evidence is lost."

Nancy leaned over and whispered back in Solo ear. "That's a good thing If it's true. You want me to fight it trying to get yawl out the evidence the D.A has?"

"Fight it like they don't have it Ma."

"This is the case people vs Daniel Dawson, Jayquan Gibbs, Vera Bookman, Jerome Gibbs. In the murder of Albert Simmons."

"How do your clients plea Ms. Gibbs?"

"Not guilty for all my clients your honor."

"People on bail, Mr. Murray?"

"I ask that all four defendants be remand."

"Your honor to remand all of my clients is cruel and usual punishment. The indictment states Vera Bookman was kidnapped. Jerome Gibbs was on the scene but had no gun. Jayquan Gibbs was on the scene but had no gun. Daniel Dawson was on scene, with a gun."

"Vera Bookman is R.O.R, Jerome Gibbs and Jayquan Gibbs, Bail is set at a half million each. Daniel Dawson is remand. Is the people ready for trial?"

"Yes, your honor we are."

"Is the defense ready for trial?"

"No your honor, the defense have not received a copy of this so call video of this murder."

"Your honor, I have a copy of the video right here for Ms. Gibbs."

"Court officer please take that tape from Mr. Murray and give it to Ms. Gibbs."

Once Nancy had the tape in her hand the judge began speaking again. "Trial is set two days from today, court is adjourned."

*****

Back in the bull pen Pit was piss. For the first time in his life he wanted to stump a hole in Solo and Supreme head. Noticing the foul look on Pit face Supreme walked over to him.

"Why you look like you ready to go to war?"

Standing up Pit looked in Supreme face with disgust. "Nigga, I thought your mother was cool people. She through me under the bus in court. I'm remanded, you two mother fuckers got a bail, and Vera is out on a fucking R.O.R. So it's just leave me in prison to take all the weight huh?"

"You know it's not even like that Pit" Solo said walking over to them.

"Really, I can't tell! Yeah, I was the one that murdered that nigga. But If I remember right. I murdered that nigga protecting your wife mother. Solo you told me to murder that nigga. Now I'm being set up to take the weight for everything."

"Pit, I really don't like the way you talking."

"You think I give a fuck what you like right now Solo! I don't like the fact that your mother shitted on me in the court room. I don't mind taking the weight, but I do mind being forced to take the weight. I know that's your mother and her duty is to look out for her two sons. But I will be damned…."

"Our mother duty is not only to look out for her sons, it's to look out for the family. You family Pit, be easy, all you have to do is sit tight and my mother will have you out in no time."

Walking up to the bull pen the officer whacked the bars with his stick. "Dawson get ready the D.A want to speak to you about a plea deal. Jayquan and Jerome Gibbs step forward your bail has been posted.

Opening the bull pen to let Solo and Supreme out. Solo looked back at Pit. "Be easy my nigga, don't be stupid" Solo said.

"You and Supreme go and enjoy your freedom while yawl still have it. In the meantime I have a meeting with the D.A in a few minutes.

"You talking like you about to rat on niggas" Supreme said walking back over to Pit.

Stopping Supreme, Solo pushed Supreme out the door of the bull pen. Walking away from the bull pen Solo and Supreme heard Pit yell out, "C.O, hurry up and get that D.A down here so I can talk to him and go to sleep."

After posting Solo and Supreme bail Nancy sat in her car in the court parking lot with Vera.

"Nancy do you think you can win this case?"

"Vera nothing is promising. Me winning or losing this case all depends on what's on this video tape."

"Nancy, Solo said, that detective made the evidence in this case disappear."

"Vera if the evidence has disappeared then what am I holding in my hand? Whatever is on this tape the D.A is very sure of his self that he has already won this case. We need to see what's on this tape, so we know what were up against."

Walking outside of Manhattan Tomus Supreme was royally pissed off by Pit comments.

"Big Bro I know you not tripping off what Pit said in the bull pen?"

Turning around Supreme looked at Solo like he had just lost his mind. "Did you hear what I heard in there, or are you fucking deaf Solo? Pit was talking about ratting all of us out."

"Supreme, Pit is just pissed off. He know were not gonna leave him for dead. I've known Pit since I was ten years old. Pit is not gonna rat on me. Which means he's not gonna rat on you. If he rat on you, then he has no choice but to rat on me."

"Solo it sure as hell sound like he's ready to eat the cheese to me. Since you know Pit longer than me. Make sure when he rat all of us out, you be the one to murder him."

"Supreme I trust Pit with my life. Killing him is like me killing you and that's something I won't do."

"You won't do it, or you can't do it?"

"Trust big Bro, trust in Pit like you would trust in me."

"Is that your way of saying you can't kill Pit? That I'm gonna have to do it after he rat on all of us?"

"Supreme, I'm not gonna go back and forth with you."

Getting in the back seat of Nancy car. Although Solo was defending Pit to Supreme. In the back of his mind he felt like Pit was ready to rat them all out as well.

"Buckle up, the three of you are going to my house with me so we can see what's on this video tape" Nancy said starting up her car.

"Daniel Dawson" Jack asked stepping in front of the bull pen.

"That's me" Pit said stepping up to the bull pen bars.

"I'm sure you remember me from court this morning. I'm Mr. Jack Murray the D.A in your case. I want to discuss a plea deal with you. Right now you're looking at fifteen years to life. If you take this case to trial and lose, which you will lose. You will be facing 25 years to life. We can save each other sometime If you cop out now. I'm willing to offer you ten years flat. If you write a statement against Vera, Jerome, and Jayquan. So what do you say? Are you willing to take that plea?"

Looking in Jack face Pit spit in his face. "If you don't know what that mean, it mean take your deal and shove it in your ass" Pit said laying back down on the bull pen bench.

Taking his handkerchief out his pocket Jack wiped the spit off his face. "I'm gonna enjoy sending you to prison for life."

Walking away from the bull pen Jack had a big smile on his face. Laying down on the bench Pit mind began to wonder. The plea deal Jack had just offered him was a good deal for a body. Although he was mad. A rat he was not and never would be. Loyalty, respect, and trust, was the team he was in. Even though he was mad with the way things had gone down in court. He still had faith his team would look out for him.

*****

Hearing her cell phone ranging Tonya picked it up and saw the name Gail on her cell phone screen. Taking her phone in the bathroom for privacy, Tonya press talk.

"Hello…. I'm in L.A…. with all I did in New York. I don't plan on coming back to New York for a while…. For what? I see…. I'm sorry to hear that Gail. Are you sure? Well of course New Jersey is not the same as New York. You want me to be what? Well in that case New Jersey here I come. I'll see you soon Gail."

Getting off the phone with Gail. Tonya called a meeting. Goody, Levi, TG, Nicole, Debra, China, Cam, Henry, and Mellow. All of them took a seat in the living room.

"Everyone I just got off the phone with Gail. She wants me to come to New Jersey and meet with her."

"I don't think that's a good idea for us to go back to New Jersey or New York right now. Especially after all we did to the Gibbs family" Nicole said.

"Nicole your right, that's why we all are not leaving L.A. Only me and Goody are going to New Jersey. The rest of you are staying right here. The Gibbs family don't know anything about Nicole house here in L.A. Which mean you all have nothing to worry about. Me and Goody are not stepping foot in New York. That is until we have everything under control. When we get everything under control, we will send for all of you to come to New York. In the meantime we will be in New Jersey at Gail house. Only a fool that want a war with Gail would step to me or Goody at Gail house. Gail has offered me a sweet temporary position that I just can't turn down. Goody let's roll."

*****

As the judge walking in the court room everyone stood to their feet. "You may all be seated" the judge said taking his seat behind the bench. "Today is the first day of trial. People vs Daniel Dawson, Jerome Gibbs, Jayquan Gibbs, Vera Bookman. This is the murder trial of Albert Simmons. The people will start with their argument, followed by the defense opening argument."

Standing up Nancy cleared her throat. "Your honor may I approach the bench?"

"Ms. Gibbs I've been told a lot about you. For whatever reason, every time you take a case. Your cases somehow are dismissed before they go to trial or dismissed the first day of trial. Whatever tricks you have in that pretty little head of yours are not going to work on me. So have a seat Ms. Gibbs."

"Your honor my clients…."

"I said have a seat Ms. Gibbs! Mr. Murray, you may start with your opening argument." Taking her seat Nancy watched as Jack kept a smile on his face during his whole opening argument.

"Ms. Gibbs you may start with your opening argument."

"Your honor, the defense do not wish to start with an opening argument."

"Is that right Ms. Gibbs" Approach the bench Ms. Gibbs." As Nancy approached the bench the judge removed the mic from his mouth. "Ms. Gibbs I've been on this bench a long time. Which mean I'm far from stupid. I know what you're trying to do. If you think you're going to get your clients a mistrial, for misrepresentation. You have another thing coming. Playing tricks in my court room is a fast way to lose your license to practice law."

"Your honor with all due respect. I have not ever got a client off by a mistrial. So I see no point in doing that today."

"I'm glad we have a understanding Ms. Gibbs, now step back."

Taking her seat once again Supreme leaned over and whispered in Nancy ear. "Ma, I think the judge has a hard on for you."

Leaning over Nancy whispered back in Supreme ear. "He can get his dick hard all he want, but he's not getting any of this pussy. He'll be going home with blue balls today."

"Ms. Gibbs you may call your first witness."

"Your honor, I have eleven affidavits statements. All witnesses that have stated that all four of my clients, were all at a family get together on the day this murder was committed. I do not wish to question these witnesses. I believe each of their statements are clear. Yet if the people wish to cross question them, their all in this court room today."

"State their first names for the record Ms. Gibbs."

"Beverly, Rome, Sierra, Tone, Khia, Tymel, Erykah, Jo-Jo, Tameka, Stephanie, Lloyd."

"At this time, all eleven statements will be placed in the file of this case as exhibit three. Mr. Murray at this time would you like to cross question any of these witnesses?"

"Not at all your honor."

"Any other witnesses Ms. Gibbs?"

"No your honor, the defense rest their case."

"Have it your way Ms. Gibbs. Mr. Murray you may call your first witness."

"Your honor the people don't have any witnesses. At this time, the people would like to show the jury exhibit one."

Setting up the T.V in the court room. The court officer put the tape in the V.C.R. "Jury this is the video of Mr. Albert Simmons being murdered. In this video you will see Mr. Daniel Dawson shoot Mr. Simmons multiple times. You will see Vera Bookman hit Mr. Simmons. You will see Jerome Gibbs and Jayquan Gibbs stand there as bodyguards for Daniel Dawson."

Pressing play Jack stood away from the T.V. Bright as day and loud as a plane taking off. The show Fat Albert played on the T.V in court. "Your honor, is this a joke or what? Are we at a trial or at a day care center? If I wanted to watch a re-run T.V show I would have stayed home" Nancy yelled standing up.

"Court officers remove that tape from the player immediately. Mr. Murray what is the meaning of this?"

"Your honor this is a mix up. I'm sure my clerk mixed up the tapes with one of her children tapes."

"Your honor I ask at this time that the charge of murder be dismissed on all four of my clients. Clearly there's no witnesses that put my clients on the scene of this murder. Yet I have eleven witnesses that state my clients were with them the day this murder took place."

"Not so fast Ms. Gibbs. We will take a thirty minute recess. In that time Mr. Murry will collect the correct tape which is exhibit one in this caser. I shall see you all back in my court room in thirty minutes not a minute later."

Running out the court room like he was on fire. Jack ran across the street to the D.A building where his office was at. He wasn't sure how the tape got mixed up. What he did know was he had a backup copy of the tape in his desk. Inside his office Jack open his top desk drawer. Snatching the tape out the drawer. He read the label on the tape to make sure he had the right tape this time.

"Albert Simmons murder exhibit one." Whoever switched the tape thought they had him. But he would be damned If he lost a second case to Nancy. With the tape in his hand. Jack ran back across the street into the courthouse.

"Court is back in session. Mr. Murray you may preside."

Standing up Jack placed the tape in the V.C.R. "Ladies and gentlemen of the jury. I apologize for the mix up earlier."

Pressing play Jack moved away from the T.V. Seeing what was on the T.V screen all twelve jury members grabbed their mouth in shock. Nancy jumped out of her seat. "Your honor! This is ridiculous! The people have went to a children T.V show, to now an adult porno tape."

"Court officers remove that tape now! Mr. Murray have you lost your damn mind! How dear you make a joke of my court room!"

"Your honor I don't understand how…."

"You don't understand! Mr. Murray, I see no evidence that these four defendants were involved in committing this murder. I have no other choice but to grant Ms. Gibbs motion to dismiss this case against these four defendants. Case is dismissed on the grounds of lack of evidence. You four are here by free to go."

Looking over at Pit, Solo wicked at him. Standing up Pit gave Solo a hug. "My bad for doubting you" Pit whispered in Solo ear.

Chapter 21

Walking up to Trina hospital room Nancy was standing in front of the door.

"Ma, what are you doing here?"

"Jayquan I'm gonna head on home. Call me If you need to talk."

Before Solo could get another word out Nancy was halfway down the hallway. Going inside of Trina hospital room Solo notice the hospital bed was empty. Looking over at the window Solo saw Vera sitting in the chair with her head in her hands.

"Vera where is Trina?"

Picking up her head Vera looked at Solo as tears ran down her face. "She's in the morgue with the child that died before her and the child that died after her."

Hearing that Trina had died Solo grabbed a hold of the hospital bed and sat down. Solo felt like he had just been hit by a car. He was finding it hard to breath.

"What…. What happen Vera?"

"Solo, Trina began bleeding again this morning. The doctors couldn't stop her from bleeding, and she bleed to death. A hour after she died her daughter died. The doctor said, the baby just stop breathing, the baby lungs wasn't fully developed. Where were you Solo?"

"Vera when I was released from jail last week. All week me and Supreme had to handle a few things that's why I didn't come to the hospital right when I was released."

"I'm not talking about this past week! Where were you the day Trina was shot by that woman! Why were you not home with your family! This is your fault that my daughter is dead."

Vera words hit Solo like a ton of bricks. Although Trina was in the drug game because she wanted to be. And even though he wasn't the one that shot Trina. Solo did feel like it was his fault. Standing up Vera placed Trina gold chain on the hospital bed next to solo. Reaching around her neck Vera took her chain off and placed it on the bed as well.

"I know your Trina husband, but I'm her mother. I think it's best that I cremate Trina and take her ashes home to my house."

In his heart Solo felt that a funeral would be better. So everyone could say their goodbyes to Trina. Yet going with Vera wishes was the lease he could do feeling Trina death was his fault. Agreeing with Vera, Solo picked up the two chains and walked out the hospital.

*****

Five days Brandy had sat in jail. Her first time in jail and a place she never wanted to come back to. Two days she sat in jail confused to why she was locked up. The third day Jack Murray offered her a plea deal of two months' probation. A deal that she turned down. The fourth day she down with her court appointed lawyer. During that sit down her lawyer showed her the video tape of her and Desean. The tape was clear to her how Desean set her up. To her lawyer and D.A the tape was clear that she was guilty of what she was being charged with. Seeing no other choice. She agreed to take the plea deal Jack offered her.

Being brought in the court room Brandy stood beside her court appointed lawyer.

"Ms. Brandy Cooper. It comes to my understanding that you have took your plea of not guilty back, and now are pleading guilty to the charge against you. Is that correct?"

"Yes, your honor."

"Ms. Cooper before I sentence you. I would like to explain a few things to you. To report a rape and have someone charged for rape. It's a very serious matter. You should be ashamed of yourself for lying that you were raped, and for having that man arrested. Let today be a lesson to you that the law works both ways. One that commit a crime the law will fall on their head. And one that lie and say a crime was committed the law will fall on them as well. With that said. I hereby sentence you to two months' probation. Court is here by adjourned."

Five days in jail was all Brandy needed to get her mind right. Two times she tried to play Desean, and both times he played her in the end. Clearly his game was tighter then hers. Although she was mad for being put in jail. She wasn't mad at Desean; she was mad at herself. If she wanted to keep her apartment and keep money in her pockets. She knew she had to step her gold digging ways up a notch. Brandy knew that Desean would think he had the upper hand over her now. But she had learned from her mother a long time ago. "Have an income and use niggas money to have fun. That way your rent and bills are paid, and you can fuck whoever you want" her mother use to always tell her. Remembering that, that's what made her mind up for her. Instead of going home after she was released from jail. Brandy went straight to Love it or Hate it and applied as a stripper. Of course with her body she was higher on the spot.

*****

In Solo house it was dark even though it was day light outside. Walking through out Solo house Beverly and Supreme found Solo laying down in his bed. Sitting on the right side of the bed. Beverly wrapped her arms around Solo. Not saying a word Solo rest his head on Beverly chest. Beverly could feel her shirt becoming wet. Which meant Solo was crying.

"It's my fault that Trina is dead Bev."

"No it's not and I don't want to ever hear you say that again. My cousin knew what she was getting into years ago when me and her stepped in the drug game. You didn't kill her, Tonya killed her. If you, me, or anybody else want to blame someone for Trina death Tonya is the one to blame."

Wiping his eyes Solo looked over at Supreme. "Gail has been text messaging me for the past two weeks none stop. Have she been text messaging you to Supreme?"

"Yeah, she want you to meet with her A.S.A.P. I tried calling her to see why, but she won't answer the phone. She just keep texting the same message over and over. I know we are all going through something right now. From losing Jay and Trina, but we can't lose our drug connect to Solo. You're the head of the Gibbs drug contract. If you want me and Bev to take a drive out there to New Jersey with you to meet with Gail, we will."

"Yeah, that would be good If yawl go with me. I don't want to take that drive by myself. Where's Rome?"

"I sent him, Pit, and Tone to go get Little Supreme."

"Supreme, you think they can handle that situation by their self?"

"Solo, I told them to call us If they feel they need back up."

"Okay well, it's been over two weeks Supreme. When are we going to start planning Jay funeral?"

"Mommy already took care of that. She had him cremated."

"Sure she did Supreme. What did she do swipe her house. Take all the dust, put it in a cup, and put it on the shelf of her fireplace in her living room?"

Supreme and Beverly bust out laughing. "Solo, Mommy feel what she's doing is best until we get things under control. So until then we have to go along with her wishes. In the meantime get dressed so you can go see Gail."

*****

Since hearing the news that Solo and Supreme had been locked up two weeks ago. Bill had been following Jo-Jo learning his schedule. Before Bill got hooked on crack. He was one of the best private detectives in New York city. While focusing on Jo-Jo schedule. Bill hadn't got the news that Solo and Supreme had been released 24 hours after their arrest. Morning, noon, and night, Bill watched Jo-Jo make drug drop offs to Soundview projects and Webster projects. Finally he had found out that Jo-Jo had all drugs stared in a rundown house that he called his, dirt house. Checking out the dirt house Bill had found out a way to get inside the dirt house. Not only did he find a way to get into the dirt house. He also realized the best time to break into the dirt house would be late at night. He knew there was a lot of drugs in that house and he wanted all of it. The only problem was he didn't want to get caught by Jo-Jo, or any member of the Gibbs drug family breaking into the dirt house. Bill sat down on the ground behind an old abandon car. Tonight was the night he plan to break into the dirt house. With a few hours to go before it got dark outside. Bill leaned against the car and went to sleep.

*****

Stepping inside of Gail house, nine women showed Solo, Beverly, and Supreme to the dining room. Looking at the woman sitting at the head of the dining room table. Solo, Beverly, and Supreme, then began looking at each other confused. They wanted to make sure of what they were seeing. From across the table Tonya looked at the three of them with a face of stone. The guilt of Trina death came flowing through Solo veins in a rage.

"Bitch, you got the nerve to be just sitting there like you don't have a care in the world. My son, my wife, and my two unborn children you got at. You think shit is sweet?"

Pulling out his gun Solo started walking towards the dining room table. Stopping him in his tracks. One of the nine women stripped him of his gun, whacked Solo in his left shoulder with it, and Solo fell hard on the floor face first. Jumped to Solo aid Supreme grabbed for the woman neck. Ducking Supreme hand the woman turn around and chopped Supreme in his neck dropping Supreme to the floor as well. Pulling out her gun Beverly aimed for Tonya head. Just as fast as Beverly pulled out her gun. Three of the women strike like lighten. One snatched the gun out of Beverly hand. The other two women took Beverly by her arms ramming her into the wall and slammed her on the floor face first. Solo, Supreme and Beverly, all laid on the floor looking up at the nine women standing over them. Things had just happen so fast they didn't know what to say or do.

As the three of them laid on the floor. Tonya cleared her throat to get their attention.

"Now that's all out the way. Let's say you three take a seat so we can discuss a few things."

Standing up first Solo looked in the face of the woman that put him on his face. She looked back at Solo with no emotion written on her face. Standing up Supreme helped Beverly up to her feet. Not wanting a repeat reaction Solo turned his attention back towards Tonya.

"Where the fuck is Gail at!"

"Gail where abouts are no concern to you or anyone else for that matter Solo. As of three weeks ago. I was placed in this position as the acting queen of the ocean. Which means I'm your boss and your drug connect now. It has also come to my attention. That you're gonna be in need of a new shipment of drugs in a few days. So If I was you, I would put my pride to the side. Also know If you or your team come at me again. Know your life and their life I will take. Let today be a lesson to you Solo. Don't fuck with me! I will chew your ass up and spit you out. Now let's get down to business. Shall I put you down for your regular shipment and payment?"

"Bitch If you think I'm gonna do business with you. You are outta your fucking mind. When Gail is back in that seat tell her to give me a call."

"Have it your way Solo. But know you are under contract with the ocean. Get caught buying from another drug connect and you will be in the ground before you can sell those drugs. Ladies! Please show the three of them to the door."

Getting back in the car in front of Gail house, Supreme looked over at Beverly.

"You okay baby girl?"

"Hell no! Ain't no bitch in this world ever put their hands on me like that. It was like them bitches had supernatural strength."

"Those nine women are trained assassins" Solo and Supreme both said.

"Now what?"

"I'll tell you what Bev. Me, you, and Supreme are going to the dirt house right now. We gonna snatch up all the drugs we have left. Split what we have left between our two drug spots. When were done selling all the drugs we have. Were gonna shut down our two drug spots until Gail give me a call."

"Solo, what If Gail never call…."

"Then Bev were out the drug game permanently." Starting up the car Solo headed for the highway.

Sitting in the back seat Beverly pulled out her cell phone and called Rome. Telling him everything that had just happen at Gail house, she also told him what solo plan was. Placing her cell phone back in her pocket. Beverly looked at Supreme and Solo sitting in the front seats of the car. Looking in the mirror Supreme saw the look on Beverly face. A look that he knew oh to well. A look that said, this shit is far from over.

"What's on your mind Bev" Supreme asked.

"Supreme, on everything I love I swear to god I'm gonna beat fire out of Tonya If that's the last thing I do."

"Beat, you don't want to kill her" Solo asked surprised at what Beverly had just said.

"I don't want that bitch dead. No, no, I want to put my foot in that bitch ass. Killing her would be to easy."

"With Gail on her side right now Bev, that's gonna be hard to do."

"Solo, that Gail shit ain't gonna last. Soon as Gail take her place back. I'm gonna beat fire out of Tonya ass."

Turning around in his car seat Supreme looked at Beverly. "Bev how about this. You beat her ass and when you done, me and Solo put a bullet in that bitch head. How does that sound?"

"Like music to my ears."

Still sitting in the dining room Tonya began thinking to herself. Tonya knew Solo would refuse to do business with her. She also knew like any other good drug dealer. What Solo next move would be. And that was go to his stash of drugs, get it all, and sell it all. All of which Tonya was counting on for her next move against the Gibbs family. Pulling out her cell phone Tonya dialed Goody cell number.

"Hello" Goody said answering his phone.

"Goody, good news. Solo has refused of Jo-Jo dirt house."

"Goody, did you set the dirt house up like I told you?"

"Of course, it's enough explosives around that house to make it raise to heaven."

"Good work, set the trip wire and get the hell out from around that house."

Hanging up with Tonya, Goody got out his car and set the wires in place. With everything looking good Goody got back in his car and drove off.

*****

Waking up in the back yard of jo-Jo dirt house. Bill took a hit of crack. To Bill, he felt he could think better when he was high. Standing up from behind the abandon car. Bill dusted the dirt from the ground off his clothes. Taking another hit of crack Bill began walking towards the dirt house back door.

Pulling up in front of Jo-Jo dirt house. Solo, Beverly, and Supreme, got out the car. With two empty duffle bags in each one of their hands. The three of them began walking towards the dirt house.

Tripping the trip wire around the house. Jo-Jo dirt house exploded in a ball of fire. The sound of the explosion shook the whole block. As the smoke from the fire cleared. The inside and around the house was completely destroyed.

Chapter 22

"I wanna go home" Little Supreme yelled at the top of his lungs.

Snatching him by his little four year old arm. Nicole dragged him to the room she had set up for him in her house. Walking in the room Nicole pushed him down on the bed.

"Listen here and listen good. You are home."

Threw tear full eyes Little Supreme got off the bed and looked up at Nicole. "I wanna go home to my Daddy and mommy Sierra."

"That bitch is not your mother. I'm your mother!"

"No you not, Mommy Sierra is my Mommy."

"Say her name one more time and I'm gonna slap the shit right out of you."

Seeing him opening his mouth Nicole raised her hand in the air Dearing him to say Sierra name again. Breathing heavy in anger he was scared to say Sierra name again.

"My Daddy is gonna come and get me."

"Boy please! Your Daddy ain't gonna come and get shit. Rome don't know where you at. So get use to this house because this is your house now."

Walking over to the toy box in the room Little Supreme kicked it over. "I wanna go home!"

"Since you want to through a fit. Let's see how you like staying in your room for the rest of the night." Closing the door Nicole walked back downstairs in her living room.

Pulling up in front of Nicole house Rome pulled out his cell phone. Going on the internet on his cell phone like Solo showed him. Rome put in the tracker code to Little Supreme chain. The same address that popped up on Solo phone in the hospital. Was still the same address that was popping up on his cell phone. Little Supreme gold chain that was around his neck was still putting him at the L.A address he was now in front of.

"How sure are you that your son is in that house Rome" Pit asked.

"One hundred percent sure, his chain tracker put him in that house" Rome wanted to say. Yet he promised Solo he wouldn't tell the team, that Solo is tracking everybody in the family and on the team by their chains. "Uncle Solo told me this is the address."

Not wanting to question Solo words Pit pulled out his gun. "Well youngen let's do this then."

Seeing high been car lights flash twice behind their car. Rome, Pit, and Tone, turned around in their car seat and looked out the back car window.

"Holy shit, is that who I think that is" Tone said still not believing who he was seeing in the car behind them.

"Unfucking believable" Rome said tucking his gun back in his pants. Getting out the car Rome walked over to the car behind his car. "Sierra what the hell are you doing here" Rome asked.

"I'm here for the same reason you are. Now are we all gonna go up in this house and get Little Supreme or what?"

Looking in the back seat of Sierra car Rome almost fell out in the middle of the street. "Sierra, you bugging. You brought our one year old daughter, and Solo son with you."

"What was I supposed to do Rome? Leave them home in New York by their self? Their sleep, so let's go in the house, get our little man, and get the hell out of here."

"No, what your gonna do is take your ass home, and let me and the fellas handle this."

Rolling down the car window just a little. Sierra snatched her car keys out the engine and got out the car. Seeing Sierra walking towards the house Rome shook his head in disbelief. Pulling his gun out he waived in the air. Seeing the signal Pit and Tone jumped out the car. Running pass Sierra, Pit, and Tone ran full speed into the house door. Knocking the door off the hinges.

Running up in the house Pit and Tone let off a shot towards the ceiling. Caught off guard Levi, Henry, China, TG, Nicole, Mellow, Debra, and Cam, stood frozen in shock. Walking in the house side by side. Sierra and Rome walked into the living room. Pit and Tone made everyone in the house lay on the floor, as they held them at gun point. Walking over to Nicole, Rome grabbed her by her hair.

"Bitch where is my son?"

"None of your damn business."

Pulling out his gun Rome press it against Nicole forehead. "I'm gonna ask you are more fucking time. Play cute again and I'm gonna forget you are the mother of my son. And I'm gonna put a hole right in your head."

"He's upstairs" Nicole said not wanting Rome to make good on his statement. Looking over at Sierra, Sierra was already halfway up the stairs. A minute later Sierra was coming down the stairs with Little Supreme in her arms. Seeing them coming down the stairs Pit, Tone, and Rome, put their guns behind their back.

"Daddy" Little Supreme yelled seeing Rome.

"Hey L.S, you all right Little Man?"

"Yeah. I told you my Daddy was gonna come and get me" Little Supreme said looking at Nicole who was laying on the floor.

Soon as the house was clear of Sierra and Little Supreme. Pit, Tone, and Rome went into a rage. Walking over to Nicole, Rome went off.

"Bitch, you tried this kidnapping shit before, and you got the nerve to do it again. What is your fucking problem?"

"You don't have to worry about me doing it a third time. You can have that little disrespectful bastard."

Pushing Rome to the side Tone stepped over Nicole and bent down in front of Debra. "Bitch, you thought you were real slick getting in good with my boy Bullet, and then you set Bullet up to be murdered."

"I…."

"POP!" the sound Tone gun made as the bullet from his gun ripped through Debra skull.

Walking back in the house Sierra walked over to Nicole. Little Supreme told me, you told him you was going to hit him If he said my name again to you."

"Damn right, you not his…." Snatching the gun out of Rome hand. Sierra went upside Nicole head with it.

"Bitch, you may have birthed him, but I'm more of a mother to him then you will ever be. Snatching the gun out of Sierra hand Rome pushed her towards the front door.

"Yo, let's roll, we got what we came for" Rome yelled over his shoulder walking out the door.

Tone, and Pit looked at each other, then looked at all that still laid on the floor. Walking over to TG, Tone put a bullet in his head. Walking over to Levi, Pit put a bullet in his head.

"The rest of you mother fuckers be lucky we are leaving you with your life" Pit said.

Walking out the door Pit and Tone got in the car with Rome. Pulling off Rome and Sierra beeped their car horns. Getting up off the floor Cam, Henry, and mellow ran upstairs to get their guns. Running out the house they saw no one.

*****

An hour into the drive back home to New York. Rome switched seats with Pit so Pit could drive. Getting out the car Tone made Sierra get in her passenger seat and he got in her driver seat. Trying to get some rest Sierra heard Rome cell phone start ranging.

"Hello…. Hey grandma…. Were about a few hours away. Why? What! Oh my god. What happen? All of them?"

Hanging up the phone Rome stared down at the cell phone in his hand. Looking over his shoulder into the back seat Pit noticed that Rome had a weird look on his face.

"Rome why you looking like you just lost your dog? Who was that on the phone?"

"Pit…. Pit that was Grandma Nancy. She said…. She said there was a explosion at jo-Jo dirt house."

Hearing that Pit pulled over to the side of the road. Not knowing what was going on but seeing Rome car pulling over. Tone pulled Sierra car over to the side of the road as well.

"What type of explosion Rome" Pit asked looking in Rome face.

"Pit all grandma said was, the explosion was bad."

"Was any one at the dirt house when it exploded?"

"Yeah, grandma said, Solo, Beverly, and Supreme, all died in the explosion."

Pit eyes grew large in shock looking at Rome. Opening the car door Tone stuck his head in the car. "What's the problem? Why yawl pulled over?"

Still in shock to what he just heard. Pit slowly turned his head towards Tone. "Tone, Nancy just called Rome and told him that Solo, Supreme, and Beverly just died in a explosion at jo-jo dirt house."

*****

Driving into New York Pit and Tone parked in front of Jo-Jo dirt house. Getting out the cars Pit, Tone, Rome, and Sierra walked up to the house. The house looked like a total lost. The frame of the house was still standing because the house was made out of brick. Everything else was burned to ashes. House windows and car windows that were around the dirt house were busted out. No doubt the reason was from the dirt house exploding. Yellow police tape still waived in the air around the house. Rome looked at the dirt house in a daze. The Gibbs family drug operation was official over in his eyes. He was now the oldest Gibbs in his family besides his grandmother Nancy. Remembering what his mother Beverly told him on the phone about Solo plan to shut everything down. Rome pulled out his cell phone and called the rest of the Gibbs drug team speaking to everyone he told them all to meet him at Nancy house for a meeting next week.

*****

Walking in her living room Nancy stood beside Rome. Pit, Lloyd, Tone, Sierra, Tameka, Vera, Stephanie, jo-Jo, Khia, Tymel, and Erykah. All of them sat in Nancy living room, while Quinn, Lisa, and Little Supreme played upstairs in the guess bedroom.

"Grandma maybe you should start off this meeting."

"I really don't know where to begin so I'll stick to the facts. A week ago I got a call from detective Price. He told me that it was an explosion at jo-jo dirt house, and Beverly, Supreme, and Solo, were there when it happen, and they had died. When I went down to the morgue to identify them. They were burned so bad the only way I could I.D them was from the gold chains that were around their neck."

Nancy placed all three gold chains on her fireplace shelf. "Me being the mother of Solo and Supreme, and Stephanie being the mother of Beverly. We both agreed there's no point in having a funeral for them when we won't be able to have open caskets for them. As we speak the three of them are being cremated. Tomorrow I have to go to the funeral home to pick up their ashes. I have buried so many people that were close to me in my life. That I refuse to bury any more. So when I pick up their ashes tomorrow. I'm getting on a phone to go to Jamaica, so I can spread their ashes on a nice, beautiful beach."

Rome watched as Nancy walked Tameka, Vera, and Stephanie to the door so they could leave. For the first time in his life he noticed that his grandmother was getting old. He didn't know If having five deaths in the family all within one moth had weighed her down, or If her age was catching up to her. What he did know was that Nancy looked tired. In no way could he take losing her to right now. It would be too much for him to bare.

Standing up Rome cleared his throat to get everyone attention in the living room. "From what I was told by my mother before…." Rome closed his eyes for a few seconds with the thought that he would never see his mother Beverly again. "She told me the Gibbs drug connect has been cut off. So we no longer have a drug connect. And from the look of Jo-Jo dirt house. Whatever drugs we had left is now gone. Me being the oldest person that holds the Gibbs name on the drug team. I guess that puts me in charge now. Khia having her own contract, will keep her spot at Joe's store, and will pay my rent for renting that spot. Soundview and Webster projects drug spots are officially shut down. With that said the Gibbs family is officially out the drug game. As you all know I own the Bank's hotel and I guess now I also own the club, Love it or Hate it. Any job any one of you want in those two spots let me know and the job is yours. In the meantime next week I'm gonna go over to Soundview and Webster and clean those apartments out."

Hearing what Rome had just said. Pit and Tone both looked at each other. Standing up they both had the Same thing on their mind and said it out loud.

"We know Tonya had something to do with all of this. When the fuck are, we gonna get back at her?"

"Were not…."

"What the fuck do you mean were not" Pit yelled.

"Word the fuck up! My two boys didn't die in vain for nothing" Tone roared.

"Listen, If you two want to get pay back do you. But don't use the Gibbs name to do it."

Like a raging bull Tone and pit rammed Rome into the living room wall.

"Boy, the two niggas that died, raised you, and looked out for you all your life. And you wanna let their murder go unpunished?"

"Get off me!"

Pushing Tone out the way Pit picked Rome up off his feet and slammed him against the wall even harder. "What the fuck do you mean get off you? What the fuck are you going to do Rome? I know damn well you heard what me and Tone bot said. I should kill your ass right here and now for the stupid shit that came out your mouth."

Standing up Tymel tried to get between Rome and Pit. Pulling out his gun Tone put it to Tymel head. "Back the fuck up little nigga!" Standing up Khia walked up to Tone. "Bitch you can get it to" Tone yelled turning his gun towards Khia head.

Walking back into the living room Nancy couldn't believe what she was seeing. Tone gun was out and against Khia head. Pit had Rome against the wall up off his feet. Walking over to the scene that was about to turn deadly. Nancy swung her hand hard to the left and swung it hard to the right. Slapping Tone and Pit in their face they both saw stairs.

"Have you two boys lost your damn mind?"

"Sorry Ms. Nancy" Tone said tucking his gun under his shirt.

Letting go of Rome, Rome feet met the living room floor once again. "Sorry Ms. Nancy" Pit said.

Looking at Tone and Pit, Nancy looked at each person in her living room. All that was in the living room stood quite. It was so quite one would have been able to hear a mouse piss on the floor.

"You should all be a shame of yourself. Respect has always been a big part in the Gibbs blood line, and on the Gibbs drug team." Looking around the living room Nancy wanted to see If her words were sinking into everyone. Hearing movement downstairs in the basement. Everyone head turned towards the basement door in the hallway.

"Grandma it sound like someone is in your basement."

"No one is in my basement Rome."

"I heard it to Ms. Nancy, someone is in your basement" Pit said standing up.

"Listen here, I said no one is in my basement. That sound yawl just heard came from upstairs. Those are the kids playing up there."

"No, I heard that noise come from downstairs to" Sierra said sure of what she had just heard the noise come from.

"You know what, I can't deal with all of this right now. Sierra this maybe a lot to ask for. But I'm gonna need you to look after Quinn until I get back from Jamaica."

"Sure Nancy, I don't have a problem with that."

"Good, now all of you get out my house so I can get some rest. I haven't went to sleep in a week since this all happen."

Getting up Rome and Sierra went upstairs to get the kids. Tymel, Erykah, and Jo-Jo, followed Khia out the house. Standing up Tone, Pit, and Lloyd, walked over to Nancy.

"Ms. Nancy, you don't look to good, are…."

"Thanks for letting me know I'm getting old and my looks are going Tone."

"Ms. Nancy, I didn't mean it like that. It's just that you look very tired. Are you sure you are okay?"

"I'm fine."

"Do you want us to go down to your basement and make sure…."

"No I don't want you to go down to my basement. If you don't mind, I want all of yawl out my house. I'm tired, I need some rest for my trip to Jamaica tomorrow."

Seeing Rome and Sierra walking down the stairs with the kids. Nancy walked everyone to the door. Locking her house door Nancy leaned against the door and took a deep breath. The whole situation was beginning to take its toll on her body and soul. First Jay, then Trina, then

Trina baby girl, then Solo, Beverly, and Supreme. All six of them were working her nerves big time. Needing a short nap Nancy headed up stairs to her bedroom. Walking up the stairs Nancy heard a few more noises coming from the basement.

"Quite the hell down, down there so I can take a nap" Nancy yelled stumping her foot on the stairs.

Walking in her bedroom Nancy kicked off her shoes and got in her bed. Laying her head down on the pillow Nancy closed her eyes. Within seconds she felt like her body was floating on a cloud.

*****

Walking downstairs Nancy felt like she was still floating on a cloud. She wasn't sure If the nap she had just took gave her back her energy, or If she was still floating on a cloud because she was dead. One thing she did know was she wasn't tired any more. Walking in her kitchen Nancy saw Solo, Supreme, Beverly, Jay, and Trina holding her baby girl in her arms. Nancy got the answer to her question whether she got her energy back or if she was dead.

"Ma, you ready to go" Supreme asked.

Pulling out her car keys Nancy looked at all of them. "I sure am, Jamaica here we come." Taking the baby out of Trina hands Nancy looked at the baby. "Hey Emma Gibbs, you are so beautiful." Handing Trina back the baby they all got in the car. "Everybody buckle up, Because it's gonna be a long ride" Nancy said starting up the car.

Chapter 23

Sending Pit, Lloyd, and Jo-Jo, to clean out the Webster project apartment. Rome took Tone with him to clean out the Soundview project apartment. Walking inside the apartment, Tone and Rome stood still in shock when they got to the living room. Sitting on the couch with his eyes closed. Mellow guided Nicole head up and down as she was giving him a blow job.

"What the fuck" Rome yelled pulling out his gun.

"How the fuck did yawl get in here" Tone yelled pulling out his gun as well.

"This is Tonya drug spot now, and we run it" Mellow said with one hand on the back of Nicole head, and the other on his gun.

"Oh really" Rome said walking towards the couch.

Grabbing a hold of Rome arm Tone stopped him. Wondering why Tone stopped him. Rome looked at Tone, and Tone pointed over to the kitchen. Coming out the kitchen Cam and Henry had their guns out.

"Four against two, so step. Because If I have to stop getting my dick sucked, shit gonna get crazy" Mellow said still guiding Nicole head up and down in his lap.

Far from a punk, and far from stupid. Tone knew when and how to pick his battles. Having no other choice Tone decided to let them win this battle. Pushing Rome out the door Tone closed the door behind them.

"Aww" Mellow moaned holding the back of Nicole head in place. Busting his nut Mellow pulled his penis out of Nicole mouth. "You swallowed that" Mellow asked looking down at Nicole. Looking up at Mellow, Nicole shook her head yes. "Let me see". Sticking her tongue out Nicole open her mouth wide. "Good girl" Mellow said patting the right side of Nicole face.

Driving over to Webster projects Rome and Tone drove in silence. Pulling up in front of Webster projects Rome and Tone spotted Pit, Lloyd, and Jo-Jo, standing outside. The look on their face told them that Pit, Lloyd and Jo-Jo, was angry.

"Yo, yawl not gonna believe this shit. Me and Pit went up to the apartment and…."

"We already know, it's the same shit over at Soundview. Get in" Tone said just as angry as they were.

Getting in the car all four of them looked over at Rome. Sitting in the driver seat Rome stared at the steering wheel. Pulling out his cell phone Rome called his house.

"Sierra take the kids over to my grandmother Stephanie house and head over to my grandfather store." Hanging up Rome dialed Khia cell number. "Khia this is Rome. Are you at Joe's store…. Good, is Tymel and Erykah there with you? Good, stay put, me and the fellas are on our way to the store. We all need to have a serious meeting. I'll be damn If I'm gonna just let that bitch Tonya push my family to the side and take over all of what the Gibbs family built."

Getting off the phone with Rome. Khia went to the back office of the store, closed the door, and sat down at the desk. Her mind had been in deep thought ever since she got the news that Solo had died. Her mind went into deeper thought after she had left Nancy house a week ago. Hearing that the Gibbs family no longer had a drug contract with Gail. Khia felt she owed a favor to the Gibbs family. Especially after all the hell she had put them through when she was beefing with the Gibbs family. The best idea she could come up with. Was suppling the Gibbs family with drugs threw her drug contract with Gail. Suppling Rome with drugs he would be able to keep his two drug spots open. Feeling her cell phone vibrating in her pocket. Khia pulled her phone out her pocket and saw a number she had never seen before.

"Hello…. Who is this? Gail, why are you calling me from a new number? I see…. Please tell me you are joking? You think my mother is planning what? Okay, okay. Thanks for the heads up."

Hanging the phone up Khia looked at her watch. Grabbing her car keys, she ran out the office, and out the store.

*****

Driving through the streets Khia parked her car in front of a public park. Getting out the car she walked into the park and started looking at all the men who were in the park and started looking at all the men who were in the park. One by one she sat down next to them and asked them one question. "How old are you?" When she found a man that was the age she was looking for. She found out his name was Carl freemen. Khia asked him for three favors. In return she told him she would give him ten thousand dollars and she would have sex with him. Looking at Khia, Carl couldn't deny that Khia was beautiful, yet at the same time he thought she was out of her mind.

"Listen here young lady, I don't…." Khia pulled a stack of money out of her purse. Looking at the stack of one hundred dollar bills. Carl jumped up to his feet. "Girl let's go, what are we waiting for" Carl said snatching the stack of money out of Khia hand.

*****

Five hours ago Rome had shut down Joe's store for the meeting. In the store back office Rome, Pit, Tone, Sierra, Tameka, Lloyd, Tymel, Erykah, and jo-Jo, all sat down with patience's. Before Rome got to the store, he called Khia and told her to stay put in the store. Yet when he got to the store five hours ago. Tymel and Erykah told him that Khia ran out the store in a hurry before he got there. Calling Khia cell phone multiple times Rome kept getting her voice mail. Here it was five hours later and Khia had still not come back to the store. Rome was out of patience's and was now beyond pissed off. Far as he was concern Khia better have a good excuse to why she left. When he told her to stay put. Because If she didn't, he was going to shut Joe's store down for good and make her find a new spot to sell her drugs.

Sitting down behind the desk in the back store office. Rome felt his cell phone vibrating in his pocket. Pulling out his cell phone he looked at the number and didn't know it.

"Hello…. Speaking. Who is this? What's your address? I'm on my way." Standing up Rome put his cell phone back in his pocket.

"Where are you going to Rome" Sierra asked.

"I'll be back, all of you just sit tight."

Watching Rome walk out the store. Tone and Pit looked at each other confused.

*****

Pulling up in front of Gail house Khia called Gail on her cell phone. Telling Gail that she was in front of her house. Gail told Khia, she would be there in twenty minutes. Hanging up with Gail, Khia looked over at Carl who was sitting in her passenger seat.

"Carl stay put I'll send for you when I need you."

Getting out the car Khia knocked on Gail house door. Walking in Gail house nine women showed Khia to the dining room. Sitting at the head of the dining room table. Tonya looked at her daughter Khia and smiled.

"Khia, what a pleasure to see you."

"Tonya, the pleasure is all mind mother."

"Khia, If you're wondering why I'm sitting here and not Gail. It's because I'm now the acting queen of the ocean appointed by Gail herself."

"I'm very aware of all of that mother."

Both of them were being sarcastic towards the other.

"Khia I'm sorry to hear about your little stay at the hospital a month ago. I tried to come see you, but I wasn't allowed up to your hospital room."

"That's funny that you say that considering you the one that put me in the hospital in the first place mother."

"You put your damn self in the hospital when you crossed me Khia. I hope your stay at the hospital taught you not to ever cross your mother again."

"Oh mother my stay at the hospital taught me a lot. Just like you dropping off the face of the earth for 21 years taught me a lot. It taught me how to be better than the one that taught me the game."

Hearing Khia last statement Tonya let out a short laugh. "Khia, you still have a lot to learn. It's just too bad I'm no longer willing to teach you. Every time you get a little idea that you have me in that little pretty head of years. I will always be around to put you in your place. You know why?"

"Why mother?"

"Because I'm the parent and you will always be my child no matter how old you get."

"You know what mother ? You may be on top of things now, but I'm gonna enjoy watching you have no position at all."

"It's funny that you say that Khia because I was saying the same thing about you."

Walking in the dining room Gail looked at Tonya and Khia. "I'm sorry to interrupt your meeting." Following Gail in the dining room Rome stood behind Gail. "Tonya thank you for filing in for me. Yet I'm in good health again and it's about time I take my place once again."

Standing up Tonya could see the smile on Khia face. A smile that she was ready to wipe off.

"Look a here, look a here, it look like you no longer have a position mother."

Taking her seat at the head of the dining room table. Paying Tonya and Khia no mind Gail turned her attention over to Rome. "Rome I'm more then sure you know who I am, so there's no need to tell you about me. From what I know Solo is no longer around. Yet that does not end the Gibbs drug contract. The Gibbs drug contract goes to you Rome." Pulling out a business card Gail slid it across the table. Catching the card Rome picked it up. "Rome when you need a shipment of drugs give me a call. Ladies! Show Rome to the door."

While the nine women showed Rome to the door. Gail looked over at Tonya and Khia giving them her full attention.

"Gail If you don't mind, I would like to pay you for a new shipment of drugs. Being that I'm the queen of the Sams drug contract" Khia said.

Hearing Khia say what she had just said Tonya bust out laughing. "little girl you thought you were the queen of the Sams drug contract. Oh Goody" Tonya yelled. Walking in the dining room Goody stood beside Tonya. "Khia my daughter meet my husband, who is now your stepfather."

Looking over at Gail, Tonya had a smile on her face. "Gail, If you don't mind can you read those two new lines Trini added into the Sams contract, that my daughter Khia never changed when she took over the Sams contract."

Pulling out the Sams contract Gail cleared her throat; "Trini, upon my death as the holder of the Sams drug contract. The contract is to go to the second oldest Sams and not the oldest Sams."

"Khia, Goody is five years older than me, and he took my last name. Which makes Goody the oldest Sams, me the second oldest Sams, and you the third oldest Sams. That also makes me the queen of the Sams drug contract and not you Khia. How does it feel not to have a position at all Khia?" Khia looked over at Gail. Stepping in front of Khia, Tonya snapped her fingers in Khia face. "Don't look at Gail look at me and answer my question. How does it feel not to have a position at all Khia?"

"Gail can you get your women to go out to my car and bring in my friend" Khia said.

"Sure, ladies!"

Two minutes after the nine women left the dining room, they were back in the dining room with Carl. Not knowing anyone in the room but Khia. Carl stood close to Khia.

"Mother meet my husband Carl Sams. He's two years older than you. Which makes him the second oldest Sams, and the holder of the Sams drug contract."

With a look of shock written on Tonya face, Tonya looked over at Gail. Stepping in front of Tonya, Khia snapped her finger in Tonya face. "Hey, don't look at Gail, look at me. Now I want you to answer your own question mother. How does it feel not to have a position at all? You know what mother hold your answer. Because I believe the holder of the Sams drug contract have something he would like to say."

Looking over at Carl, Carl pulled a piece of paper out his pocket. A paper that Khia wrote on for him to read. "As the king of the Sams drug contract. I'm choosing to step down as the King and put Khia Sams to run the Sams drug contract."

"So order, Khia is now the holder of the Sams drug contract" Gail said.

"Gail as the holder of the Sams drug contract. I would like to take Trini two lines that he added to the contract, out of the contract. I would like to add these lines in the Sams drug contract. In no way shall Tonya Sams ever become the holder of the Sams drug contract, or anyone that she shall marry ever become a holder of the Sams drug contract."

"You bitch" Tonya yelled jumping on Khia taking her down to the floor. On top of Khia, Tonya wrapped her hands around Khia neck.

"Ladies" Gail yelled. Four of the women pulled Tonya off of Khia. Holding her neck Khia stood up from the floor. "Tonya get a hold of yourself in my house. I warried you when I gave you my position. I told you to make up with your daughter. Instead you used my position to continue to beef with your daughter. Now look at you, you are left with no position. The drug game is meant for men to run. As women in the drug game we have to work extra harder to be respected in the drug game we have to work extra harder to be respected in the drug game. Beefing with another woman will get you nowhere Tonya in this game. You beefed when there really wasn't a beef, now you really have a beef with her. My best advice to you Tonya, is use your head and get back in the game."

"Looking over at Khia, Tonya began speaking to Gail. "Gail, you taught me well and my head is always in the game. My daughter may think she won, but the game is only beginning."

Gail looked over at Khia. "Khia, you have the Sams drug contract. Call me when you want to pick up your new shipment of drugs. Ladies! Show Khia and Carl to the door."

With Khia out of Gail house. Tonya sat down at the dining room table across from Gail. "Life is a chest game Tonya. You said I taught you well, well make me a believer. What's your next move?"

Going in her pocket Tonya pulled out a envelope and her wallet. Taking her I.D out her wallet Tonya slid it across the table at Gail. Picking it up Gail read the name on the I.D.

"Tonya Sams" Gail said sliding the I.D back across the table at Tonya.

Taking another I.D out her wallet Tonya slid it across the table. Picking up the I.D Gail read the name on the I.D. "Tonya Jones" Gail said sliding the I.D back to Tonya.

"Gail as of now I'm going by my husband last name." Opening the envelope Tonya pulled out six birth certificates. Picking up the birth certificates Gail began reading the names on the birth certificates. Nicole Jones, China Jones, Cam Jones, Mellow Jones, Henry Jones, Goody Jones.

"Good move making everyone on your team change their last name. Folding the birth certificates Gail slid them back across the birth certificates Gail slid them back across the table.

"Gail, you've known me for years. Which also mean you know I'm not a rat or an informant. So at this time Gail I would like to ask you for a Jones family drug contract?"

"Tonya before I give you my answer. I want you to answer a question for me. Why do you want this drug contract Tonya?"

"Because I wanna put the Gibbs and the Sams drug operations out of business."

"Tonya clearly you were right I did teach you well. With that said you are now the holder and queen of the Jones family drug contract."

Signing the new contract with Gail. Tonya stood up and walked out of Gail dining room with Goody following behind her. Walking outside Tonya spotted Khia and Rome in their cars parked across the street. As Goody got in the passenger seat of Tonya car. Tonya got in the driver seat, staring up the car Tonya pulled up beside their cars.

'I'm gonna enjoy taking down the Gibbs, and Sams drug operations. Get ready for war" Tonya yelled speeding off down the block.

Chapter 24

One Year Later

Sitting in his living room Rome got up and walked over to his wall unit. Finding the video tape he was looking for. Rome held the video tape in his hand. No matter how hard he tried to get over Beverly, Supreme, Trina, Jay, and Solo death, he just couldn't. He missed Solo, Jay, and Trina without a doubt. But most importantly he missed his mother Beverly and Supreme the most. Looking at the video tape in his hand. It was Beverly and Supreme 18th wedding anniversary party that was recorder in Love it or Hate it. Although they had been married for 26 years. They only recorded their 18th wedding anniversary party. Putting the tape in the V.C.R Rome pressed play. Looking at the T.V screen Rome had to admit for the first time in his life. What everyone had been saying about Beverly and Supreme for years. Beverly did look a lot like the singer Mary J Blige, and Supreme looked a lot like the singer Usher. Not only did they like those two singers. They both could also sing just like those two singers. Seeing DJ L-Boogie beating on the mic Rome turned the volume up on the T.V and sat back down on the couch:

"As you all know I'm L-Boogie on your ones and twos. Yawl know why we here, to celebrate Supreme and Beverly 18th wedding anniversary! These two are ready to show you all why they been together all these years. Both ready to sing a do-wet called, Do Anything!" Walking out on the stage. Beverly made every guy in the club mouth drop wide open. Wearing a one piece white spandex cat suit, with thigh high white Italian leather stiletto boots. Beverly spotted Supreme sitting in a chair in front of the stage. Taking the mic in her hand she let her voice fill the air:

"You! Told me a thousand times!

That you would be mine oh mine!

Do everything for you! But in your smile, I still can't find!

Now you tell me this, this is something that I missed.

And all'll I did! Is for you to love me for me and I'll love you for you.

I don't wanna do, I don't wanna do, anything else!!!!!

No, no, no!!!!!"

Pulling his mic out his back pocket Supreme let his voice fill the air:

"Now I know I'm gonna make love to you!

So lady! Open up your heart!

And let me in where I belong!"

Looking in Supreme eyes Beverly continued:

"If loving you is all that I have to do!

Then it won't be wrong baby!

Because we belong together."

Taking each other hand they song at the same time:

"Together!!!!!

We will be as one!"

Turning off the video tape Rome wiped the tears from his eyes. Somehow, he knew he had to move on. Beverly, Supreme, and Solo, was never coming back, they were gone. Leaving his head back on the couch Rome closed his eyes. A whole year bad past since he lost all of them. Within the past year so much had changed. Rome and Sierra decided to move into Beverly and Supreme house. With Solo and Trina both gone, leaving their six year old son Quinn without parents. Doing what was right Sierra and Rome took on the responsibility to raise Quinn, along with their two children five year old Little Supreme, and their two year old daughter Lisa. The lost time Rome spoke to his grandmother Nancy was a year ago. After Nancy had all that died cremated. She told everyone that she was taking all the ashes to Jamaica. So she could spread the ashes on a nice beach. Nancy had also told Rome she would call him when she came back home from Jamaica. In the meantime she told him not to call her because she wanted to be left alone. Yet that was a whole year ago, she didn't called him, and to his knowledge she still haven't come back from Jamaica. Being that his grandmother had lost not only her husband, but all three of her children. Rome decided to obey his grandmother wish and give her some space.

Standing up Rome took the tape out the V.C.R and put the tape back inside the wall unit. Being that Rome was now the oldest Gibbs in the drug game. He now had control of the Gibbs drug contract with Gail. Yet the way he was handling the Gibbs drug operation. He knew the Gibbs drug team wasn't happy with the way he was running things. Khia was running her drug contract out of his grandmother store. The only money he was seeing from that spot was the rest Khia was paying him for renting the store. The Gibbs Soundview project spot had been taking over by Tonya. It was now the Jones drug spot. The Gibbs Webster projects spot had also been taking over by Tonya. It to was now the Jones drug spot. Both of those spots he wasn't seeing any money from. Owning the Bank's hotel and the strip club Love it or Hate it. Rome started selling his drugs out of these two spots. Something that Solo and Supreme would have a fit over If they were alive. No way in the world they ever sell drugs out a legal business that was owned by the Gibbs family. Rome knew he had to get a drug spot and stop selling drugs out his hotel and strip club.

Pulling out his cell phone Rome took a deep breath. It was time he started running the Gibbs drug operation like a true Gibbs. Solo and Supreme once told him, "A good businessman is hated by more people then who loves him. And sometimes a good businessman have to make a deal with the devil himself." In Rome case he knew it was time to make a deal with the devil herself and send the devil seed on her way. Calling Gail, Rome asked her to contact Tonya and Khia to set up a meeting at Love it or Hate it in two hours. Hanging up with Gail, Rome called Tank the strip club bartender, and told him to shut down the strip club. Hanging up with Tank, Rome called everyone on the Gibbs drug team. He told them all, to come to the strip club tomorrow at 9 a.m. for a meeting, and make sure that they are suited up and guns loaded." Grabbing his car keys Rome headed over to the strip club.

*****

"I don't think you having a meeting with Rome is a good idea grandma" Nicole said.

"I agree Tonya, at lease let the whole Jones team go with you to this meeting" Goody added in.

"I will be fine going to this meeting by myself."

"How do you know this is out a set up for him to murder you Tonya?"

"Goody only a fool would contact Gail to set a person up to be murdered. I'm sure Rome know that. Believe me If I don't make it back to this hotel sweet tonight a live. Gail will have Rome murdered first thing tomorrow morning. For putting her in the middle of a set up to have someone murdered. Gail made that clear to me and she made that clear to Rome before she called me. What Gail don't know, and what I don't know, is why Rome want to meet with me. Now like I said I'm off to go handle this meeting with Rome. In the meantime. I want you two to get the whole Jones team together for a meeting in two hours. Also get Desean over here for our meeting as well." Grabbing her car keys Tonya walked out the hotel sweet.

*****

After getting a phone call from Gail, telling her that she had to go to Love it or Hate it to have a meeting with Rome. Khia picked up the phone and called Rome. Getting no answer Khia called again and still got no answer. To Khia it made no sense to her that Gail called her instead of Rome himself. There was no beef believe the two of them for him to have to go through Gail to have a meeting with her. Not only was it strange that Rome asked Gail to call her. It was even stranger that now Rome wasn't answering her phone calls. Placing her cell phone back in her pocket. It was clear the only way Khia was going to find out what was going on. Was for her to go meet up with Rome at Love it or Hate it. Grabbing her car keys Khia walked out the store back office.

"Tymel, Erykah, you two hold down the store. I have to go have a meeting with Rome."

"A meeting, is everything all right Ma" Tymel asked.

"To be honest with you I don't know. All I can tell you is I should be back in an hour." Giving both of her children a kiss on the cheek. Khia walked out of the store and got in her car.

*****

Going back and forth trying to play the other. Brandy and Desean both decided to hang up their game cards and decided to get together. At least that's what they said to the other. Yet truth be told they were still using their game cards on each other just in a different way. Not only was Brandy making a lot of money as a stripper in Love it or Hate it. She was also ranking in a load of money from Desean. Not only was Desean lining her pockets because they were in somewhat of a relationship. He was also paying her to run drugs out her apartment in Webster projects.

In Desean eyes he was a boss that have always known how to talk the talk and make money. In no way did Desean see Brandy as his girlfriend. To him Brandy was ugly, all she had was a phat nice ass that he loved to fuck. If giving her a few dollars to fuck her in her asshole, made her feel that they are in a relationship. So be it Desean felt. Long as Brandy continued to let him run drugs out her apartment and let him fuck her in her asshole. Desean didn't care who Brandy told that him and her are in a relationship. He would play along as he was making money. He was making 15,000 dollars a week running drugs out of Brandy apartment. Giving Brandy a thousand dollars a week was in no way hurting his pockets. Being the only man still standing from the blood gang Red-Money. Desean recruited four young blood guys, Buddha, Trouble, Demon, Tracy, to join the Red-Money crew was all sent to prison. Leaving Smoke as the only Red-Money member free on the streets. All four of the new members Desean recruited were eighteen years old. Desean liked all four of them, yet Trouble reminded him of his self when he was eighteen. Which made Desean make Trouble the second man in charge of the Red-Money set. Being the big homie of the Red-Money set Desean called all the shots.

A whole year together and getting fucked in her asshole every day. Brandy no longer felt pain when Desean wanted to have anal sex with her. When she first agreed to deal with Desean on the regular. She didn't know how she was going to deal with him always wanting to have anal sex. Especially with him having a 13 inch penis. Yet her working in a strip club around nothing but women that danced and fucked for a living she was taught a trick to talking big dicks. A bottle sat on Brandy nightstand. Inside that bottle was lubrication mixed with baby oral gal. The lubrication made the dick slip in and the baby oral gal made the inside of her asshole go completely numb. Every time Desean wanted some ass. Brandy gave herself a quick squirt up the asshole of her special lub mix and placed her ass up in the air. To Desean, he liked a female face down, ass up, and shit on his dick. To Brandy If she was going to deal with him. She liked it face down, ass up, butty hole numb before he stuck it in.

Inside Brandy bedroom Desean had a tight grip on her waist as he drilled his penis in and out of her asshole doggy style. "Yeah bitch, take this big dick" Desean yelled.

Letting go of Brandy waist not missing a mump, Desean slapped Brandy on both of her ass cheeks. Grabbing her by the waist once again Desean pumped in and out of her even harder. So hard that Brandy could feel Desean balls slapping up against her pussy. "Shit bitch, shit on my dick bitch" Desean yelled.

Going in deep as he could go inside of her Desean let loose busting his nut inside her asshole. "Fuck" Desean moaned feeling his nut sack going empty.

Coming out the bathroom Desean walked into the kitchen. Seeing his four home boys sitting at the table Desean gave them a head nod. Walking up behind Brandy Desean slapped her on her ass as she was cooking on the stove.

"I gotta step out for a few hours. Make sure you have that ass ready for round two when I get back."

"It's always ready big Daddy. Where you going?"

"I have to get a re-up from my connect. I also have to have some type of meeting with my connect. Trouble you in charge while I'm gone."

Walking Desean to the door Trouble walked back into the kitchen. Pushing Brandy out the way he cut the stove off.

"Bitch stop acting like your ass is deaf. You heard big homie say I'm in charge, and you know damn well what go down when I'm in charge. So take your ass to the back room, get out those clothes, so I can tear that pussy up bitch."

Hearing Trouble words made Brandy pussy get wet immediately. Moving fast pass Trouble, Brandy ran to her bedroom. Turning around Trouble looked at Buddha, Demon, and Tracy who was still sitting down at the table.

"Keep the drugs flowing out and keep the money flowing in while I go get this nut out of me" Trouble said walking out the kitchen.

Hearing the door close to Brandy bedroom. Tracy, Demon, and Buddha, all looked at each other. Although they were all shaking their heads at the whole scene. It wasn't a secret to the three of them that Trouble was having sex with Brandy behind Desean back for the past seven months.

"Trouble know damn well that's foul to be fucking that bitch" Tracy said.

"You sound made stupid, Trouble ain't foul. Brandy is a bonafide whore and should be treated as such" Demon said.

"True that Bro, she may have a phat ass, I just can't see myself fucking that ugly bitch" Buddha added in.

"That bitch is beyond ugly" they all said laughing.

*****

Stepping out of Brandy building Desean felt his cell phone vibrating on his hip. Looking at his cell phone Desean blood pressure went up immediately. It was a number that had been calling him almost every day, since Smoke and the other Red-Money crew members were all murdered. He knew the number and who was calling him from the first day he got the call. From then on, every time he saw the number, he refused to answer the call. Desean thought he made his self-clear to the caller the first time he got the call. Clearly the caller wasn't getting the message. Pressing talk on his cell phone Desean put the cell phone to his ear.

"You have a collect call from an inmate…. BaBa….In Clinton correctional facility. Press one to accept, two to decline the call."

"What BaBa" Desean asked pressing one.

"What BaBa" BaBa repeated annoyed. "Nigga, I been calling you every day for months and you haven't been answering the phone."

"That's because I been busy BaBa."

"Busy my ass, you been busy avoiding my phone calls. Smoke played the same games that you're playing now Desean. Me, Leevon, Just, and Dutch have been starving in this shit whole for years. Smoke refused to do the right thing by us. Your now running the Red-Money blood set, and you feel that you don't have to do right by us either. Nigga you better know we ain't gonna be in this mother fucker forever. So If you know like I know you would want to start doing right by us. Otherwise when we get the fuck out. You and those new niggas you put under the Red-Money gonna have a beef that you can't win."

"Is that a threat BaBa?"

"Threat, nigga I don't make threats, I speak the truth. So like I said, you and them niggas under Red-Money better start putting money on our books."

"BaBa do you know dial?"

"Dial" BaBa repeated confused.

"Yeah nigga, dial tone" Desean yelled hanging up his cell phone. "I wish the fuck I would put money on their books. I never grind in the streets with any of them niggas before. Them niggas are Smoke peoples, Smoke problem, Smoke is dead, and them niggas are not my problem" Desean said out loud placing his cell phone back on his hip.

Chapter 25

Walking in Love it or Hate it, Tonya spotted Rome sitting at a table by his self. Taking a seat at the table across from Rome, Tonya crossed her legs, and looked at Rome with an evil smirk on her face. Looking back at Tonya, Rome could see the evil glowing off her skin.

"Shall we get this meeting started or are we just going to look at each other?"

"Tonya this meeting will start when the third party of this meeting get here."

"I see, Gail didn't tell me I would be meeting with two people."

"Tonya that's because the only person you need to listen to is me."

"Well since I have to wait can I at lease get a drink?"

Before Rome could answer Tonya, Tank placed a glass in front of Tonya. Looking down at the glass Tonya looked up at Tank and smiled. "I see you remembered I like a Vodka on the rocks." Not responding to Tonya Tank walked back behind the bar. Taking a sip Tonya placed the glass back on the table. "That Tank have never been a man of words when it comes to me. I guess I'm to much women for him."

"That's what you think Tonya? Did you ever think your just not Tank type?"

"Type" Tonya repeated with a laugh. "Rome when it comes to a type. I'm every straight man type. I'm like a fine bottle of wine. I keep getting better looking with age. So when are me and you going to do the nasty?"

"Never! I'm married and you're not my type."

"Rome I've had sex with your grandfather Joe. I even had sex with your father Supreme. I mean your stepfather Supreme. And let me tell you the sex get better down the Gibbs generation line. Sex with Joe was good. Sex with Supreme was great. I'm more than sure sex with you would be excellent. Rome let me give you some advice. Never say never, especially to me because I always get what I want."

"Tonya, I would never touch you."

"Rome, you will never touching me, you can take that statement to the bank and cash that check. Because I don't like for a man to touch me that's why I always tie my sex partners up. I find it more enjoyable to me that way."

Seeing Khia walk into Love it or Hate it, Tonya looked at her in disgust. Being that the feeling was mutual Khia gave Tonya the same look of disgust. Taking a seat at the table Khia gave Rome a evil look.

"I'm glad you could join me Khia."

"Rome what the hell is going on?"

"Well now that you both here, I can explain why I asked you both to meet with me. Three names in the Bronx rang bells, the Gibbs, the Sams, and the Jones. It's enough money in the Bronx for all of us to eat without stepping on each other toes. Tonya, I called you here to set things straight. Soundview projects have always belong to the Gibbs family, not to you. Webster projects was a trial run for the Gibbs family. You can have Webster projects. As for Soundview projects vacate it within the hour, or my team will kill every one of your people that are in Soundview projects."

"Rome to be honest with you running both projects is becoming to be a pain in my ass. I can agree to vacate Soundview and just run Webster projects. But know If your team come to Webster projects. My team will not hesitate to put them in the ground with the rest of your family."

"Tonya don't think for a minute that I don't think you had something to do with Jay, Solo, Beverly, Trina, and Supreme deaths. I can't prove it, but when I do. You will be going in the ground next to your family. Far as I'm concern my meeting with you is over."

Rome turned his attention over to Khia. "Khia, I called you here to tell you, you need to find another drug spot. As of today your team selling out my grandfather store is over."

"Rome, Solo agreed that I…."

"Khia your agreement with Solo has nothing to do with me. I run the Gibbs drug operation now. I subject you knock Mike down off his throne and take over Courtlandt projects. Your Mike supplier, yet he's running a whole projects like he has a drug contract. I know your team is small Khia. With that said If you need help taking over Courtlandt projects from Mike. The Gibbs family will be more than willing to help the Sams family take those projects from Mike. Call me If you need our help Khia."

"Call you Rome, huh? I been calling you all day and you were not answering my phone calls."

"Khia that's only because I wanted you to just come to the meeting. Me not answering your calls was just a one hour thing today. If you need my team help, I'm here for you."

"Thanks for the offer Rome, but I know how to take shit over without needing help from another drug family. I didn't get the Sams drug contract from being stupid. Ain't that right mother" Khia asked looking over at Tonya.

"Khia, I will admit you are far from stupid. I guess that has something to do with all I have taught you. You crossed me once, and I put your ass in the hospital. Then you had the nerve to cross me again and steal the Sams drug contract from me. As you can see, I still was able to get another drug contract with Gail. So you didn't stop shit when it comes to me. Yet do keep in mind you crossed me for a second time, and it will not go unpunished. I just haven't made up my mind to what I want to do to you this time. Clearly me banging your damn head against the ground didn't teach you not to cross your mother." Standing up Tonya walked out the strip club.

"Khia…."

"Rome, I've heard enough for one day. Business is business and I understand. Your grandfather store will be vacated today as you wish. As for your help I don't need it. Mike and his team I can handle with my eyes closed and one hand behind my back."

"Khia, the Gibbs family is also willing to help you If you need us to help you with the Jones family."

"Rome, my mother hate is not just towards me, it's towards your family as well. Just because my mother didn't show her hate towards you don't mean it's not there. My advice to you Rome is don't sleep on my mother. She know more tricks then Whodenee himself." Picking up her purse Khia walked out the strip club.

*****

Taking a deep breath Tonya closed the door behind her. Taking off her stiletto heels Tonya let her feet sank into the soft carpet of her hotel sweet. Walking into the living room sweet the whole Jones drug team was sitting waiting for her. Nicole, Mellow, China, Cam, Henry, and Goody, all looked up at Tonya. Yet Tonya eyes were focus on Desean who was sitting in the corner.

"Desean I'm so glad that you could make it to this meeting" Tonya said walking over to Desean. "I wanted you here at this meeting to let you know the business deal me and you have. Is no longer valid. From this day on I'm not your drug supplier. You and your teamwork for me and yawl are a part of the Jones drug family."

"Tonya I'm gonna have to decline your new business deal. I work for me, not for others."

"Oh I'm sorry Desean. I don't want you to think that I'm giving you that choice. So let me make myself clear. You have two choices. Either you are a part of the Jones drug family. Or you and your team can clear out of Webster projects, and you no longer have a drug connect."

"There are my two choice? It sound more like your forcing me…."

"Let me stop you there Desean. You may see it as your being force. I see it as offering you a better opportunity to make more money then you are making now. You can still run your team and give orders to your team Red-Money. You can still sell drugs out the apartment you are selling out of. The only thing that changes is now you take orders from me. If the Jones family got beef, your crew has beef, and If your crew got beef, then so does the Jones family. Are we clear Desean?"

"Crystal clear Tonya" Desean said threw his teeth.

"Tonya could tell Desean wasn't happy at all, nor did she care. "I'm glad were on the same page Desean." Walking away from Desean, Tonya open the hallway closet, and pulled out four duffle bags of crack cocaine. Dropping all four bags at Desean feet Tonya looked at him. "Your uses to a half of a duffle bag. Which gave you a money cut of 15,000 dollars a week. Four full bags will now give you a money cut of 120,000 dollars a week. Desean know that there is a war coming to the Jones drug family very soon. When I don't know, but I'm more then sure it's coming. So make sure that you and your team know that your down with the Jones drug family." Turning around Tonya looked over at Cam and Mellow. "You two will be making the drop offs to Desean spot, and picking up my cut from Desean. In the meantime help Desean to his car with those bags."

With Desean, Cam, and Mellow out the hotel sweet. Taking a seat Tonya closed her eyes and leaned her head all the way back on the chair. She now had a total of eleven members on her team. Twelve including herself. The deal that Rome and she agreed on was a sweet deal. A deal to her that sounded too sweet. If there's a hidden agenda behind the agreement they made earlier. Tonya wanted to be more than ready for the war going up against the Gibbs family. With Solo and Supreme being dead she knew the Gibbs drug family was weak. Rome may have been taught by two of the best in the drug game. Yet Tonya saw herself as a veteran of the drug game. Going up against the Gibbs family again. This time she wanted to make sure she didn't leave any of the Gibbs drug members alive. Her crew was now even stronger, and now all she had to do was wait for Rome to make his next move.

Opening her eyes Tonya notice all eyes in the living room sweet was on her. Cam, and Mellow was even back in the living room looking at her. Standing up Tonya placed her heels on her feet.

Nicole, China, get to work cooking that new work I got from Gail. Henry, Goody, get a move on it and go over to our private spot in Webster projects. Cam, Mellow, when Nicole and China finish cooking. I want you two to cut and bag up. Make sure you two are ready just in case our spot or Desean spot need a re-up."

Seeing Tonya walking to the door of the hotel sweet Goody called out to her. "Where are you off to Tonya?"

"Goody, I have to go buy myself a wild card for the war that will soon be coming our way."

"Tonya If you're so sure that Rome is not gonna stick to the deal that you two agreed on. Why wait? Why don't we just ambush the Gibbs team at their club or at their spot in Soundview projects?"

"Because Goody If Rome is running game on me. We would be walking into a ambush trying to hit them in their spots. So I have no other choice but to wait until Rome make his move. In the meantime I will prepare for the war by putting a strong team together. When he make his move when I make my move back against him. He will be confused not knowing who is against him or how many he's up against. Now If you done with all your questions, I have some where to go."

*****

Inside Courtlandt Projects hallway, Khia, Tymel, and Erykah, stood in front of Mike drug spot apartment door.

"Ma are you sure this is a good idea" Erykah asked a little bit unsure on the move they were about to make.

"Erykah, you been in the drug game for a short while. In that time you haven't really seen a takeover. Just follow my lead, don't show fear, keep a stone face, watch my back. If someone inside this apartment pull a gun or reach for one. Put a bullet in their head. Are we clear Erykah?"

"Yeah" Erykah said taking a deep breath.

Looking over at Tymel, Khia notice that he was calm. "I'm more then sure I don't need to tell you Tymel to follow my lead. My mother raised you. So I'm more then sure you know how a takeover goes down."

"I'm ready Ma, I got your back, let's do this."

Knocking on the door Khia mind flashed back to when she was younger. She remembered when her father Carlos sent her mother Tonya to take over a spot when she was ten years old.

With the scene in her mind of how her mother did it, Erykah and Tymel following her. Mike lead the way through the apartment to the living room. In the living room sat Mike crew, Terry, Joey, and Codie. Taking the duffle bag off her shoulder. Khia through it at Mike feet. Following suit Tymel through the two duffle bags that was on his shoulder at Mike feet as well. Taking the duffle bag off her shoulder Erykah through her duffle bag at Mike feet as well.

"Mike your uses to a bag of work. As you can see, we brought you four bags. Mike it's been a change in plans when it comes to the deal me and you have."

"How so Khia?"

"Well for one your no longer running Courtlandt projects anymore, I do. I'm no longer your supplier, you and your teamwork for me now. This spot is no longer owned by you, it's owned by the Sams drug family."

"Bitch If you don't get your stupid ass out of this spot talking that stupid shit. I'll put a fucking bullet in your head" Joey yelled jumping up to his feet pulling out his gun.

"POP!"

Just as fast as Joey got on his feet, his body fell back on the couch. The bullet to his forehead from Erykah gun killed him instantly. Although Tymel and Khia was shoch they didn't let it be seen on their face. Codie and terry on the other hand stood frozen in shock staring at Joey lifeless body.

"Khia this shit is unnecessary coming up in here killing people" Mike said with his voice shaking in fear not knowing what was going to happen next. "Khia, I been running this spot for years. You know I don't work for anybody but myself."

"Mike that all sound good but that all ends today. This is my spot now, you and your teamwork for me now. If you don't like this new deal. You and the rest of your team can join you boy Joey on the other side. So what's your choice?"

"This shit ain't right and you know that Khia."

Looking over at Erykah, Khia spoke in a raw tone. "Erykah maybe you should help Mike understand the words that just came out my mouth."

Pulling out her gun again Erykah pointing her gun at Mike head. "Wait! Fine Khia will take your new deal."

"Wonderful Mike, now let's get down to business. Erykah is now the cook of the weight. Tymel will get the weight from Erykah and run it to this spot. Mike, you have the morning shift. Terry, Codie, you two have the night shift. The afternoon will be run by Tymel. In the meantime, Terry, Codie, Mike, you three get Joey body and get rid of it."

Picking Joey body up. Mike, Terry, and Codie, took Joey body to the back of the projects and left it in the grass. Walking back in the building the three of them waited for the elevator. Mike could feel Terry and Codie eyes on him. He was trying his best not to look over at them.

"Tell me you have a plan to stop this crazy bitch from taking over our spot Mike" Codie asked.

"Codie right now there's nothing we can do. We just lost one of our members. On top of that Khia is the person that was supplying me with drugs. If we kill her, we lose. If we walk away and get a new spot, we don't have a drug supplier, we lose."

"So you saying we fucked all around the board and we have to deal with this crazy bitch" Terry asked.

"In the meantime, yes. Terry until we can find a team we can roll on and take over their spot, money, and drugs. Yes, we have to deal with her."

*****

Getting off the elevator Brandy went straight to her mailbox. Opening the mailbox Brandy pulled out a stack of bills and an envelope addressed to her from Clinton correctional facility. There was no need to look at the inmate name on the envelope. Because she already knew who the letter was from. For over eight years Ba-Ba had been sending her a letter once a week. Yet not once had she ever wrote him back. Although she never wrote him back, she always read his letters. Taking a seat on the stairs in the lobby. Brandy open Ba-Ba letter and began reading it:

"Dear: Brandy

You already know who I be so no need to state my name. Shorty I'm beyond surprised at how you left me in prison for dead all these years. You got a lot of answering to do when I come home. Me and you were high school sweethearts. For years I kept your pockets lined with that green, up until the time I got sent up north to do a bid. Them crackers gave me a sentence of ten years, good time out in eight in a half years. You act like gave me life and forget all about me. I'm most deafly gonna put my foot in your ass when I came home. You forgot about me and started fucking my little brother Smoke. Smoke get murdered and now you fucking this dude name Desean. You better let that nigga Desean know what he's up against. Me and my brother Leevon started the Red-Money blood set. We left Smoke to hold down the set until we get out. Now where the fuck this nigga Desean come from, I don't know and don't care. Smoke may have put him down on the team before he died, and Desean is the only one left out that set. But that nigga better know he's a second and third generation of Red-Money. Yet the first generation of Red-Money is all a live and in prison doing time. We all got the same time up north and we all get out the same time. We got eight years in and some change. Me and the boys will be out very soon. And when we come home, we coming back to run Red-Money. As for you I'm not even that mad at you, because I know I left you out there with nothing. Which mean you have to do you to be straight. Just know who your real man is. Because when I come home your mine bitch.

Love always

Your Husband Ba-Ba

Walking in Brandy building Tonya watched as Brandy read a letter sitting on the steps. Looking at the envelope in Brandy left hand. Tonya notice the envelope had a prison address on it.

"Hey Brandy, I hope I'm not interrupting your letter reading" Tonya said walking up to Brandy.

"Not at all" Brandy said balling up the letter and envelope. Throwing it across the lobby Brandy stood up from the steps. "Hey Tonya, what you doing in the neighborhood?"

"Well I came by to see you Brandy."

"Me, see me for what?"

"Well to me you seem like a smart young lady. A lady that like to make a lot of money. I need a female such as yourself on my team. Something like a silent partner."

Far from stupid Brandy backed up and looked at Tonya for a few seconds. "Tonya in other words what you trying to say is that you want me down with your team, but you don't want anyone to know I'm down with your team."

"Exactly Brandy, not even those that are in my team."

"How much money are we talking about Tonya?"

"Brandy it's kind of hard to put a number on this business deal. It's more like the price is up to you to charge me."

Hearing Tonya last comment Brandy sat back down on the stairs. "You telling me I have to through a number out at you? This job that you want me for has to be real deep Tonya. What exactly do you need me to do?"

"I need you to become one hell of a actress."

"Actress" Brandy repeated confused.

"Yes, Brandy an actress. A good actress, study the roll, look the part, sound like the character and become the character. If you're willing to do all of that. I'm willing to pay the cost of everything and I'm willing to pay your fee."

Taking the big yellow envelope from under her arm. Tonya pass the envelope over to Brandy.

"Everything you need to know, and study is in that envelope. If you down with everything give me a call in a week or two. Because we need to get things started as soon as possible. Just to let you know this is not a game. Let me through a number out at you Brandy. I'm willing to pay you 500,000 dollars." Brandy eyes open wide in shock. "If you not down no hard feelings. Either way this is our little secret. Just call me when you make your decision Brandy."

Turning on her heels Tonya walked out the building. Not sure what was inside the envelope. Brandy stuffed the envelope down her pants. Getting on the elevator Brandy took the elevator up to the last floor in the building. Getting off the elevator Brandy walked out onto the roof of her building. Pulling out the envelope she began reading threw the papers that was in the envelope. The more she read the more shock she became. It was almost like she couldn't believe what she was reading, and what Tonya was asking her to do. After reading everything Brandy placed all the papers back inside the envelope. Looking up at the sky she wondered what her mother would say or do in a situation like this.

Chapter 26

Inside the police station officers and detectives stop what they were doing when they saw the district attorney walk into the police station. It was no secret when the district attorney graced the police station with his presents. He wasn't there to bring them all milk and cookies. When he showed his face it was to rip into their Captain. Walking pass everyone without a word. Jack walked into Captain Morris office and slammed the door closed. Yelling at the top of his lungs. His words were muffled and no one outside the office could understand what Jack was yelling about. Five minutes later Jack made his exit out Captain Morris office and out the police station. Seeing the Captain door open again all in the station began to act as If they were busy.

"Lopez, Price, in my office now" Morris yelled.

"Captain you wanted to see us" Detective Price asked with Lopez by his side.

"Both of you close the door and have a seat. Let me first say to you both. I don't enjoy getting my ass chewed out from a D.A. Especially about a year old case that I thought was closed and handled by you two my best two detectives."

"What case would that be Captain" Lopez asked.

"The Albert Simmons murder! Can you two explain to me. How an easy case such as that one end up without someone going to prison?"

"Well…."

"Shut up Price! A video tape of the murder was mailed to our police station. A video tape that was clear as day to who was murdered, who did it, and who was there when it happen. How did that video tape go missing!"

"Captain with all due respect me and Price did our job. We both hand delivered that video tape to the district attorney our self. Now what happen to that video tape once it was in the district attorney hands. Is not our problem, it's his."

"You think I don't know that Lopez!"

"Captain If you know then why are you mad at us?"

"Because I just got my ass chewed out! Not only did that video tape go missing. Even If that video tape pop up. Double jeopardy has attached to this case. Which mean the defendants that have been charged in this murder can no longer be charged.

"Once again Captain I don't understand why you are mad with us when we did our job as the detectives on that case."

"I'll tell you Lopez why I'm mad! Because Mr. Jack Murry strongly believe that you two played a part in fucking up his case. Going over his records he saw that detective Lopez and detective Price, paid his office a visit signing his office logbook the day before his case went to trail. He believes your visit to his office was to tamper with the video tape of Albert Simmons murder of course I told him that's ridiculous for him to think such a thing. Now of course I backed you two up against Jack. But I really would like to know why did you two go to his office the day before that case went to trail?"

"Captain I don't…."

"Captain we went up to Jack office that day to see If he needed me and Lopez to testify at the trail."

Detective Lopez looked over at Price confused. He remembered that case, he also remembered that him and Price never went up to Jack office together the day before that trail. Clearly something was up, and it was clear to him that Price was trying to cover up something.

"Captain we would have gave Jack a call like we normally do. But we were in his area and stopped in his office to ask him in person. Jack wasn't there so me and Lopez asked his desk clerk."

Satisfied with the reason Price gave him. Captain Morris told them to get out his office and get back to work. As Lopez and Price sat back down at their desk. Lopez kept his eyes glued on Price. "Price, I want to know what that was all about in the Captain office?"

"Lopez, I don't know, but I'm getting sick and tired of Morris trying to get into our ass. When the D.A come down here and get into his ass."

"I'm sick of that as well Price. But that's not what I'm talking about. Do you care to explain to me why you lied to the Captain, about me and you going to the D.A office the day before that trail?"

"It wasn't a lie Lopez. I did go up there to…."

"You went up there, okay so explain how my name got signed into that logbook at the D.A office that day?"

"Lopez, we sign each other names all the time when were on a case."

"Right Price, when were on a case. Not when we are not together."

"Lopez, I'm so use to signing both of our names, it was a slip of the pen. Now I'm gonna step out and go get something to eat. You want me to pick you up something too?"

"No, I'm fine Price standing up Price walked out of the police station.

Sitting down at his desk Lopez thinking to his self. The number one rule in law enforcement is protect your partners back. Him and Price had been partners for the past ten years. With Price having twenty years on the police force, and Lopez having twenty three years on the force. With two more years to go before Lopez could retire. In no way was he going to let anyone take his retirement check from him. For the past three years Lopez had been feeling that Price has been into something illegal. That something he was sure had something to do with that Gibbs family. Although the number one rule was protect your partner. Lopez also knew the number one rule to retiring is protect your own ass. With all the years Lopez had on the police force. He knew in the illegal business sometimes you can have a good run. Yet a long or short run, it all ended the same way, with someone going down hard. In no way did he want to go down. Standing up Lopez walked into Captain Morris office and closed the door.

"How can I help you detective Lopez" Morris asked looking up from the paperwork on his desk.

"Captain, I need to tell you something about detective Price."

*****

Looking around Clinton prison yard, Bab-Ba spotted his brother Leevon, and his two boys Nest and Dutch sitting at a table. Walking up to the table Ba-Ba gave them each a pound with his fist. Taking a seat at the table with them all three guys eyes seem to be on him. Ba-Ba knew they wanted to know what moves they were gonna have to make when they all got release. Not wanting to string them along any longer. Ba-Ba got straight down to business.

"Listen fellas I been writing Brandy a letter every week since we been on lock. Truth be told she haven't wrote me back yet. I'm not gonna give up on Brandy. Yet that bitch has a lot to answer to when we all touch the town. As for this nigga Desean that's running around with our Red-Money blood set name. I been calling that nigga every day since Smoke died. Two times I spoke to him. The week Smoke was murdered and once last week. Both times that nigga blew me off like I'm a no body."

"So what's the plan when we get out Ba-Ba" Leevon asked.

"The plan is clear Leevon. When we get out were gonna step to Desean."

"Do you think this Desean guy is gonna step down from running Red-Money" Dutch asked.

"Dutch I'm not thinking shit, I don't care, that's what's gonna happen. Either he step down, let me and Leevon run Red-Money, with everyone taking orders from us. Or he can go in the ground and the niggas he put down on the Red-Money team can follow him in the ground."

"Ba-Ba this situation sound like we will be going to war when we get out" Nest sated.

"Nest, If a war is what Desean want then a war is what he will get."

*****

Coming out the bathroom in Tone house, Lloyd walked into the living room and saw that Tone was asleep in his recliner chair. Looking at the coffee table in front of Tone. Lloyd noticed that Tone wallet was on the table. Looking around the living room nervously Lloyd picked up the wallet. Taking two hundred dollars out the wallet. Lloyd placed the wallet back on the table. Placing the money in his pocket Lloyd made his way over to the house door fast. Sweet poured from his forehead as he got in his car. Although he felt bad for stealing from one of his drug family members. He was out of money and he needed money bad.

Hearing his cell phone ranging woke Tone up. "Talk to me" Tone said placing his phone to his ear.

"Where the hell are you and Lloyd, did yawl forget that we are having a meeting today" Rome said yelling threw the phone.

"Were on our way now" Tone said hanging up on Rome. Standing up Tone placed his wallet in his pocket. Calling out Lloyd name a few times Tone realize Lloyd wasn't anywhere in his house. Looking out his living room window Tone notice Lloyd car was gone as well. Annoyed that Lloyd left without waking him up. Tone pulled out his keys, locked his house up, jumped in his car and hit the road. Ten minutes into his drive he noticed that he was low on gas. Pulling into a gas station Tone pulled out his wallet. Looking in his wallet his wallet was totally empty of money.

"What the hell" Tone said out loud checking his pockets. Confused about what happen to the two hundred dollars he placed in his wallet earlier in the day. Tone jumped back into his car and pulled off even more pissed off. This was the fifth time this month he somehow lost money out his wallet.

*****

One by one, Tone, Pit, Sierra, Jo-Jo, and Tameka all walked into Love it or Hate it. Stopping at the bar they all got a drink from Tank and sat down at the table with Rome. Taking one last sip of his drink Rome stood up.

"I'm more then sure you all wondering why I wanted you all here this early in the morning. Well wonder no more let's get this meeting started. We got hit hard when Solo, Supreme, and Beverly died. This past year the Gibbs drug operation has been running reckless. As of today the Gibbs family will start running our drug operation like we been doing. I gave Khia the boot out my grandfather store. I gave Tonya the boot out of Soundview projects. I asked you all to suit up with your bullet proof vest and have your guns on you for today."

As Rome spoke Tone and Pit looked at each other then looked at Rome. "Are you telling us that you had a meeting with Tonya" Tone asked.

"Yeah, I met with her and Khia yesterday."

Standing up Jo-Jo walked over to Rome. Nigga are you stupid! Why the fuck would you have a meeting with Tonya without your team? What If she brought her team with her and they murdered you Rome?"

"I thought about all of that Jo-Jo. That's why I went through Gail to set up the meeting with Tonya. When a meeting is set up with Gail name in it. If blood is shed Gail will shed their blood. Now back to what I was saying. I asked yawl to suit up and make sure you have your gun. The reason is because If Tonya renege on the agreement me and her made. Were gonna kill everyone she got in our Soundview drug spot."

"Now that's what the fuck I'm talking about" Pit and Tone yelled jumping up to their feet. Rome pushed them both back down in their chair.

"Take it easy I'm not done yet. This is the set up so listen good. Our Soundview spot will be run by Tone, with Lloyd help."

Looking around Rome notice that Lloyd wasn't even sitting in on the meeting. Rome had been so into getting the meeting started that he didn't notice Lloyd not being in the meeting.

"Where the hell is Lloyd at Tone?"

"The hell If I know!"

"Tone when I spoke to you earlier. You told me that you and Lloyd was on your way to the meeting. Which mean yawl were together."

"I thought we were Rome until I realize he left my house while I was sleep."

"Well make sure you fill Lloyd in on everything I say in this meeting Tone."

"Will do."

"Good, now back to what I was saying. Our store drug spot will be run by Pit, with…."

"Let me stop you there Rome. I can run the store with the help of my Pitbull dogs."

"Pit this is serious…."

"Rome believe it or not Pit is serious, Pit got his dogs trained. He used to have then dogs of his selling drugs out the Soundview apartment to the fiends" Tone said laughing.

"Cool Pit, If you think you can run the store with the help of your Pits, do you. In the meantime Sierra will run the Banks hotel. I will run Love it or Hate it. We have a out of town crew called, Legends. The Gibbs family have been the drug suppliers of Legends for the past year. Thanks to Tameka putting that deal together for our drug team. They come to New York and Tameka make the drug drop to them."

"Where are they from? What are their names? Have you met them Rome" Pit asked.

"No I haven't met them. Tameka handles their meet and greet. Their names are Lucky and Neal. There from Baltimore…."

"Tell me you joking Rome! Baltimore niggas! Baltimore niggas and New York niggas don't get alone!"

"Pit calm down…."

"Calm down my ass Rome! Did you forget what happen to your uncle Gutta? Niggas from Baltimore murdered Gutta!"

"Pit, I remember all of that, how could I forget? That's why I have them coming to New York and Tameka not going down to Baltimore."

"Rome it's not about where they pick up at. It's about Baltimore niggas can't be trusted."

"Tone, Tameka has told me that she has known these guys since she was a child. Yes, I haven't met them, but I trust Tameka to make the right choices. If she feel these guys are on the up and up. Then I'm good with the deal. At the end of the day Tameka is the only one dealing with these guys. Which mean If shit go wrong, Tameka will be the only one with her head on the chopping block."

"Okay that's cool, but I still feel that we should see what these guys look like Rome" Pit said.

"In time that will come Pit, but in the meantime, Tameka will handle the deal with these Baltimore guys."

"In other news as we all know Jo-Jo dirt house was taking down in that explosion. It's been a year since that explosion. The soundproof basement survive that explosion. As for the rest of that house a lot of work had to be done to repair it. Thanks to Jo-Jo, his dirt house has been fully repaired. Which mean will start staring our drugs there once again. Jo-Jo is still our runner. So Pit, Tone, when you need a re-up call Jo-Jo. At this point in time we have a total of seven members of the Gibbs drug family. I don't think I need to tell you that we need some new members to join our drug family. Seven members is the lowest members we have ever had in our drug family. Although we are strong, we need to be even stronger. You never know If we have to go to war with another drug team. So If you know anyone that you believe can be trusted. Let's get them on our team."

Wrapping up the Gibbs drug meeting, Rome gave Tameka two duffle bags of raw cocaine, and sent her to meet up with the Baltimore guys. Giving Pit two duffle bags of crack cocaine. Rome sent him to his grandfather store so that he could set up shop. Sierra on the other hand went to go pick up the kids from school, so she could head over to the Bank's hotel. As for Tone and Jo-Jo, Rome told them to get in the car so the three of them could head over to Soundview projects.

*****

Not having to go to work Rihanna laid on her couch with her remote control in her hand. Channel after channel Rihanna changed trying to find something to watch on T.V. Hearing her doorbell Rihanna got up. Looking out the peep hole in her door. Rihanna was shocked to see that it was Lloyd on her doorstep. Opening the door Rihanna looked at Lloyd with a annoyed look on her face. She had been calling his phone once a week since Davon had been murdered. Which was over a year now. Not once had Lloyd picked up any of her phone calls. Looking at Rihanna, even in sweatpants and a sweatshirt, Rihanna still looked beautiful to him.

"Are we just going to look at each other or are you going to invite me in your house?"

"I'm not sure, I'm still undecided."

"Well let me decide for you" Lloyd said brushing pass Rihanna as he walked into her house.

Sitting down on Rihanna couch Lloyd picked up the T.V remote. Walking over to Lloyd Rihanna snatched the T.V remote out Lloyd hand.

"I been calling you like crazy and you been refusing to answer my phone calls. You pop up at my house after a whole year and act like were the best of friends."

"Listen Ri-Ri…."

"Don't call me that Lloyd."

"My bad Rihanna, listen I been dealing with a lot this past year."

"You think you're the only one that been going through things this past year Lloyd? I lost the man I loved damn near all my life."

"Rihanna we both lost Davon. Davon was my best friend; we grew up together. Hell not only did I lose Davon. I lost two other close friends to me Solo and Supreme. I know if I answered the phone for you Rihanna, I would feel even worst. I was so close, and I couldn't stop Davon from being murdered. I feel fucked up that I couldn't save him, Ri-Ri."

"I told you to stop calling me that" Rihanna yelled upset that he kept calling her by the nick name Davon gave her years ago. Seeing the tears rolling down Rihanna face. Lloyd got up and wrapped his arms around Rihanna.

"Davon may have gave you that nick name. But I been calling you Ri-Ri just as long as Davon. I'm more then sure you know I have always had the hots for you Ri-Ri."

Pulling back from Lloyd Rihanna looked into his eyes. Although Rihanna felt the same way about Lloyd. Rihanna felt trying to get with Lloyd would somehow be disrespecting Davon.

"Lloyd you were Davon best friend, and I don't think…."

"Ri-Ri, you were Davon number one woman. I'm more then sure Davon would be fine with his right hand man taking care of his number one girl."

Looking closer in Lloyd eyes Rihanna noticed that they were glassy like. Busting out laughing Rihanna pulled all the way away from Lloyd. "Here I am thinking that you are sincere with the words coming out your mouth. And you are high as a kite Lloyd."

"That weed I smoked earlier may still have me tripping. But you know the saying, a drugged mind make the lips speak the truth. The truth is I want you to be my girl Ri-Ri."

"Lloyd, I really don't know about a me and you."

"So you telling me I have to think for you a second time today Ri-Ri?"

"What…." Stopping Rihanna in mid-sentence Lloyd grabbed a whole of Rihanna pulled her close and stuck his tongue down her throat.

The touch of Lloyd tongue on hers got Rihanna panties instantly wet. Her body wanted him; her body needed him. Davon was gone and never coming back. Feeling like she should be happy once again. Rihanna kissed Lloyd back, and within seconds they were both out of their clothes.

*****

Getting a call from Brandy, Tonya got in her car and rushed over to Webster projects. Pulling up to the building Tonya called Brandy and told her to come downstairs. Sitting in the driver seat Tonya watched as Brandy walked out her building. Tonya hoped to herself that Brandy wanted to meet with her today to agree to the business deal she offered her a week ago. As Brandy walked over to Tonya car. Tonya began talking to herself in her head. "Brandy is the right skin color, the right height, the right weight. Her butt is a pinch bigger. But that can be taking down with no problem with a little bit of exercise. Her hair is the right length, wrong color, that can be changed with no problem with hair die. A week of vice lessons and her voice will be perfect. But my god she is so damn ugly. If she know like I know she better had taking me up on my offer. Because she down sure need this plastic surgery."

"Hey Tonya, how are you" Brandy said getting in the car with Tonya.

"I'm good, yet I hope to be great after I hear the decision you made to my offer."

"Well Tonya wonder no more. I'm willing to help you. But…."

"I knew there would be a, but. So hit me with it, but what?"

"Well you said that you would be willing to pay me 500,000 dollars. After reading everything you gave me. I'm thinking more like you should pay me one million dollars."

A million dollars to Tonya was like giving away a dollar to a bum in the street. Yet life was a game and Tonya knew exactly how to play it.

"Brandy a million dollars is a lot of money. But I can do a million. Just know I will not except any half stepping from you Brandy. So do we have a deal or not?"

"Yeah, we have a deal, but when do I get my money?"

"Today" Tonya said reaching behind her car seat. Picking up a bag Tonya placed it on Brandy lap. "As you wish that's your million dollars."

"How did you know that I would ask you to pay me a million dollars?"

"Brandy, I'm far from stupid. I knew you would double what I offered you. Just like I'm far from stupid I also don't play games when I make a business deal with someone. Take my money and don't do what you are paid to do. I promise you that you will meet your maker on the other side. Now I suggest you put that money in a safe deposit box in a bank. Because If you put it in the bank, the bank will red flag your account and contract the I.R.S. And of course you won't be able to show proof to where you got this amount of money from, and the I.R.S will take all of it. So our first stop is the bank, then the plastic surgery. I already scheduled you an appointment with the best plastic surgeon in New York today. Three days you should be in the hospital. From there you will recover in a private sweet in the Trump hotel. During your recovery you will undergo voice lessons, study T.V monitors, and get your hair dyed another color. Within two weeks to three weeks you should be fully recovered from your surgery, your voice should be fully changed, and all your studying should be complete. Then will come your first acting job. Any questions Brandy?"

"Yeah, Tonya If I want to undo the surgery that I'm about to go under after our business deal is over. Is it even possible to undo this surgery, and go back to the old me?"

"Sure, you will have to pay out your own pockets to do that though. This surgery is costing me 100,000 dollars. But you know what Brandy? If you do a good job, I'll pay for you to undo this surgery. Are you ready to begin Brandy?"

Taking a deep breath Brandy looked at Tonya. "Ready as I'm ever gonna be."

With a wicked smile on her face Tonya started up her car and took off burning rubber.

*****

Walking into the bank Brandy told the bank clerk, that she would like to open a safe deposit box. Passing Brandy a form, Brandy placed three names on the form that would have rights to the safe deposit box. She placed her name, the name Tonya wanted her to go by, and she placed Ba-Ba name on the form as well. Passing the clerk back the form. The clerk took Brandy to the back of the bank where all the safe deposit boxes were at. Giving Brandy her safe deposit key. The clerk closed the room door and left Brandy alone. Pulling the money out the bag Brandy placed all the money inside the box. Pulling a envelope out her pocket she placed it inside the box as well. Locking the box Brandy left the room. Walking out the bank Brandy got back in the car with Tonya.

"Are you ready to get your new face" Tonya asked.

"I'm more than ready, let's do this.

"About damn time because I'm sick of looking at your ugly ass" Tonya said in her head as she drove.

"I know this bitch can't be trusted, and I just made a deal with the devil. But god please watch over me through this whole business deal" Brandy said to herself looking out the car window.

Chapter 27

Up in Love it or Hate it, Rome sat down at the bar. "What can I get for you Rome" Tank asked.

"Tank hit me with a soda no liquor for me tonight."

Placing a soda in front of Rome, Tank looked at Rome trying to read his mind. Picking up on Rome vibe Tank cleared his throat. "You know Rome I have to say. I was a little bit worried about you, but it seems like you're getting your head back in the game."

"Why, and how so Tank" Rome asked picking up his soda to take a sip.

"Well Rome when the two kings and queen fell a year ago. You went into a depression. You were running the Gibbs drug operation reckless. You were letting that devil in heels Tonya take over the Gibbs drug spots. Yet you pulled yourself out of that depression a month ago and put things back in order with that meeting. I have to say I'm proud of you Rome. I'm more then sure that Solo, Supreme, and Beverly, are proud of you too."

"Thanks Tank, I needed to hear that."

"So tell me Rome how are things going at your two drug spots?"

"To be honest with you Tank I don't know."

"Why is that Rome?"

"Well as of today it's been a month that both spots have been back up and running. Today I plan on going by both spots to see If things are running smooth."

"I see, so basically your giving Pit and Tone a month to get things in order."

"Yup! And today that month is up. If things are running smooth, they can continued to run the spots I gave them to run as they see fit. If the spots are not running right, I will be making changes today."

"Look at you talking like a true king. But let me ask you this Rome. How is the money flow from those two spots? Is it coming in low or high?"

"Tank, I have to say Soundview is pulling in more money than when Solo was running the show. As for Joe's store the money is coming in big as well. The store is bring in more money than Soundview projects. Which is crazy."

"How so?"

"Well Tone and Lloyd run Soundview and Pit run the store by his self."

"By his self, didn't he say something about he's gonna have his Pitbull dogs helping him?"

"Tank be real."

"No you be real Rome. Don't underestimate Pit and the Pitbull dogs he train." Changing the subject Tank began talking about the strip club. "Rome, I heard that you hired three new strippers."

"I had to Tank, Ke-Ke quit a month ago. Jill never came back after Cassie cut her face. Brandy worked for two weeks and never came back. So three gone, three new."

"What are their names?"

"Lexus, Cinnamon, and Jazzie. Their up on stage next. If they do a good job tonight, they stay. If their whack they will be out and replaced tomorrow." Seeing the lights go dim in the strip club Rome turned around in his seat towards the stage.

Beating on the mic DJ L-Boogie put the mic to his lips. "Fellas we have three newcomers coming to the stage. These three ladies want me to make it known to all of you. Their pussy is ready, their pussy is wet, and their asses are phat. And all they want to know is are you fellas ready to spend that money?'

All the guys stood up in the strip c lub and yelled out, "hell yeah."

Letting the music play the music came out the speakers full force. Running out on the stage wearing nothing but things. Lexus jumped on the right pole of the stage, leaving Jazzie to jump on the pole on the left side of the stage. Standing in the middle of the stage with her ass to the crowd. Cinnamon raised both of her hands in the air. Coming down the poles, Lexus and Jazzie wrapped their feet around the poles, and reached their hands out to Cinnamon. Grabbing a hold of their hands the three of them began making their ass cheeks clap. All the guys in the club went crazy throwing money in the air. Like monkeys in heat the three of them began swinging each other around the stage onto the poles making their asses clap even louder. Ending with the three of them stacked on top of each other in a doggy style position bouncing their ass cheeks up and down. Turning around in his bar stool Rome looked at Tank, and Tank looked back at Rome.

"Their staying" Rome and Tank both said. Getting up Rome walked out the strip club.

*****

Driving in the car with Tameka, Anton looked out the car window as Tameka pulled into his driveway. Turning off the car Tameka looked over at Anton.

"You know Anton, me and you talked about damn near everything over dinner tonight. Yet there is one thing we didn't talk about."

"And what's that Tameka?"

"Anton how have things been going between you and Jason? Has there been any more problems with Jason mother and father?"

"Tameka, me and Jason have been together for almost two years now. Things have always been good between me and him. As for his father Dennis I only had one run in with him and that was last year. I haven't heard from him since. As for his mother Ruth. The last time I saw her was last year. Yet I get a phone call from her almost every day. Her phone calls sound like a old broking record. She yell out the same thing every time I answer the phone for her; My son is not gay! He's mentally ill and your taking advantage of him! I will get my son out your house and that's a promise! Tameka, I wish that woman would just leave me and Jason the hell alone."

"What do Jason say when his mother call harassing you?"

"He take the phone from me and tell his mother, I love Anton, he loves me, stop calling here Ma. Then he hang up on her. Tameka enough about my life. My relationship with Jason has now been talked about. Yet there is something else me and you haven't talked about over dinner tonight Tameka. How have you been getting along since Jay murder?"

"Anton all I can say is I finally found a man that excepted me for being born a man and is now legally a woman. He married me and now he's gone."

Anton looked at Tameka for a few seconds then shook his head. "Tameka before you became my sister, you was my brother. I know you like a book Tameka. I get the feeling that there's more to this Jay being murdered thing."

"Anton I'm gonna tell you something but you have to promise not to tell anyone" Tameka said facing Anton.

"Tameka we are family you know I wouldn't repeat anything you tell me."

Taking a deep breath Tameka told Anton everything when it came to what happen a year ago with Jay. When Tameka was done Anton grabbed his mouth in shock. "Tameka you have to tell Rome."

"Anton, I was told to keep my mouth closed."

"By who, Nancy or Tonya?"

"Anton how can you ask me a stupid question like that after everything I just told you? Who the hell do you think told me to keep my mouth closed?"

"Your right Tameka that was a stupid question to ask you. Yet I do have another question for you."

"What?"

"Are you still living in Jay house?"

"Yes! That's my damn husband house!"

"Okay calm down Tameka. I'm just surprised that the Gibbs family didn't make you get out Jay house."

"Anton what the hell is wrong with you? Have you heard anything I just explain to you? Key words, Jays house, not the Gibbs family house. Anton, I love you, but talking to you right now is like talking to a brick wall. So it's time to end this conversation. I love you, now get out my car, and go be with that sexy ass man of yours."

"Thanks for taking me out to dinner, love you too, and I will keep what you told me to myself" Anton said. Giving Tameka a kiss on the cheek Anton got out the car. Watching Tameka drive off Anton went into his house.

Walking in his bedroom Anton found Jason laying in the bed watching T.V. Just the sight of Jason was a turn on for Anton. Especially when Jason laid in the bed with the covers covering his lower body only showing his muscular chest. As Anton took off his clothes to take a shower. Jason penis became erect making the cover left up from his lower body. From the corner of his eye Jason watched Anton go into the bathroom. A minute later he then heard the water from the shower. Five minutes later Jason snatched the cover off his lower body. He felt Anton was taking to long in the bathroom. Completely naked Jason jumped out the bed, open the bathroom door, and snatched the shower curtain open. In shock Anton jumped.

"You scared the shit out of me Jason."

"Miss me with all that I scared you shit. You in here playing in water when I got a hard dick and I want to play up in you."

"I was almost…." Not giving Anton time to finish his sentence. Jason snatched Anton out the shower and threw him over his shoulder.

Walking in the bedroom Jason threw Anton on the bed. Aggressive was a turn on for Anton and Jason knew exactly how he liked it and how to give it to him. The faster Jason fucked him the harder he became. Flipping Anton over Jason took Anton penis into his mouth. Up and down, up and down, faster and faster Jason sucked as he stroked Anton penis. Holding the back of Jason head in place Anton shot his load. Sitting up Jason spread Anton legs wide open and spit Anton cum in the crack of his own ass hole. Not missing a beat Jason filled Anton whole with his penis once again fucking him even harder than before.

*****

In Soundview projects Rome walked into his private drug apartment. Walking into the living room Rome saw that Tone and Ke-Ke was glued to the T.V. Clearing his throat to get their attention Tone and Ke-Ke both jumped.

"I hope I'm not interrupting your movie time. Standing up Tone gave Rome a pound and mushed Rome in his head.

"Kill all that you interrupting shit nigga. What brings you out this way Rome?"

"I'm just checking on things."

"Well breathe easy nigga everything is running smooth as butter Mr. Boss man."

Rome looked over at Ke-Ke. "Is Pit here?"

"No, and before you get to thinking something that's not true Rome. Let me give you the run down to why I'm here…."

Rome held his hands up stopping Ke-Ke in mid-reason. "Why is she here Tone" Rome asked looking over at Tone.

"Pit asked me to put Ke-Ke and Ke-Ke son Tre down to help me run Soundview. So…."

"Wait a damn minute so that's why you quit stripping in the club?"

"Yeah, it was time to retire, I been doing that for years. Plus I'm making more selling money selling drugs then taking off my clothes."

Understanding Ke-Ke reasoning Rome looked back over at Tone. "Tone did I hear you say Ke-Ke son works here at this spot?"

"Yeah."

"Tone how old is he like eight or nine years old?"

"Rome, Tre is eleven years old and little homie is a pro. Keep in mind Tre did bust off a shot at Wayne a few years back. A shot that would have killed Wayne If Pit didn't grab the gun from Tre."

"Ke-Ke, are you cool with your son selling drugs?"

"Rome, I been teaching my son the game from the age of four. Need I say more?"

"I guess not."

"Good, because me and you need to talk about something that's private" Tone said looping his arm around Rome shoulders. Walking Rome to the back room Tone closed the door.

"What's so private that you need to talk to me about Tone" Rome asked sitting on the bed.

"Rome something is up with Lloyd."

"Something like what?"

"Something like I haven't seen or heard from him in over a month."

"And you just telling me this! He could be dead Tone!"

"Be easy Rome, Lloyd is not dead."

"How do you know that If you haven't seen or heard from him in a month?"

"Because he keep going to my house and taking money out my stash."

Hearing what Tone just said Rome went into deep thought. Hearing Tone say that Lloyd was stealing from him. Rome realized he may have a serious problem with Lloyd. The situation seem bigger then him just missing that meeting a month ago.

"Tone how much money has Lloyd stole from you?"

"In total about ten thousand dollars."

"How much is your stash?"

"It's in the millions. Rome I'm really not sure what's going on with Lloyd. All I know is he's stealing my money. Because I have him on camera going in my stash multiple times. Curiosity killed my cat, and I went over to Lloyd house and open up his stash box. To my surprise his stash is completely empty. Normally Rome If someone was stealing from me. I would kill them first and ask questions later. But this is Lloyd, and Lloyd been down with our team for years. The crazy shit is Lloyd is taking a hundred dollars to two hundred dollars at a time out my stash, not the whole thing."

"Listen Tone don't worry about Lloyd. I'll get up with him and see what's going on with him."

"A'ight? Rome do something because If Lloyd keep this stealing shit up. I'm gonna take his ass in the back of my house and put his ass to sleep like they did old yellow."

"I'm gonna handle it" Rome said walking out the apartment.

*****

Pulling up in front of his grandfather store, Rome was shocked to see that Pit had replaced the store front sign on the store. Rome was used to seeing the sign read, "Joe's store." Seeing the sign read, "Dog pound" Rome shook his head in disbelief. Getting out the car Rome walked into the store and was stopped at the door by four Pitbull dogs. Rome eyes grew large when he realized the dogs were not allowing him to go past them. Looking around the store Rome notice four doghouse set up in the store, with windows where the doggy doors should have been on the dog houses. He also notice that all he saw was dogs and Pit was nowhere in sight. All four dogs took a seat in front of Rome and barked. Jumping back Rome hit the back of his head on the store door.

"Who that out there" Pit yelled from the store back office.

"Pit, it's me Rome, come out here and get these damn dogs!"

"Bitches be easy" Pit yelled walking up to the front of the store. Hearing Pit voice and words all four dogs walked away from Rome.

"Pit are you selling drugs in here od dogs" Rome asked giving Pit a pound with his fist.

"Both Mr. Boss man. Yet I only sell dogs that I feel have been fully trained. Let me show you around Rome to how me and my dogs run shit around here."

Walking around the store Pit explain to Rome the way the store was set up. "Take a look Rome, I have four dog houses, in the back of the dog houses is a back yard for the dogs to play. The dog houses have a window in front of the houses, and a doggy door in the back of the houses."

"I see that Pit, but what's with the signs above the dog houses?"

"That's for the drug buyers. House one, has a sign with the number, one, on it. Fiends go to that house when they want to buy one bag. House two and three has a sign with the number, 2, on it. That's for fiends that want to buy two bags. House four has a sign with the letter, B, on it. That's for buyers that want to buy a brink of cocaine." Rome looked at Pit like he was crazy. "You looking at me like I'm crazy, but the system works well. I bag the drugs up and my dogs do the rest of the work. My male dogs do the selling, and my female dogs keep the store safe. My dogs follow four commandments in this store and when their sold."

"Such as what Pit?"

"Be easy bitches, Kill, Shake down, Hit the wall."

"Pit, I don't want to ask, but I would really love to know. Who collect the money, you or the dogs?"

"That's a stupid as question Rome! The dogs collect the money."

Rome through his hands in the air hearing enough. "That's it Pit, this shit all sound crazy. As of today this shit stops."

Seeing two female fiends walk into the store. Pit pulled Rome behind the cash register. Putting his finger to his lips for Rome to shut up. Pit pointed to the two fiends for Rome to watch them. Rome watched as the four female dogs let the fiends walk over to the dog houses. The white female walked up to doghouse one. Placing her money on the windowsill. The dog sniffed the money, then snatched the money into the doghouse with his right paw. The dog then hit his head on the windowsill and a bag of crack fell from the top of the window into the fiend hand. In shock Rome turned his head towards Pit. Pit turned Rome head back towards the dog houses with his hand for Rome to continue to watch the Spanish fiend. Just like the white female fiend. The Spanish female fiend put her money on the windowsill of doghouse two. The dog in the doghouse sniffed the money, barked, stock his head out the dog window and bit the Spanish female hand. Hearing the woman scream the dog let the female hand go. Rome looked in horror while Pit bust out laughing. Standing to their feet the four female dogs chased the Spanish female fiend out the store.

"Pit you have to shut this shit down. You can't have these dogs biting people."

"Why the fuck not" Pit yelled walking over to the doghouse. Snatching the money off the windowsill he handed it to Rome.

"This ain't real" Rome said looking at the money that Pit handed to him.

"No shit Rome, that's why the dog bit that bitch for trying to give him fake money."

"You telling me the dog knew this was fake money, how?"

"Rome dogs are smart. Especially when you train them right. The smelling sense on a dog is very high. You can train dogs to find drugs, find dead bodies, or to pick the sent up of a missing person or criminal. Understand this Rome all money has cocaine residue in each bill. Why the government make their money with cocaine in the thread they make money with, I don't know. But hey it works for me and my dogs."

"Pit that's why…."

"Yes Rome, I taught the dogs how to tell money from fake money. If they don't smell cocaine on the money you give them, they will wild the fuck the fuck out. And before you ask, they are train to know what bills you are giving them too."

"How, you know what I don't even want to know. Somehow this is all working out. Keep up the good even want to know. Somehow this is all working out. Keep up the good work Pit." Walking out the store Rome shock his head in amazement.

*****

Walking in his house it was completely dark. Although it was late Rome was surprised that he didn't hear the kids making noise throughout the house. Having Solo son and his own two kids for the past year all living in his house. His house had never been this quite. Feeling uneasy Rome pulled out his gun and began walking through his house with light feet. Every room he checked and found that the house was completely empty of Sierra, Quinn, Little Supreme, and Lisa. Tucking his gun under his mattress Rome turned on his bedroom light, sat down on his bed and called Sierra.

"Hello."

"Hey baby, where are you and the kids?"

"I just dropped them off at your grandmother Stephanie house. I'll be home in about five minutes."

"Okay I'll see you when you get home."

Hanging up the phone Rome took a deep breath of relief and looked over at the wall. Looking at the calendar on the wall Rome jumped up off the bed. "Holy shit" Rome yelled noticing it was Sierra birthday. "Damn it, I can't believe I forgot her birthday is today. Think, think, she'll be home in five minutes."

Running to the hallway closet he pulled out a box of long white candles. Running back in the bedroom he sat them up around the room. Lighting the candles, he ran in the bathroom and set up a few candles in there and lit them up as well. Threw bubble bath liquid in the tub he turned the water on. Running downstairs he got a knife from the kitchen and ran out the house into the back yard. Living in Supreme and Beverly house since their death. He took over taking care of the roses Beverly always grew in the back yard.

"Sorry Ma, but I have to do it" Rome said looking up at the sky.

Grabbing two rose bushes Rome chopped them from the dirt they were in. Running back in the house Rome threw the knife in the sank. Running up the stairs to the bedroom. He ripped up a few roses and threw them on the steps all the way to the bedroom. Ripping up a few more he threw them on the bed. Running into the bathroom he threw a few in the tub and cut the water off. He then threw the rest of the roses around the bedroom and the bathroom. Hearing Sierra car pull up in the driveway. Rome ran back in the bedroom and ripped off all his clothes like he was on fire.

Walking in the bedroom Sierra face lit up light a Christmas tree. With one leg cocked up on the bed and a rose in his mouth. Rome looked at Sierra with a smile on his face as R.Kelly 12 play CD played sex me softly in the room. Spitting the rose out his mouth at Sierra, she caught it in midair.

"Happy birthday baby girl."

Helping Sierra out her clothes he picked her up and carried her into the bathroom and laid her down in the tub. Washing her up, he dried her off, and carried her back into the bedroom. Laying Sierra down on the bed. He spread her legs apart and buried his face inside her sweet love box. Rome tongued her hot hole with his thick tongue until he could taste her sweet cream. Getting on top of her Rome looked into her eyes.

"You know I love you right?"

"Yeah, and I also know you forgot it was my birthday today."

"I did baby girl and I'm so sorry" Rome said kissing Sierra on her neck.

"When did you realize it was my birthday?"

"When I got off the phone with you."

Sierra bust out laughing. "Damn boy you must really love me. You put all this together in five minutes?"

"I must love the hell out of you. Hell, I cut up my mother roses for you. If she was alive, she would kill me for cutting up her roses."

"Well Rome there's only one thing left to do."

"What's that?"

"Make your wife cum a few more times for her birthday."

"You ain't said nothing but a word baby girl."

Sliding his thick long dick inside Sierra nice and slow. Rome began kissing and sucking on her neck. As Rome talked dirty softly in Sierra ear he pumped slowly inside her. Picking up the speed he began bouncing up and down on top of her like a true porn star. Up and down he bounced. She could feel his balls slapping against her between her legs. The faster he fucked her the harder his dick seem to get inside of her. One orgasm, two orgasm, by the third orgasm Rome was pumping so fast and hard inside of her that she was losing count of her orgasms.

*****

Waking up the next morning to someone banging on the house door. Anton grabbed his robe to answer the door. Opening the door seeing who it was took the smile completely off Anton face. Ruth stood face to face with Anton with two tall guys behind her.

"Ms. Marshall it's early in the morning and I'm not really in the mood for your nonsense."

"Read and weep you son of a bitch" Ruth yelled slapping a paper on Anton chest. Taking the paper in his hand Anton saw that it was a court order from a judge.

"Sir we have been appointed by the judge to remove a Jason Marshall from your house and take him to the site ward in St. Barnabas hospital" one of the tall guys said.

Trying to walk pass Anton, Anton stopped all three of them. "This has to be a joke; Jason is not a child. He's 43 years old."

"Sir If you read the court order, you will see that Jason Marshall is mentally ill and is under the care of his mother due to his illness."

Pushing Anton out the way the two guys followed Ruth up to Anton bedroom. Standing at the front door in shock. Anton could hear Jason screaming and fighting upstairs. Two minutes later the two tall guys were carrying Jason down the stairs wearing only a white straight jacket. Pushing Anton to the side once again. Ruth lead the way out the house, as the two guys carried Jason. Anton watched as Jason penis swung in the air as they carried him to the car. Slamming the door closed Anton ran over to his phone. Picking up the phone he called Erykah.

Chapter 28

Waking up Rome had a lot on his mind. He was happy that both of his drug spots were running smooth. Yet he couldn't shake that he may have a problem with Lloyd. Pulling out his cell phone Rome jumped on the internet. Putting in the code that Solo gave him a year ago. Rome pulled up Lloyd chain tracker map history. Looking up Lloyd map history for the past year. Rome looked at his cell phone screen confused. Four to five times every day for the past year. Lloyd had been going to Webster projects to their old drug spot apartment. Which was strange considering that Tonya had taking over that spot for the past year. Lloyd had also been going over to Davon old girlfriend Rihanna house for the past month. Turning off his cell phone Rome went into deep thought. Two reasons popped into Rome head to why Lloyd could be going over to Webster drug apartment. One, to get some insight into how Tonya was running her crew. Something that Rome didn't give Lloyd promise to do. Two, Lloyd is double crossing the Gibbs family now working for the Jones drug family. Rome wasn't sure which one fit Lloyd. Yet one thing Rome did know was he needed to find out what was going on with Lloyd.

After jumping in the shower Rome got dressed and got into his car. Pulling out his cell phone Rome jumped on the internet and pulled up Lloyd chain tracker map history again. Looking at his phone screen Rome notice that Lloyd had just left Webster projects, and was now heading over to Rihanna house. Turning his phone off Rome started up his car and hit the road.

*****

Pulling into Rihanna driveway Lloyd cut off his car and took off his seatbelt. Seeing Rihanna car already in front of her house. Lloyd became even more annoyed. He was hoping that he would beat her to her house so he could do his thing. Seeing no other choice he reached into his pocket and pulled out what he had just brought earlier. Going under his car seat he pulled out a paper bag. Wrapping the aluminum foil around the spoon, he poured one of his crack pages into the spoon. Adding a little bit of water into the spoon, Lloyd pulled his lighter out his pocket.

Firing up his lighter under the spoon, Lloyd watched it turn into a milky like liquid. Pulling a cotton ball out the bag he placed it over the liquid. Filling the syringe Lloyd eyes began to bulge. Taking his belt off he wrapping it around his arm. Slapping his arm, he found a vein, and stuck the syringe into his arm.

As the drug traveled threw his veins Lloyd body began to calm down. Leaning his head back on the car seat headrest. Lloyd licked his lips and closed his eyes.

Seeing all that he needed to see Rome got out his car and pulled out his gun. Walking over to Lloyd car Rome smashed Lloyd car door window with his gun. Jumping up in his car seat in shock vomit shot out of Lloyd mouth onto his dashboard. Tucking his gun in his pants Rome stuck his hand threw Lloyd car door window and snatched Lloyd threw the car window. Rome movements were happening so fast Lloyd was beyond confused to what was going on. Landing hard on the ground Lloyd tried to pull his gun out the waistband of his pants. Snatching Lloyd gun from him Rome went upside Lloyd head with it twice. Grabbing Lloyd by his shirt Rome held the gun to Lloyd head.

"You haven't answered your phone in a month, you been missing for a month, you been stealing money from Tone. Why, because you using drugs!"

Looking in Rome face not only was Lloyd embarrassed, he was ashamed that someone from his team caught him getting high.

"Lloyd, you know better than this shit! The number one rule in the drug game is don't get high off what you sell."

Hearing the commotion outside of her house. Rihanna ran out her house and saw that Rome had his gun to Lloyd head.

"Rome what are you doing?"

Paying Rihanna words no mind Rome dragged Lloyd to his car. Throwing Lloyd in the passenger seat Rome got in the driver seat and pulled off. Confused at the whole scene Rihanna watched as Rome speeded off. Looking over at Lloyd car Rihanna saw that Lloyd car door window was broken.

Driving at top speed Rome refused to say a word to Lloyd as he sat in the passenger seat. Thirty minutes later Rome pulled up to, McKenzie rehab center. Getting out the car Rome snatched Lloyd out the car and dragged him into the rehab center. Lloyd held his head down with vomit on his shirt as Rome dragged him up to the front desk.

"Ma'ma, I'm here to check my friend into rehab today" Rome said to the receptionist.

"Rome…."

Pulling out his gun Rome snatched Lloyd by his shirt and held the gun to his head. "Say another word and I'm gonna blow your fucking head off your shoulders. Be lucky I didn't do that when I caught you shooting that shit. The receptionist at the desk looked at Rome in shock as Rome held a gun to Lloyd head. "How much money to check him in " Rome asked looking over at the receptionist.

"Fifteen hundred a week."

Rome pulled a stack of money out his pocket and slammed it on the desk. "That eight thousand dollars for a month stay. The extra money is for you to call me If he try to leave."

Snatching the pen out the receptionist hand. Rome wrote down his name and cell phone number on a paper that was laying on the desk. Turning around Rome leaned over and whispered in Lloyd ear. "This is our little secret. When you get out of here you better be done with getting high. If not I'm gonna end your life myself for breaking the number one drug dealer rule."

Saying all he needed to say Rome tucked his gun back in his pants and walked out the rehab center. Picking up his head Lloyd looked over at the receptionist. Placing the paper that Rome wrote on in her pocket the receptionist stood up. "Come with me Sir."

Walking in a small room Lloyd took a seat on the bed. Stepping inside the room behind Lloyd the receptionist closed the door. "My name is Amber Bell. What's your name?"

"Lloyd."

"Well Lloyd there's a book of rules on your nightstand that you must follow while you're here. A counselor will talk to you tomorrow morning. If you don't mind me asking. How long have you been using drugs?"

"A little over a year."

"Lloyd was today the first time that guy that brought you in here caught you using drugs?"

"Yeah."

"I have to say Lloyd I been working here for almost ten years. I've see almost everything since I been working here. But today is the first time a person brought someone in at gun point. If that's not friendly love I don't know what is. Try not to disappoint him and complete your month stay here. Also keep in mid I have your friend number and I will use it."

*****

161 family courthouse Erykah and Anton took their seat behind a wooden desk in the court room. Jason took his seat behind the middle desk with a court appointed lawyer. Jason, mother and father, Ruth and Dennis took their seat at the third desk in the court room. As Anton spoke to Erykah he could feel Ruth eyes burning a hole in his face. Paying no attention to Ruth grilling him Anton continued to whisper to Erykah.

Seeing the judge walk into the court room everyone stood up. "You may all be seated" the judge said taking his seat behind the bench. "This is the case of Jason Marshall. I have to say this case is a first for me as a judge. Mr. Jason Marshall is 43 years of age. Due to his mental health, his mother Ms. Ruth Marshall legally over see his wellbeing. According to court papers filed. Ms. Marshall is requestion that her son legally be ordered to take his medication, and if he refuse, she want him to be placed in a hospital site center. At the point in time Mr. Jason Marshall is in a hospital site center. Mr. Anton Fisher has filed court papers as well. According to those papers Mr. Fisher is requesting that Jason be released from that hospital and allowed to live with him. Let's began agreements starting with Mr. Jason Marshall. Mr. Jason Marshall have you been taking your medication since you been at the hospital?"

"Yes."

"How long were you off your medication?"

"For two years your honor."

"How long have you been living with Mr. Fisher?"

"Two years."

"Who do you want to live with now?"

"Anton."

"Ms. Ruth Marshall you may argue your case. Why do you feel your son need to be home with you?"

"My son is mentally ill. Without his medication my son does not think straight. He gets his self into problems, sometimes legal problems. Yet when he is on his medication he think straight."

"Mr. Anton Fisher you may argue your case. Why do you feel Jason should live with you?"

"We have been living together for the past two years. In that time Jason has not been on any medication, nor has he got into any trouble whatsoever."

"I'm ready to make my decision in this matter. It is highly unusual that a court order a 43 year old man in the care of another. Yet due to the mental health of Mr. Jason Marshall the court has to do so. I have looked threw Jason medical history. There's not a doubt in my mind that Jason may have mental health issues. Yet off his medication, or on his medication. There is no record of Jason doing harm to his self or to another person. Yet due to the serious mental health issues that Jason has. I find that Mr. Jason Marshall should legally remain under the care of his mother."

"Thank you, god," Ruth yelled out.

"Your honor If I may speak" Erykah asked standing up.

"You may Ms. Sams."

"How can you rule a married couple to be split up without their permission?"

"Ms. Sams, I don't follow your question."

"Your honor, Mr. Fisher and Mr. Jason Marshall are married. And have been married for the past eight months. I'm more then sure that your honor is aware same sex marriage is legal now in New York. With that said your honor has to respect their marriage."

"Do you have proof of this marriage?"

Erykah pulled a marriage certificate out her briefcase and handed it to the judge. The judge looked at the certificate.

"In light of this new evidence. I have no choice but to grant Mr. Jason request to live with his husband Mr. Anton Fisher." Passing out Ruth fell out the chair hitting the floor.

*****

"You asked to see me captain" Price said sticking his head in Captain Morris office.

"Yeah, come in and close the door." Doing what he was told Price took a seat. "Price something has been brought to my attention regarding you. Price, me and your father came into the police force together. Before your father died, I told him I would always look out for you as If you were my own son. What I was told can get your badge taking from you If I report it. Instead I'm gonna give you a chance to make things right."

Looking at Morris, Price had a confused look on his face. A look that was pissing Morris off by the second.

"How long did you think you could take a pay off from a drug family before it got back to me Price?"

"Captain...."

"Price don't you dear try to play me like I was born yesterday by denying what I just said. You are on the Gibbs pay roll. Since you are in good with that drug family. Here's what you're going to do. If you don't know, find out Price. Find out where their drug spots are, where they store their drugs, and I want that information on my desk before Friday. Because come Saturday this police station will be raiding their spots and taking down the Gibbs drug family. Are we clear detective Price?"

"Yes Captain."

"Good, because If we are not clear. Know that your job maybe on the line, so no tipping the Gibbs family off."

Leaving Morris office Price went inside the police station bathroom. Calling Rome he told Rome they needed to meet up. In response Rome told Price to meet him at the strip club in two hours. Getting off the phone with Price, Rome continue to drive in his car. He had just dropped Lloyd off at the rehab center. Rome still had a lot running through his mind. Tone and Pit was right, he needed to see what these two Baltimore guys looked like that Tameka was doing business with. Yet he didn't want Tameka to think he didn't trust her. How could he find out what they looked like without stepping on Tameka toes? Like a light switch being turned on. Rome knew what needed to be done. Something he should have done a long time ago when he put Tameka down with the Gibbs drug team.

Pulling up to his grandmother Nancy house, Rome notice that her car was in the driveway. Although Rome gad agreed to give Nancy some space. He felt a year was enough space. He hadn't heard or seen his grandmother in a year. Getting out the car he let his self into the house. A foul odor hit him in his face like a ton of bricks when he walked in the house. Walking in the living room Rome turned on the light switch and nothing happen.

"No lights, I guess grandma isn't back in New York" Rome said to himself walking over to the fireplace.

Picking Beverly, Supreme, Trina, Solo, and Jay, gold chains up off the fireplace shelf. Rome put them in his pocket. Following the foul odor to the kitchen Rome looked at the garbage. Opening the lid to the garbage the foul odor got even stronger. Pulling the garbage bag out the trash can, he tied it up. Carrying the bag outside Rome locked his grandmother house back up.

In Love it or Hate it Rome sat in the back office. He called Tameka, Ke-Ke, and Ke-Ke son, and told them to come over to the club. While he waited for them and detective Price to get to the club. Rome jumped on the internet on the computer in his office. Putting in the code that Solo gave him. He changed Solo tracker to Tameka name. He changed Supreme tracker to detective Price name. He then changed Jay name to Tre, and Trina name to Ke-Ke. Turning off the computer just in time. Tameka, Tre, and Ke-Ke walked into the office. One by one Rome through a chain at them.

"Put those on, don't take then off, you are officially apart of the Gibbs drug team. If you ever take those chains off that will tell me, you want to be murdered. I hope we clear." Placing the chains around their neck the three of them gave Rome a hug. "Tameka you have to meet up with those Baltimore boys today, right?"

"Yeah."

"Well you better get a move on it then. Tre, Ke-Ke, Tone told me you two are doing a good job over there in Soundview." As the three of them walked out the office detective Price waled in the office.

Closing the door Price took a seat. "Here's your chain being that you are a part of my team, and your payment for this month for looking out for my team." Passing the chain and the envelope to Price. Price out the chain on and put the envelope in his pocket. "So Price what did you want to meet up with me for?"

"Well I just wanted to see If were on the same page."

"The same page about what?"

"Well Rome in order to keep your team page."

"The same page about what?"

"Well Rome in order to keep your team out of prison. I have to know…. Ummm…. Where your drug spots are…. and where your drugs…. are stashed. That way…. you know…. I can keep the police off your ass."

Hearing the way Price was studdering raised flags in Rome head. Solo told him years ago, "Price is paid to keep us out of prison, not to know our business. He maybe on the payroll, but he's still a pig, and a pig will eat anything."

"Price it's good to know your looking out for my team. Well here at Love it or Hate it, is one of my drug spots. The Banks hotel is where I store my drugs. Last but not lease the store now called Dog-pound is my second drug spot."

Standing up Price gave Rome a pound with his fist. "I have to run Rome but be assure I'll keep those spots free of police."

"I'm sure you will Price" Rome walking Price to the door.

After watching Price leave the strip club. Rome called Pit and sat down at the bar. "What up Boss Man?"

"Pit heads up, I believe we may have police on our ass and your store will be hit."

"Rome they can hit it, but best to believe they not gonna get a nut. Me and my dogs know how to bark."

"Pit to hell with your dogs, I'm serious. I don't know when, but I believe the police is gonna raid that store. Hello…. Hello…." Rome looked at his cell phone. "I know damn well he didn't just hang up on me?" Rome looked over at Tank in shock. "Can you believe Pit just hung up on me?"

"Yeah, I can believe that Rome. You said, to hell with his dogs. You know how Pit feel about his Pitbull dogs."

"Tank this is serious."

"He know that Rome. Pit heard what you said so be easy. Now tell me what's going on?"

Telling Tank what he told Price. Tank gave him a weird look. "What's with that look Tank?"

"Rome if you feel Price is setting you up to be raided. Why would you give up Pit store, your hotel, and this club?"

"Because Tank the Banks hotel is clean just like this club. There's no dirty money or drugs they will find."

"That's true, but what about Pit store?"

"Tank I rather one person go down then the whole team. Yet I gave Pit a heads up to clean that spot out. That way nothing will be caught in a raid."

"Rome normally when a person believe that they are going to be raided. They give the rat wrong addresses to raid. You gave him two legal businesses and one dirty spot."

"Tank if Pit listen to my heads up. If the police do raid, they will be raiding three clean spots."

"Rome...."

"Tank what do I have a degree in?"

"Business management."

"Exactly Tank! I know what I'm doing. When I took over this strip club. I turned it into a strip club slash night club. Which now make even more money. I run Soundview projects; it's now making more money than when Solo was running it. I run that store. I took it from Khia, and it's bring in way more money then what I was seeing out of it when Khia had it."

"That's all true Rome, but a good businessman don't send the police to raid their spots."

"They do Tank, especially when their clean businesses. With them being clean, them being raided, the police finding nothing. I'm gonna sue the hell out of the N.Y.P.D."

"Oh, I see your frame of thinking now. Every time I talk to you Rome you surprise me."

"Well I'm glad I could surprise you once again Tank. Now if you will excuse me Tank. I have to go give Erykah a call to get her started on my lawsuit."

Standing up Rome walked back into the club back office. "That damn boy got both of his parents inside of him. He get the smarts from his father Solo and get the wicked from his mother Beverly" Tank said to his self, letting out a short laugh.

*****

Walking into Morris office Price slapped a paper on his desk. "What's this" Morris asked picking up the paper.

"It's what you wanted Captain. That's two drug spots and the place where they store their drugs."

Picking up the phone Morris got the D.A on the phone. Telling Jack the information he had. Jack told him he would get the warrants for the raid on those three spots. Hanging up the phone Morris patted Price on his back.

"You did good Price, come next week that whole damn family will be in prison."

"I hope so Captain, because If they're not. I might be in the ground come next week. Captain If they find out I still them out."

"Price it's not good for a man to worry. We got them and there's not a damn thing they can do about it."

"I hope your right Captain."

*****

Getting off the phone with Erykah. Rome jumped on the internet and pulled up Tameka tracker map history. Looking at the computer screen Rome was confused. To him it look like Tameka was heading to Baltimore, instead of her meeting up with the Baltimore guys in New York. He told her that she could do business with them in New York, not in Baltimore. Jumping off the computer Rome pulled out his car keys. He wanted to know the true deal about these Baltimore guys Tameka was hooked up with. The only way to do that was to follow her to Baltimore. Walking out the club Rome got in his car. Burning rubber Rome speeded out the club parking lot.

*****

Hearing a knock on her hotel room door. Brandy open the door to see that it was room service. "About time you got here I'm starving."

"Here's your food Ms. Sams and here's your mail."

Taking the food and the mail Brandy slammed the door closed. While recovering from her surgery Brandy thought long and hard to herself. Tonya plan was sweet but coming up with a plan of her own. Brandy felt her plan sounded better. A plan that she would keep from Tonya until the time was right. For the first time in over eight years, Brandy wrote Ba-Ba. Telling him of the plan she was working on she was waiting for his response. Flipping through the mail she spotted a letter from Ba-Ba. Opening the letter Brandy began reading it. It was clear that Ba-Ba was still upset with her. Yet it was also clear that he was down with her plan. He wasn't too sure about having plastic surgery, but said he was down with it if that was going to make them millionaires. To Brandy surprise Ba-Ba wrote on the bottom of the letter, "I'll see you in two days." Although that was good news for the plan she was putting together. She was still somewhat scared to come face to face with Ba-Ba, after all the years she had shitted on him.

Ripping up the letter Brandy threw it in the garbage. Flipping through the rest of the mail Brandy found the envelope she had been waiting for. It was from the D.M.V addressed to Mr. Wayne Sams. Opening the envelope Brandy pulled the I.D out the envelope. "I'm gonna love fucking your fine ass" Brandy said kissing the I.D card.

Hearing a knock at the hotel door Brandy threw all the mail in the top draw of her nightstand. Opening the door Tonya brushed pass Brandy and walked into the hotel sweet. Taking a seat on the couch Tonya kicked off her high heels. Opening the folder that was on her lap. Tonya began pulling out paper after paper.

"Hello to you to Tonya" Brandy said taking a seat next to Tonya.

"Girl fuck the hellos; we need to get down to business. Today I set up a meeting between you and Gail for tomorrow. Which mean I have to make sure you are prepared. Have you been studying all the home videos I gave you?"

"Yes."

"Have you been looking and studying the T.V monitors to the cameras that are set up in my hotel sweet?"

"Yes Tonya, I have."

"Good, stand up and let me have a look at you Brandy."

Standing up Brandy stood like a model taking a picture. Standing up Tonya looked over Brandy body, then stared at her face.

"Perfect! You look just like her. Here's the name you will be going by and here are the answers to the questions that Gail may ask you. Get some sleep were driving to New Jersey early in the morning." Slapping Brandy on her butt Tonya walked out the hotel sweet.

Chapter 29

Across the street from where Tameka chain tracker had her pen pointed. Rome tried his best to swallow the lump that was forming in his throat. This was his second time ever being in Baltimore in his whole life. The first time was when the whole Gibbs family came to Baltimore to kill the guys that murdered his uncle Gutta. Here he was back in Baltimore. To his surprise at the same house of the guys that they murdered, for murdering Gutta. He watched from his car as Tameka walked in the house with two duffle bags. Multiple thoughts began to run through Rome mind. "What the hell is going on? Is she planning to set the Gibbs family up like Monique did to Gutta? Are these guys that she's doing business with related to the guys we murdered for murdering Gutta? If they are do, she know that? Fuck, what is this all about?"

Breaking his thoughts Rome saw Tameka walking house with two guys. Rolling down his car window so he could hear what they were talking about. Rome heard Tameka call one of the guys by his name, "Lucky." Turning to the other guy she called him by his name, "Neal." Looking closer at both of the guys face. Rome had never seen them before. Seeing Tameka giving them both a hug, Rome watched Tameka get in her car and drive off. Rolling up his car window Rome wait for both guys to go back in their house.

"This will be the last time she will be making a drop off to them. Believe that. Come next month no drop for them." Starting up his car Rome pulled off heading back to New York.

*****

Walking in Gail dining room Khia took a seat across from Gail. "First things first Gail, hello."

"Hello to you to Khia."

"Gail although I love to see you. Please explain why you asked me to meet with you so early in the morning? I was out cold when you called me."

"Well Khia there's an old saying. When starting off a day bad, the rest of that day will only get worse."

"I heard that saying before."

"You've heard that before, well you will know the true meaning of that saying today."

"Gail, your starting to scare me. Why did you call me to meet with you today?"

Gail took a deep breath and let it out slow. "Khia, I'm sorry to tell you this but I have no choice. As of today you are no longer the queen of the Sams drug operation."

"Gail how is that possible! I clearly stated in the Sams drug contract that Tonya…."

"Khia, Tonya is not the one claiming the Sams drug contract."

"If not her then who?"

"Me" Brandy said walking into the dining room.

Looking at Brandy as If she was seeing a ghost. Khia whole body began to sweet. "How…. how…. how is this…. she's…. she's dead."

"Khia that's rude to say a person is dead when you see that person right in your face" Brandy said walking over to Khia.

Turning her face towards Gail, Khia eyes looked as If they were going to pop out at any minute.

"Khia, you have one last trump card left to use. You just have to figure out what that trump card hold. I know what it hold, yet I can't tell you due to my position" Gail said.

"Gail, what is going on here" She is dead, I watched the casket close, I watched the dirt go over the casket. She is dead."

"Are you gonna keep saying I'm dead, or are you going to get up and give your big sister Melissa a hug?"

Seeing that Khia was looking at her in a daze. Brandy placed her hand on Khia shoulder. Jumping up from the table Khia ran towards the dining room door. Stopping her in her track Tonya stood in her way.

"What a beautiful sight seeing both of my daughters in the same room. I have only one question for you Khia. How does it feel not to have a position at all?" Pushing Tonya to the side Khia ran out of Gail house. "I told you I would get you back for crossing your own mother" Tonya yelled at Khia back side.

Hearing Gail clear her throat Tonya turn around giving Gail her full attention. "Tonya If you would excuse yourself. I need to have a one on one with Melissa."

"No problem Gail. Melissa, I will be outside in the car waiting for you."

"Okay Mommy" Brandy replied.

Twenty minutes later Melissa was walking out of Gail house. Getting in the car with Tonya, Tonya pulled off. Stopping at the red light Tonya bust out laughing.

"Did you see the look on Khia face when she saw you? I thought for sure she was going to have a heart attack. My god I almost feel sorry for what I did to her. I think I should call her and make sure she's all right."

Pulling over to the side of the road reality began to set in for Tonya. Foe the first time in her life she was beginning to feel she took things too far. Having Brandy have plastic surgery to look like her dead daughter Melissa. At first the look on Khia face was funny. Yet in her mind replaying the look Khia had on her face. It hurt her that she hurt her only living daughter. Pulling out her cell phone she dialed Khia number.

"Hello."

"Khia are you okay?"

"Ma everything is a joke and war with you. I'm only beefing with you because you keep beefing with me Ma. How is this possible Ma? I put Melissa in the ground myself years ago."

"That's not important Khia. Listen, this beef between me and you is getting way out of hand."

"How is Melissa still alive Ma!"

"Khia…."

"I want to know Ma!"

"Khia, I can't tell you that."

"You can't tell me! Well Ma let the fucking war between me, and you continue."

"Khia…."

"Watch your back bitch."

"Excuse me, have you not learn to stop crossing your mother Khia?"

"I haven't learned shit!"

"Have it your way Khia. Just know Courtlandt projects no longer belong to you. It belongs to your sister Melissa. Move your team out or I'll have them all murdered."

Hanging up Tonya put her phone back in her pocket. Starting up the car Tonya looked over at Brandy. "I must say Brandy you deserve an award with your actress skills. Yet there's a whole lot more work to be done. Such as us taking over Courtlandt projects."

*****

Pulling up to her house Tameka out his gun and ran up behind Tameka. Hearing someone running up behind her Tameka tried to turn around. Yet she was pushed in her house with so much force she fell to the floor. Slamming the door closed, Rome grabbed Tameka by her hair, and held his gun to her head.

"Rome what is wrong with you?"

"What's wrong with me! The question is what the hell is going on with you Tameka! I told you to meet with them Baltimore boys in New York, not go to Baltimore. Who are those guys Tameka!"

"Their friends of mine I told you that."

"Tameka the only reason why I haven't put a bullet in your head yet. Is because my cousin Jay loved you. But I swear to god If those guys from Baltimore are trying to kill one of the Gibbs drug members. Mark my words I will kill you myself. Do you understand me?"

"Yes."

"That drug deal you have going with those Baltimore niggas is over as of today. The Gibbs are no longer their drug contact. And If I ever find out that you went back to Baltimore your dead. As of tomorrow report to Soundview projects because that's where you work now." Letting go of Tameka, Rome walked out the house slamming the door behind him.

Getting up oof the floor Tameka called the Baltimore number she had.

"Hello…. It's me Tameka. Listen, I don't know how Rome found out, but he know I went to Baltimore to drop those drugs off to yawl. Yeah, I'm wearing a Gibbs drug family chain. What does that have to do with anything? What do you mean you know how he found out I went to Baltimore? How? Why can't you tell me? He just had a gun to my head. I thought he was going to kill me. Fine!" Hanging up the phone Tameka took off her high heels and threw them across the living room. I'm getting sick of this lying shit" Tameka yelled out loud.

*****

Like clockwork at 8 p.m. on the dot police raided all three spots. The Dog-pound store, Love it or Hate it, and the Banks hotel. Detective Price and Captain Morris headed up the raid at the Banks hotel. Clearing out the hotel of all customers. Captain Morris made all the employees of the hotel line up in the lobby of the hotel. Searching them all the police officers found nothing.

"Can I ask what is going on" Sierra asked.

Snatching Sierra up by her shirt Morris slammed her into the wall. "you can't ask shit. Stand there and keep your fucking mouth closed. Tear it up fellas, every room, closets, and carpet, open it, rip it up" Morris yelled out to the uniform officers.

An hour later with over twenty police officers. The Banks hotel came up clean of no drugs. "Damn it" Captain Morris yelled calling Jack.

Jack Murry choose to head up the raid on love it or Hate it. He had a score to settle with the Gibbs family. He was sick of being beat in the court room every time he went up against Nancy Gibbs. He wanted to see the look on Rome face when he had him caught by the balls. Clearing the strip club out. Jack ordered the uniform officers to tear the club up until they found the drugs. Rome sat in a chair along with Tank watching the officers tear his club apart. Seeing a smile on Rome face Jack walked over to him.

"When I find all the drugs you been pushing threw my streets in here. I'm gonna wipe that pretty boy smile right off your face. You want to call your grandmother now or later?"

Not saying a word back to Jack. Rome continued to smile looking directly into Jack face. An hour later the uniform officers came up empty handed. "You got to be shitting me" Jack yelled calling detective Lopez.

Heading the raid on the Dog-pound store. Lopez ran up in the store with twenty uniform officers. Ten female Pitbull dogs ran to the store door barking. Jumping back all officers pulled out their gun.

"Shake down" Pit yelled at the top of his lungs standing up from behind the cash register. Officers looked in shock as over thirty Pitbull dogs ran towards the four dog houses. Jumping over the dog houses, dogs ran in and out of the dog houses. A minute later they all began barking.

"Calm these fucking dogs down before we start shooting them" Lopez yelled trying to be heard over all the barking.

"Hit the wall" Pit yelled. Hearing Pit commandment each dog ran over to the left wall, lining up they all sat down and stop barking.

Lopez looked at the dogs in amazement, then looked over at the uniform as well. Turning his attention back at Pit, he looked at him for a few seconds before he spoke.

"Do I have to call animal control down here?"

"Not at all detective, what seems to be the problem" Pit said with a face of stone.

"If one of them dogs jump or attack one of my officers. It will be shot to death. I have a search warrant to check this store for drugs."

"Drugs" Pit said in a shock tone. "Feel free to check, you will not find drugs in here."

"Tear it up boys" Lopez yelled out. An hour later each officer walked up to Lopez and told him they found nothing.

Down at the police station Jack Murry ripped into Captain Morris in his office. With the office door wide open. Every officer in the police station could hear Jack words loud and clear.

"I have to go back to my boss, and the judge I got these warrants from. I have to tell them both in the raids we found nothing. Their gonna want someone job for this fuck up Morris. And your job sounds real good right about now."

"Jack, I don't know what happen today. But I swear I will get to the bottom of this."

"Morris, I want a head on my desk in an hour" Jack yelled walking out the police station.

"Price get in my office now" Morris yelled. With his head hanging low Price walked in Morris office. "Am I stupid Price?"

"No Captain."

"You tipped that Gibbs family off, didn't you?"

"No! They gave me wrong information Captain."

"Wrong information! Price put your gun and badge on my desk your suspended."

"For how long?"

"Until I tell you to come back to work so I can fire you."

"Captain, I didn't tip them off, but I'm sure they know I set them up now. When they get a hold of me their gonna kill me."

"Price, you can't be serious! You tip them off and you have the nerve to act like you need my help to hide out. Get out my damn office, and out my police station!"

Walking out the house station Price saw Erykah walking up to the police station. Bumping Price in his chest hard with her shoulder. With disgust written on her face Erykah looked at Price.

"You are a dead man walking, enjoy your life while you still have it."

Sweat began to pour down Price face. Walking over to his car Price hands began to shake as he tried to open his car door. Walking in the police station Erykah walked up to the desk.

"How can I help you Ma'ma" Captain Morris asked.

"My name is Erykah Sams I'm a lawyer. I believe you have three of my clients here."

"What are their names?"

"Rome Gibbs, Sierra Gibbs, and Daniel Dawson A.K.A Pit."

"They're not under arrest Ms. Sams."

"I know that! Yet they are being held. Get my damn clients out here right now so I can take them home."

"Detective Lopez, go get those three people from the raid" Morris said.

Two minutes later Pit, Sierra, and Rome, was walking up to the front desk.

"Captain Morris one more thing."

"Yes, what is it Ms. Sams?"

Pulling a ten page document out her briefcase Erykah slammed it on the front desk. "Consider yourself and your whole police department served. Notice of lawsuit from Rome Gibbs against this police station and the N.Y.P.D."

Pushing Pit, Sierra, and Rome, out the police station Erykah walked them to her car. Picking up the ten page document Captain Morris mouth fell open in shock.

"He's suing the N.Y.P.D for thirty million dollars" Morris said looking over at Lopez.

"Erykah we need to hurry up and get over to the Dog-Pound store" Pit said.

"Pit be easy, Rome gave me keys to all three spots. I locked them all up before I came to the police station."

"That's nice, but we need to hurry up over to the store before all of my dogs die."

Seeing the weird look on Erykah face. Pit snatched the car keys out her hand and got in the driver seat. Getting in the front passenger seat Rome put his seatbelt on. Erykah and Sierra got in the back seat. Burning rubber Pit speeded out the police station parking lot.

Pulling up in front of the Dog-Pound store Pit jumped out the car. Unlocking the door to the store Pit walked into the store. All of his dogs still remand sitting in a line against the left wall. Walking in the store Sierra, Rome, and Erykah, watched as Pit ran around the store like a mad man.

"Don't just look around like yawl stupid, help me!"

"What do you need us to do" Rome asked confused.

"Rome get all the doggy bowls from behind the cash register. Place a bowl in front of each dog."

Jumping behind the dog houses Pit began kicking things out the way. The store was a complete mess due to the raid.

"Erykah, Sierra, get a plastic cup and get two gallon bottles from behind the cash register."

"What's in these bottles" Sierra asked looking at the clear liquid in the bottles.

"It's mineral oil, pour a cup full in each doggy bowl."

Doing as they were told they stood over by Rome. As the dogs drunk the mineral oil out the bowls, they kept their eyes on Pit. Finally cleaning up all the stuff from behind the dog houses. Pit pulled out a waterholes. In groups of five Pit walked the dogs over to the back of the dog houses.

"I'm confused, why did you just have all these dogs drink mineral oil" Erykah asked.

"You can't smell why" Rome and Sierra yelled covering their nose.

"Smell what, oh my god" Erykah said smelling the dogs doo-doo in the air.

"Hit the wall" Pit yelled.

Running back over to the left wall behind the doggy bowls each dog sat down. Turning on the waterholes Pit washed all the dog doo-doo down the drain. When all the dog doo-doo was washed away Pit turned the waterholes off. Throwing Sierra and Erykah a pair of rubber gloves. Pit also throw them a garbage each.

"Go behind the dog houses and bag up all the drugs. Rome help me feed the dogs so we can get out of here."

"Pit please tell me you didn't have the drugs in the dogs and they just shitted out all the drugs?"

"You want me to lie to you Rome? Because that's exactly what just happen. Niggas in prison do it so the CO's don't catch the drugs on them. I trained my dogs to do the same thing."

<u>Chapter 30</u>

In Soundview projects Rome sat with his whole team and Khia whole team. A living room full yet divided with Rome and Khia sitting in the middle of it all. Sierra, Tone, Pit, Tameka, Tre, Ke-Ke, and Jo-Jo, all sat on the right side of the living room. Tymel, Erykah, Mike, Terry, and Codie, all sat on the left of the living room. Rome cleared his throat to get everyone attention in the room. Seeing that he had everyone attention Rome began speaking.

"Listen up everyone, me and Khia called this meeting for both of our teams to sit down together. We both feel we may have a big problem on our hands. Yesterday Khia went from feel we may have a big problem on our hands. Yesterday Khia went from being the queen of the Sams drug operation, to not having a position at all."

Rome turned towards Khia for her to take over the meeting. "Yesterday, I was confused, and I'm still confused today. I don't know how, but somehow my older sister Melissa is alive. My mother Tonya took Melissa to meet with Gail. In which she did meet with Gail and now Melissa is the queen of the Sams drug contract. I saw Melissa in her casket, I saw her casket be put in the ground. I saw the dirt go over Melissa casket. That was over ten years ago. How Melissa is alive is beyond me."

Khia turned towards Rome to take back over the meeting. "Me and Khia don't know If she will get her position back. So in the meantime Khia team is now a part of the Gibbs drug family team. Right now the Banks hotel, Love it or Hate it, and the Dog-Pound store are all shut down."

"Dog-Pound will be back up and running within a week" Pit added in.

"Any way as I was saying before I was interrupted. Before all three of those spots are reopen. We need to take pictures of all the damage that was done during those raids. Those pictures will go to Erykah to help her along with the law suit I have against the N.Y.P.D. I have two drug spots and will be splitting our now team of fifteen members between those spots as followed."

"Pit will remand running the Dog-Pound store with him and his dogs only" Pit yelled out.

"Pit…."

"Rome, don't Pit me. Me and you spoke about this before Rome."

"You know what Pit with that perfect stunt you pulled at that store during that raid. As you wish I will not put any one to work with you at that store. With that said I will be splitting this Soundview spot into three shifts. Khia will run the morning shift, with Tymel and Mike helping her. The afternoon shift will be run by Tone, with Tameka, Terry and Lloyd helping him."

"Rome, I told you Lloyd…."

"Tone, I saw Lloyd, I spoke to Lloyd, and I found out what the problem was. At the point in time Lloyd is on vacation for a month. Jo-Jo will continue to be our drug runner, and Sierra will continue running the Banks hotel. As for Erykah she will be laying low since she's the only lawyer we have on hand at the moment. Erykah has her hands full with two things. Such as my lawsuit against the N.Y.P.D."

Rome turned towards Khia to speak. "Erykah is also working on a court order to have my sister Melissa casket pulled out the ground."

Looking over at Rome, Rome took control over the meeting again. "I said earlier in this meeting that, me and Khia both feel we may have a big problem on our hands. Tonya has control over Webster projects. Which I agreed to let her take over that spot. Tonya has found a way to take over Courtlandt projects, with the help of Melissa. Me and Khia strongly believe that Tonya is trying to take over all the projects in the Bronx that are money makers. Which mean she may be thinking about trying to take Soundview projects over again. Now I'm not sure if she will go against the meeting and agreement me and her made. Just be on point and on the lookout for any one of Tonya team members being in Soundview projects. With that said this meeting is over."

Standing up Rome went to the back private room. Standing up Tone followed behind Rome into the room and closed the door.

"Rome you said in the meeting that you saw and spoke to Lloyd."

"I did Tone, and I also found out what the problem was with Lloyd. A problem that me and Lloyd will keep to our self."

"Is that your way of telling me that you not going tell me what's going on with Lloyd?"

"It sure is Tone."

"I take it that I'm just supposed to forget that Lloyd stole ten thousand dollars from me to?"

Pulling out his pocket Rome through the envelope over at Tone. Catching the envelope Tone looked at it confused. "Tone that's your ten thousand dollar, plus an extra five thousand. You not being asked to forget what Lloyd did. You being asked to forgive and move on Tone."

"Rome, I'll move on when I find out why Lloyd was stealing from me."

Stepping closer to Tone, Rome looked him in the face. "Let me reword what I just said to you Tone. You're not being asked; your being told to forgive Lloyd and move on. Are we clear?"

Not backing down Tone looked back at Rome face. "Were clear that I won't kill Lloyd or put him in the hospital."

"Tone all I'm gonna say is show Lloyd brotherly love not enemy love."

"Deal" Tone said giving Rome a pound with his fist.

*****

Parking in front of Clinton correctional facility Brandy waited in her car for Ba-Ba to be released. Seeing Ba-Ba walk out the prison with Leevon, Nest, and Dutch, following behind him. Brandy beeped her car horn and rolled down her car window. Confused to who the woman was that was waiving them over. Leevon looked over at Ba-Ba.

"Who the hell is she" Leevon asked.

Pulling out the picture that Brandy had mailed him of what she now looked like after her surgery. Ba-Ba looked at the picture then at the woman inside the car waiving them over. "That's Brandy A.K.A Melissa" Ba-Ba said with a smile.

Ba-Ba had told them that Brandy had plastic surgery. Yet he didn't show them the picture that she had mailed him of herself after the surgery.

"Damn big bro, she look good as a motherfucker now" Leevon said.

Getting out the car Brandy wrapped her arms around Ba-Ba. "Damn you look good sweetheart" Ba-Ba said hugging Brandy back.

Letting Ba-Ba go Brandy looked over at Leevon, Nest, and Dutch. "What up fellas? Where's the love at?"

One by one three of them gave Brandy a hug. "Brandy girl, you look good as hell" Leevon said.

"Thank you, brother, in law. Come on yawl get in the car."

Driving away from the prison Brandy began breaking down her plan to all four of them. "From now on don't call me Brandy any more. From here on out get use to calling me Melissa. What's good about my plan is that the Gibbs family, the Sams family, the Jones family, and Desean and his team don't know what any of you look like. Just like myself, Ba-Ba will be going under the knife to get a new face. Right now I'm the queen of the Sams drug contract. I have a drug contract with one of the biggest drug lords in the world. Her name is Gail. With Ba-Ba new face and who he's about to become. Ba-Ba will become the king of the Sams drug contract. I will explain more about how things go with the contract and Gail later. In the meantime know that I now run Courtlandt projects when it comes to selling drugs. A spot that Ba-Ba will soon be running when he is fully recovered from his surgery. Which will be in about two weeks."

"In two weeks I'll be having the surgery" Ba-Ba asked.

"No, today you will be having the surgery, in two weeks you will be fully recovered from the surgery. I want this takeover to be done as soon as possible. I schedule your surgery for today Ba-Ba at the same place I had my surgery done at."

Pulling up to the medical plastic surgery center. Brandy looked over at Ba-Ba. "Are you ready to do this?"

"Not yet, there are a few things we need to discuss Melissa."

"Such as what Ba-Ba?"

"Who do this woman Tonya have helping you run Courtlandt projects?"

"Two guys by the name of Henry and Good, that I will meet for the first time today."

"Brandy, I mean Melissa. Melissa, you do know when we take things over. This Henry and goody guys are out, and my team will be running Courtlandt projects."

"I know that Ba-Ba, that's my whole plan. When you take over Tonya and her team will be pushed out."

"Melissa what If this Tonya woman tell this Gail woman that you're not who you are supposed to be, and neither am I?"

"Ba-Ba she can't tell Gail that because If she do that would mean that she lied to Gail. And lying to Gail will get Tonya Jones drug family contract canceled. Another things Ba-Ba. Until we take over the Sams drug contract fully. You boys have to wait to take over the Red-Money team from Desean."

"Wrong Melissa, Leevon is going to handle the take over from Desean while I'm in surgery. Because If were gonna go up against this Jones drug family. We don't need to be watching over our shoulder for Desean team to get at us too."

"Ba-Ba what if Desean and his team refuse to let you run Red-Money?"

"Then Melissa they all have two choices, stop using Red-Money name or they can all go in the ground. Yet if they do join us that will make our crew even stronger to go up against this Jones drug family."

"That's all cool by me Ba-Ba. Now are you ready to do this?"

"No, two more things Me-liss-a. I know your plan Melissa, but what plan do Tonya think you have with her?"

"Well she wanted me to get control over the Sams drug contract from Khia. Which has been done. Tonya also want me to re-write the Sams drug contract in a month making her the queen of the Sams drug family contract."

"I understand, last but not lease Melissa. I didn't forget how you shitted on me and the boys for eight in a half years."

"Ba-Ba…."

"Shut up! I'm not done talking! I didn't forget Melissa. Yet with this sweet plan you came up with all is forgiving between me, you, and the fellas. Now I'm ready to go in this place and get this surgery over with."

After dropping Ba-Ba off at the medical plastic surgery center. Leevon told Brandy to drive to Webster projects. So that him, Nest, and Dutch could have a talk with Desean and his team. Pulling up to Webster projects Brandy gave Leevon her apartment keys and three guns. With the apartment keys in hand Leevon got out the car with Nest and Dutch following behind him. Using the key that Brandy gave him. Leevon, Nest, and Dutch, walked in Brandy apartment. An apartment they hadn't been in over eight in a half years. Seeing no one in the living room. Leevon did a quick peek into the kitchen and saw five guys sitting at the Kitchen table. "Jackpot" Leevon whispered pulling out his gun. Following suit Dutch and Nest pulled their gun out as well. Ba-Ba had gave Leevon the run down that there was five members of the new Red-Money crew. There wasn't a doubt in Leevon mind that all five members were all sitting in the kitchen. With that quick peek in the kitchen. Leevon saw one guy sitting at the head of the table counting money, which had to be Desean. Leevon also saw two guys cutting up drugs, and two other guys bagging up drugs.

With guns pointing, Leevon, Nest, and Dutch ran up in the kitchen. "Listen up" Leevon yelled making all five of them jump in shock at the table. Letting off a shot at the wall Leevon told them all not to move. "The next shot I let off in this mother fucker. The bullet is going in one of your heads."

Walking over to Desean, Leevon put his gun to his head. "I take it your Desean and you run Red-Money?"

"Yeah."

"That shit ends today! My name is Leevon and my brother name is Ba-Ba.

Hearing the name Ba-Ba, Desean heart began beating fast. Yet on the outside he remand calm.

"Fellas, Ba-Ba would have made this meeting were having, but he had some other business to handle. Which mean I'm in command."

"Listen I don't know a Ba-Ba, you or these other two niggas, what's all this about" Tracy asked annoyed that a gun was pointed to his head.

Not liking Tracy tone Dutch whacked Tracy in his face with his gun. "Let that be a lesson to keep your fucking mouth closed" Dutch said looking down at Tracy. Dutch looked over at Leevon to continue to speak.

"Fellas, Ba-Ba is the founder of Red-Money. Me, Ba-Ba, Dutch, and Nest, were all in prison for eight in a half years. Our little brother Smoke put Desean on. When Smoke died Desean took over and put you all on. As of today Ba-Ba runs Red-Money. When my brother Ba-Ba is not around I'm in charge. Now here's the deal you five guys can continue to be down with Red-Money. Or you can drop your red flags and walk away now. Know if you stay, you take orders from us. If you walk keep walking or you will find yourself in the ground. So fellas, make your choice."

Standing up Desean threw a stack of money to Buddha, Trouble, Demon, Tracy, Leevon, Nest and Dutch. Desean threw the duffle bag strap over his shoulder. Seeing Desean walking out the kitchen Trouble stood up.

"Where you going big homie" Trouble asked Desean.

"I'm out, I don't take orders from people I don't like or don't know. Yawl can stay, yawl can keep the rest of the drugs."

"If you out then so am I big homie" Trouble said following Desean out the apartment door.

Seeing Desean and Trouble walk out the apartment. Leevon turned his attention back to the kitchen table. "What choices are you three gonna make?"

"I'm staying" Buddha said.

"I'm staying to" Demon said.

Standing up Tracy stood face to face with Leevon. "Them two niggas can bounce. Like I said earlier I don't know Ba-Ba, you, or these two other niggas. With Desean and Trouble stepping down puts me in charge."

"POP" the sound Dutch gun made. The bullet ripped through the side of Tracy head killing him instantly.

"Damn Dutch, why you kill him? His speech was just getting good."

"Leevon, I was getting sick of hearing that nigga talk. He spit more shit out his mouth then a baby shit out their ass."

Stepping over Tracy body, Leevon, Nest, and Dutch, sat down at the kitchen table. "here's the deal you both will meet Ba-Ba in two weeks. Until then this is how things will be running. Continue to get the drugs from this Tonya bitch. When it comes to paying her, dead her on her cut. For two weeks Buddha you are in charge of running this spot. Give that Tonya bitch the run around when it comes to her receiving her money cut. In the meantime myself, Ba-Ba, Nest, and Dutch, will be laying low for two weeks. Have all the money that this house make in total the next time you see us."

Standing up from the kitchen table Dutch tie a garbage bag around Tracy head. Standing up Leevon took the stack of money out Tracy pocket that Desean gave him and put it in his own pocket. Standing up from the table Nest picked Tracy body up and through his body over his shoulder. Walking out the apartment the three of them took Tracy body with them. Opening the staircase Nest threw Tracy body down the stairs. Walking down the stairs the three of them stepped over Tracy body. Walking out the building the three of them got back in the car with Brandy.

Picking Ba-Ba up from the hospital Brandy took all of them back to her hotel sweet. Laying Ba-Ba in the bed Brandy looked down at him as he slept. She couldn't wait until the bandages came off his face. Ba-Ba always looked good to her. Yet the picture of Wayne got her juices flowing. With Ba-Ba now looking like Wayne, Brandy couldn't wait to have sex with him. Feeling someone looking at him Ba-Ba grabbed a hold of Brandy hand.

"My face hurt like hell shorty."

"That pain will go away in a week and then you can take the bandages off your face. Your face will look swollen, but that will all go away before your second week is up, and then you will be up and running just like me."

Seeing that Ba-Ba had fell back asleep Brandy pulled the covers over him. Walking in the living room off the hotel sweet Brandy laughed. Dutch, Nest, and Leevon, looked up from the T.V and looked at Brandy.

"What's so damn funny" Nest asked.

"Yawl! Yawl been in prison for the past eight in a half years and you out and watching T.V. Order some room service and charge it to the hotel sweet. Order some body massages, I hear they end with a happy ending.

Brandy last comment about happy endings, Dutch jumped up off the couch and grabbed the hotel phone. "Room service, let me get two pizza pies with extra cheese. Four cheeseburgers, a pan of French fries, and four two liter Pepsis. And hit my room in a hour with three of your finest female massagers" Dutch said into the phone.

Going in her purse Brandy pulled out three stack of money. Throwing a stock of money at each of them Brandy closed her purse. "Make sure yawl go buy yourself some clothes. I have to go meet up with Tonya. I shall be back later on tonight."

*****

In Courtlandt projects Tonya lead the way into Khia old drug spot apartment. Brandy, Goody, and henry, followed Tonya into the apartment.

"Goody, Henry, get to cleaning up this place." Tonya took Brandy to the kitchen and sat down. "Do you have the number that Gail gave you?"

"Yes, I do Tonya."

Placing a bag of money on the table Tonya pushed it across the table at Brandy. "Give Gail a call and tell her you need a shipment of weight A.S.A.P."

Doing as she was told Brandy made the call to Gail. While Brandy talked on the phone. Tonya placed a new house door lock on the kitchen table. She then placed two set of keys on the table. Getting off the phone with Gail, Brandy looked over at Tonya.

"Take both set of keys Brandy. Those are the keys to this apartment. One set is to the old locks, the other set is to the new locks. Hopefully when you come back over here Henry will the locks changed. If not, you will still have the old keys to get in. So what did Gail say?"

"She said okay, gave me the address to where I have to pick the weight up at in an hour."

"Good, do you know how to cook cocaine into crack?"

"Of course Tonya."

"Good, because that's your job here. Go pick up the weight, bring it back here, cook it, and go back to the hotel. Henry and Goody will do the bagging and selling. That weight should hold this spot for a month. Next month me and you will go to Gail and you will turn the Sams drug family contract over to me. The money made in this apartment Goody will hold it all in the back room to be picked up next month by me."

"So today is the only day I need to be at this apartment?"

"Yup, after today all you have to do is lay up in that hotel sweet, I got you Brandy. In a month I'll give you a call so we can meet with Gail, after that your job is done Brandy."

Picking the bag and two set of keys up off the table. Brandy placed her sunglasses on her face. "I'll see you in a month" Brandy said walking out the apartment.

Walking in the kitchen Goody and Henry sat down at the table across from Tonya.

"Are you sure you want to kill that girl after that meeting next month with Gail" Good asked.

"I'm more than sure Goody. I gave her that face and with my gun shall I take that face right back when I shoot it off. No way in the hell will I allow her to walk around for life wearing my daughter beautiful face."

"Tonya, I thought you said Brandy want to have surgery to put her face back to what she use to look like" Henry said joining in the conversation.

"Henry that's what she said. Believe me when I tell you Henry. Ain't no way in the world is that girl gonna go from ugly, to beautiful, back to ugly again. So in the ground she will be going next month." Standing up Tonya looked over at Henry. "Henry make sure you change the locks on this apartment door that way Khia can no longer get inside this apartment." Spinning on her heels Tonya walked out the apartment.

Chapter 31

Two Weeks Later

Brandy, Leevon, Nest, and Dutch, all sat in the living room of Brandy hotel sweet. To say they were all becoming annoyed was a understatement.

"Ba-Ba has been in that bathroom for almost an hour. What is he doing in there" Nest said cutting off the T.V.

Standing up Brandy went into the bathroom and closed the door behind her. With the bandages still on his face he stood on front of the bathroom mirror. Walking up behind Ba-Ba, Brandy wrapped her arms around his waist and rest her head on his back.

"Ba-Ba it's been two weeks since you had the surgery. You could have took the bandages off your face a week ago. Why haven't you took them off yet?"

"Because…."

"Because what Ba-Ba?"

"Because taking these bandages off mean that's truly the end of me."

"Ba-Ba, having a new face doesn't me your gone. Think of it as up grading yourself. You have always been a king to me Ba-Ba. And today is that day that you step on the throne as king. You have the face, your face is fully healed, and it's time to use it."

With Brandy help Ba-Ba took the bandages off his face. Looking in the mirror at his self Ba-Ba smiled. He looked just like the picture of the man Brandy had showed him before his surgery. Looking closely at his self in the mirror. Ba-Ba always thought he was a handsome man. Yet he had to admit with his new face he looked a pinch better.

"Are you ready to take on the world with your new face?"

"Yeah."

"Good, because I scheduled a meeting with Gail for today for me and you. Did you memorize all the answers to the questions I told you Gail will ask you?"

"Brandy, I got this, trust me." Handing Ba-Ba his new I.D card the both of them walked out the bathroom.

As Ba-Ba stepped inside the living room, Leevon, Nest, and Dutch stood up. "Damn bro you look like a whole different person" Leevon said looking at Ba-Ba.

"That's the whole point when you get a new face to look like a new person. Now today is the day we get down to business. As of today were running Courtlandt projects full force. Which mean this Henry and Goody guys have to go. I'm sure when this Tonya chick get the news that were taking over, she's gonna flip out. Which mean today is our last day staying in this hotel sweet." Ba-Ba turned around and looked at Brandy. "Are you sure there's no way this Tonya chick can take the Sams drug contract from us?"

"Not that I know of, but with a contract there's always a loophole somewhere. All I know is she can't go directly to Gail and tell Gail were not who we say we are. Otherwise her head will be on the chopping block for lying to Gail."

"Okay, let me think, you said this Gail woman only do business threw contracts. Do Tonya have a lawyer?"

"Her granddaughter Erykah is a lawyer. But from what I'm told their not on speaking terms."

"That's what all people say when their mad at each other Brandy. When money talks, all the rest of this shit go out the window. Which mean we have to do our homework on Erykah because she has to go."

"Ba-Ba are you sure about this? Erykah is not only related to the Jones, she's also related to the Sams and Gibbs families."

"Good, then all of them can go to one funeral. Here's the game plan for today. While me and Brandy are having a meeting with Gail. Leevon pack up all of our things and find us some where new to rest our heads. Dutch, Nest, go check out our corner where we Red-Money use to sell drugs. See if we can set up a drug shop there again. Also check on this Erykah girl. I want to know what's her schedule from Monday through Friday. When all of that is done. I want yawl all to meet up with me and Brandy."

*****

In Love it or Hate it, Rome sat down at the bar. "Tank hit me with a henny on the rocks."

Placing the drink on the bar in front of Rome. Tank shook his head at Rome and smiled at him.

"What's with that smile on your face Tank?"

"Rome every step you take you surprise me every time. Three of your spots got raided two weeks ago and all three of them are back up and running better looking than before. The Banks hotel was a four floor hole in the wall. You redoing it over, it look like a up class hotel. The Dog-Pound store is back up and running. The inside of that spot look like a doggy heaven now. Then look what you did to this club. It was already a strip club slash night club. You redoing the club over you added a second floor to this club. Night club on the first floor, strip club on the second floor. So tell me Rome, when are these three spots gonna be open for business?"

"Tank, Pit reopen the store last week. Sierra reopen the Banks hotel yesterday. And today Love it or Hate it, open tonight. I have something I have to handle today. So I'm gonna need you to hold the club down Tank."

"Rome not a problem I can handle things up in here."

Seeing Jo-Jo, and Tymel walking in the club. Rome stood up and walked to the club back private office. Taking a seat down behind his desk. Tymel and Jo-Jo walked in the office and closed the door. Jumping on the computer Rome pulled up detective Price chain tracker map history. Seeing that Rome was focus on the computer screen. Jo-Jo and Tymel stood quite at the office door. From the time Price left the police station he had been laying low at his house. Picking up his desk phone Rome blocked his club phone number and called Price cell phone.

"Hello."

"Price, I think me, and you need to see each other face to face."

"Rome listen…."

"No you listen! You're on the Gibbs payroll to keep my team out of prison. Instead you thought you were slick by helping set those three raids up. Lucky for me I picked up on you growing into a rat. Now it's bad for you because I know you are a rat, and I have to give you some rat poison. I can't have a rat around my team Price. So can I come over to your house right now, so I can give you the rat poison I have for you?"

"Rome, you think I'm gonna give you my home address so you can come murder me?"

"Price, you don't have to give it to me, I already have it."

Hearing Rome resight his home address Price hung up the phone. Running around his house like a bat out of hell. Price grabbed a few things, money, a wig, sunglasses, and his gun.

Running out his house he jumped inside his car. Speeding off Price hit the highway. After Price hung the phone up, Rome watched closely at the computer screen. It was clear that Price was on the move. Yet Rome didn't have a clue where Price was heading. Becoming impatience Tymel cleared his throat to get Rome attention. Paying Tymel surceased attempt to get his attention no mind. Rome continued to look at the computer screen.

"Ummm hello, earth to Rome. You called us to come over here to see you. Did you call is over here so you could just pay us no attention" Jo-Jo said.

Seeing on the computer screen that Price had checked into the Banks hotel in room six. Rome yelled out "Unfucking real" and slammed his fist on the desk. "How stupid can he be to try to hide out from me in the hotel I own" Rome said to his self in his head. Turning off the computer Rome looked up at Jo-Jo and Tymel. "You know why I called you two over to this club to meet with me?"

"Why" Jo-Jo and Tymel both said really wanting to know the answer.

"Because the three of us are going to go murder detective Price."

"Rome, you really think Price is going to stay in his house after what you just told him over the phone?"

"Not at all Tymel. Price is at the Banks hotel in room six."

Tymel and Jo-Jo looked at each other confused. "Why would he check into a hotel room in the hotel you own after what he did?"

"Tymel, why, I can only guess is because he's not thinking straight. Yet him not thinking straight works in our favor. Let's roll!" Standing up Rome walked out the office and out the club, with Jo-Jo and Tymel following close behind him.

*****

Pulling up on the old street corner where Red-Money use to sell drugs at. Nest and Dutch got out the car. Looking up and down the block they didn't see any one outside selling drugs. Although they hadn't been on the block in over eight in a half years. Not a lot had changed except for one thing. Joe's store that was always closed for business, was no longer Joe's store, it wasn't closed for business either anymore. It was now named, Dog-pound.

"Hey, let's say me and you go buy a dog for our new drug spot" Nest said to Dutch.

Not responding to Nest, Dutch lead the way into Dog-pound store. Four female Pitbull dogs ran over to the store door stopping them in their tracks. Hearing the dogs barking Pit stood up from behind the cash register. Looking at the two men that had just walked into his store. Pit could tell they were not fiends because they were to clean. Which only left three other reason to why they were in his store. One, to buy a dog. Or two, to buy a large amount of drugs. Or three, to try to rob his store.

"What can I do for you two fellas" Pit asked.

"Me and my boy are looking to buy two Pitbull dogs."

"Bitches be easy." Hearing those three words come out of Pit mouth. The four female dogs walked away from the store door, letting Dutch and Nest walk freely around the store.

As Dutch and Nest walked around the store looking at the dogs. It didn't take Pit long to notice they both had a gun tucked in their pants under their shirt. In the hood guns on a person meant that person is into the drug game. And to Pit a drug deal that wasn't down on his team was nothing more than a threat to his team.

"So fellas your looking to buy female dogs or male dogs?"

"My man no need to be all professional calling us fellas. My name is Nest, and this is my boy Dutch. Were, looking to buy two male Pitbull dogs."

"Okay, okay, well Dutch, Nest. The dogs that are for sell are in the back room, follow me. Following behind Pit into the back room. Dutch and Nest picked out two male Pitbull dogs. Paying Pit, Dutch and Nest left the store.

*****

Gail sat at her dining room table looking across the table at Brandy and Ba-Ba. Tapping her finger on the table Gail tried her best to figure out the problem that was nagging at her mind. She too thought that Melissa had been murdered just like Khia thought. If her memory was right Melissa was murdered by Solo. Yet here she was alive for the second time sitting before her. This time she wasn't sitting alone, she was sitting with her brother Wayne Sams. Wayne Sams who Gail also thought had been murdered. Murdered by Trina, Solo wife.

"Melissa, I understand in the drug world, we lie, we go into hiding. Sometimes we even leave people thinking we are dead. Yet you two were written off years ago as had been murdered. Normally I would question your reasons of going M.I.A. But since I know your mother Tonya very well, and Tonya brought Melissa to my house. I will not question both of you going M.I.A for years. So what can I do for you Melissa?"

"Gail as you know I'm now the queen of the Sams drug contract. With my brother Wayne being older than me. I think it's only right that he take his place back as the king of the Sams drug contract since he's older than me."

"Is that what you want again Wayne?"

"Yes Gail."

"Well so ordered, Melissa you are no longer the queen of the Sams drug contract. Ladies! Please show Melissa and Wayne to the door." The nine women that showed Brandy and Ba-Ba into the house appeared in the dining room. Standing up Brandy and Ba-Ba began walking out the dining room. "Wayne" Gail called out.

Turning around Wayne looked at Gail. "Yeah?"

"Come over here."

Walking over to where Gail was seated Ba-Ba leaned over to see what she wanted. Looking at Wayne neck Gail noticed he didn't have no sign of a scare. Wayne how is your ass hole?"

"Huh" Wayne said confused to why Gail would ask him such a question.

"I said how is your ass hole?"

"Gail, I'm not sure what you mean by that. But I can a sure you I don't play that fruity shit. Ain't nobody ever played up in my butt hole Gail."

"Are you sure about that Wayne?"

"I'm positive Gail."

"Are you telling me you have never been raped by multiple men Wayne?"

"Hell no!"

"Ladies, show them to the door."

Sitting at the dining room table alone Gail began thinking to herself. Wayne didn't have a clue to what she had asked him. Nor did he have a scare on his neck which a scare should have been on his neck. Going down memory lane in her head Gail remembered what Solo told her years ago. "Wayne set his wife Train up to be raped. For that he had multiple men rape Wayne and had Trina cut Wayne throat from ear to ear. Then they dumped Wayne body in the truck of Wayne car and left his car in the Banks hotel parking lot." In no way did Gail feel Solo would have lied to her about what his team did to Wayne. Gail also knew it could have been a possibly that Wayne could have served what Solo team did to him. Yet what bothered her was Wayne didn't have a clue to the rape question she asked him. Nor did he wear a scare around his neck that should have been on his neck. Then another thing popped into Gail head. Maybe Solo did all of that to someone he thought was Wayne. Gail pushed that thought out her head just as fast as she thought it. She knew for a fact that Solo knew exactly who Wayne was and what he looked like. So there was no way Solo could have done all of that to the wrong person. Gail then also remembered Solo telling her "He shot Melissa in her head in her hospital bed." How could Solo believe that two people he had a hand in killing, be so much alive years later? That was the big question running through Gail mind. A question that only Solo could answer. A answer she wanted to know, yet knew she wasn't going to get it any time soon from Solo. Something about Melissa and Wayne stepping back on the scene just wasn't sitting well with her. For now she would have to go with the flow. Yet she plan to put her team on the job in the meantime to put the missing pieces together in this puzzle.

*****

Meeting up in front of Webster projects Dutch, Nest, and Leevon, got in the car with Brandy and Ba-Ba. Seeing the two dogs that Dutch tied to the pole on the sidewalk. Ba-Ba looked at Dutch threw the car mirror as he got comfortable in the back car seat.

"Where the hell did you get those two mutts from Dutch?"

"Me and Nest brought them earlier for our new drug spot in Courtlandt projects."

"I see, well while you two were buying dogs. Did you happen to handle that business that you were told to handle?"

"Yeah, we did, what the hell you think we can't do more than one thing at a time nigga?"

Not liking Dutch tone Ba-Ba turned around in his car seat facing Dutch. "Who the fuck do you think you talking to like that Dutch!"

"You nigga, you deaf" Dutch yelled back not backing down.

"Hey, both of you chill the fuck out. You know we don't beef between each other and were not gonna start today" Leevon said cutting the tension in the air fast. "Dutch what did you and Nest find out today?"

Dutch waived at Nest to talk still feeling some type of way about the way Ba-Ba was talking to him. Taking the lead Nest started running down everything him and Dutch found out earlier. "Ba-Ba, me and Dutch hit the old block we use to sell weight on. Not a lot has changed over there. Yet we did find out the new store that has open up on that block sell drugs. That's where we brought those two dogs from. We also found out from a few fiends in that area. That the Dog-pound store is a front. The owner sell drugs out that store. We also found out about that chick Erykah. Every Friday she make it her busines to be in the courthouse on 161st in the Bronx. Me and Dutch spoke to one of the desk clerks in one of the court houses. Me laying down my Mack daddy skills on the female clerk. She told me Erykah is working on two cases. A lawsuit against the N.Y.P.D. And another case trying to get some type of court order from a judge. I asked the clerk do any one of those cases that Erykah is working on have anything to do with a contract. She told me, no. So Ba-Ba If you want Erykah dead. The best time to do so is on Friday when she's at the courthouse. We can catch her before she go in the courthouse or when she come out the courthouse."

Ba-Ba sat in the car quite for a few seconds processing everything that Nest had just told him.

"All right here's the plan. We gonna go get these young Red-Money niggas. Taking them from Webster projects to Courtlandt projects and officially bring the old and new Red-Money team together. Together were gonna take over the Courtlandt projects drug spot. And Dutch since you want to be slick out your mouth today. You and Nest can go handle Erykah next Friday."

"Ba-Ba let me tell you something."

"First off stop calling me Ba-Ba, get use to calling me Wayne. And that goes for everyone in this car. As for you telling me anything Dutch. Keep it to yourself because I don't want to hear it. Remember I run Red-Money, ain't shit change from eight in a half years ago. So check the way you talk to me. You got that Dutch?"

"Yeah, I got it, and just like you said ain't shit change. You run Red-Money, but you gonna respect me like you been doing" Dutch said getting out the car. Turning to Brandy, Ba-Ba told her to stay in the car. As Ba-Ba got out the car Nest and Leevon followed him.

Inside Webster drug spot apartment. Stepping inside the apartment Ba-Ba introduced his self to the young Red-Money crew. He told Buddha and Demon, he was Ba-Ba, yet they are to call him Wayne. He then told them to pack up all the drugs and money inside the apartment. When they were done, they locked the apartment up and headed downstairs to the two cars waiting. Dutch, and Nest, got in Brandy car with the two dogs they brought earlier in the day. Ba-Ba took Dutch car keys and jumped in Dutch driver seat. Leevon helped Buddha and Demon put the drugs and money in the truck. When they were done, they got in the car with Ba-Ba. Hearing Ba-Ba beep the car horn giving the signal that he was ready to roll. Brandy started up her car pulling off leading the way to Courtlandt projects.

*****

Standing at the front desk Sierra smiled when she saw Rome walk into the Banks hotel. Instead of receiving a smile in return from Rome. Sierra got a displeased look from Rome. Walking up to the front desk Tymel and Jo-Jo stood close behind Rome.

"Do you have any idea Sierra who you let in this hotel and didn't notify me that they were here?"

"Rome, we get a lot of people that come into this hotel a day. So why are you coming up in here pissed off at me?"

"Because Sierra although a lot of people come in this hotel. It's not every day that detective Price, a person that has a hit on his head rent a room here."

"Rome, I been at this desk all day. He didn't rent a room here."

"Oh he did Sierra, he's in room six."

Thinking quick Sierra slammed her fist on the top of the desk. "Shit that was that weirdo that came in here with a long black wig wearing sunglasses. I was trying so hard not to laugh at how funny looking the guy looked. That I didn't pay any attention to his face. I'm so sorry Rome."

Leaning over the desk Rome kissed Sierra lips. "Everybody slip once in a blue. Lucky for you baby girl your husband is on the job hard body. Just know you gonna receive a punishment for slipping today."

"A punishment" Sierra repeated not sure If she heard Rome correctly.

"Yeah, a punishment, when you get home tonight, I'm gonna give you a spanking on that cute little butt of yours."

Hearing enough of the freaky talk Jo-Jo pushed Rome towards the elevator. Looking over his shoulder at Sierra, Rome gave her the Gibbs million door smile and licked his lips. Smiling back at Rome, Sierra threw Rome a set of keys to room six.

Getting off the elevator, Rome, Jo-Jo, and Tymel, placed rubber gloves on their hands. "What's the plan Rome" Tymel asked.

Paying Tymel question no mind Rome unlocked the hotel room door and looked at Tymel and Jo-Jo. "There is no game plan."

Walking inside the room they found Price sleeping in a chair with the T.V on. Closing the door the three of them stood in front of the chair. Clapping his hands to wake Price up Rome pulled out his gun. Half sleep Price open his eyes. Seeing Rome, Tymel, and Jo-Jo, standing before him. Price eyes grew large in fear. Going in his top pocket Rome pulled out a attachment to his gun. Screwing the silencer on his gun Rome eyes burned a hole through Price Dearing Price to make a move.

"Rome please for the love of god don't do this."

Pointing the gun at Price head, Rome fired one shot landing a bullet in the middle of Price forehead.

"Damn Rome that was cold. Didn't you hear him pleading for his life" Tymel said. Turning his head Rome looked at Tymel as if he had just spoke a language he couldn't understand.

"Lighten up I'm fucking with you" Tymel said pulling out two large garbage bags. He placed one bag around Price upper body and handed the other bag to Jo-Jo. Jo-Jo lifted Price lower body up into the garbage bag. Taping the bags up around Price body. Tymel and jo-Jo picked Price body up and looked over at Rome.

"Now what" both of them asked Rome. Picking up Price car keys Rome told them to follow him.

Placing Price in the back seat of his own car. Rome got in the driver seat and pulled off. Following behind Price car inside of Rome car, Tymel and Jo-Jo made sure they stayed close. Driving for twenty minutes Tymel and Jo-Jo wasn't sure where Rome was driving to. That's until Rome made a sharp right in Price car driving down the block towards the 34th police station. Driving Price car up on the sidewalk of the police station. Rome got out the car leaving Price car door open as he got in the car with Tymel and Jo-Jo. Pulling off nice and slow Jo-Jo drove two blocks away from the police station and made a sharp left. Finally feeling they were in the clear Jo-Jo pulled over. Turning around in the car seat Jo-Jo looked Rome in his face.

"Have you lost your damn mind! Why hell would you drive his body to the police station? Are you aware you just murdered a cop and drove him to the police station he work for?"

"I'm aware of all of that Jo-Jo. Just like I'm aware Price is a rat. I killed the rat, the lease the police station can do is do something with the rat body."

Jo-Jo couldn't help but to laugh at Rome response to his question. Shaking his head in disbelief Jo-Jo started the car back up. "Rome I'm starting to worry about you" Jo-Jo said as he began driving again.

"Why is that Jo-Jo?"

"Because slowly but surely your starting to turn into Solo. Cold hearted, loving, sweet, yet very deadly."

"Well Jo-Jo, I may have been raised by Supreme, but do keep in mind Solo was my blood father. Now let's call it a night."

*****

Leaving Brandy downstairs in the car parked in front of Courtlandt projects. Ba-Ba took the keys from Brandy that Tonya gave her. With the keys in hand Ba-Ba lead the way to Tonya drug apartment in Courtlandt project. A drug spot that Khia took from Mike. A drug spot that Tonya took from Khia. A drug spot that will be taking over by Red-Money now. Using the key Ba-Ba let his self-inside the apartment. Following close behind Ba-Ba, Leevon, Dutch, Nest, Buddha, and Demon, all walked into the apartment as well. Seeing five guys walk into the living room. Henry and Goody looked at each other confused then looked back at the five guys that stood before them. While the rest of the Red-Money team held court in the living room. Dutch walked down the hall of the apartment until he found the bathroom. Finding the bathroom Dutch placed the two dogs inside the bathroom and closed the bathroom door.

Pulling out their guns each one of the Red-Money team members held them at their side. "What the hell is this" Goody said.

Each one of the Red-Money team looked over at Ba-Ba. Stepping in front of Goody, Ba-Ba let his words bounce off the apartment walls. "I'll tell you what this is about. It's called a takeover by Red-Money. We can do this the easy way or the hard way."

"Oh really" Goody said standing up. "Take over my ass! This here drug spot is owned by Tonya. So If you know like I know. You and these damn goon looking mother fuckers better beat your damn feet the hell up out this apartment."

Seeing Henry stand up beside Goody, Leevon walked over to his brother Ba-Ba. One thing ran through all four of their minds, and that was pop off. Reaching back each one of them threw a knockout punch at the other. Seeing the explosion of blows being thrown. The Red-Money team jumped to help their two big homies. Although it was eight guns in the living room fully loaded. A full blown brawl began to break out inside the apartment. Six against two, yet Goody and Henry continued to hold their own still on their feet. A brawl that they were sure they could win. Yet for each two punches they gave, they received six punches back. A fight that seem to last for hours, really only lasted two minutes. Goody and Henry found their self on the floor being kicked and stumped on. A kicking and stumping match that lasted way past the point of them being beat on conscious.

Picking Henry and Goody up off the floor. The Red-Money team threw down the stairs in the projects staircase. Walking back inside the apartment. Ba-Ba pulled out his cell phone and called Brandy. Telling Brandy to come up to the apartment Ba-Ba hung up. Leevon went to the back room and began counting up the drugs and money Tonya team left in the apartment. As Buddha, Demon, and Nest, cleaned the apartment up. Dutch began changing the locks on the apartment door. Walking inside the apartment with four bags full of drugs and money from Webster projects. Brandy dragged the bags in the back room to Leevon. An hour later Leevon had a total count of the drugs and money. Walking in the kitchen Leevon found everyone sitting at the kitchen table.

"Speak on it little bro what we got" Ba-Ba asked. Leevon passed a piece of paper. Opening the paper Ba-Ba read it to his self, "a million dollars to be split between me and you. Another million dollars to be split between the team members. We have enough drugs to hold this spot down for a month. Which will bring in another million dollars." Ba-Ba nodded his head at Leevon and put the paper in his pocket. With a duffle bag on his shoulder Leevon walked around the table putting two stacks of money in front of Buddha, Demon, Nest, Dutch, and Brandy. Standing up Ba-Ba looked out the kitchen window. He watched as E.M.T's loaded Henry and Goody body into two ambulance. Clearly someone had found them in the staircase and called 9-1-1 to help them. Ba-Ba could see from the window that Henry and Goody were still alive. Yet the beating they took Ba-Ba didn't see them as a threat, because they would both be laid up for at least a week. The only threat he saw coming his way was Tonya. Especially when Tonya found out that her second drug spot in Webster projects was robbed and shut down. That her Courtlandt projects drug spot had been taking over. Three million dollars of her money had been taking. And to top it all off that Brandy crossed her.

Chapter 32

A week had passed since detective Price was murdered. Coming from the cemetery Captain Morris walked into his police station and went straight to his office. Taking off his police jacket he sat down behind his desk. Many thoughts ran threw his mind. He felt like Price death was his fault. He had pushed Price to cross a dangerous drug family. He thought that Price had cross him by giving the Gibbs family a heads up on the raids. Price swore up and down to him that he didn't tip the Gibbs family off about the raids. Price had also told him that he would need protection from the Gibbs family. So angry with the thought that Price was lying to him, he brushed off Price cry for protection. Now Price was dead with the blood of Price on his hands. Before Price father died, he promised Price father that he would look out for Price as If he was his own son. He failed to keep his promise and he had to make things right. Somehow, some way, he had to make the Gibbs family pay for Price death, by taking the Gibbs family down.

Standing up from his desk Captain Morris stuck his head out his office door. "Lopez get in here" Morris yelled.

"Yes Captain, what can I do for you?"

"You can start by pulling up every case that has something to do with the Gibbs family."

"Every case" Lopez repeated to make sure he was hearing the Captain correctly.

"Yes, every case Lopez. As of right now you are in charge of a private investigation against the Gibbs family. I want you to look through every case. Find me loopholes, find D.N.A, find connections, find anything that I can use to put the whole Gibbs family behind bars for life. Lopez when you find it report it directly to me."

*****

Walking into Tonya bedroom Nicole sat down on the bed next to Tonya. "Grandma, I did everything you told me to do. But we have a few problems."

"A few problems like what Nicole?"

"Well for one your second drug spot in Webster projects. No one is answering the phone. I called all day yesterday and all day today."

"I'll call Desean later, what's the other problems?"

"The same problem with Webster is the same problem with your Courtlandt projects drug spot. All day yesterday I called over there and got no answer. Today I called over there and the phone number was disconnected."

"I'll call Goody later and see what's going on. Anything else?"

"Yeah, Goody never brought the money over here last week like you told him to. How much money was he supposed to bring?"

"I believe about three million."

"Grandma you been maxing and relaxing up in this hotel room getting massages all day long. That I don't even think you notice that Goody and Henry haven't been in this hotel suite in a whole week."

"Nicole sometimes a woman has to take some time. I don't look this young because I have good jeans. I look this young because I take time out my busy schedule to pamper myself."

Getting out the bed Tonya kicked Nicole out her bedroom. Reaching for the phone on the nightstand it began ranging before she could pick it up.

"Hello.… Yes, this is Tonya Jones.… Yes, I'm the wife of Goody Jones.… What! I'm on my way." Hanging up the phone Tonya ran around her room trying to get dressed.

Fully dressed Tonya made her way through the hotel sweet into the living room. "Mellow, Cam, let's roll" Tonya yelled walking towards the hotel room door.

From the time they met Tonya she always wear high heels. Yet seeing her with sneakers on her feet for the first time. Cam and Mellow knew something was up. Jumping up from the couch they tucked their gun in their pants and followed behind Tonya.

"What's going on Tonya" China asked.

"Good is in the hospital and the doctor said him and Henry was beat up pretty bad. I'm gonna head over to the hospital and see what happen to them."

*****

With one eye swollen shut Henry tried his best to watch T.V from his hospital bed with his one good eye. Yet his one good eye kept wondering over to the guy he had to share a hospital room with. Henry knew he looked messed up from the beating he took last week. But the guy in the bed next to his bed made him want to vomit looking at the sight of him. The man had burns all over his body that were trying to heal. Curiosity was killing Henry to want to know what happen to the guy in the next bed.

"Hey ummm, brother man."

"Yeah" the man said in a raspy tone.

"I don't mean to be in your business. But what's your name and what the hell happen to you?"

"The names Bill, and they say god don't like ugly. I tried to steal from some drug dealer stash house. Them mother fuckers had the place rigged with explosions. Long story short my ass got caught in fire. I'm lucky to be alive. It was eye opening for me. I'm done with smoking crack. I have a year and some change clean of drugs."

Walking inside the hospital room Tonya turned her face fast when she saw Bill. The look of him was terrifying. Seeing the reaction Tonya gave him when she walked in the room. Bill sat up in his hospital bed.

"Don't be turning your nose up at me Miss lady. I may not have any hair on my head and patches of my skin is all burned up. But I'm lucky to be alive."

"You may think you're lucky. But whoever did that to you, you should have begged them to kill you. Instead you have to walk around for life looking like a damn beef jerky."

Pulling the hospital curtain up to block the sight of bill, Tonya walked over to Henry bed. "What the hell happen to you and Goody?"

"He didn't tell you Tonya?" With a quick hand Tonya slapped Henry upside the head.

"Damn Tonya, quite it, my damn head still hurt like hell."

"As if the fuck I give two shit about your down head hurting Henry. You think I would be asking you what happen If Goody told me? Goody is on pain medication and is out cold. So once again what the hell happen to you two?"

"Tonya about six guys came up in the spot talking about a Red-Money take over. Shit got out of control real fast. Before I knew it, they were stumping on our heads up in that apartment. We must of pass out, because the next thing I remember we were being loading up in the back of the ambulance."

Looking at Henry for a few seconds Tonya shook her head in disbelief. "You said they came up in the apartment, which mean they didn't force their way inside the apartment. Explain to me how six guys just walked inside an apartment Henry?"

"The hell if I know Tonya."

"You want me to tell you how Henry?"

"How Tonya?"

"By you not changed those locks on the apartment door like I told you to."

"Shit" Henry said remembering he never changed the locks on the apartment door like Tonya told him to.

"That got damn Khia had this done to yawl. She caught you two Jackasses slipping…." Tonya stopped in mid-sentence. "Wait a damn minute! Did you say a Red-Money take over?"

"Yeah, two guys that's down with those Red-Money niggas you got selling in Webster was with these other four guys."

"Damn it" Tonya yelled. "Khia is behind this and she got to the Red-Money team to flip on me. Now it all make sense to why both of those spots are not responding to Nicole phone calls."

"Tonya If that's the truth what's our next move?" Pulling out her cell phone Tonya dialed Khia phone number.

"Hello."

"Don't hello me you little bitch! I'm about to give you a war your ass will never forget for the rest of your life."

"Ma I really don't have time for this. I don't know what the hell you are talking about. And to be honest with you I really don't care. You wanted the Sams drug contract, you now have it. You wanted Courtlandt projects, you now have it. Now leave me the hell alone because I'm sick of this nonsense with you Ma." Hanging up on Khia, Tonya called Desean.

"Hello."

"Desean, I warned you from day one not to cross me."

"Tonya…."

"Shut up! How dear you flip on me and join Khia team!"

"Tonya, I don't know what Khia has to do with why your calling me Red-Money stepped on the scene and me and Trouble walked away from everything."

"Desean, you run Red-Money! What the hell are you talking about Red-Money stepped on the scene?"

"Tonya, a guy name Ba-Ba and Leevon are the head of Red-Money blood set. They were in prison for eight in a half years, with two other guy's name Nest and Dutch. All four of them are out of prison now and their taking over everything. They made me step down from running Red-Money and they took over the Webster drug spot I was running."

"If that's the case Desean why didn't you call me, and I would have brought my team over there to put these guys in their place."

"Tonya point blank me and Trouble are out the mix. You deal with the drama."

"Oh I'm gonna deal with it, you can count on that. When I'm done dealing with it. You can count on me dealing with you and Trouble as well." Hanging up the phone Tonya placed her cell phone in her pocket.

Taking a seat in the chair next to Henry bed. Tonya looked at Henry and rolled her eyes at him. Walking in the hospital room Cam and Mellow looked at Tonya.

"So what's the deal" Cam asked.

Looking at Cam and Mellow, Tonya rolled her eyes at them as well. Pissed off was a understatement. Her blood was so hot she felt like it was cooking her skin. Three million dollars gone, and she would be damn if she let it go that easy. Seeing Tonya stand up, for the first time since they known Tonya. Mellow and Cam could see all in Tonya face why people called her the devil in female form. Looking over at Henry, Tonya wanted to slap him again. Instead she chose to use her words this time.

"In two days the doctors said, they will be releasing you and Goody. I'm giving you two one day after that to rest up. Come four days from today were going to war against these damn Red-Money guys. Until then I'm gonna go get up with Melissa. I'm gonna get a shipment from Gail under the Jones contract, and I'm gonna have Melissa get a shipment under the Sams contract." Walking out the hospital room Mellow and Cam followed behind Tonya out the hospital.

*****

Desean walked back and forth in his living room. For the first time since he been in the drug game. He didn't have a wild card to play. Every time he had in the drug game; he found a way out the drama by the help of Solo. With Solo being dead he didn't have any one to turn to for help to save his own life. In so many words Tonya words were clear. She was going to kill him soon as she handled the Red-Money team. With Rome running the Gibbs family and Rome not knowing him. Desean couldn't ask the Gibbs family for help. With Khia running the Sams family, and him crossing Khia a few years ago. Desean couldn't ask the Sams family for help. He had two options, go back to Red-Money and help them take Tonya down. Or try to get back down with the Jones family, and help Tonya kill the Red-Money team. Thinking more to his self. Desean felt either way when it was all said and done. No matter which one he went back to they would murder him once they took out the other side, because they would feel he couldn't be trusted. Walking in Desean living room. Trouble watched Desean walk back and forth in the living room in deep thought.

"Yo you a'ight Desean?"

Stopping in mid-walk Desean looked over at Trouble. "Hell no I'm not a'ight! I just got off the phone with Tonya a few minutes ago. From what she said to me. She want both if us dead. Trouble for the first time in my life I feel like it's about to come to an end. For right now me and you are safe. Don't know body know where I live except me and you. But it's only a matter of time before Tonya find a way to get my home address."

"So Desean what are we going to do?"

"Stay put in this house Trouble until I come up with something to beat Tonya at her own game.

*****

Inside the Trump hotel Tonya went to Brandy hotel sweet. Seeing a hotel maid inside the sweet. Tonya walked inside the room. In seconds Tonya notice all Brandy things were gone. "Excuse me Miss, where is the lady that's renting this hotel sweet?"

"She's gone, she checked out last week with her four male friends."

Hearing what the maid said Tonya pulled out her cell phone and called Brandy cell phone. "Hello."

"Brandy where the hell are you?"

"Tonya what a surprise. I been meaning to call you. How have you been Tonya?"

"Brandy why did you check out the hotel? Where are you?"

"Tonya, I checked out the hotel because me and your business deal is over."

"No the hell it's not Brandy! Next week our business deal is over. Until then your ass is supposed to be in this hotel sweet. So what you need to do is get your ass back over here to…."

"Tonya our business deal is over. My boyfriend is running the Sams drug contract now."

"Your what? What the hell are you talking about Brandy?"

"I'm talking about me going to Gail house last week and getting the Sams drug contract turned over to my boyfriend. Tonya do me a favor and go to hell."

Hanging up the phone Tonya head began spinning. "Please tell me this bitch didn't go to Gail house" Tonya said out loud.

"I don't know Gail."

"Bitch get the fuck out" Tonya yelled pushing the maid out the hotel room.

Slamming the hotel room door close Tonya sat down in the chair. Feeling like she was about to lose her mind Tonya began talking to herself. "This has to be a joke. This bum bitch Brandy crossed me! She turned the Sams contract over to her boyfriend. That's impossible! The only way she would be able to turn the Sams drug contract over to someone. Is if she marry someone and gave them her last name. She said her boyfriend not her husband. So how the hell did she turn that contract over?"

Jumping up Tonya ran out the hotel at top speed. Jumping in her car she hit the highway to New Jersey. It was only one way to find out who has control over the Sams drug contract. The only way Tonya was going to find out if what Brandy said was true. She needed to talk to Gail. An hour and a half later Tonya pulled up to Gail house. Knocking on Gail door nine women showed Tonya to the dining room. Taking a seat across from Gail at the dining room table. Gail sat at the head of the table looking at Tonya with a face of stone. All the years Tonya had been going to Gail house. Not once had she ever seen a T.V in Gail dining room. Yet for the first time ever there was a T.V set up in the corner. Normally when Tonya came to Gail house always greeted her with a warm hello. This time she was just staring at Tonya not saying a word.

"How have you been doing Gail?"

"Tonya what brings you to my home?"

"Well I was wondering…."

"Wondering what Tonya?"

"Gail has there been a change in the Sams drug contract such as a new holder?"

"Tonya, you should know better than to ask me about another family contract. The only contract you should be concern about is the Jones contract that you are the holder of."

"Gail me and you have known each other for many years."

"We have Tonya that's why I want to show you something."

"Show me what?"

"I'll get to that in a minute Tonya. Tonya you brought Melissa to my house to claim the Sams drug contract from Khia. To my knowledge Melissa has been dead for many years. How did she come to still being alive?"

"Gail come on you know the game. I went into hiding for over twenty years. Everyone that knew me thought I was dead all those years."

"Yes, but I knew you were still alive Tonya all those years."

"Gail, Melissa was in hiding, I knew she was alive."

"I see, well Melissa came to my house a week ago with another person."

"Another person like who?"

"Wayne Sams your oldest son." Hearing her oldest son name Tonya broke out in a cold sweat. "Melissa turned the Sams contract over to Wayne. Tonya to my knowledge just like Melissa. I thought Wayne had been dead for many years as well. Can you explain where Wayne has been all these years Tonya?"

"I can't Gail."

"You can't or you won't Tonya?"

"I can't Gail because I thought he was dead myself. This has to be some type of mix up Gail. My son Wayne is dead."

"I beg to differ" Gail said pressing power on the T.V. Looking at the T.V screen Tonya saw Brandy and Wayne sitting with Gail at her dining room table. In shock Tonya pass out and fell out the chair.

Two of the nine women that showed Tonya into the dining room rushed into the dining room. Helping Tonya up they sat her back in the chair and began fanning her with their hands. Opening her eyes Tonya looked over at Gail.

"Tonya it's clear to me that you hide Melissa and used Melissa to get back at Khia. It's also clear that Melissa hide Wayne from you and used him to cross you by making him the king of the Sams drug contract. I'm not sure but it looks like Khia may have beat you again. Or it's Melissa who's into this stunt by herself creating a beef of her own with you. My advice to you Tonya has always been the same since you came back on the scene. Make up with your children and end this beef between you and them. I'll also tell you one more thing. I don't believe Khia has anything to do with this power move of the Sams drug contract."

"I have to go; I have to get out of here" Tonya said standing up.

Tonya legs felt like wet noodles as she walked to her car. Getting in her car Tonya rest her head on her car steering wheel. Tonya knew for sure now that Khia had nothing to do with any of this take over situation. Gail was right about two things. She needed to make up with her children, and that was Khia and Jo-Jo. The only two children she had that was truly still alive. The other thing Gail was right about Melissa had crossed her. Better yet Brandy had crossed her. Picking her head up from the steering wheel Tonya didn't have a clue how to fix this situation. Clearly Brandy got someone to have plastic surgery to look like Wayne, just like she had Brandy get plastic surgery to look like Melissa. Just like that Tonya realized that she had giving Brandy the keys to a drug kingdom. Punching the steering wheel Tonya started up her car. In no way could she tell Gail the deal she made with Brandy. Lying to Gail was like getting a paid trip to a hole in the ground. Even if she made up with Khia. Khia wouldn't be able to get the Sams drug contract back from Melissa without telling Gail that Tonya lied to Gail.

"I have to get up with Brandy and this guy that she has playing as if he's Wayne. And when I find them, I have to kill them both to get that contract back into my family, but how" Tonya said pulling off.

Chapter 33

It had been a week since Goody and Henry were attacked in the Courtlandt projects drug spot. Their body still ware the bruises, but they were both feeling back to the old them. With guns fully loaded Tonya, Goody, Henry, Mellow, Cam, Nicole, China, got out the car in front of Courtlandt projects. Walking through the projects to the drug spot building. Tonya lead the way with Henry in last place with two guns in his hands. Walking in the building the seven of them got on the elevator.

Demon was giving the job of, look out, from Ba-Ba. "We got company coming our way Wayne" Demon said as he looked out the kitchen window.

"How many?"

"Seven all together Wayne."

Ba-Ba had been waiting for this day for two weeks. Standing up he told the whole Red-Money team to get into place. Nest, Dutch, and Buddha, ran out the apartment and into the staircase. Demon ran out the apartment and into the apartment across the hall. Brandy took Demon place and sat in the kitchen and began looking out the window. Closing the drug spot door Ba-Ba and Leevon stood close by the apartment door.

Stepping off the elevator Tonya lead the way to the drug spot apartment door. Following behind Tonya the six of them took the safety off their guns. As Tonya raised her fist to knock on the apartment door. The door swung open and Tonya was faced with two guns in her face. Like a domino effect the apartment door across the hall open and Demon held a gun to the back of China and Nicole head. Stepping out the staircase Dutch grabbed Henry in a choke hold and held his gun to Henry head. Running out the staircase Nest and Buddha aimed their guns at Cam and Mellow head. Surrounded Tonya realized that she had just walked her team into a ambush. Yes they all had guns, yet the same amount of guns were already cocked, loaded and pointed at their heads. Looking at Ba-Ba who were the face of her dead son Wayne. Tears formed in Tonya eyes. She wanted to know who the guy was under that face. Looking inside the apartment Tonya saw Brandy sitting at the kitchen table wearing her dead daughter Melissa face.

Stepping closer to Tonya face Ba-Ba spoke in a calm tone. "You must be Tonya. I'm gonna say this one time. Keep your mouth closed, take your team, leave and never come back to these projects again."

Not backing down Tonya looked Ba-Ba in his face. "You and that bitch are wearing the faces of two of my children that are dead. You two think you're gonna get away with this shit?"

"Dutch handle that" Ba-Ba yelled out.

"With pleasure" Dutch said shooting Henry in his head.

Letting Henry body fall to the floor Dutch stepped over his body. Seeing Henry body hit the floor shocked everyone on the Jones team except Tonya. Seeing a murder of a team member and even killing a team member never ever phased her. Not blanking an eye Tonya continued to look into Ba-Ba face.

"If I have to repeat myself to you Tonya, I'll have my team kill two more of your team members."

Tonya was in the game long enough to know when she had to walk away. She rather walk away with her life to fight another day. Then to be murdered without getting her own pay back. Tucking her gun in her pants Tonya began walking down the hallway. One by one Nicole, China, Cam, Mellow, and Goody, followed behind Tonya. Each one of then stepped over Henry body and got back on the elevator. From the kitchen window Brandy watched Tonya and her team drive off.

After getting rid of Henry body all of the Red-Money team sat in the living room of their drug spot. Standing in the middle of the living room Ba-Ba clapped his hands.

"Listen up people, good job, that situation was handled very well. I believe that Tonya chick got the message, and I don't believe we will have a problem with her again. Buddha, Leevon, Demon, you three hold down the spot. Me and Melissa are going over to the new house and go get it in order for all of us to live in it. Nest, Dutch, today is Friday and that Erykah situation need to be handled today."

Standing up Nest and Dutch walked out the apartment. Giving Leevon a pound with his fist Ba-Ba and Brandy walked out the apartment as well.

*****

Inside the courthouse Erykah stood in line waiting to file her motions with the court of New York. "Next" the court clerk asked.

"Hello, my name is Erykah Sams, I'm a lawyer. I need to file…."

"You need an order to be signed by a judge, and you need to file the amount on record with the court on how much your client is suing the N.Y.P.D" the clerk said taking the papers out of Erykah hand.

"How did you know all of that?"

"Well Ms. Sams these two cases are pissing the head D.A off. And he don't mind coming down here to give me an ear full about these two cases."

"Oh really, one case is none of his concern. The other one is his fault to why the N.Y.P.D is being sued. So the next time Jack Murray come down here relate that message to him."

"With pleasure, can I through in that you said, kiss your ass too?"

"Sure, and while you at it. Tell him I also said he can lick the crack of my ass after I take a good shit." Laughing the clerk and Erykah slapped each other a high five with their hand.

Text messaging Rome, "That D.A is trying to block the two cases" Erykah put her cell phone in her pocket. Walking out the courthouse Erykah fished her car keys out her pocketbook.

"Ms. Erykah Sams." Hearing her name being called from behind her. Erykah turned around and stood frozen as her eyes grew triple their size.

"POP! POP! POP!POP!"

As Erykah body hit the ground Nest and Dutch ran down the block to their car. Jumping in their car they speeded off.

*****

A hour into moving furniture in its right place in their new house. It didn't take much dirty talk to get Ba-Ba out of his clothes. Picking Brandy up Ba-Ba carried her to their new bedroom. The last time Brandy had sex was a month ago with Trouble. She was used to having sex at least two to three times a day. Soon as Brandy told Ba-Ba that she wanted to have sex. Ba-Ba was beyond ready to handle his business. He hadn't had sex in almost nine years with a female due to him being in prison. Stroking inside Brandy long and hard from behind while she sat in a doggy style position, Ba-Ba bust his nut. Nowhere done Ba-Ba flipped Brandy over onto her back. Putting her legs over his shoulders, he slid his dick back inside of her. Stroking inside of her even harder than before. Ba-Ba grabbed a hold of her thighs and pumped even faster. In heaven Brandy looked in Ba-Ba face enjoying every inch of him inside of her. Slow stroking Brandy, Ba-Ba bent down and tongue kissed Brandy.

"Damn I missed the hell out of you shorty."

"Don't tell me, show me Wayne."

Picking up the speed Ba-Ba began fucking her faster and faster, pumping in and out of her like a mad man. Grabbing a hold of Brandy thighs even tighter, he pushed his dick inside her as far as it would go shooting his second load. Standing up straight Ba-Ba playfully slapped Brandy across her face.

"Bitch you better not ever call me Wayne again while we fucking. You hear me?"

"I was caught up in the moment Ba-Ba."

"Get caught up in the moment when we having sex again, and I'm gonna slap the shit out of you for real. Now get dressed we still got a lot of shit to do."

*****

"I'm Jill Peterson reporting live on 161st in front of the courthouse. Just a few hours ago, right here where I'm standing a lawyer was gun down. Erykah Sams walked out the courthouse and was shot four times. Police are saying that Ms. Sams died on the scene. There's a camera in front of the courthouse, yet the police are having a hard time identifying the two male shooters. The police are asking for the public help in identifying the two male shooters." After the T.V station played the video of Erykah being gun down, they went back to Jill Peterson live. "The police are asking the public to call crime stoppers If they have any information on this murder. Will be back at ten p.m."

Cutting off the T.V Khia whole body became in rage. Hearing and seeing her daughter being gun down on T.V. It wasn't a doubt in her mind her mother Tonya was the cause of Erykah being murdered. For the first time in her life Khia felt Tonya went to far and was surely going to let Tonya know that. She too was about to go to far by killing her own mother. Pulling out her cell phone Khia called Rome.

Turning off the T.V Rome pulled out his cell phone and called his grandmother Nancy cell phone. Getting no answer Rome text message Nancy, "Grandma, Erykah was murdered, she was working on two cases for me, get back to me." Sending the messages Rome phone began ranging.

"Rome they…. they murdered my…. my……"

"I just saw it on the news Khia. I'm coming to pick you up right now and were gonna meet up with the teams later at my house."

"Okay."

Hanging up the phone Khia continued to look at the T.V as the station replayed the story about Erykah being gun down.

Beyond pissed off seeing her granddaughter being shot down like a dog on T.V. Standing up in rage Tonya picked up the hotel sweet T.V and slammed it against the hotel wall. Tonya saw clearly on the T.V who the two guys were that gun down Erykah.

"They stole three million dollars from me! They stole a drug contract from me! Two of their damn members are wearing two of my damn kids' faces! And now they just murdered my damn granddaughter! That's it!"

Taking off her high heels Tonya threw them across the room. Placing her sneakers on her feet Tonya tucked two guns in the back of her pants, she then tucked a gun in the of her pants. Seeing Tonya in rage Nicole, China, Cam, and Mellow, sat in the living room terrified at what Tonya was going to do next. Seeing Tonya storming towards the hotel sweet door. Goody jumped up and grabbed Tonya in a bear hug. "Get the hell off me Goody!"

"You're not thinking straight Tonya, you need to calm down" Goody said carrying Tonya to their bedroom.

Closing the door to the room Goody locked the door. Going ape shit crazy Tonya fought Goody like a wild animal to get out the room. Pulling the gun from under her shirt. Tonya tried to shoot Goody, grabbing hold of the gun Goody slammed his body against hers as they both fell on the bed. As the gun went off Goody snatched the gun out Tonya hand and threw it on the floor.

Hearing the gun shot Nicole, China, Mellow, and Cam, all jumped in shock. Running over to the bedroom door Nicole began banging on the bedroom door.

"Grandma! Grandma are you okay!"

"We are fine" Tonya and Goody yelled out.

Hearing that they were both fine Nicole sat back down on the couch. A whole hour Tonya fought Goody like a wild animal to get out the room. Not backing down Goody refused to let Tonya out the room. By the second hour Goody had finally calmed Tonya down, took her guns, and talked her into thinking things threw before she reacted. Coming out the room Goody closed the door behind him. Looking up from the couch at Goody, the four of them grabbed their mouth in shock if they didn't know any better, they would have thought Goody was in a fight with a lion. His clothes were ripped up and his face was stretched up with knots on his forehead.

*****

After picking up Khia, Rome took her to I.D Erykah body. They then headed over to the funeral home to plan Erykah funeral. After seeing Erykah body in the morgue. Khia became a walking zombie. Rome knew Khia body was with him, but it was clear that her mind was somewhere else. Taking control Rome spoke to the funeral director and plan Erykah whole funeral arrangements. As Rome drove to his house with Khia sitting in the passenger seat of his car. Multiple things were going through Rome head. Although he grew up with Supreme as his father, he always knew Solo was his real father. With Solo being his father, and the father of Erykah. Erykah was his sister and he knew If Solo was alive. Solo would go all out for Erykah funeral. So he did the same out of respect for Solo and because Erykah was his sister. The total of Erykah funeral hit the mark at 150,000 dollars, which he paid in full. Rome also knew that Solo would flip out and paint the streets in blood for someone killing his first daughter. Something he plan to do as soon as they put Erykah in the ground.

Stopping at the light Rome looked over at Khia. Khia sat quite looking out the car window. Reaching over Rome grabbed a hold of Khia hand and squeezed it.

"You okay Khia?"

"No I'm not" Khia said back in a low tone as tears fell down her face.

"Khia not only did you lose your daughter; I lost my sister. You being her mother I'm gonna follow your lead. However you want to handle things I'll back you one hundred percent."

Turning her head Khia was face to face with Rome. Rome could see the hurt in her eyes and the rage building inside of Khia.

"The day after I put my daughter in the ground. I'm killing them all Rome. My mother, my niece, my sister and the rest of the Jones team."

"Khia when that day come, from sunup, to sundown, we gonna make that happen." As Rome continue to drive Khia went back to looking out the car window.

Walking in his house Rome walked Khia into his living room where Sierra had everyone waiting for them. Tone, Pit, Jo-Jo, Ke-Ke, Tre, Lloyd, Tameka, Mike, Tymel, Codie, and Terry, all sat in the living room. Standing up Tymel wrapped his arms around Khia.

"Ma you okay?"

Not able to find her words Khia shook her head no. Jo-Jo walked over to his big sister, before he could reach his arms out to hug Khia, Khia fell into Jo-Jo chest crying uncontrollable. Holding Khia tight Jo-Jo Walked Khia over to the couch.

"How could she have her own granddaughter murdered" Khia said looking up at Jo-Jo.

'Khia the same way me and you gonna murder her and her whole team."

Stepping out the living room Rome text message his grandmother Nancy again. "Grandma please get back at me, Erykah funeral is on Monday." Walking back into the living room Rome looked over at Lloyd. Beside the fact that he had a black eye, he looked good, and back to his normal self. The black eye looked fresh. It wasn't a doubt in Rome mind that Lloyd got the black eye today, and he got that black eye from Tone.

<u>One Week Later</u>

After Erykah wait service Khia watched as Erykah casket was loaded into the back of the funeral home hearse. Beautiful was a understatement as to how Khia looked. As her long her blew in the wind, her makeup was perfect. Yet her face had war written all over it. Tymel stood on her left, Jo-Jo stood on her right. Rome stood in front of their limo and open the door so they could get in. Behind their limo sat another limo with Tone, Pit, Lloyd, Tameka, Ke-Ke, and Tre sitting inside. In the third limo Sierra sat with the kids Quinn, Little Supreme, and Lisa. The forth limo held Mike, Terry, and Codie. As the funeral hearse pulled off so did the four limos following close to the cemetery.

An hour later they were five minutes away from the cemetery. The first time Rome looked out the limo back window. Rome thought he was seeing things. A minute later he looked out the back window again and knew for sure he wasn't seeing things. When they left the funeral home there was only three black limos behind their limo. It was now six limos behind their limo. The last limo was all white. Pulling up to the cemetery everyone got out the first four limos and headed over to the burial plot. As Rome looked over his shoulder Rome tried his best to see who was in the last three limos. Yet no one was getting out of them. Three chairs were placed in front of the burial plot. Khia sat in the middle chair holding Erykah gold chain in her hands. Tymel sat on the right and Jo-Jo sat down on her left side. Rome stood behind them as everyone else stood around them. Rome eyes stayed glued across the cemetery at the three last limos that pulled up with them. Holding his gun tight under his suit jack Rome rested his left hand on Khia shoulder.

As the preacher began to speak Rome saw the first unknown limo door open. Seeing Nancy step out the limo, he then saw the two guys he saw with Tameka in Baltimore, Lucky and Neal, get out the limo behind Nancy. Rome gripped his gun even tighter as the three of them walked over to the plot.

"The N.Y.P.D settled the lawsuit at twenty million" Nancy said giving Rome a check. Turning to Khia, Nancy bent down and gave Khia a hug. "I can't tell you how sorry I am that you're going through this Khia. I hope this helps in some way. Here's that court order you requested signed by a judge."

Taking the court order out of Nancy hand Khia stood up. "Hey, you" Khia yelled to one of the grave diggers.

"Yes Ma'ma?"

"My sister Melissa Sams plot is in this cemetery. Here's a court order. I want her dug up now. I want to see what's in that casket."

Taking the court order out of Khia hand the grave digger looked the court order over. "As you wish Ma'ma, follow me."

Walking behind the grave digger to Melissa burial plot Rome grabbed her arm stopping her. Turning around Khia saw that Rome was pointing to the second back limo. As Tonya walked towards them, Nicole, China, Cam, and Mellow followed behind her.

With all the pain and hurt Khia was feeling. Soon as Tonya reached her Khia slapped Tonya across her face. "How dear you show your face here after you had my daughter murdered!"

Holding her head high Tonya looked at Khia. "I deserve that slap but not for what you think. I deserve that slap for not being a real mother to you and for keeping this beef going between us. But I would not allow you to believe I had a hand in my granddaughter's death. I had nothing to do with this shit. Keep in mind I went against your father Carlos to allow you to give birth to Erykah."

"Then who did this Ma" Khia asked with tears in her eyes.

"Two guys from that new Red-Money team name Nest and Dutch did this. And as far as I'm concern their both a dead man walking for killing my granddaughter."

"Ma'ma were ready to dig the plot up, shall we start" the grave digger asked.

"Khia there's no need to have that done. Melissa is dead, and she's in that casket."

"Explain to me Ma why I saw her that day at Gail house?"

"That wasn't her Khia. It was a girl name Brandy that I made get plastic surgery to look like Melissa."

"You went that far to get the Sams drug contract from me?"

"Yeah, and I got double crossed by Brandy."

"Ma'ma…." Khia snatched the court order out of the grave digger hand. "Never mind, I won't be digger her up today."

As Khia and Tonya spoke Rome walked over to Nancy. "Grandma what's going on here? How do you know these two guys that came here with you?"

"I don't know them; they know these two guys" Nancy said pointing to the limo she got out of.

As Nancy pointed to the limo Rome saw the limo door open. Seeing the six people getting out the limo Rome began to go weak. Seeing that Rome looked like he was about to fall to the ground. Nancy grabbed a hold of Rome and tried to hold him up. Seeing Solo, Supreme, Jay, Beverly, and Trina holding a one year old girl in her arms walking their way. All that stood around Erykah plot looked in shock. Running from Sierra, Quinn jumped into Solo arms. "Daddy!"

As tears ran down Rome face Beverly wrapped her arms around him. "Ma, I missed you so much" Rome cried hugging Beverly back even tighter.

Putting Quinn down Solo walked over to Khia. Taking the gold chain out of her hand he placed it around her neck. With tears in each other eyes Solo and Khia hugged each other tight.

"I thought you were dead Solo. Where were you? They killed our daughter."

Not responding to anything Khia said to him, Solo held her even tighter. Hearing the white limo beeping it's car horn all in the cemetery looked in its direction. Seeing the white limo back window roll down, Gail face appeared. Khia stood frozen not sure If she should walk over to Gail limo. Taking a deep breath Khia walked over to Gail limo. Taking a white rose from Gail, Khia stuck her head in the limo window. Saying a few words to each other. Khia walked back over to Erykah burial plot. Throwing the white rose on top of Erykah casket Khia looked at everyone.

"Solo, Tonya, Rome, Gail what's to have a meeting with the three of you right now.

Getting in the limo with Gail the three of them sat directly across from her. "Rome as of today you are no longer the king of the Gibbs drug contract. Solo you are now the king of the Gibbs drug contract now that you are back." Rome and Solo nodded their head in agreement with Gail. "Tonya If I ask Solo a few questions right now. I'm more than sure I will get the answers to the questions I have. I'm also sure your death will come soon after I get those answers from Solo. Right now I don't know what's going on with the Sams drug contract. As a friend to you, I will not ask Solo anything, I'll find out another way. In the meantime Tonya. Take this advice, find a way to fix it before I find out what's really going on."

Getting out the limo Tonya, Rome, and Solo, walked back over to Erykah burial plot. Walking through everybody Solo stood on top of the middle chair in front of Erykah plot.

"Because of the death of my daughter. The Gibbs, the Sams, and the Jones are no longer enemies. We are one team. These Red-Money niggas want a war, we about to give these mother fuckers a war."

To Be Continued

www.ingramcontent.com/pod-product-compliance
Lightning Source LLC
Chambersburg PA
CBHW081337160726
48000CB00010B/3137